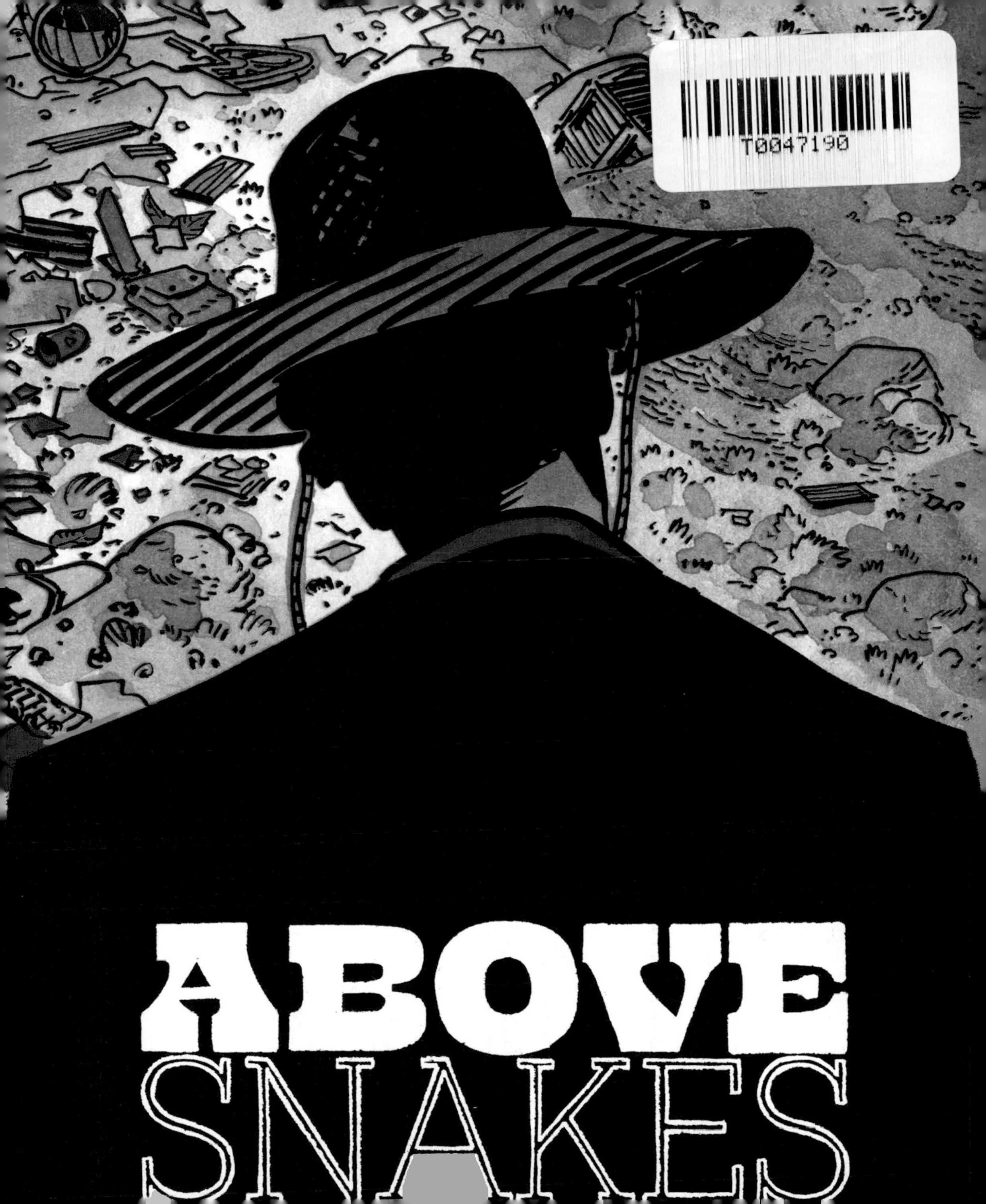

ABOVE SNAKES

ABOVE SNAKES

written by:
Sean Lewis

art by:
Hayden Sherman

lettering by:
Hassan Otsmane-Elhaou

cover painted by:
Jenny Sun
jennysunart.com

IMAGE COMICS, INC. • Robert Kirkman: Chief Operating Officer • Erik Larsen: Chief Financial Officer • Todd McFarlane: President • Marc Silvestri: Chief Executive Officer • Jim Valentino: Vice President • Eric Stephenson: Publisher / Chief Creative Officer • Nicole Lapalme: Vice President of Finance • Leanna Caunter: Accounting Analyst • Sue Korpela: Accounting & HR Manager • Matt Parkinson: Vice President of Sales & Publishing Planning • Lorelei Bunjes: Vice President of Digital Strategy • Dirk Wood: Vice President of International Sales & Licensing • Ryan Brewer: International Sales & Licensing Manager • Alex Cox: Director of Direct Market Sales • Chloe Ramos: Book Market & Library Sales Manager • Emilio Bautista: Digital Sales Coordinator • Jon Schlaffman: Specialty Sales Coordinator • Kat Salazar: Vice President of PR & Marketing • Deanna Phelps: Marketing Design Manager • Drew Fitzgerald: Marketing Content Associate • Heather Doornink: Vice President of Production • Drew Gill: Art Director • Hilary DiLoreto: Print Manager • Tricia Ramos: Traffic Manager • Melissa Gifford: Content Manager • Erika Schnatz: Senior Production Artist • Wesley Griffith: Production Artist • Rich Fowlks: Production Artist • IMAGECOMICS.COM

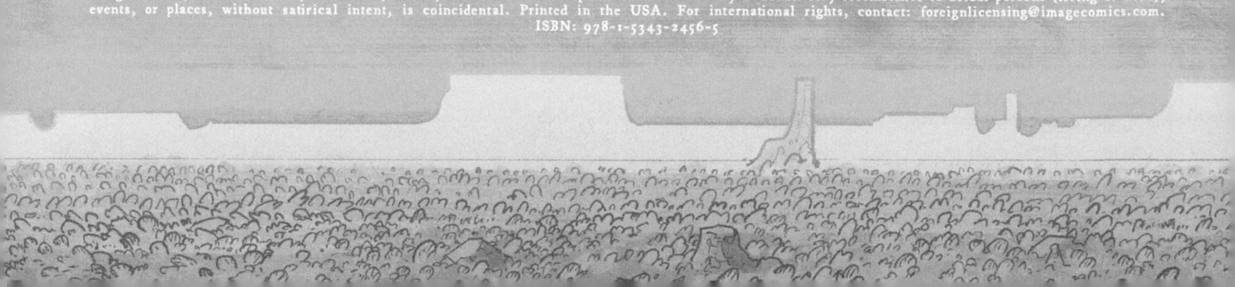

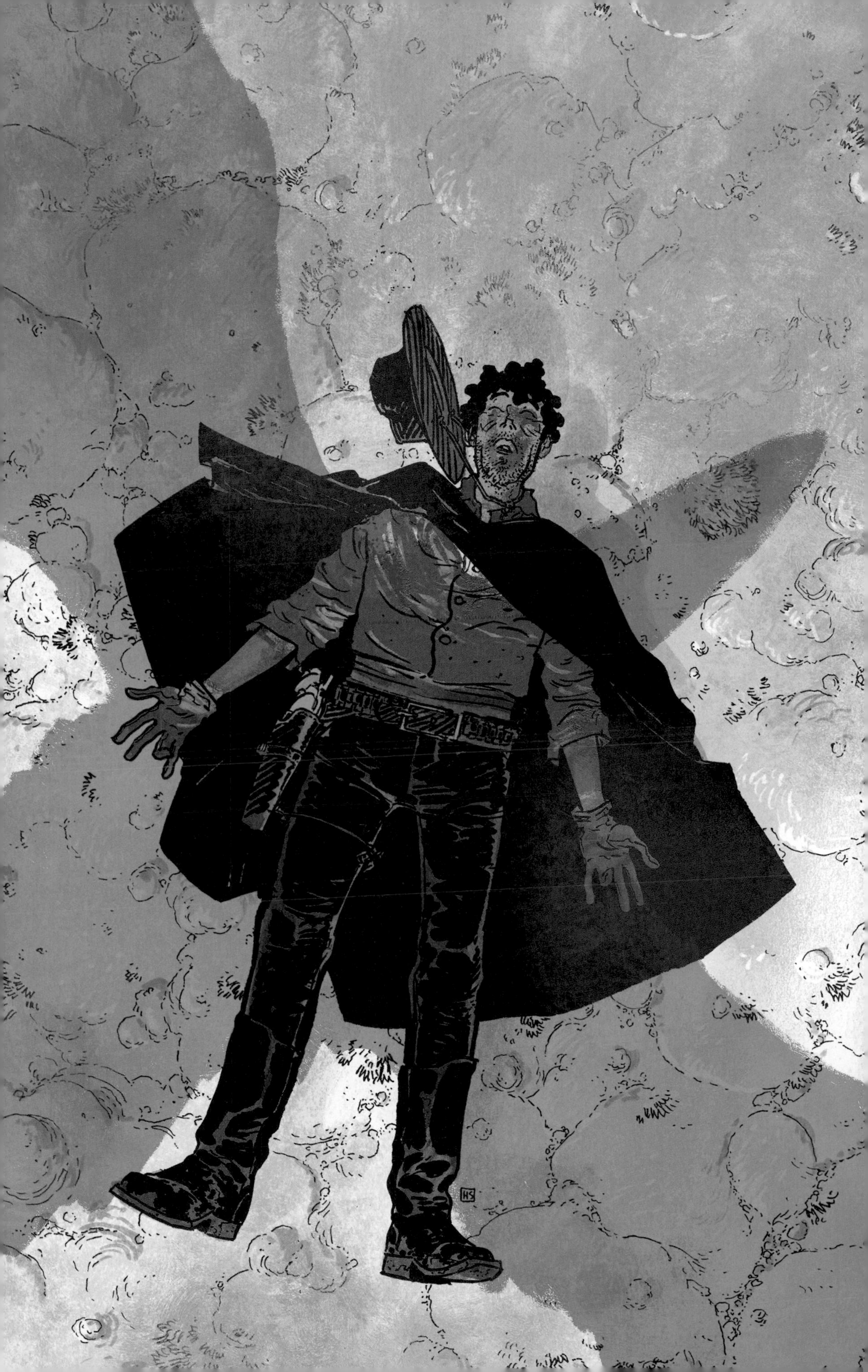

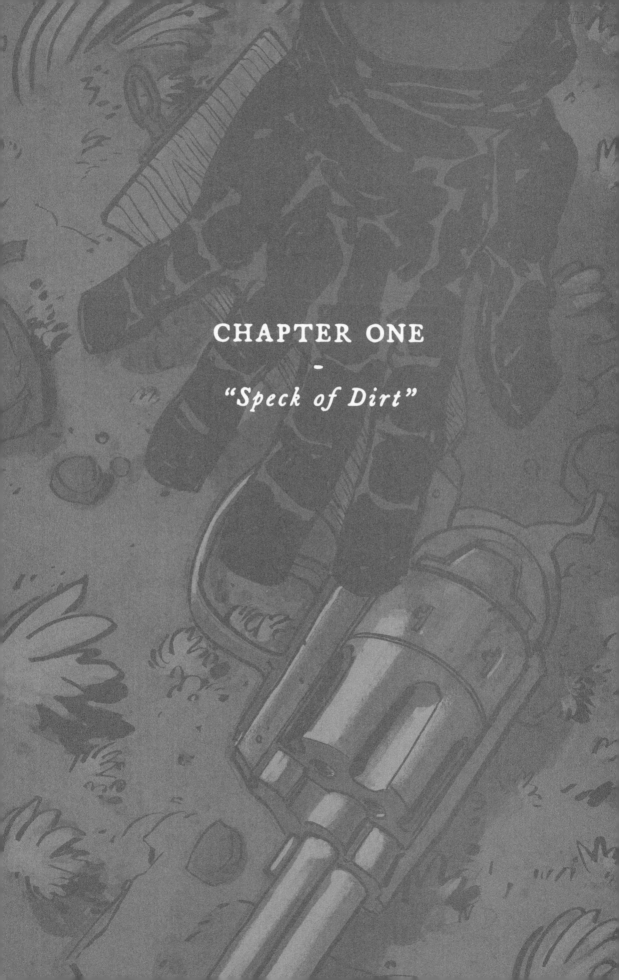

CHAPTER ONE

-

"Speck of Dirt"

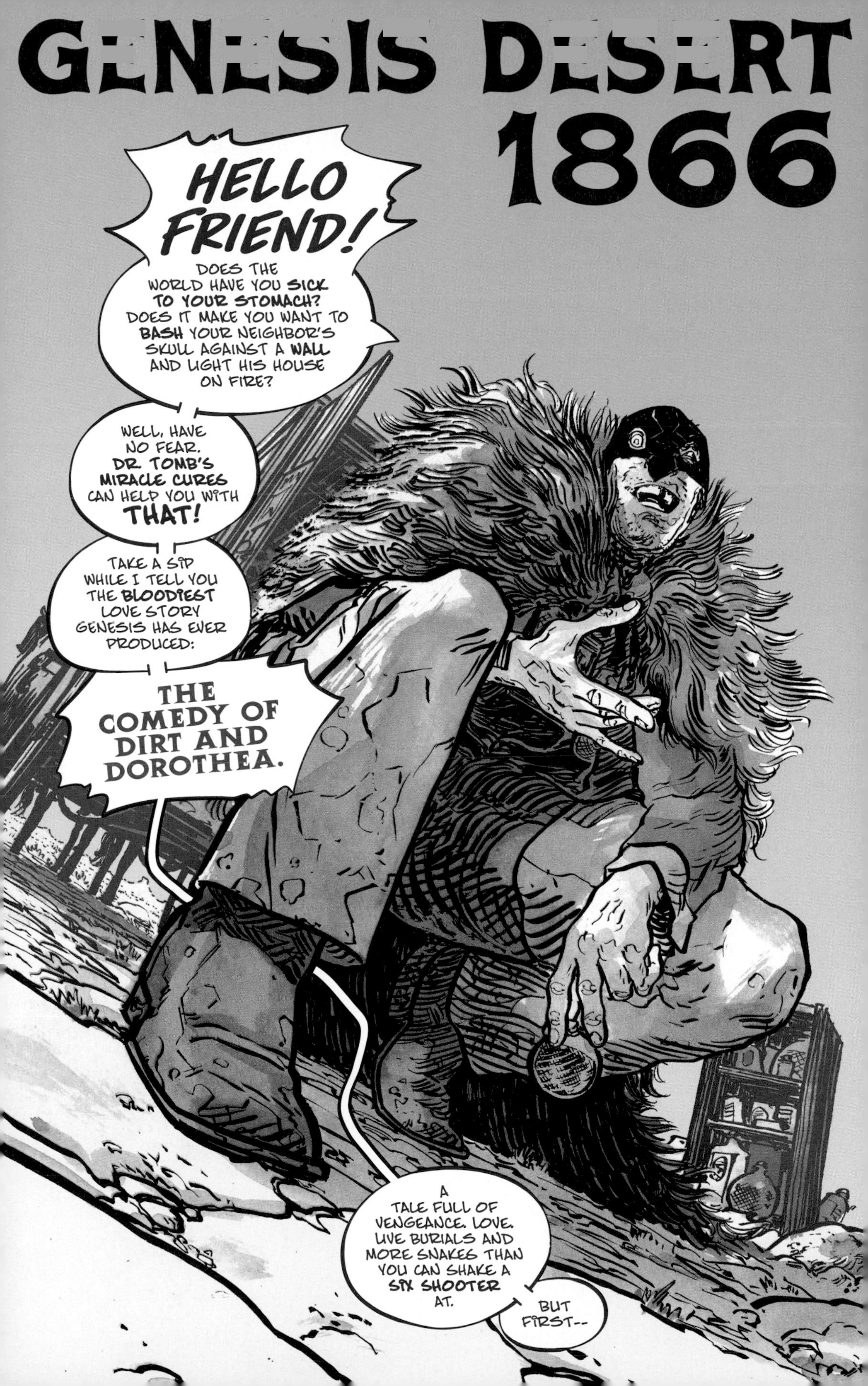
GENESIS DESERT 1866
HELLO FRIEND!
DOES THE WORLD HAVE YOU SICK TO YOUR STOMACH? DOES IT MAKE YOU WANT TO BASH YOUR NEIGHBOR'S SKULL AGAINST A WALL AND LIGHT HIS HOUSE ON FIRE?
WELL, HAVE NO FEAR. DR. TOMB'S MIRACLE CURES CAN HELP YOU WITH THAT!
TAKE A SIP WHILE I TELL YOU THE BLOODIEST LOVE STORY GENESIS HAS EVER PRODUCED:
THE COMEDY OF DIRT AND DOROTHEA.
A TALE FULL OF VENGEANCE, LOVE, LIVE BURIALS AND MORE SNAKES THAN YOU CAN SHAKE A SIX SHOOTER AT.
BUT FIRST--

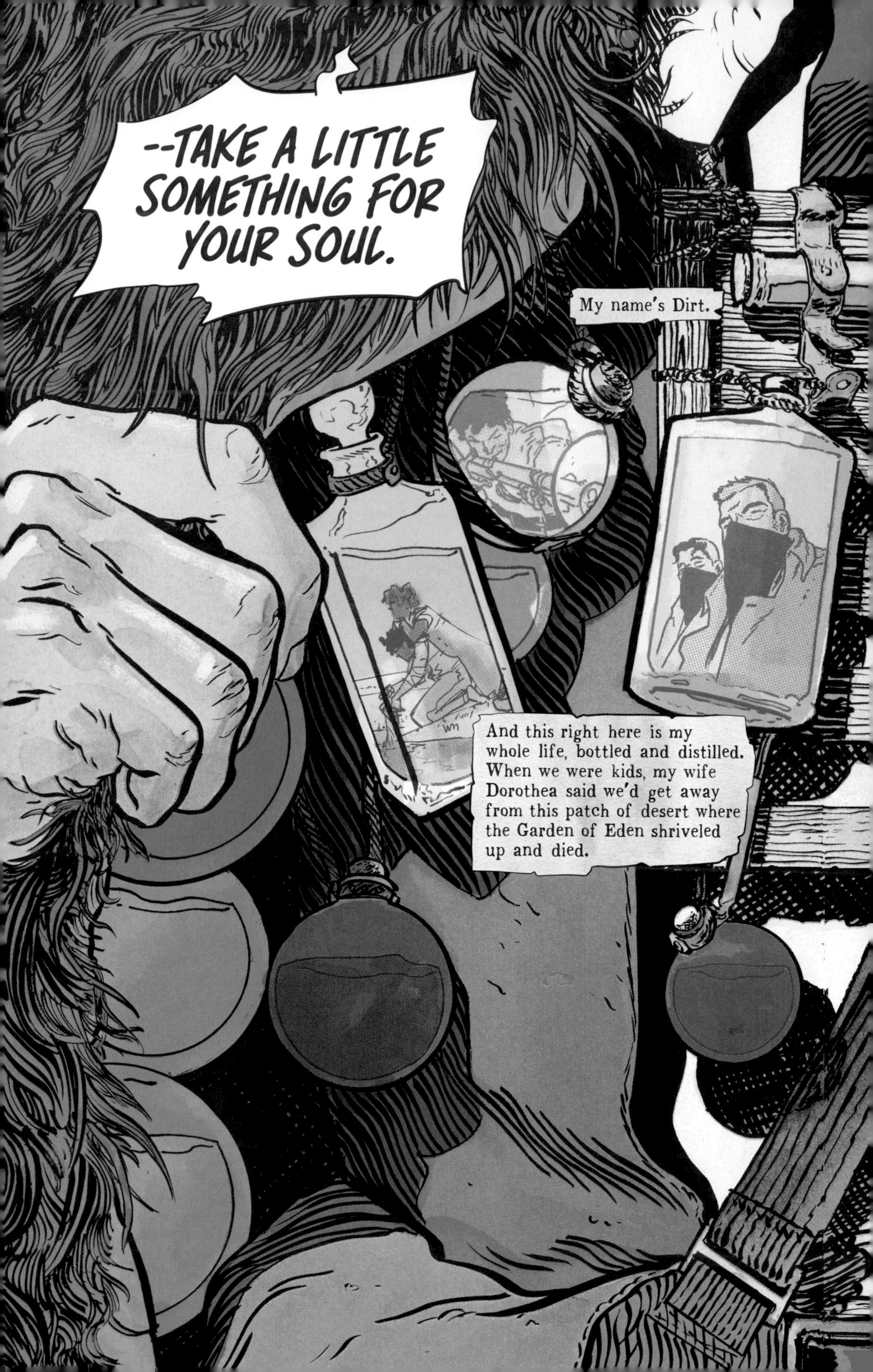
--TAKE A LITTLE SOMETHING FOR YOUR SOUL.
My name's Dirt.
And this right here is my whole life, bottled and distilled. When we were kids, my wife Dorothea said we'd get away from this patch of desert where the Garden of Eden shriveled up and died.

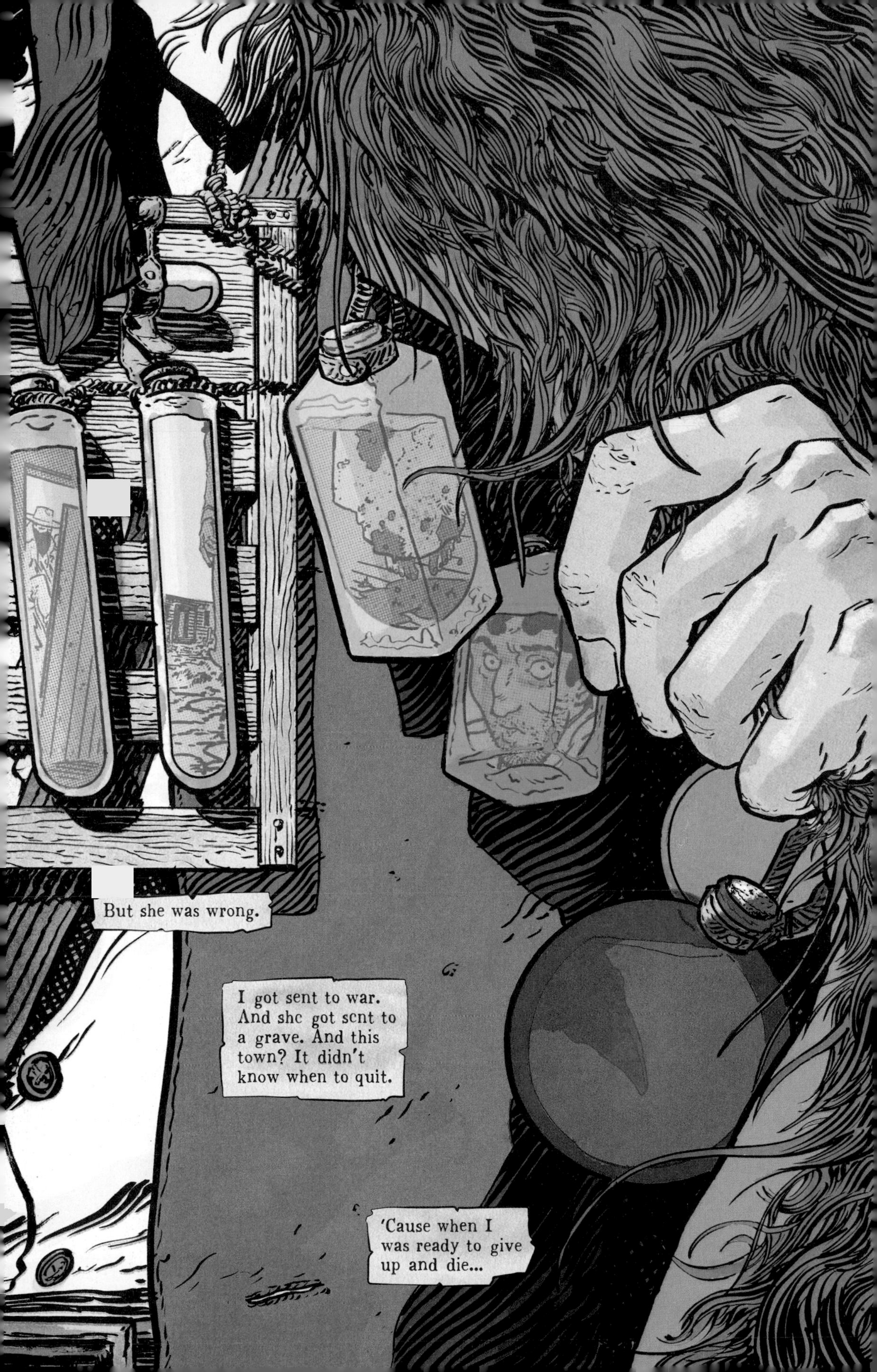
But she was wrong.
I got sent to war. And she got sent to a grave. And this town? It didn't know when to quit.
'Cause when I was ready to give up and die...

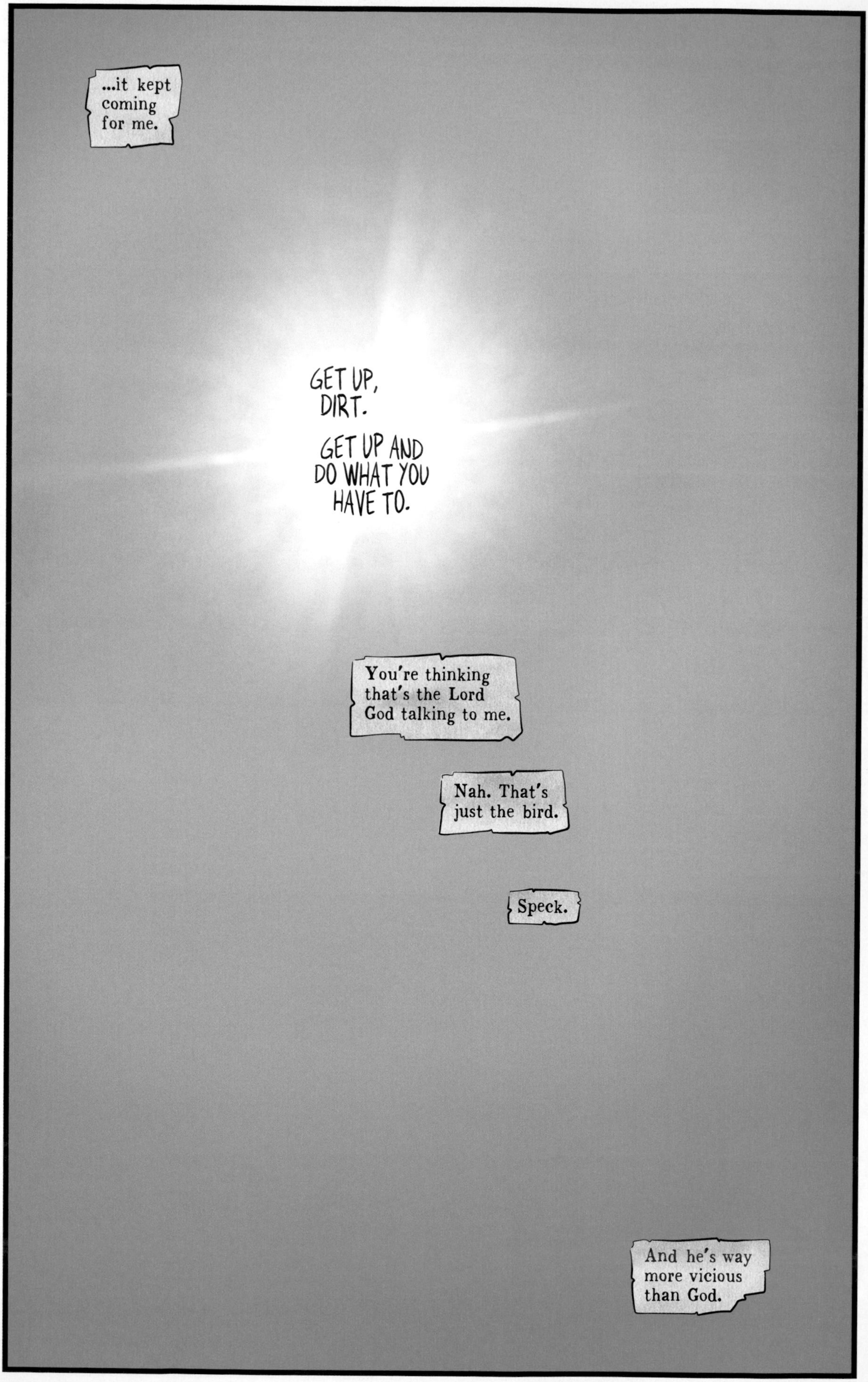
...it kept coming for me.
GET UP, DIRT.
GET UP AND DO WHAT YOU HAVE TO.
You're thinking that's the Lord God talking to me.
Nah. That's just the bird.
Speck.
And he's way more vicious than God.

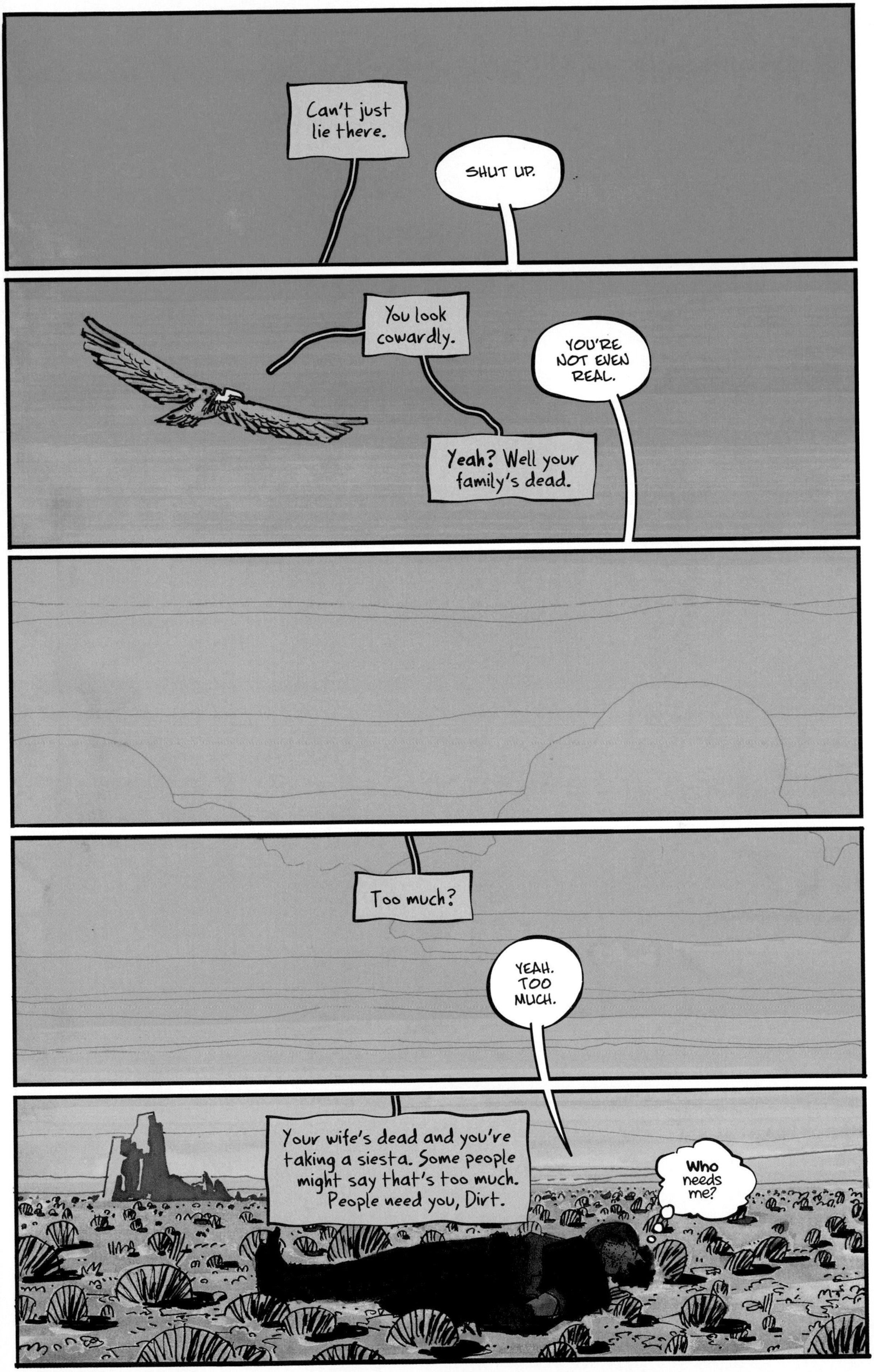
Can't just lie there.
SHUT UP.
You look cowardly.
YOU'RE NOT EVEN REAL.
Yeah? Well your family's dead.
Too much?
YEAH. TOO MUCH.
Your wife's dead and you're taking a siesta. Some people might say that's too much. People need you, Dirt.
Who needs me?

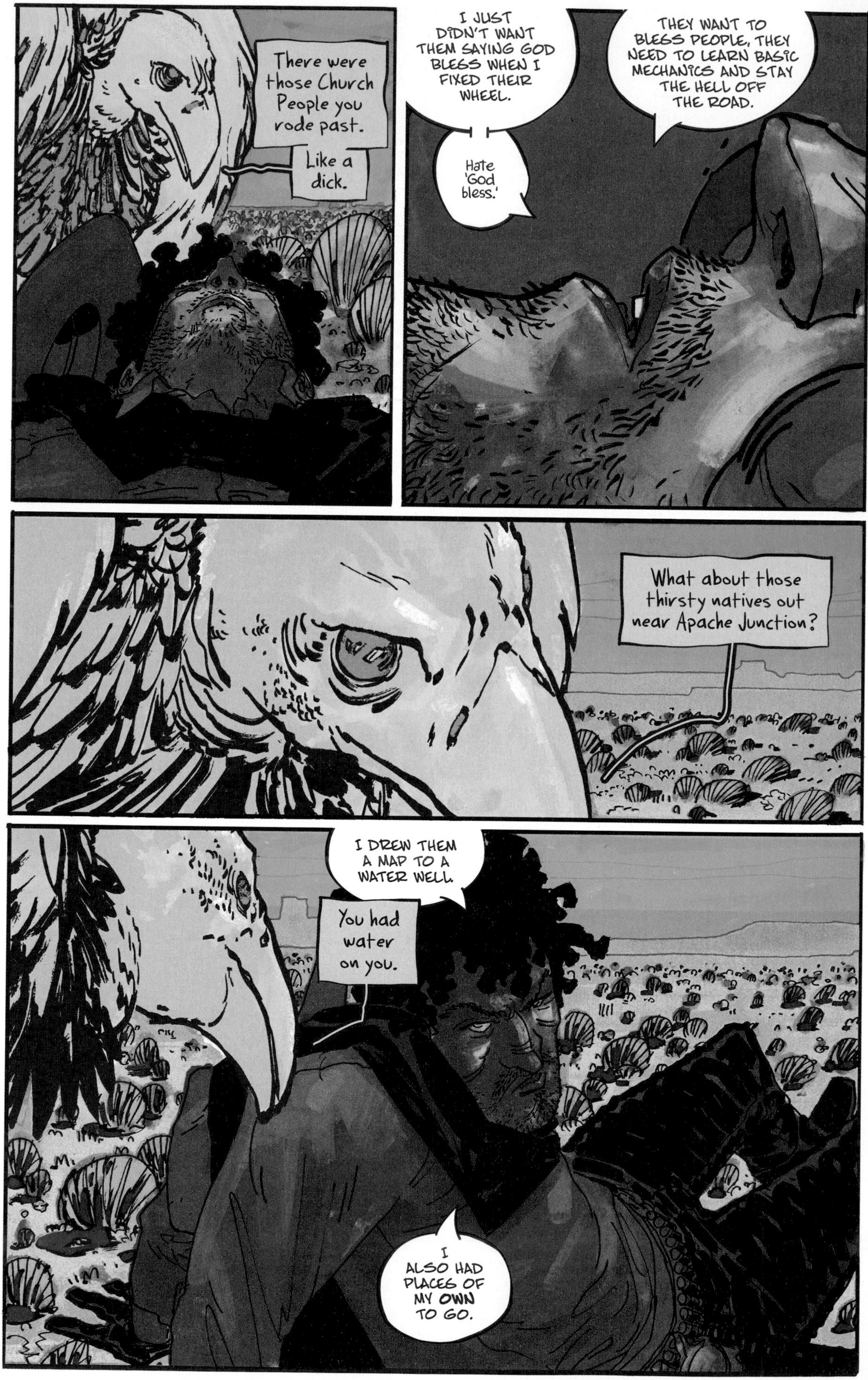

There were those Church People you rode past.
Like a dick.
I JUST DIDN'T WANT THEM SAYING GOD BLESS WHEN I FIXED THEIR WHEEL.
Hate 'God bless.'
THEY WANT TO BLESS PEOPLE, THEY NEED TO LEARN BASIC MECHANICS AND STAY THE HELL OFF THE ROAD.
What about those thirsty natives out near Apache Junction?
I DREW THEM A MAP TO A WATER WELL.
You had water on you.
I ALSO HAD PLACES OF MY OWN TO GO.

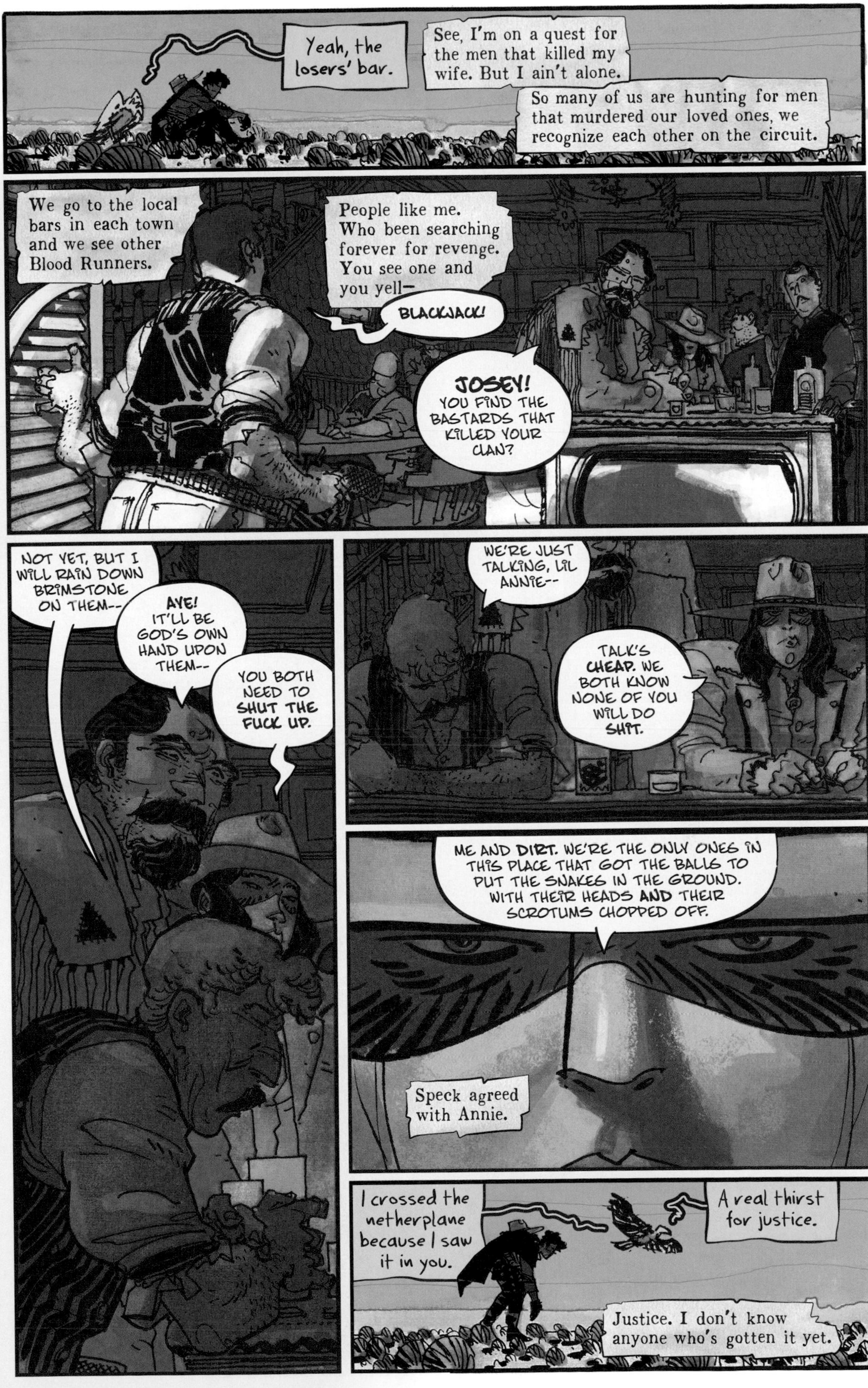
Yeah, the losers' bar.
See, I'm on a quest for the men that killed my wife. But I ain't alone.
So many of us are hunting for men that murdered our loved ones, we recognize each other on the circuit.
We go to the local bars in each town and we see other Blood Runners.
People like me. Who been searching forever for revenge. You see one and you yell—
BLACKJACK!
JOSEY! YOU FIND THE BASTARDS THAT KILLED YOUR CLAN?
NOT YET, BUT I WILL RAIN DOWN BRIMSTONE ON THEM--
AYE! IT'LL BE GOD'S OWN HAND UPON THEM--
YOU BOTH NEED TO SHUT THE FUCK UP.
WE'RE JUST TALKING, LIL ANNIE--
TALK'S CHEAP. WE BOTH KNOW NONE OF YOU WILL DO SHIT.
ME AND DIRT. WE'RE THE ONLY ONES IN THIS PLACE THAT GOT THE BALLS TO PUT THE SNAKES IN THE GROUND. WITH THEIR HEADS AND THEIR SCROTUMS CHOPPED OFF.
Speck agreed with Annie.
I crossed the netherplane because I saw it in you.
A real thirst for justice.
Justice. I don't know anyone who's gotten it yet.

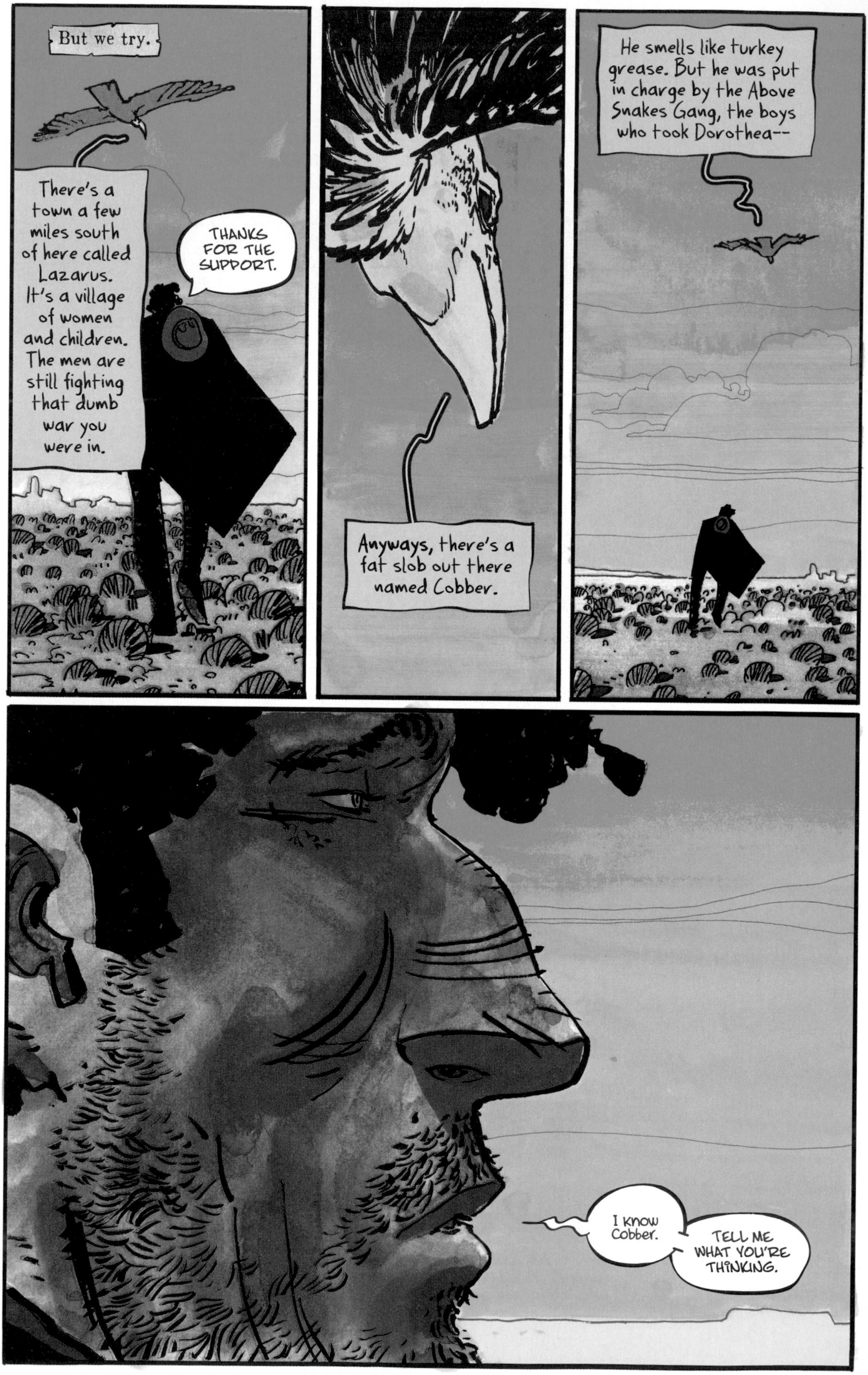
But we try.
There's a town a few miles south of here called Lazarus. It's a village of women and children. The men are still fighting that dumb war you were in.
THANKS FOR THE SUPPORT.
Anyways, there's a fat slob out there named Cobber.
He smells like turkey grease. But he was put in charge by the Above Snakes Gang, the boys who took Dorothea--
I know Cobber.
TELL ME WHAT YOU'RE THINKING.

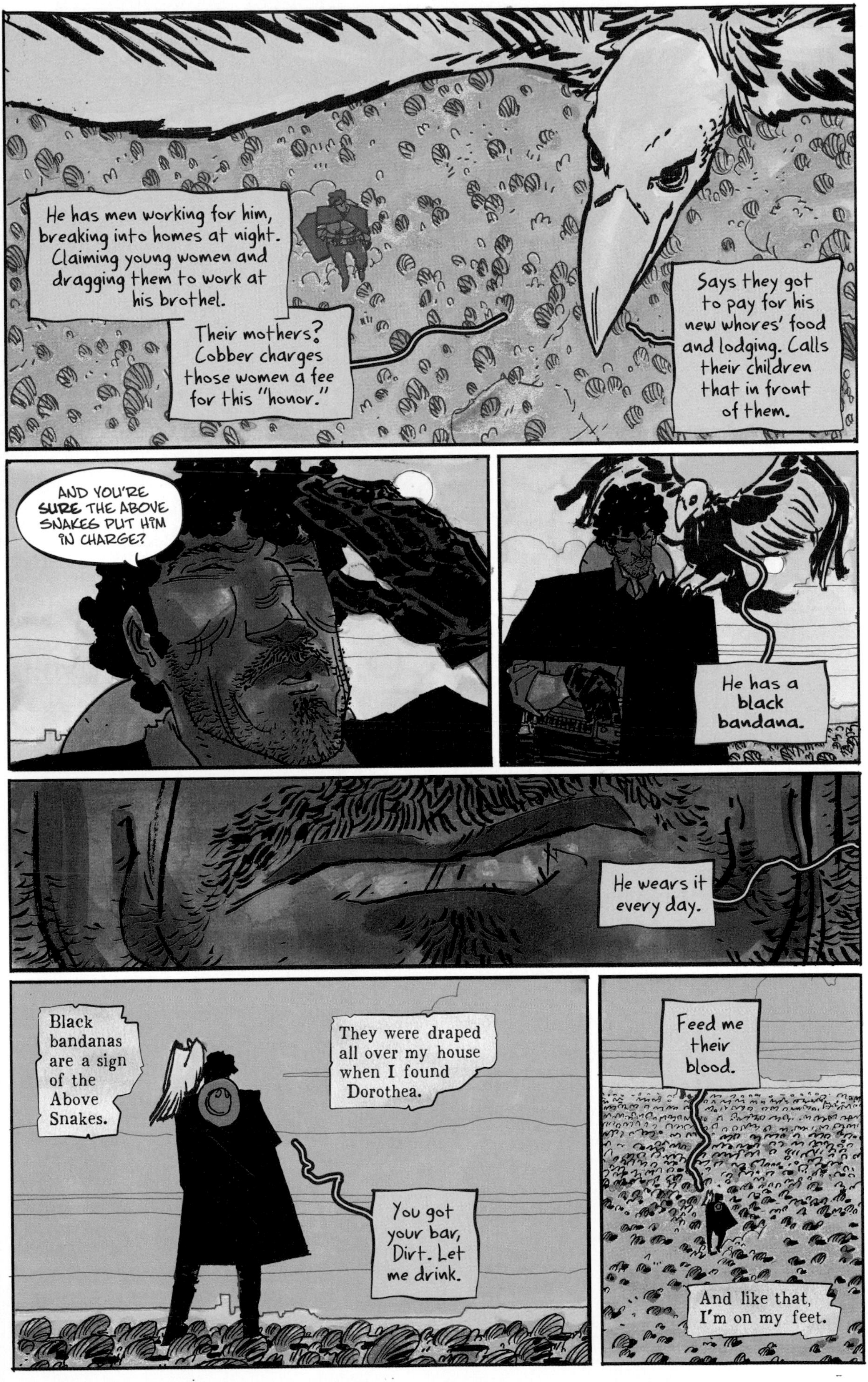
He has men working for him, breaking into homes at night. Claiming young women and dragging them to work at his brothel.
Their mothers? Cobber charges those women a fee for this "honor."
Says they got to pay for his new whores' food and lodging. Calls their children that in front of them.
AND YOU'RE SURE THE ABOVE SNAKES PUT HIM IN CHARGE?
He has a black bandana.
He wears it every day.
Black bandanas are a sign of the Above Snakes.
They were draped all over my house when I found Dorothea.
You got your bar, Dirt. Let me drink.
Feed me their blood.
And like that, I'm on my feet.

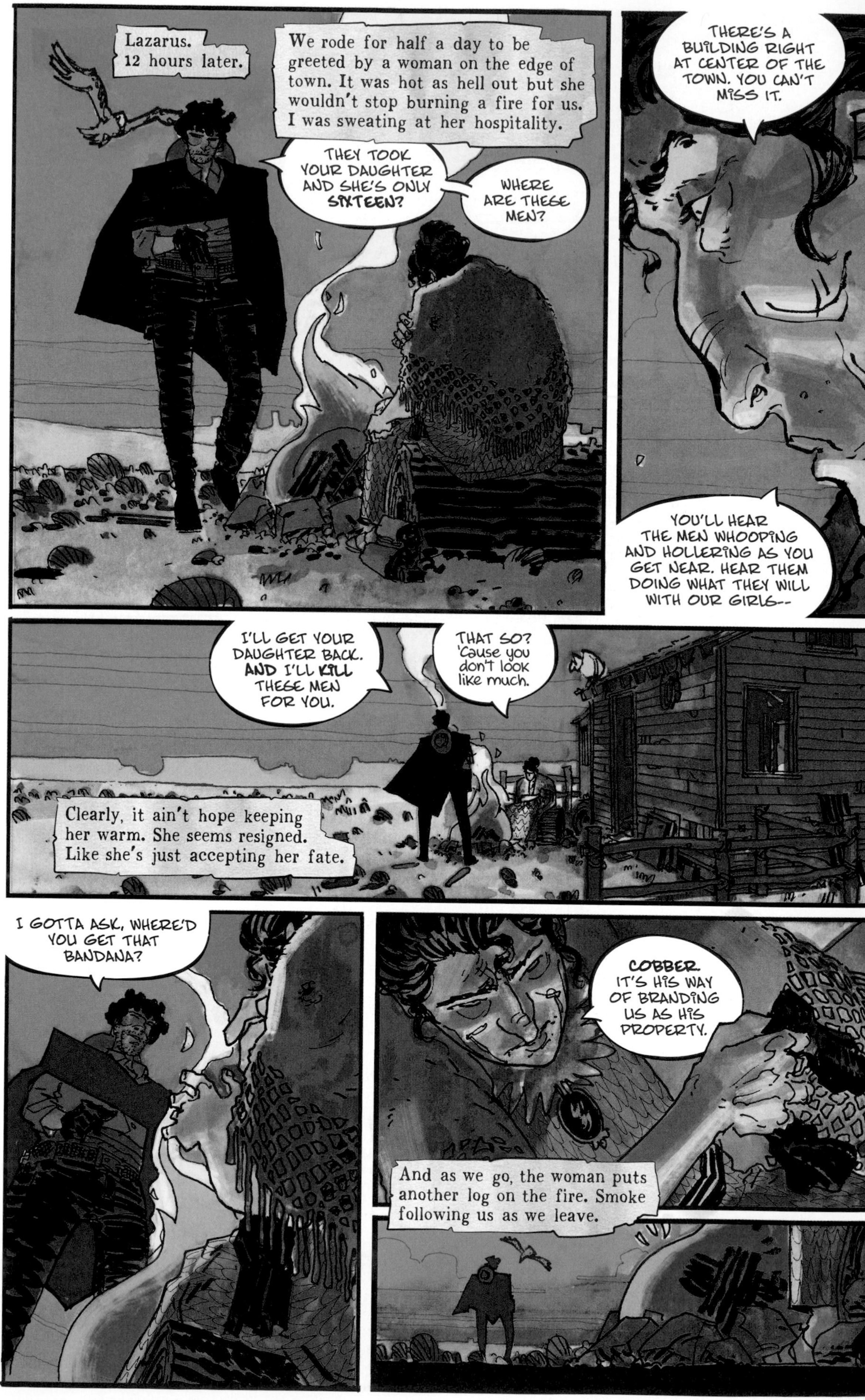
Lazarus. 12 hours later.
We rode for half a day to be greeted by a woman on the edge of town. It was hot as hell out but she wouldn't stop burning a fire for us. I was sweating at her hospitality.
THEY TOOK YOUR DAUGHTER AND SHE'S ONLY SIXTEEN?
WHERE ARE THESE MEN?
THERE'S A BUILDING RIGHT AT CENTER OF THE TOWN. YOU CAN'T MISS IT.
YOU'LL HEAR THE MEN WHOOPING AND HOLLERING AS YOU GET NEAR. HEAR THEM DOING WHAT THEY WILL WITH OUR GIRLS--
I'LL GET YOUR DAUGHTER BACK. AND I'LL KILL THESE MEN FOR YOU.
THAT SO? 'Cause you don't look like much.
Clearly, it ain't hope keeping her warm. She seems resigned. Like she's just accepting her fate.
I GOTTA ASK, WHERE'D YOU GET THAT BANDANA?
COBBER. IT'S HIS WAY OF BRANDING US AS HIS PROPERTY.
And as we go, the woman puts another log on the fire. Smoke following us as we leave.

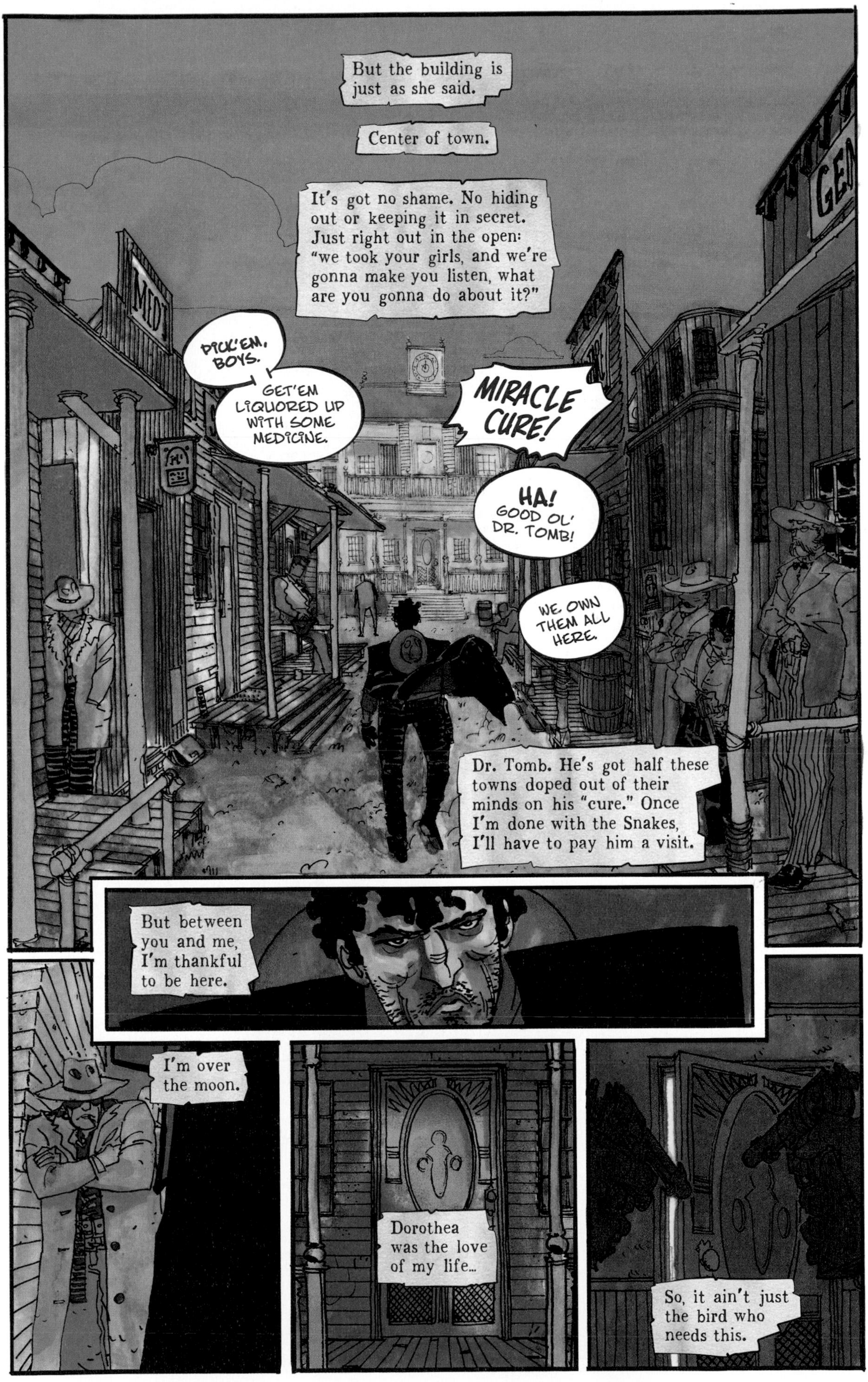
But the building is just as she said.
Center of town.
It's got no shame. No hiding out or keeping it in secret. Just right out in the open: "we took your girls, and we're gonna make you listen, what are you gonna do about it?"
PICK'EM, BOYS.
GET'EM LIQUORED UP WITH SOME MEDICINE.
MIRACLE CURE!
HA! GOOD OL' DR. TOMB!
WE OWN THEM ALL HERE.
Dr. Tomb. He's got half these towns doped out of their minds on his "cure." Once I'm done with the Snakes, I'll have to pay him a visit.
But between you and me, I'm thankful to be here.
I'm over the moon.
Dorothea was the love of my life...
So, it ain't just the bird who needs this.

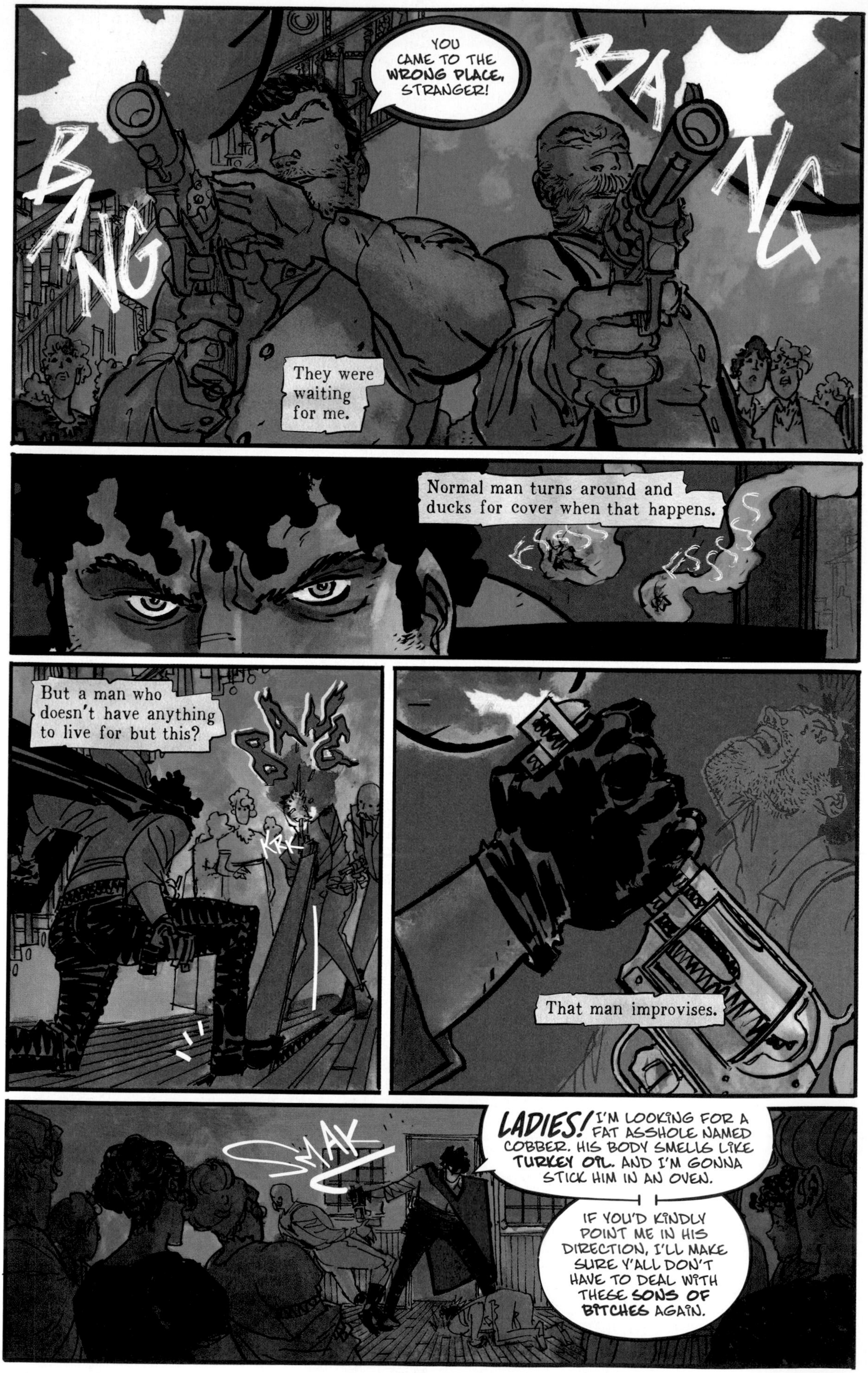
YOU CAME TO THE WRONG PLACE, STRANGER!
BANG
BANG
They were waiting for me.
Normal man turns around and ducks for cover when that happens.
But a man who doesn't have anything to live for but this?
BANG
KRK
That man improvises.
SMAK
LADIES! I'M LOOKING FOR A FAT ASSHOLE NAMED COBBER. HIS BODY SMELLS LIKE TURKEY OIL. AND I'M GONNA STICK HIM IN AN OVEN.
IF YOU'D KINDLY POINT ME IN HIS DIRECTION, I'LL MAKE SURE Y'ALL DON'T HAVE TO DEAL WITH THESE SONS OF BITCHES AGAIN.

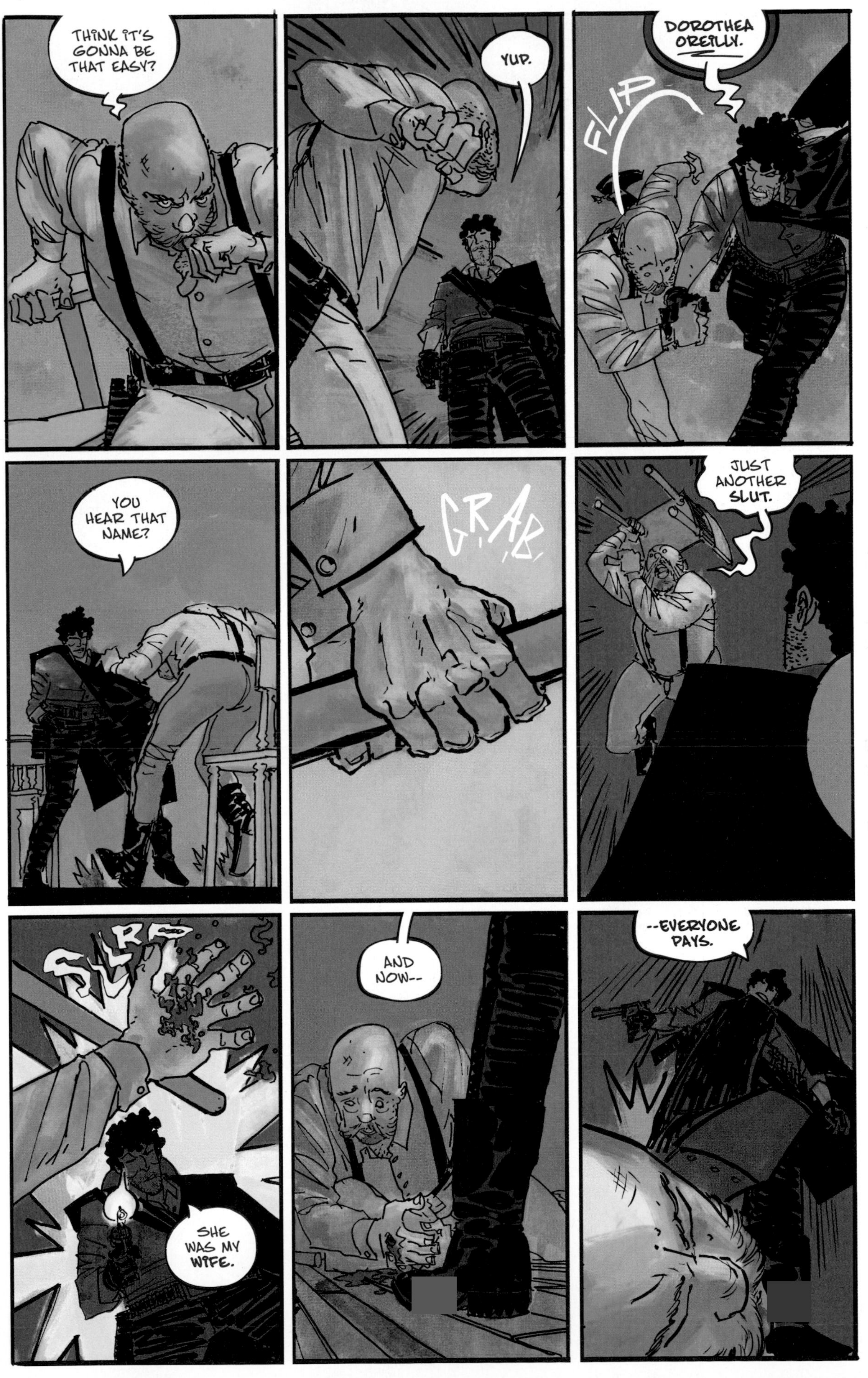
THINK IT'S GONNA BE THAT EASY?
YUP.
FLIP
DOROTHEA OREILLY.
YOU HEAR THAT NAME?
GRAB
JUST ANOTHER SLUT.
SHE WAS MY WIFE.
AND NOW--
--EVERYONE PAYS.

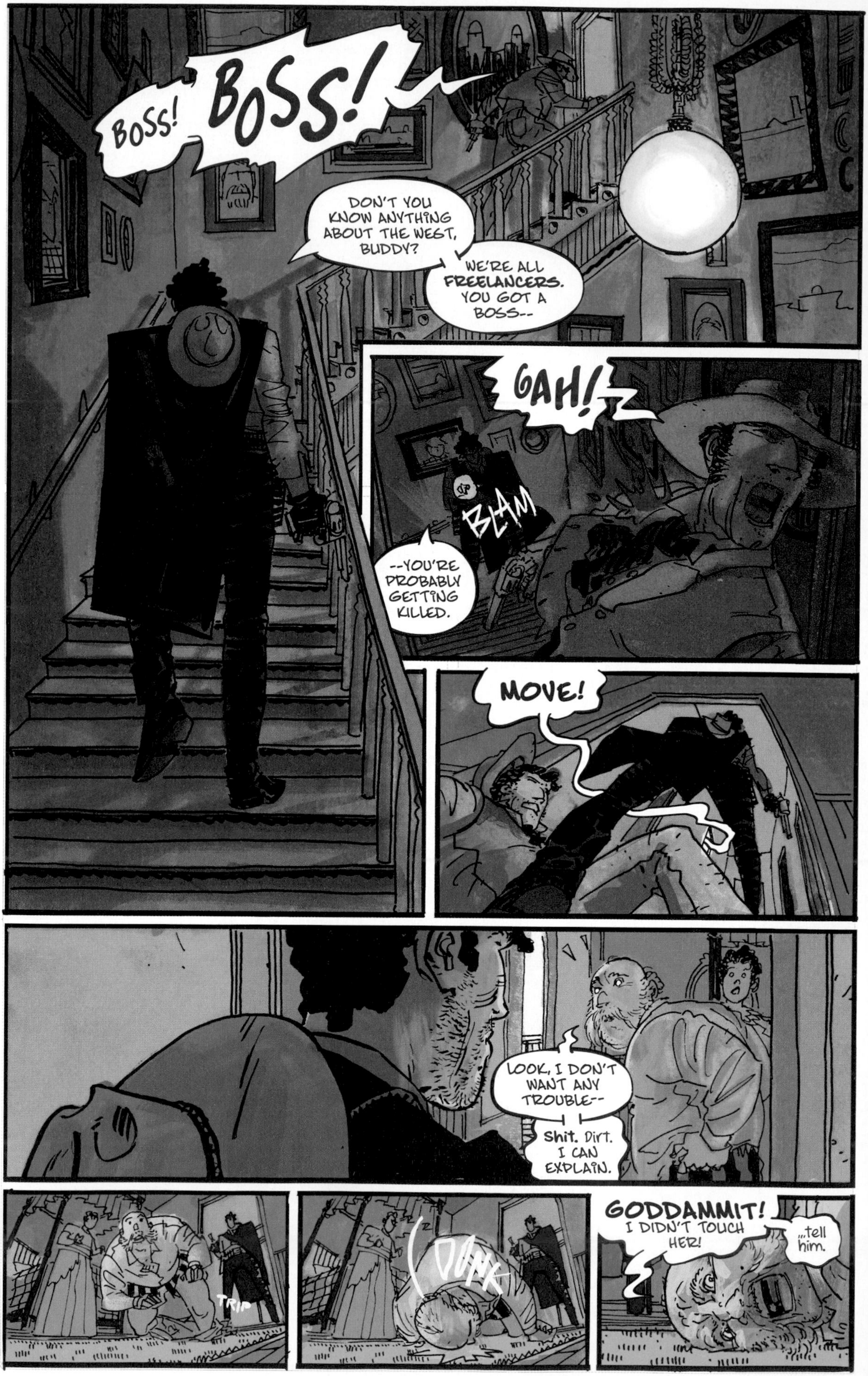

BOSS! BOSS!
DON'T YOU KNOW ANYTHING ABOUT THE WEST, BUDDY?
WE'RE ALL FREELANCERS. YOU GOT A BOSS--
GAH!
BLAM
--YOU'RE PROBABLY GETTING KILLED.
MOVE!
LOOK, I DON'T WANT ANY TROUBLE--
Shit. Dirt. I CAN EXPLAIN.
TRIP
DONK
GODDAMMIT! I DIDN'T TOUCH HER!
...tell him.

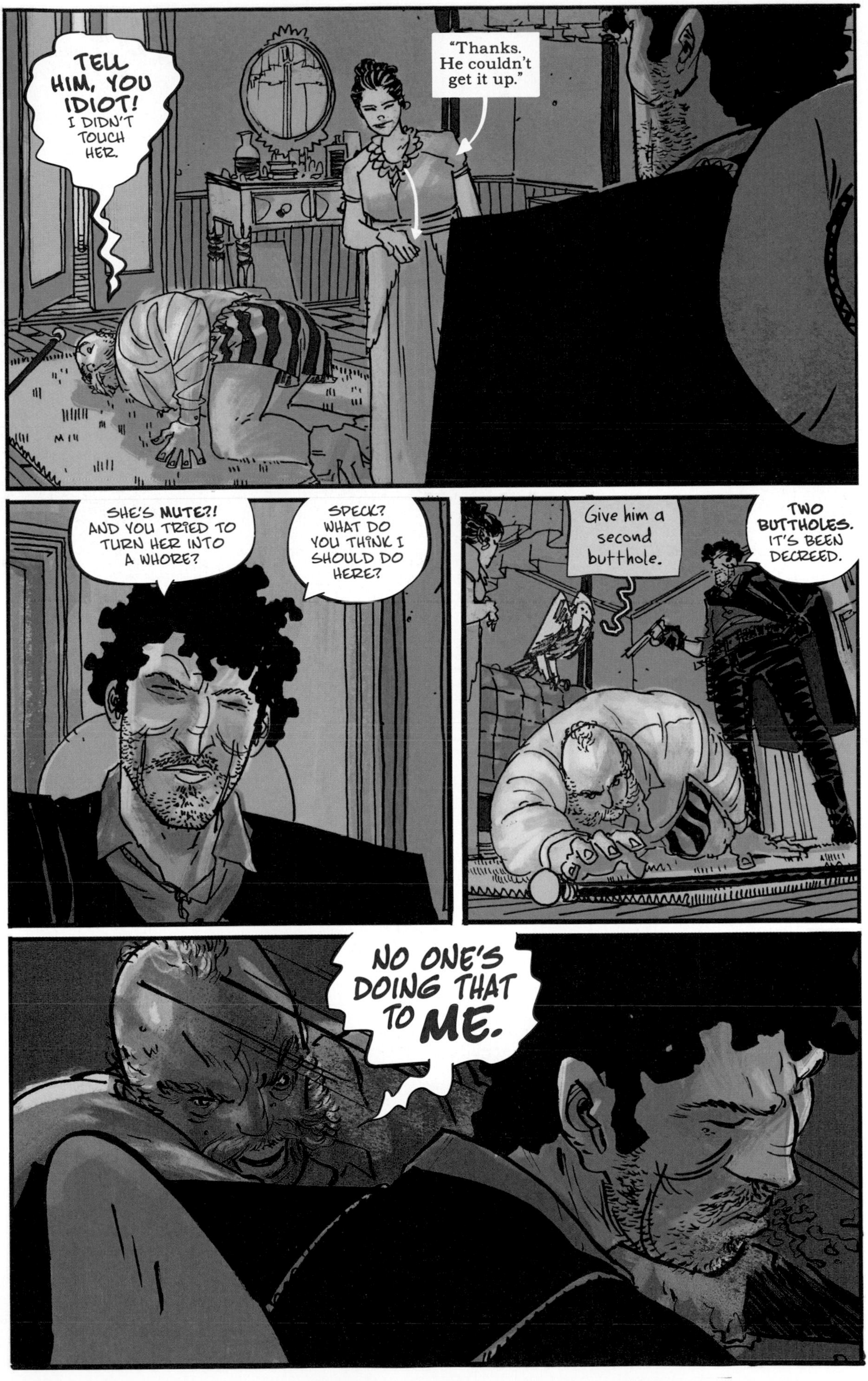
TELL HIM, YOU IDIOT! I DIDN'T TOUCH HER.
"Thanks. He couldn't get it up."
SHE'S MUTE?! AND YOU TRIED TO TURN HER INTO A WHORE?
SPECK? WHAT DO YOU THINK I SHOULD DO HERE?
Give him a second butthole.
TWO BUTTHOLES. IT'S BEEN DECREED.
NO ONE'S DOING THAT TO ME.

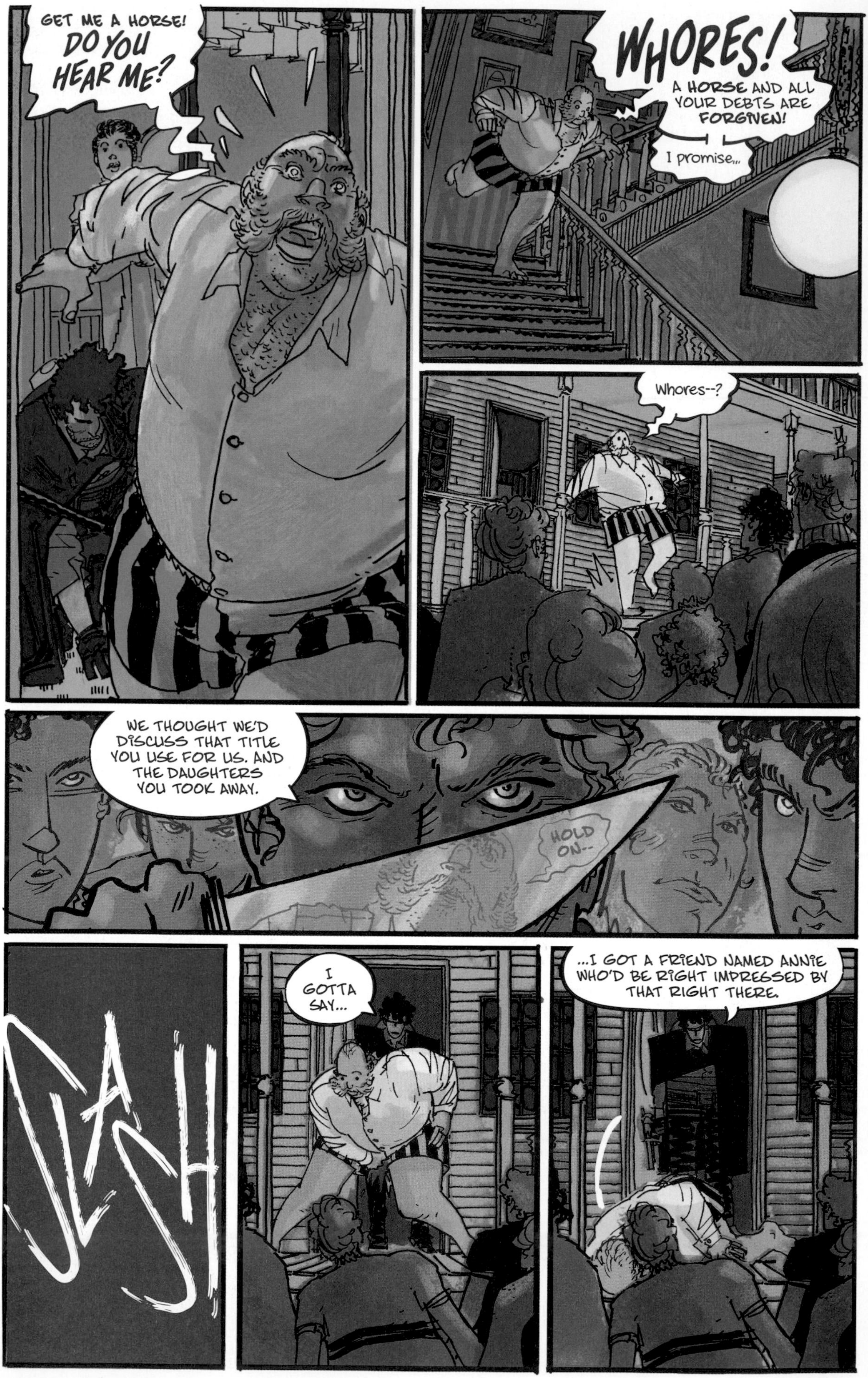
GET ME A HORSE! DO YOU HEAR ME?
WHORES!
A HORSE AND ALL YOUR DEBTS ARE FORGIVEN!
I promise...
Whores--?
WE THOUGHT WE'D DISCUSS THAT TITLE YOU USE FOR US. AND THE DAUGHTERS YOU TOOK AWAY.
HOLD ON--
SLASH
I GOTTA SAY...
...I GOT A FRIEND NAMED ANNIE WHO'D BE RIGHT IMPRESSED BY THAT RIGHT THERE.

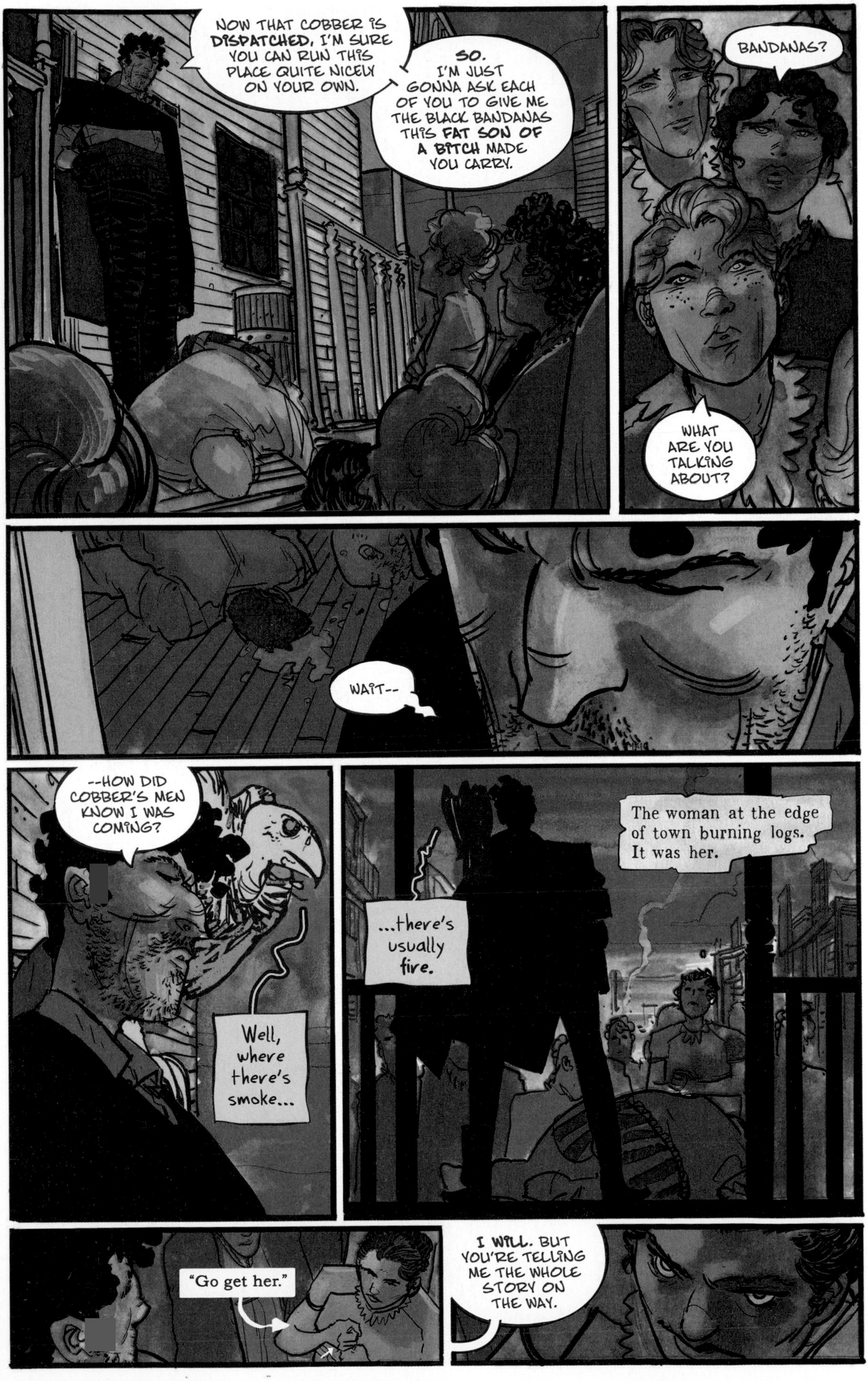
NOW THAT COBBER IS DISPATCHED, I'M SURE YOU CAN RUN THIS PLACE QUITE NICELY ON YOUR OWN.
SO. I'M JUST GONNA ASK EACH OF YOU TO GIVE ME THE BLACK BANDANAS THIS FAT SON OF A BITCH MADE YOU CARRY.
BANDANAS?
WHAT ARE YOU TALKING ABOUT?
WAIT--
--HOW DID COBBER'S MEN KNOW I WAS COMING?
Well, where there's smoke...
...there's usually fire.
The woman at the edge of town burning logs. It was her.
"Go get her."
I WILL. BUT YOU'RE TELLING ME THE WHOLE STORY ON THE WAY.

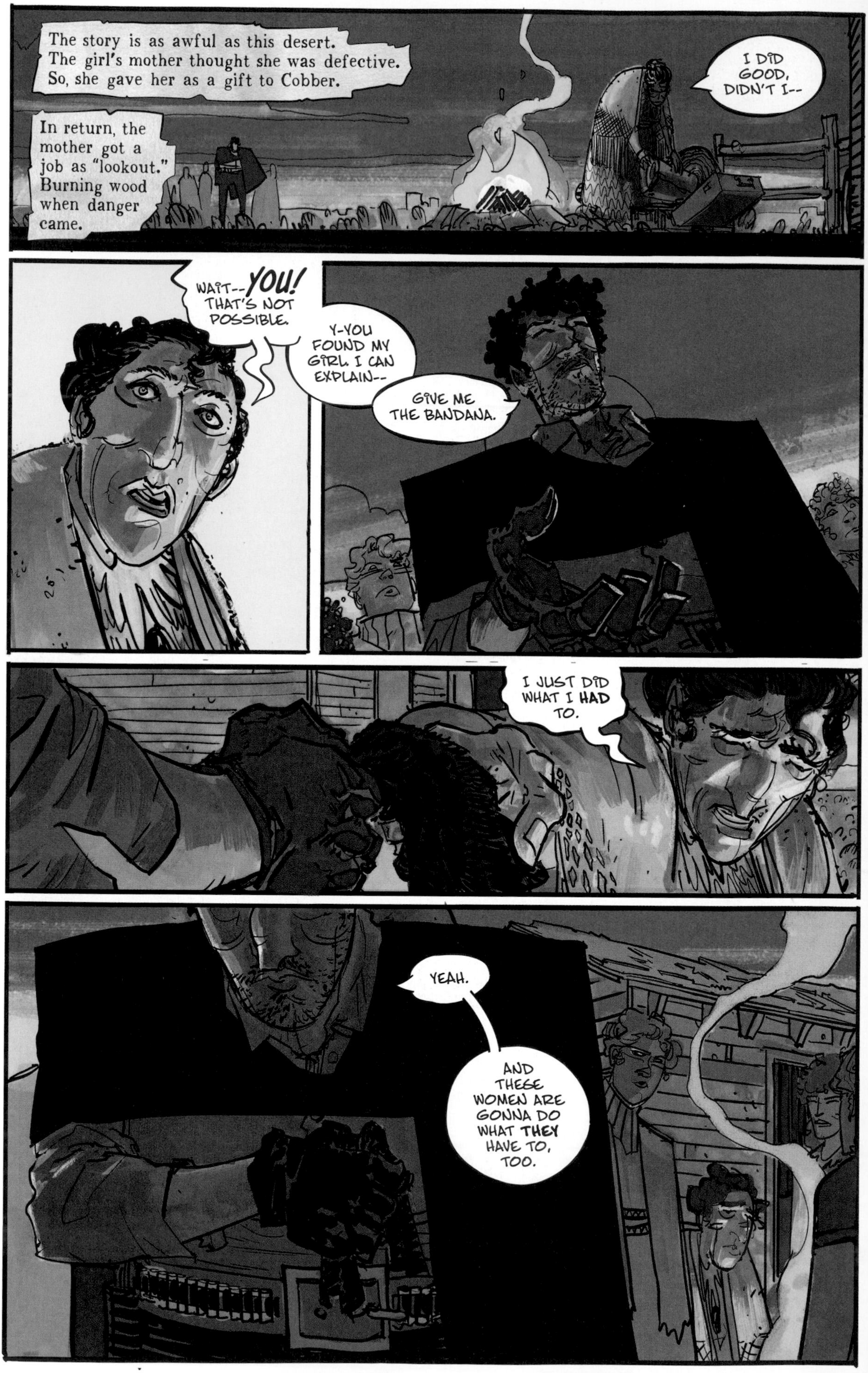
The story is as awful as this desert. The girl's mother thought she was defective. So, she gave her as a gift to Cobber.
In return, the mother got a job as "lookout." Burning wood when danger came.
I DID GOOD, DIDN'T I--
WAIT--YOU! THAT'S NOT POSSIBLE.
Y-YOU FOUND MY GIRL. I CAN EXPLAIN--
GIVE ME THE BANDANA.
I JUST DID WHAT I HAD TO.
YEAH.
AND THESE WOMEN ARE GONNA DO WHAT THEY HAVE TO, TOO.

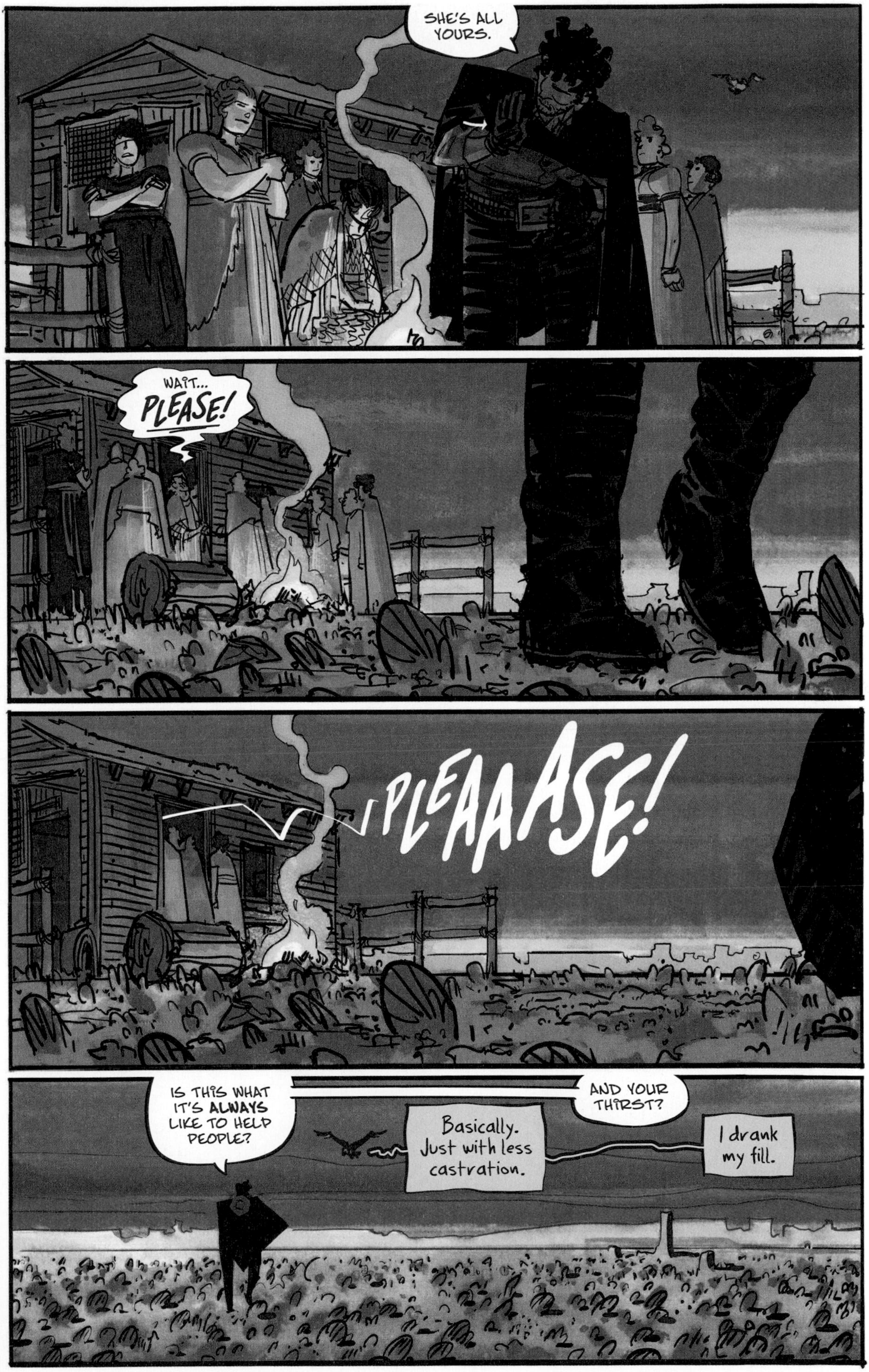
SHE'S ALL YOURS.
WAIT... PLEASE!
PLEAAAASE!
IS THIS WHAT IT'S ALWAYS LIKE TO HELP PEOPLE?
Basically. Just with less castration.
AND YOUR THIRST?
I drank my fill.

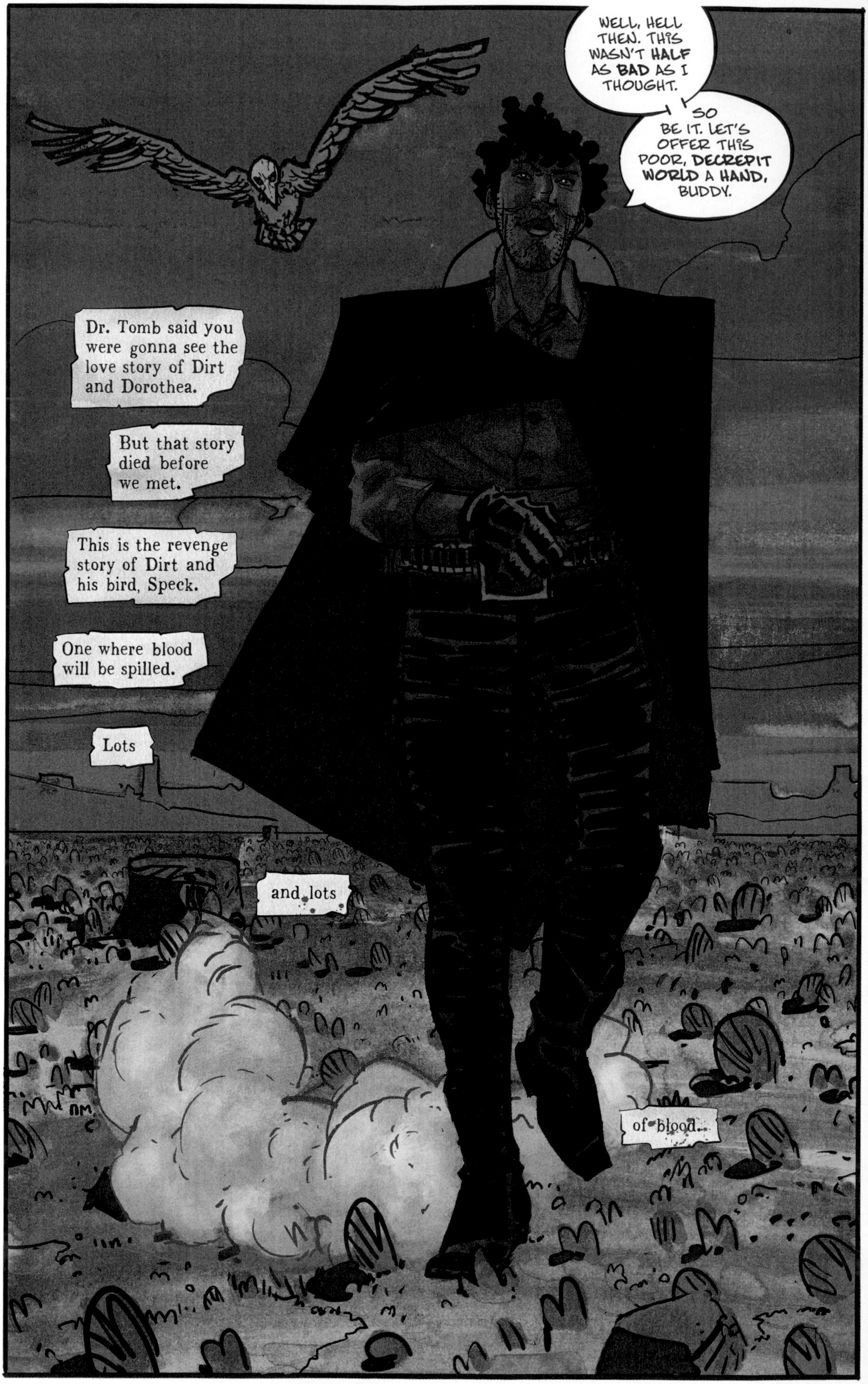
WELL, HELL THEN. THIS WASN'T HALF AS BAD AS I THOUGHT.
SO BE IT. LET'S OFFER THIS POOR, DECREPIT WORLD A HAND, BUDDY.
Dr. Tomb said you were gonna see the love story of Dirt and Dorothea.
But that story died before we met.
This is the revenge story of Dirt and his bird, Speck.
One where blood will be spilled.
Lots
and lots
of blood...

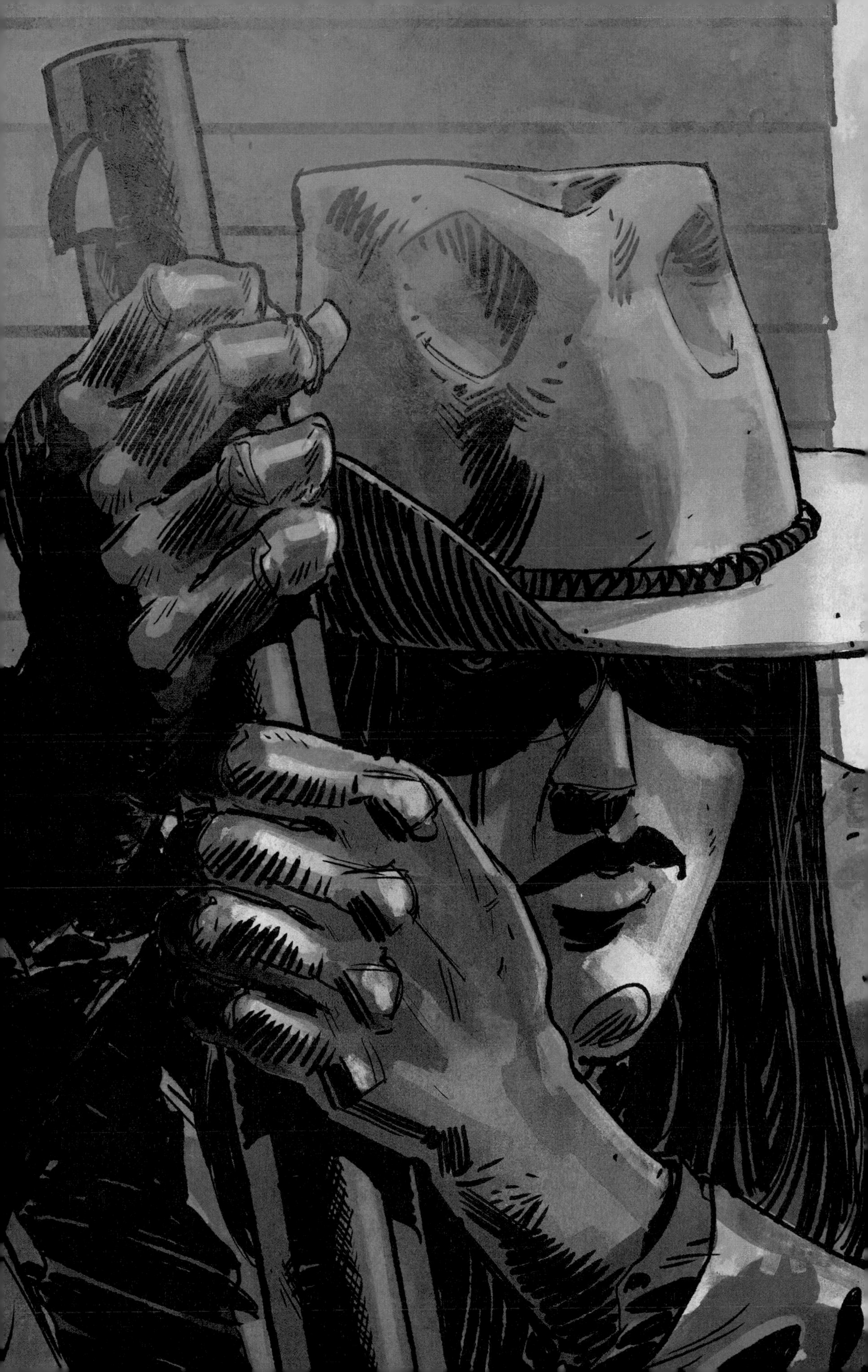

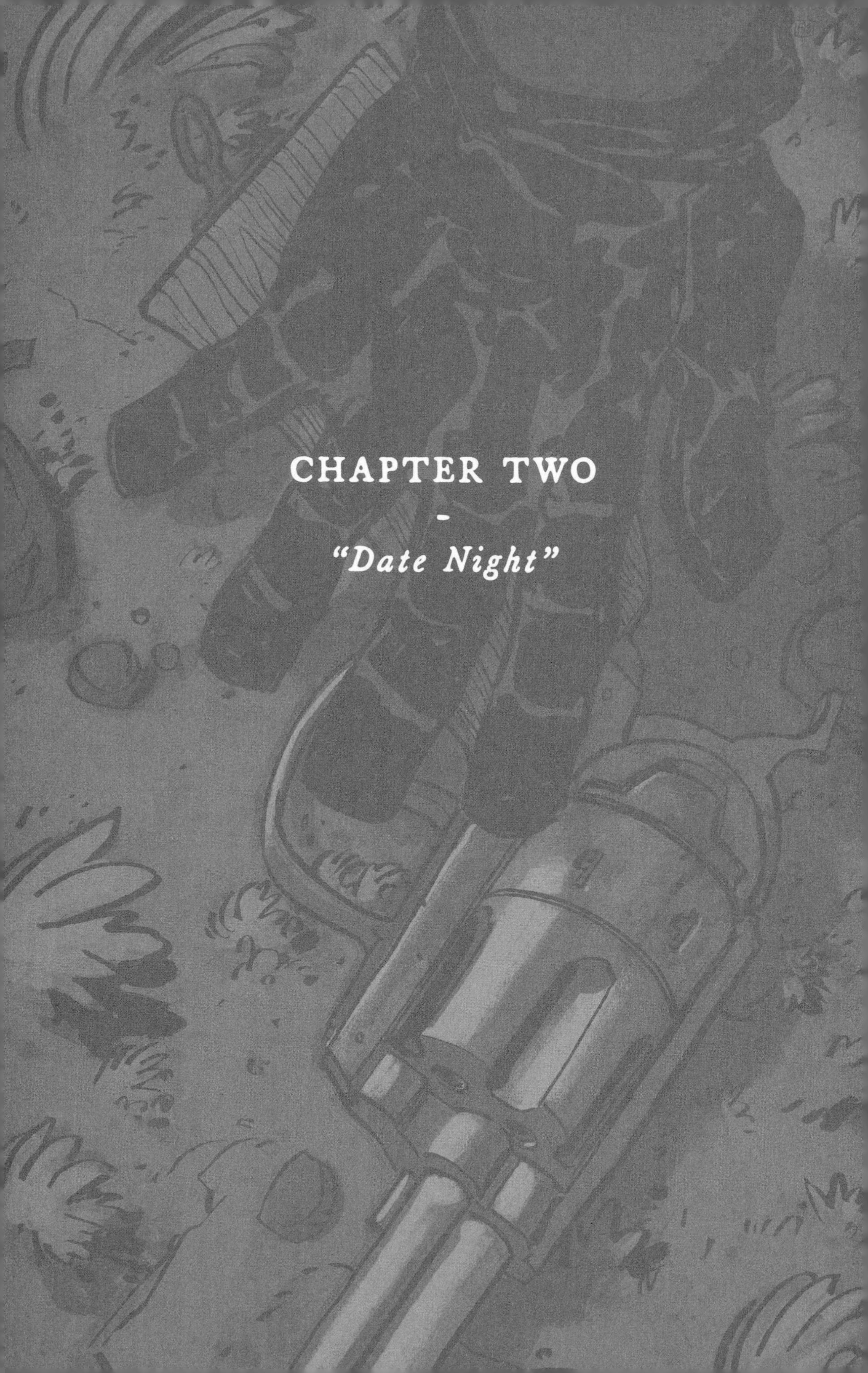

CHAPTER TWO

-

"Date Night"

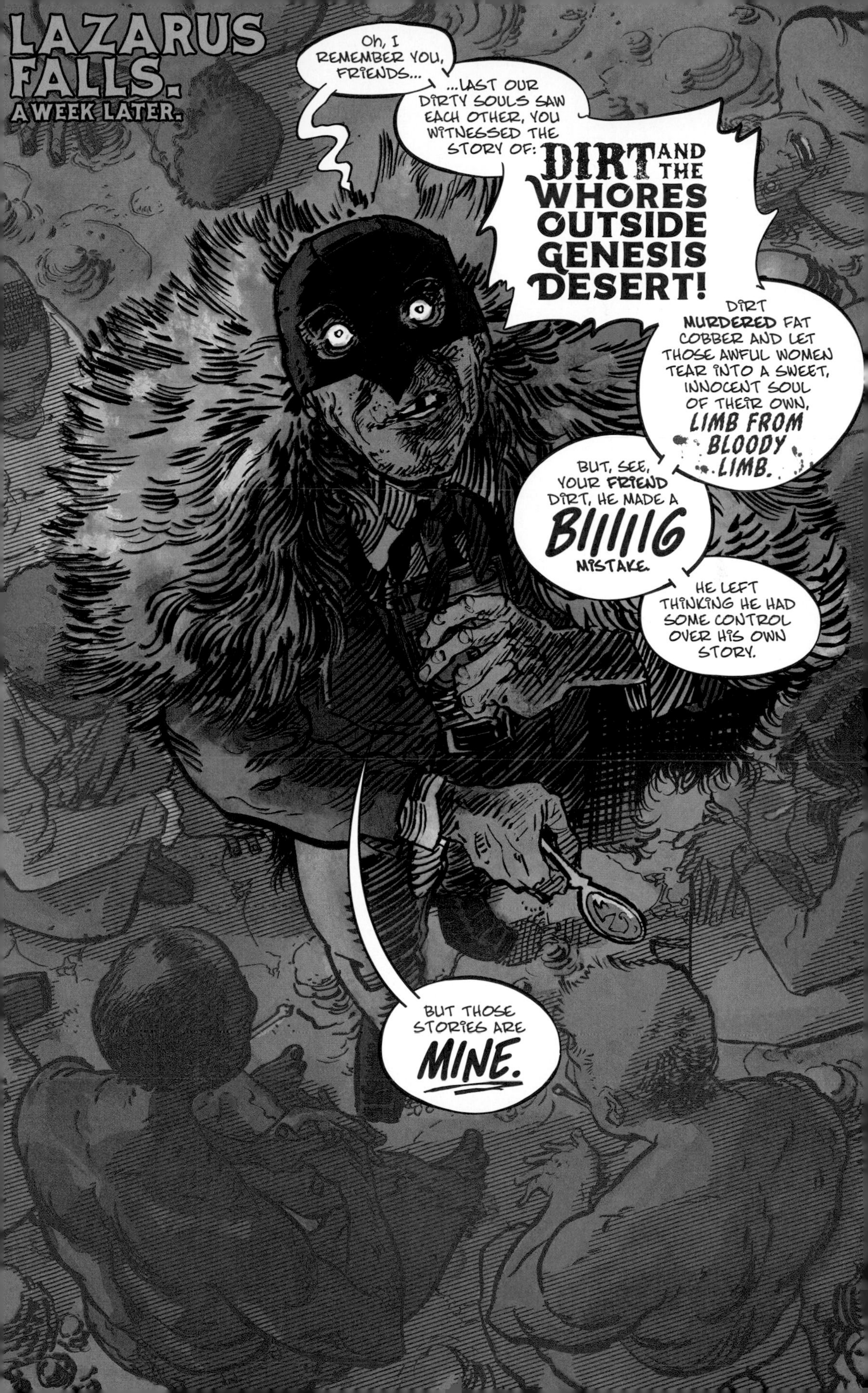
LAZARUS FALLS.
A WEEK LATER.
Oh, I REMEMBER YOU, FRIENDS...
...LAST OUR DIRTY SOULS SAW EACH OTHER, YOU WITNESSED THE STORY OF: DIRT AND THE WHORES OUTSIDE GENESIS DESERT!
DIRT MURDERED FAT COBBER AND LET THOSE AWFUL WOMEN TEAR INTO A SWEET, INNOCENT SOUL OF THEIR OWN, LIMB FROM BLOODY LIMB.
BUT, SEE, YOUR FRIEND DIRT, HE MADE A BIIIIIG MISTAKE.
HE LEFT THINKING HE HAD SOME CONTROL OVER HIS OWN STORY.
BUT THOSE STORIES ARE MINE.

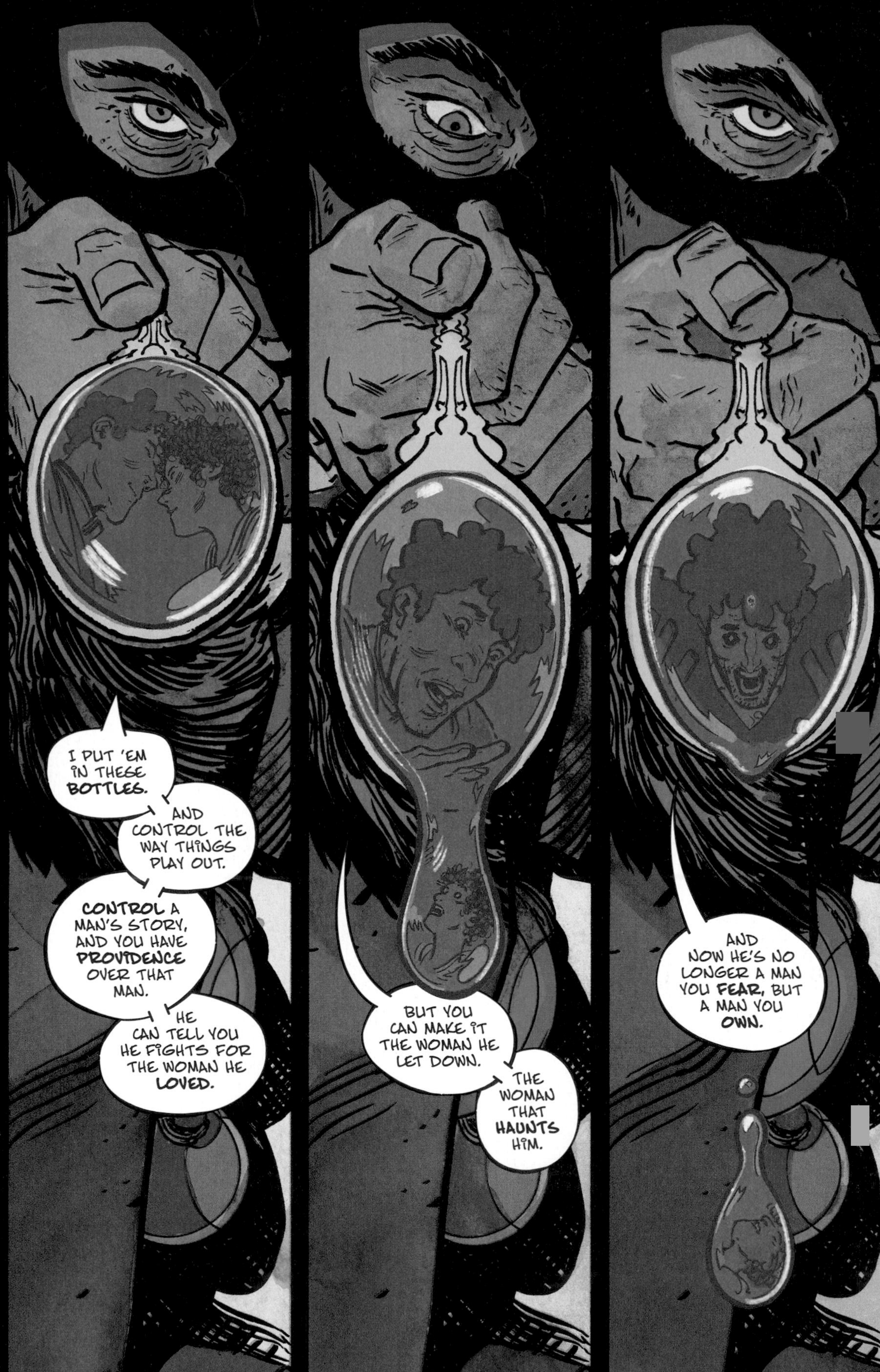

I PUT 'EM IN THESE BOTTLES.
AND CONTROL THE WAY THINGS PLAY OUT.
CONTROL A MAN'S STORY, AND YOU HAVE PROVIDENCE OVER THAT MAN.
HE CAN TELL YOU HE FIGHTS FOR THE WOMAN HE LOVED.
BUT YOU CAN MAKE IT THE WOMAN HE LET DOWN.
THE WOMAN THAT HAUNTS HIM.
AND NOW HE'S NO LONGER A MAN YOU FEAR, BUT A MAN YOU OWN.

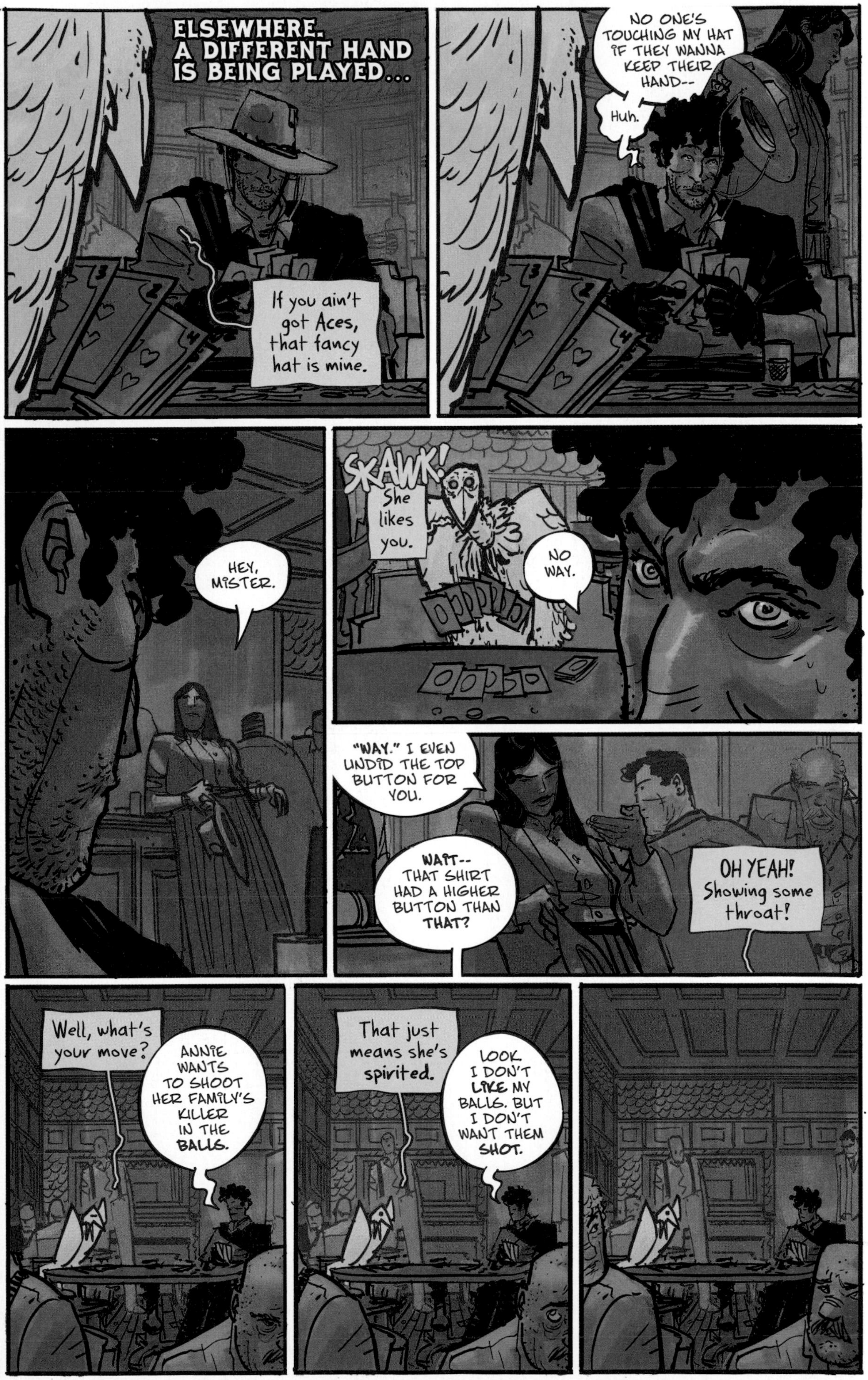
ELSEWHERE. A DIFFERENT HAND IS BEING PLAYED...
If you ain't got Aces, that fancy hat is mine.
NO ONE'S TOUCHING MY HAT IF THEY WANNA KEEP THEIR HAND--
Huh.
HEY, MISTER.
SKAWK!
She likes you.
NO WAY.
"WAY." I EVEN UNDID THE TOP BUTTON FOR YOU.
WAIT-- THAT SHIRT HAD A HIGHER BUTTON THAN THAT?
OH YEAH! Showing some throat!
Well, what's your move?
ANNIE WANTS TO SHOOT HER FAMILY'S KILLER IN THE BALLS.
That just means she's spirited.
LOOK. I DON'T LIKE MY BALLS. BUT I DON'T WANT THEM SHOT.

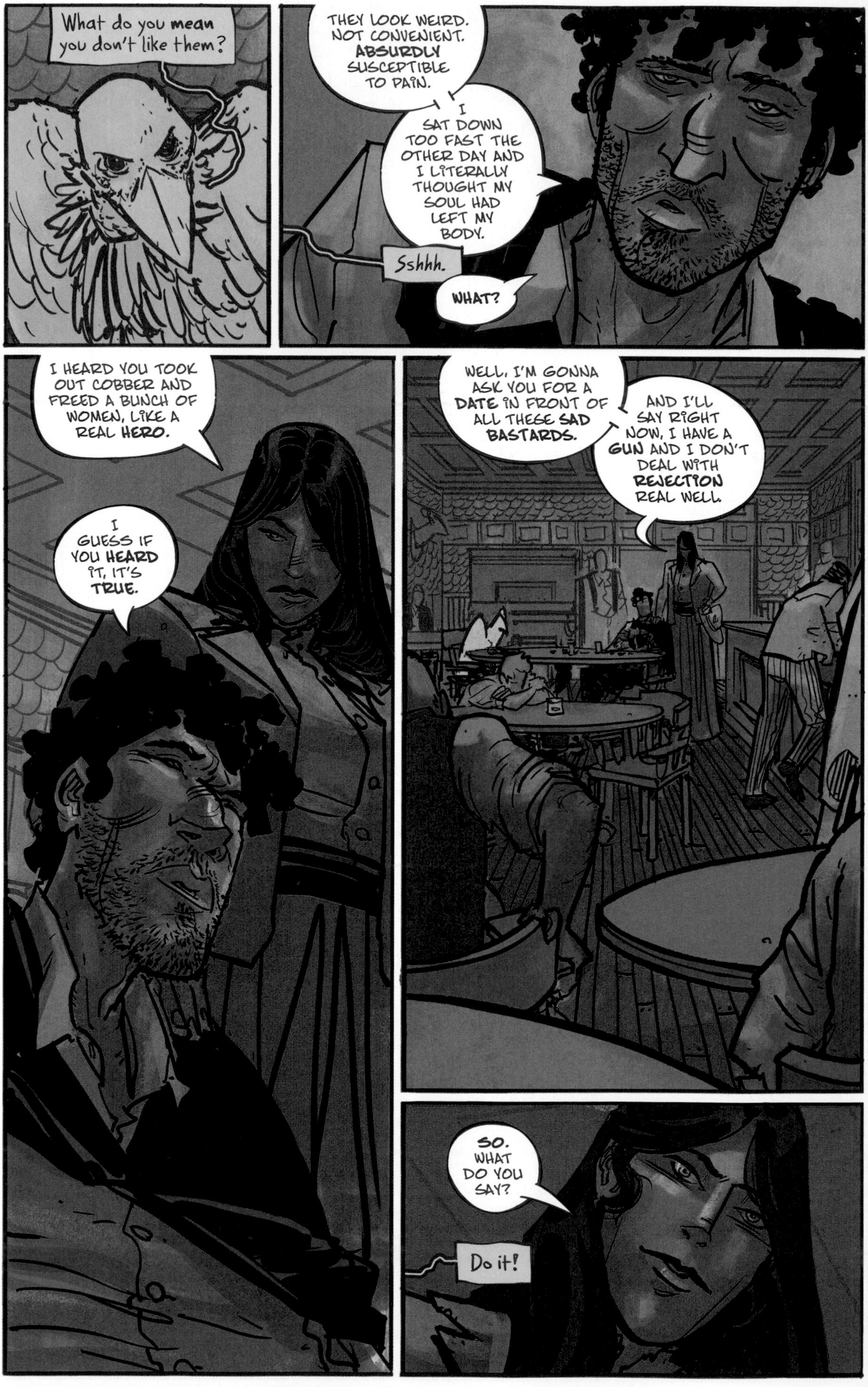
What do you mean you don't like them?
THEY LOOK WEIRD. NOT CONVENIENT. ABSURDLY SUSCEPTIBLE TO PAIN.
I SAT DOWN TOO FAST THE OTHER DAY AND I LITERALLY THOUGHT MY SOUL HAD LEFT MY BODY.
Sshhh.
WHAT?
I HEARD YOU TOOK OUT COBBER AND FREED A BUNCH OF WOMEN, LIKE A REAL HERO.
I GUESS IF YOU HEARD IT, IT'S TRUE.
WELL, I'M GONNA ASK YOU FOR A DATE IN FRONT OF ALL THESE SAD BASTARDS.
AND I'LL SAY RIGHT NOW, I HAVE A GUN AND I DON'T DEAL WITH REJECTION REAL WELL.
SO. WHAT DO YOU SAY?
Do it!

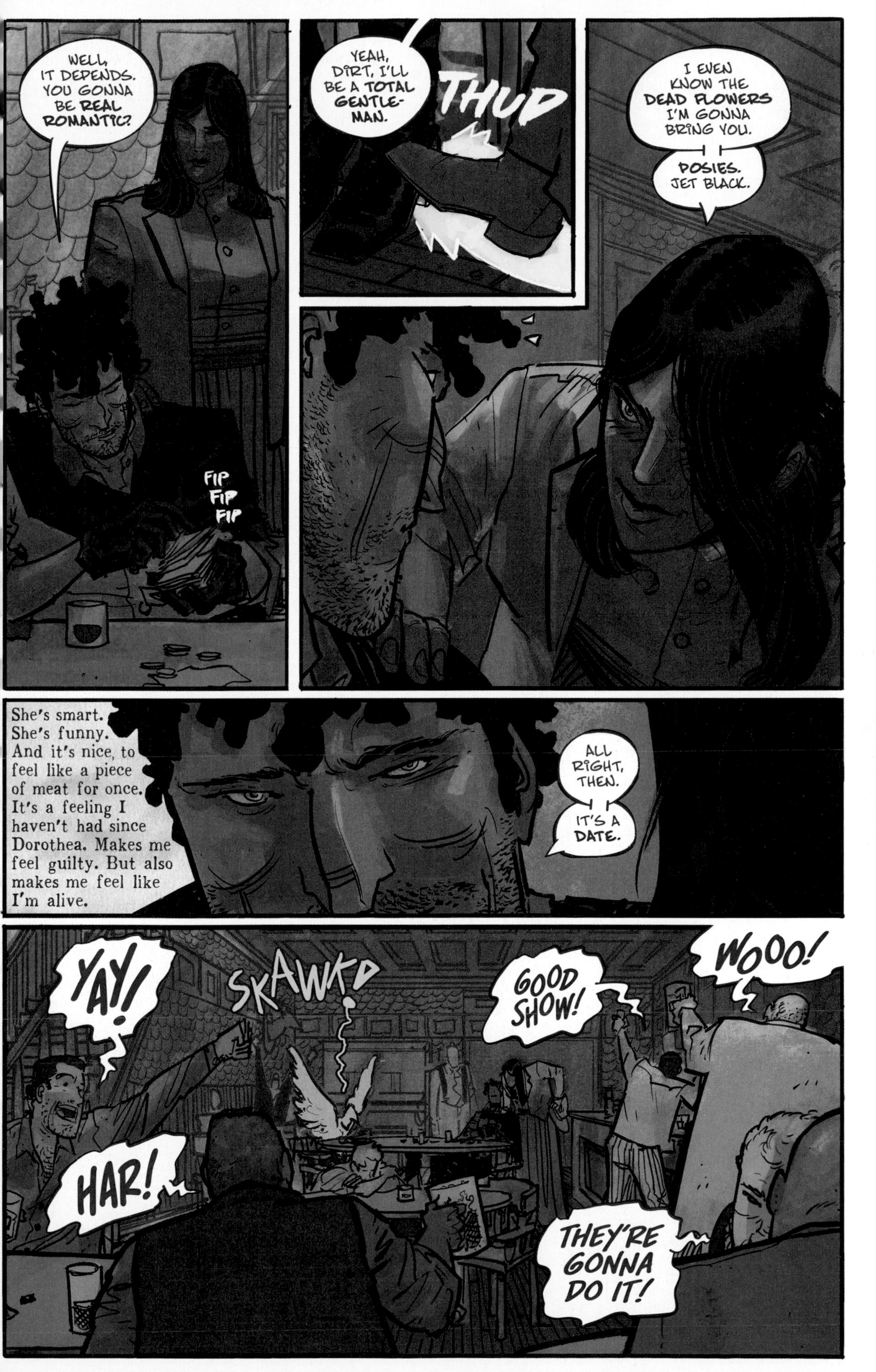
WELL, IT DEPENDS. YOU GONNA BE REAL ROMANTIC?
FIP
FIP
FIP
YEAH, DIRT, I'LL BE A TOTAL GENTLE-MAN.
THUD
I EVEN KNOW THE DEAD FLOWERS I'M GONNA BRING YOU.
POSIES. JET BLACK.
She's smart. She's funny. And it's nice, to feel like a piece of meat for once. It's a feeling I haven't had since Dorothea. Makes me feel guilty. But also makes me feel like I'm alive.
ALL RIGHT, THEN.
IT'S A DATE.
YAY!
SKAWKK
HAR!
GOOD SHOW!
WOOO!
THEY'RE GONNA DO IT!

HOURS LATER...

I can't blame them. You lost what we have and you go nuts at anything good happening in someone's future.

That's what happens when you spend most your time living... in the past.

TWENTY YEARS AGO.

JEBEDIAH DIRT O'RYAN.

MY MOMMA HATES WHEN I'M CALLED DIRT, DOROTHEA. YOU KNOW THAT.

THEN SHE SHOULD GIVE YOU BETTER HYGIENE.

PRIEST SAYS I'LL STOP SMELLING WHEN I GET CONFIRMATION.

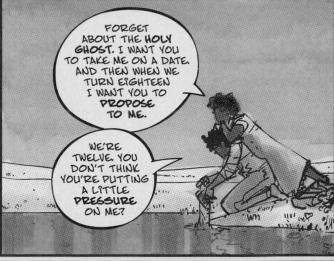

FORGET ABOUT THE HOLY GHOST. I WANT YOU TO TAKE ME ON A DATE. AND THEN WHEN WE TURN EIGHTEEN I WANT YOU TO PROPOSE TO ME.

WE'RE TWELVE. YOU DON'T THINK YOU'RE PUTTING A LITTLE PRESSURE ON ME?

NO. BUT I AM SAYING, I EXPECT SOME COURTSHIP.

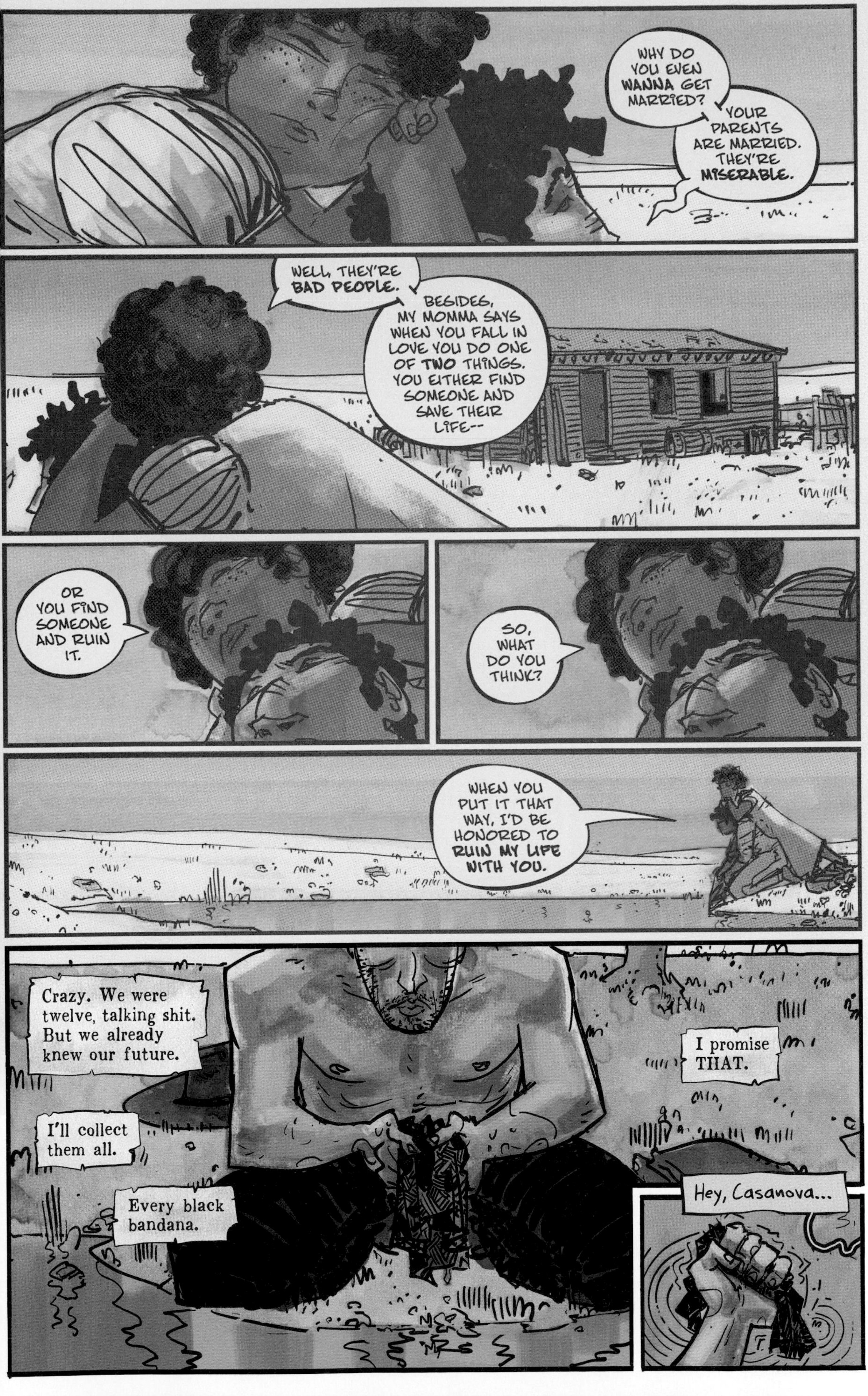
WHY DO YOU EVEN WANNA GET MARRIED?
YOUR PARENTS ARE MARRIED. THEY'RE MISERABLE.
WELL, THEY'RE BAD PEOPLE.
BESIDES, MY MOMMA SAYS WHEN YOU FALL IN LOVE YOU DO ONE OF TWO THINGS. YOU EITHER FIND SOMEONE AND SAVE THEIR LIFE--
OR YOU FIND SOMEONE AND RUIN IT.
SO, WHAT DO YOU THINK?
WHEN YOU PUT IT THAT WAY, I'D BE HONORED TO RUIN MY LIFE WITH YOU.
Crazy. We were twelve, talking shit. But we already knew our future.
I'll collect them all.
Every black bandana.
I promise THAT.
Hey, Casanova...

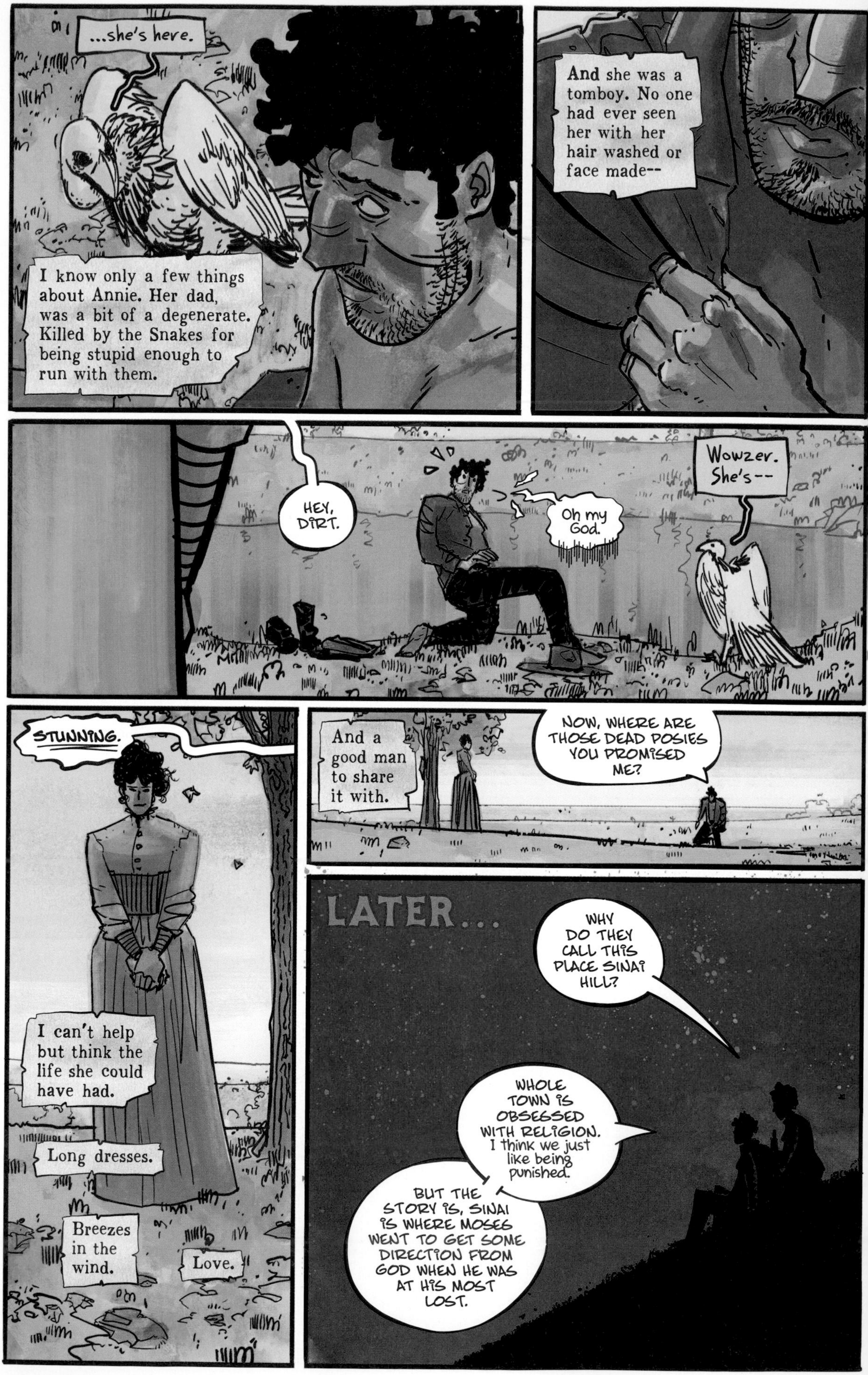
...she's here.
I know only a few things about Annie. Her dad, was a bit of a degenerate. Killed by the Snakes for being stupid enough to run with them.
And she was a tomboy. No one had ever seen her with her hair washed or face made--
HEY, DIRT.
Oh my God.
Wowzer. She's--
STUNNING.
I can't help but think the life she could have had.
Long dresses.
Breezes in the wind.
Love.
And a good man to share it with.
NOW, WHERE ARE THOSE DEAD POSIES YOU PROMISED ME?
LATER...
WHY DO THEY CALL THIS PLACE SINAI HILL?
WHOLE TOWN IS OBSESSED WITH RELIGION. I think we just like being punished.
BUT THE STORY IS, SINAI IS WHERE MOSES WENT TO GET SOME DIRECTION FROM GOD WHEN HE WAS AT HIS MOST LOST.

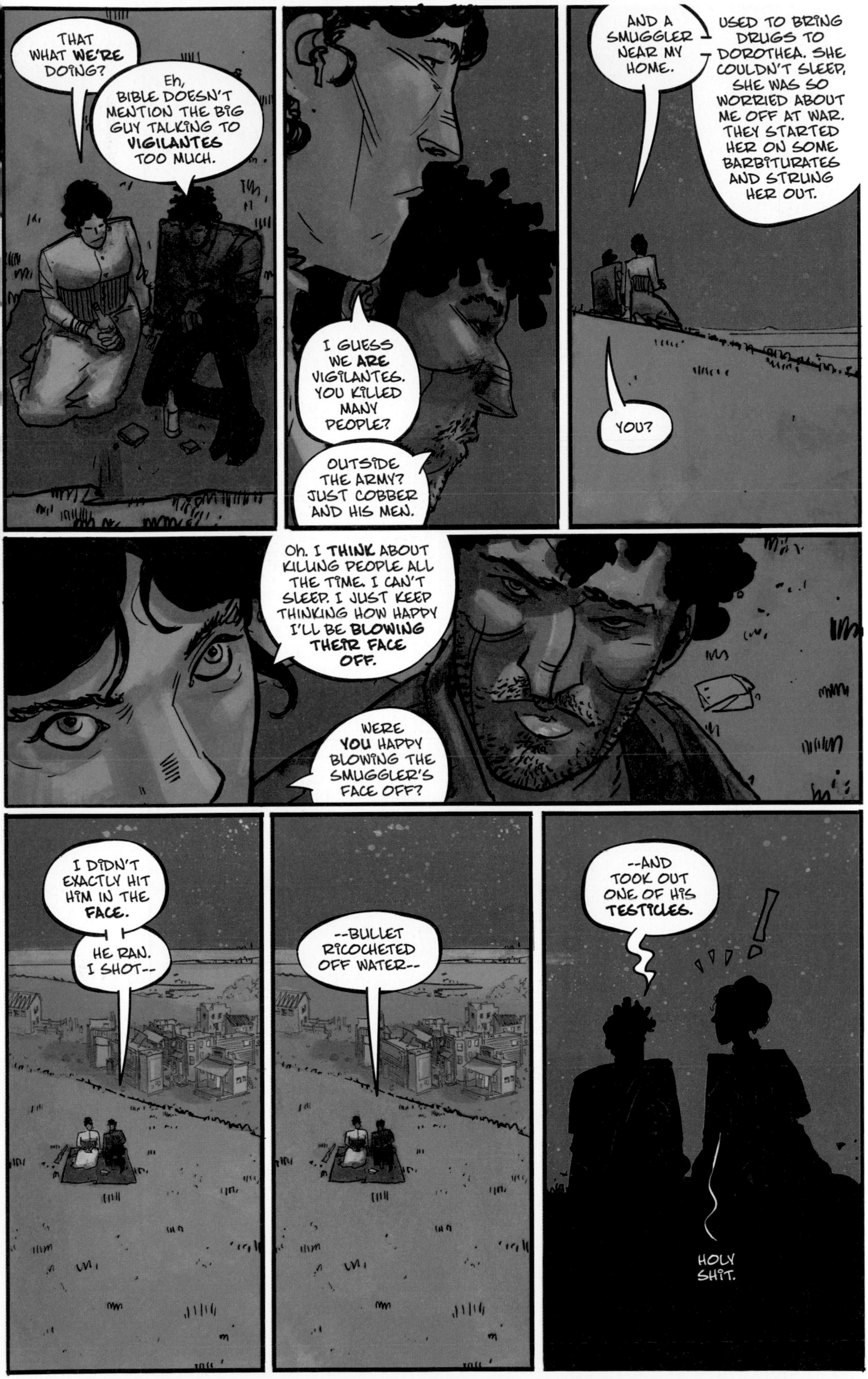
THAT WHAT WE'RE DOING?
Eh, BIBLE DOESN'T MENTION THE BIG GUY TALKING TO VIGILANTES TOO MUCH.
I GUESS WE ARE VIGILANTES. YOU KILLED MANY PEOPLE?
OUTSIDE THE ARMY? JUST COBBER AND HIS MEN.
AND A SMUGGLER NEAR MY HOME.
USED TO BRING DRUGS TO DOROTHEA. SHE COULDN'T SLEEP, SHE WAS SO WORRIED ABOUT ME OFF AT WAR. THEY STARTED HER ON SOME BARBITURATES AND STRUNG HER OUT.
YOU?
Oh. I THINK ABOUT KILLING PEOPLE ALL THE TIME. I CAN'T SLEEP. I JUST KEEP THINKING HOW HAPPY I'LL BE BLOWING THEIR FACE OFF.
WERE YOU HAPPY BLOWING THE SMUGGLER'S FACE OFF?
I DIDN'T EXACTLY HIT HIM IN THE FACE.
HE RAN. I SHOT--
--BULLET RICOCHETED OFF WATER--
--AND TOOK OUT ONE OF HIS TESTICLES.
!
HOLY SHIT.

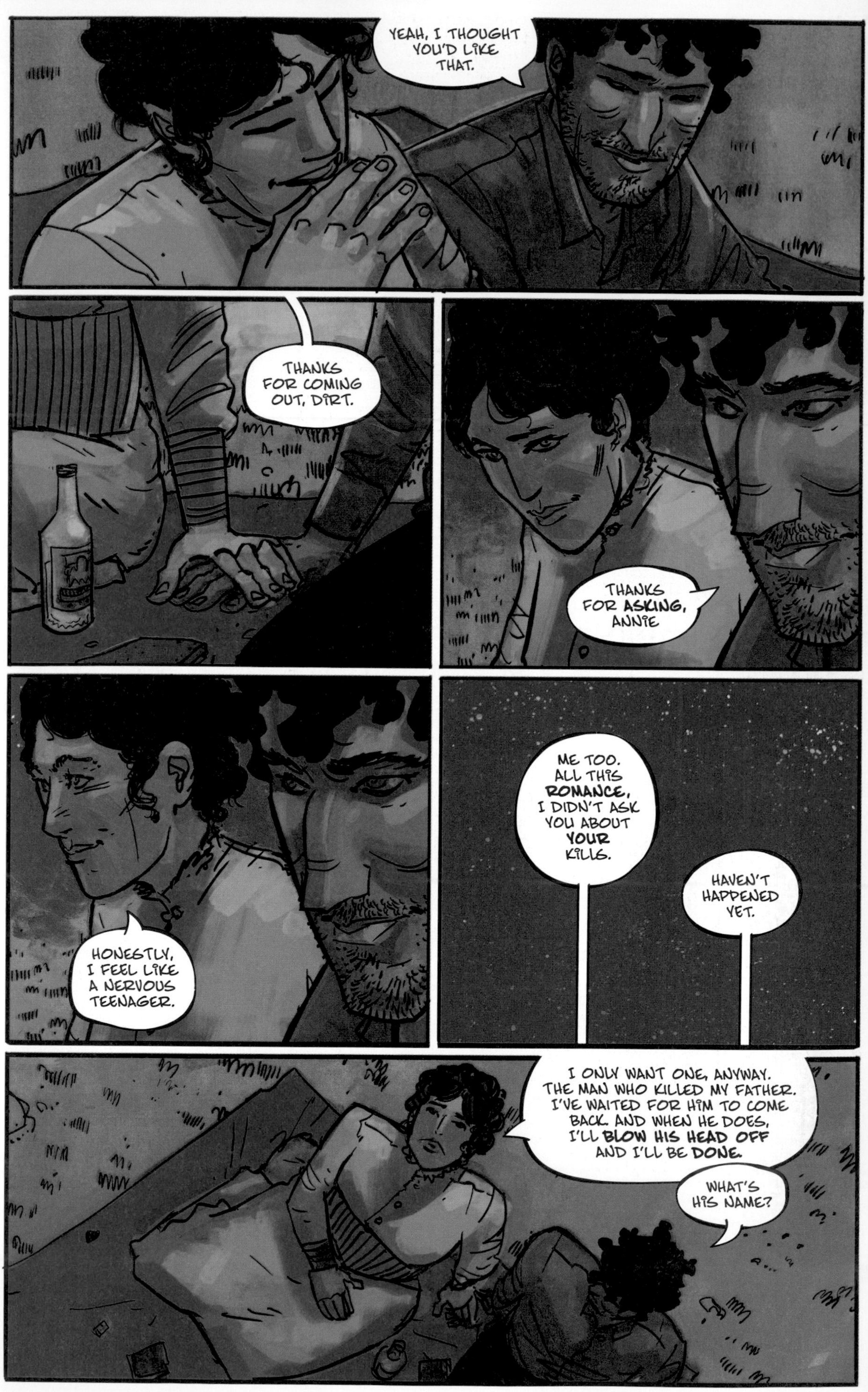
YEAH, I THOUGHT YOU'D LIKE THAT.
THANKS FOR COMING OUT, DIRT.
THANKS FOR **ASKING**, ANNIE
HONESTLY, I FEEL LIKE A NERVOUS TEENAGER.
ME TOO. ALL THIS **ROMANCE**, I DIDN'T ASK YOU ABOUT **YOUR** KILLS.
HAVEN'T HAPPENED YET.
I ONLY WANT ONE, ANYWAY. THE MAN WHO KILLED MY FATHER. I'VE WAITED FOR HIM TO COME BACK. AND WHEN HE DOES, I'LL **BLOW HIS HEAD OFF** AND I'LL BE **DONE**.
WHAT'S HIS NAME?

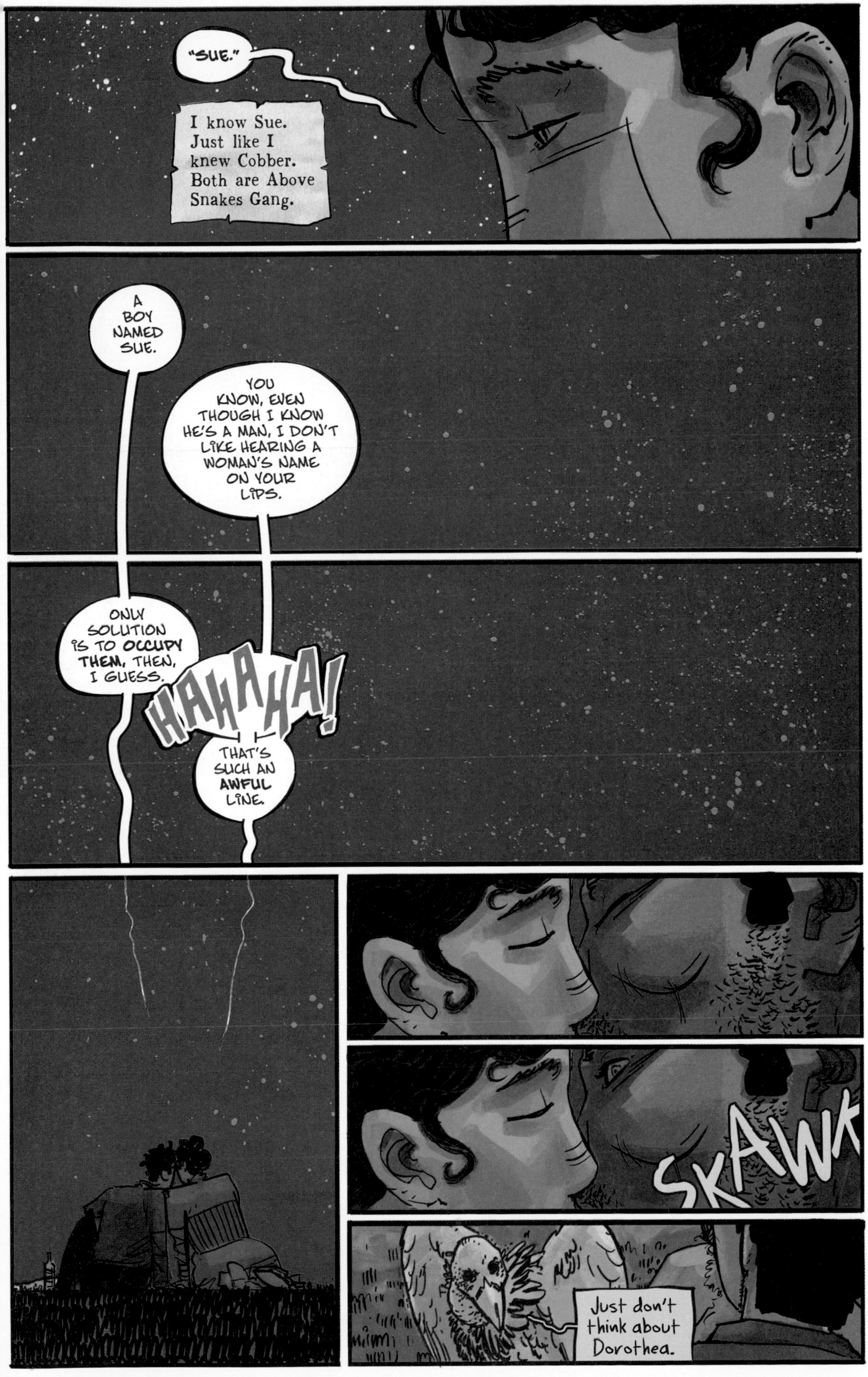
"SUE."
I know Sue. Just like I knew Cobber. Both are Above Snakes Gang.
A BOY NAMED SUE.
YOU KNOW, EVEN THOUGH I KNOW HE'S A MAN, I DON'T LIKE HEARING A WOMAN'S NAME ON YOUR LIPS.
ONLY SOLUTION IS TO OCCUPY THEM, THEN, I GUESS.
HAHAHA!
THAT'S SUCH AN AWFUL LINE.
SKAWK
Just don't think about Dorothea.

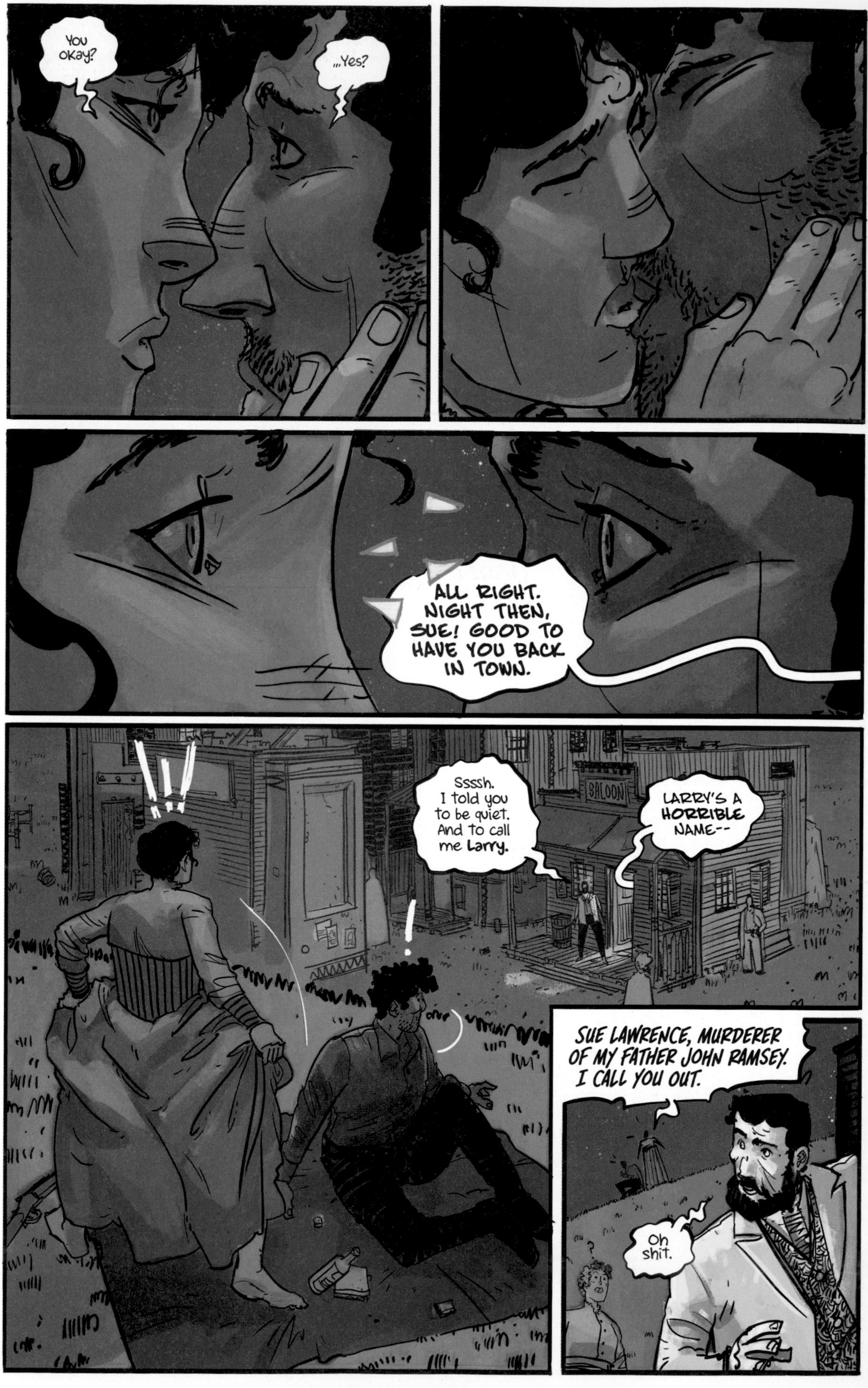
You okay?
...Yes?
ALL RIGHT. NIGHT THEN, SUE! GOOD TO HAVE YOU BACK IN TOWN.
!!!
!
Ssssh. I told you to be quiet. And to call me Larry.
LARRY'S A HORRIBLE NAME--
SALOON
SUE LAWRENCE, MURDERER OF MY FATHER JOHN RAMSEY. I CALL YOU OUT.
?
Oh shit.

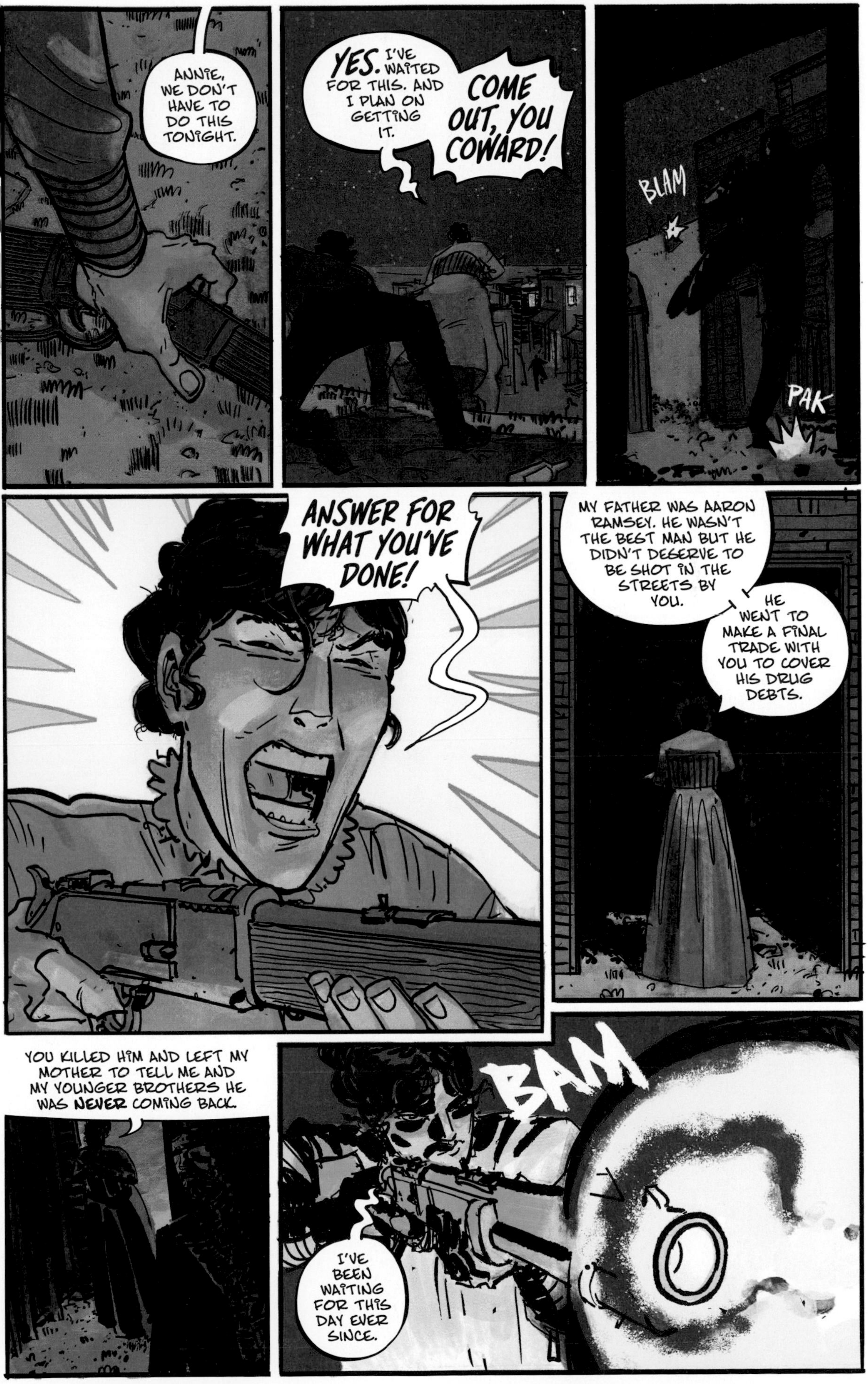

ANNIE, WE DON'T HAVE TO DO THIS TONIGHT.
YES. I'VE WAITED FOR THIS. AND I PLAN ON GETTING IT.
COME OUT, YOU COWARD!
BLAM
PAK
ANSWER FOR WHAT YOU'VE DONE!
MY FATHER WAS AARON RAMSEY. HE WASN'T THE BEST MAN BUT HE DIDN'T DESERVE TO BE SHOT IN THE STREETS BY YOU.
HE WENT TO MAKE A FINAL TRADE WITH YOU TO COVER HIS DRUG DEBTS.
YOU KILLED HIM AND LEFT MY MOTHER TO TELL ME AND MY YOUNGER BROTHERS HE WAS NEVER COMING BACK.
BAM
I'VE BEEN WAITING FOR THIS DAY EVER SINCE.

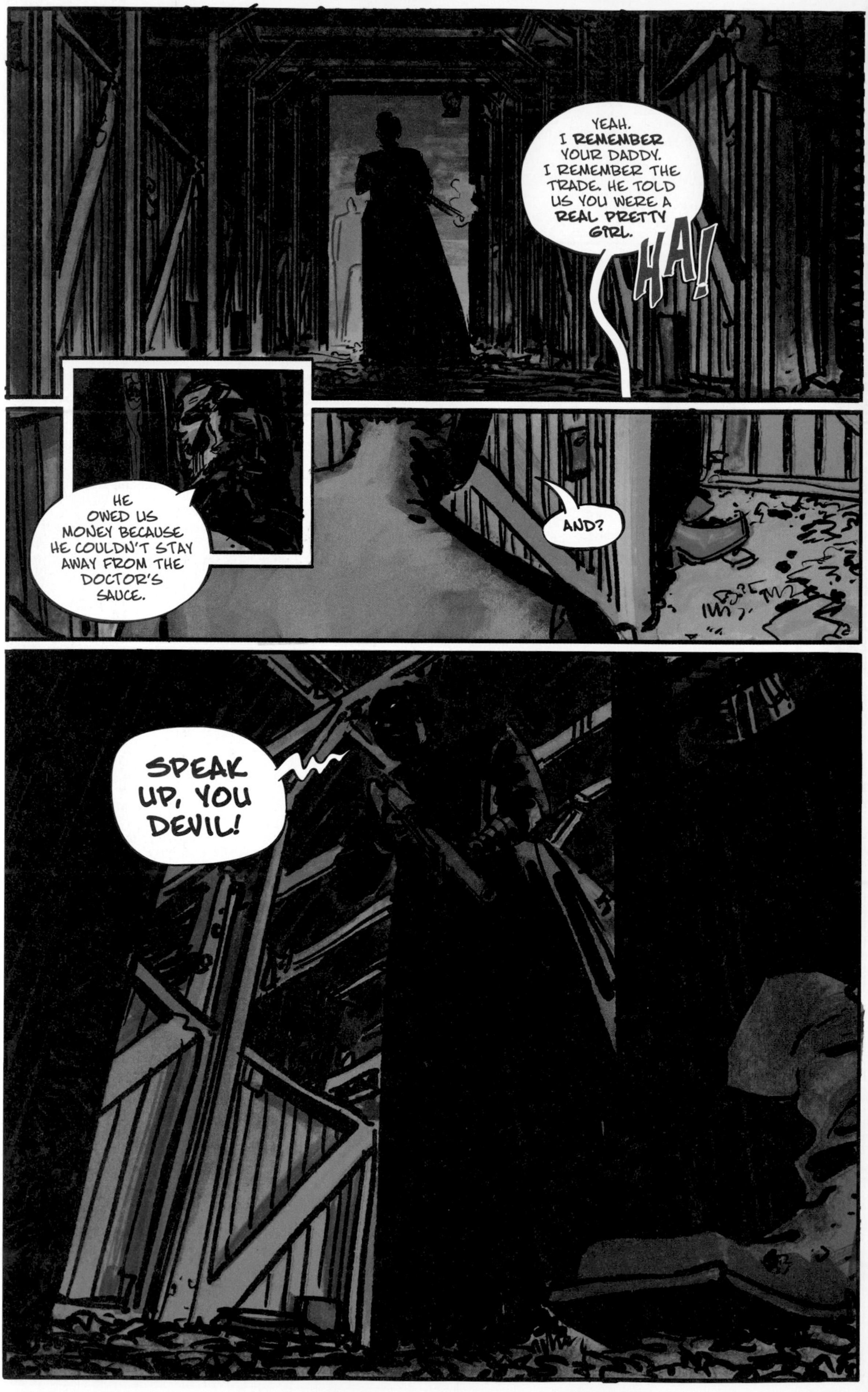
YEAH. I REMEMBER YOUR DADDY. I REMEMBER THE TRADE. HE TOLD US YOU WERE A REAL PRETTY GIRL.
HA!
HE OWED US MONEY BECAUSE HE COULDN'T STAY AWAY FROM THE DOCTOR'S SAUCE.
AND?
SPEAK UP, YOU DEVIL!

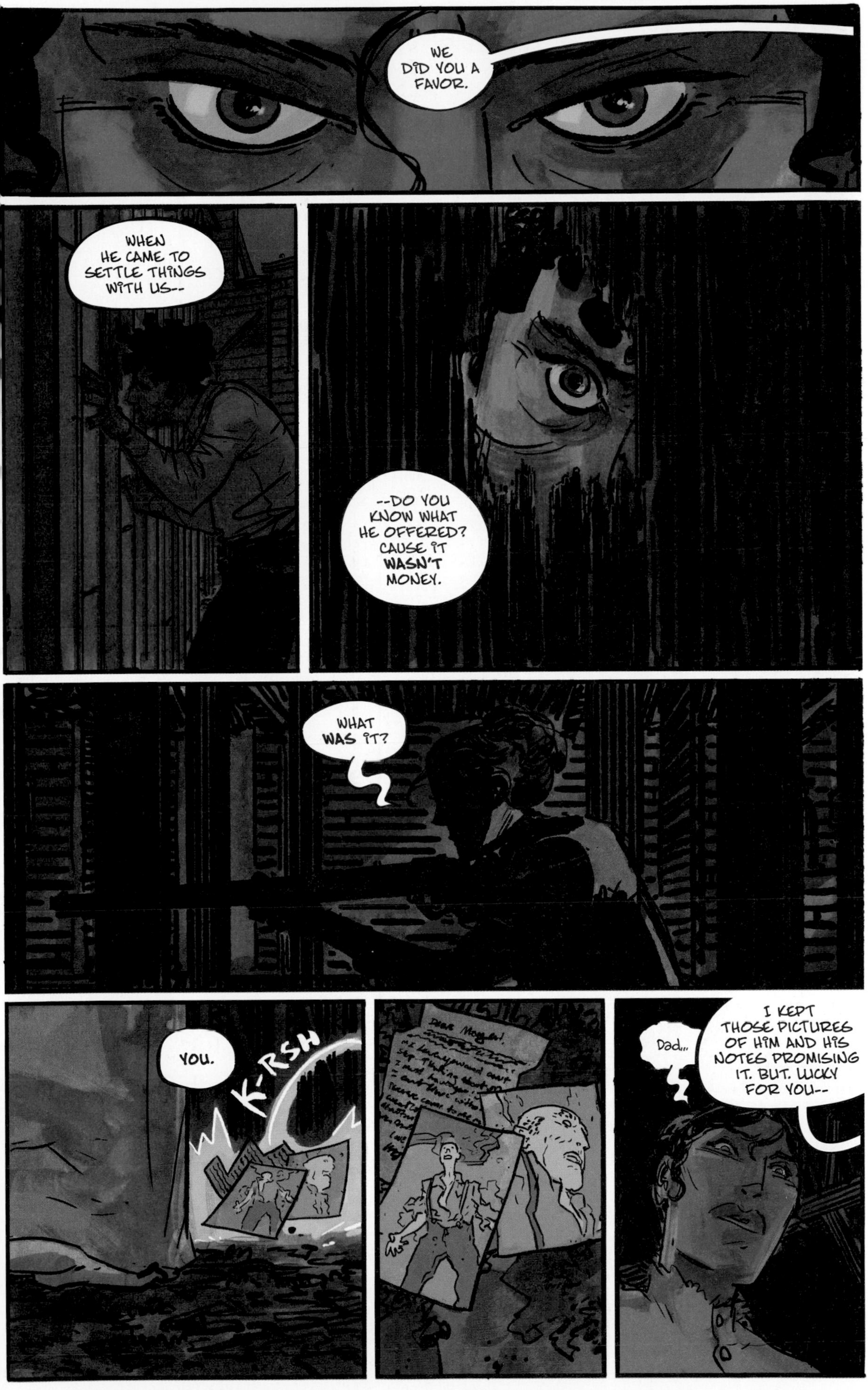
WE DID YOU A FAVOR.
WHEN HE CAME TO SETTLE THINGS WITH US--
--DO YOU KNOW WHAT HE OFFERED? CAUSE IT **WASN'T** MONEY.
WHAT **WAS** IT?
YOU.
K-RSH
Dear Morgan!
Dad...
I KEPT THOSE PICTURES OF HIM AND HIS NOTES PROMISING IT. BUT, LUCKY FOR YOU--

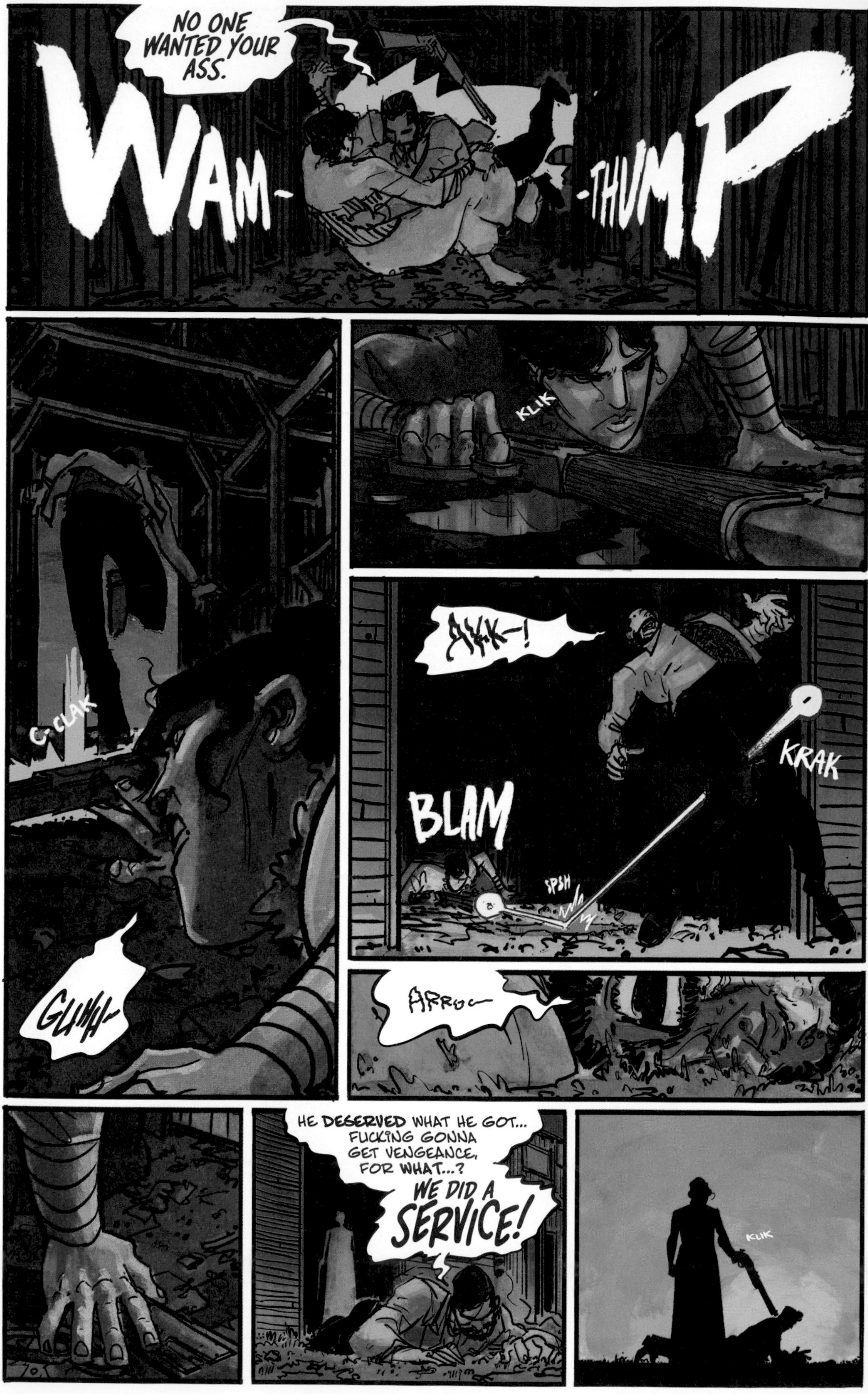
NO ONE WANTED YOUR ASS.
WAM-
-THUMP
C-CLAK
GUHH-
KLIK
AKK-!
BLAM
KRAK
SPSH
ARROG-
HE DESERVED WHAT HE GOT... FUCKING GONNA GET VENGEANCE, FOR WHAT...?
WE DID A SERVICE!
KLIK

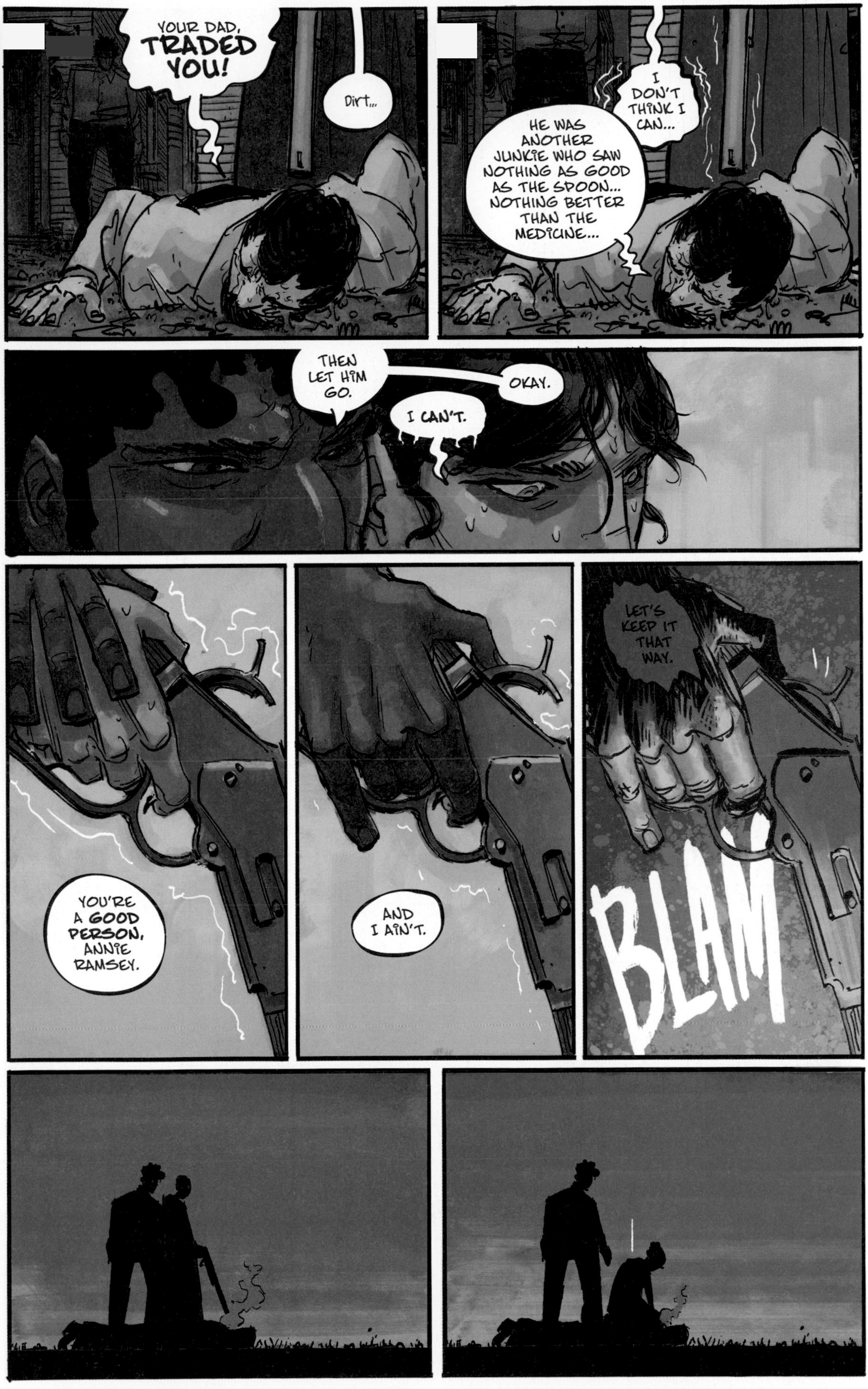
YOUR DAD, TRADED YOU!
Dirt...
I DON'T THINK I CAN...
HE WAS ANOTHER JUNKIE WHO SAW NOTHING AS GOOD AS THE SPOON... NOTHING BETTER THAN THE MEDICINE...
THEN LET HIM GO.
OKAY.
I CAN'T.
YOU'RE A GOOD PERSON, ANNIE RAMSEY.
AND I AIN'T.
LET'S KEEP IT THAT WAY.
BLAM

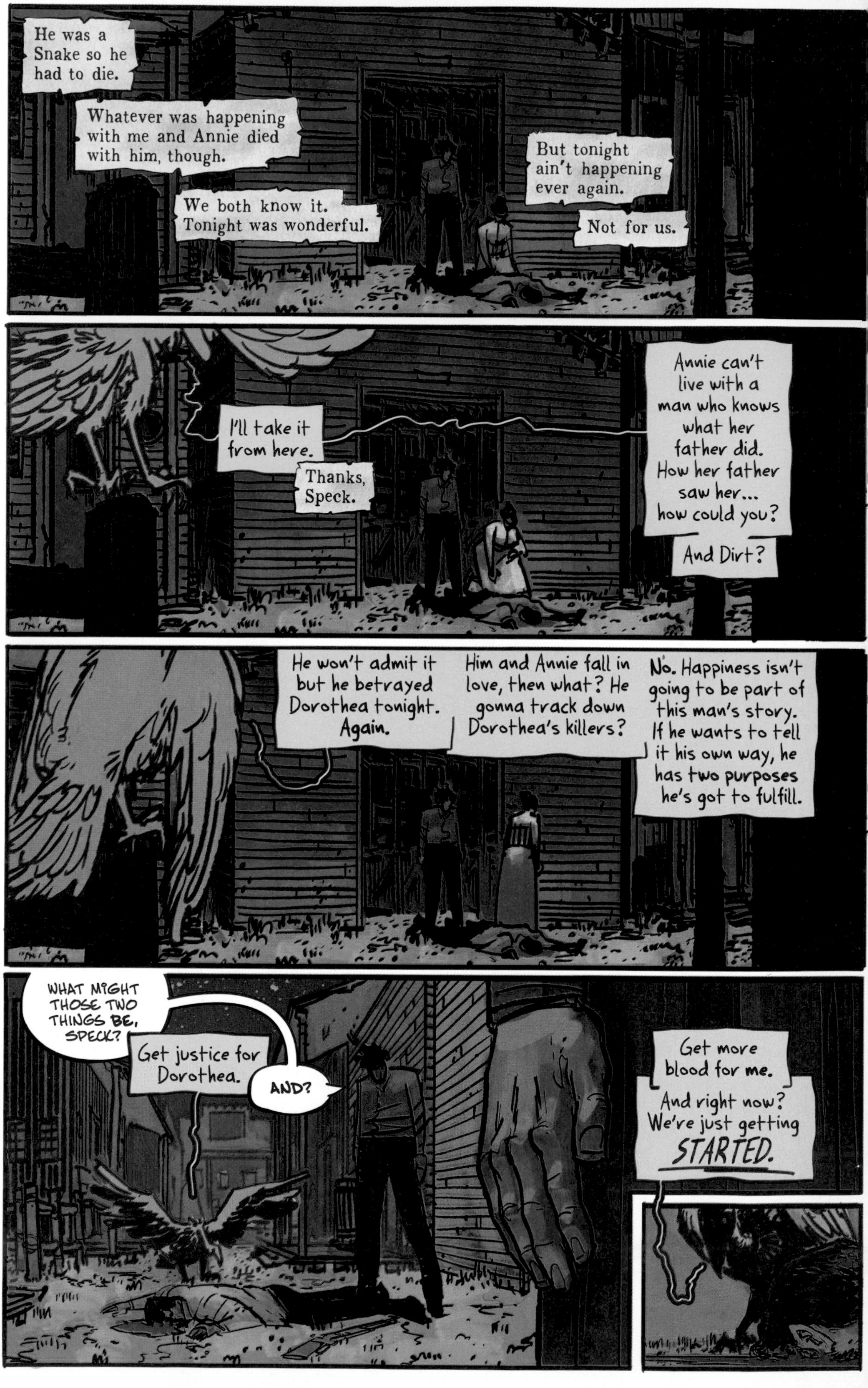
He was a Snake so he had to die.
Whatever was happening with me and Annie died with him, though.
We both know it. Tonight was wonderful.
But tonight ain't happening ever again.
Not for us.
I'll take it from here.
Thanks, Speck.
Annie can't live with a man who knows what her father did. How her father saw her... how could you?
And Dirt?
He won't admit it but he betrayed Dorothea tonight. Again.
Him and Annie fall in love, then what? He gonna track down Dorothea's killers?
No. Happiness isn't going to be part of this man's story. If he wants to tell it his own way, he has two purposes he's got to fulfill.
WHAT MIGHT THOSE TWO THINGS BE, SPECK?
Get justice for Dorothea.
AND?
Get more blood for me.
And right now? We're just getting STARTED.

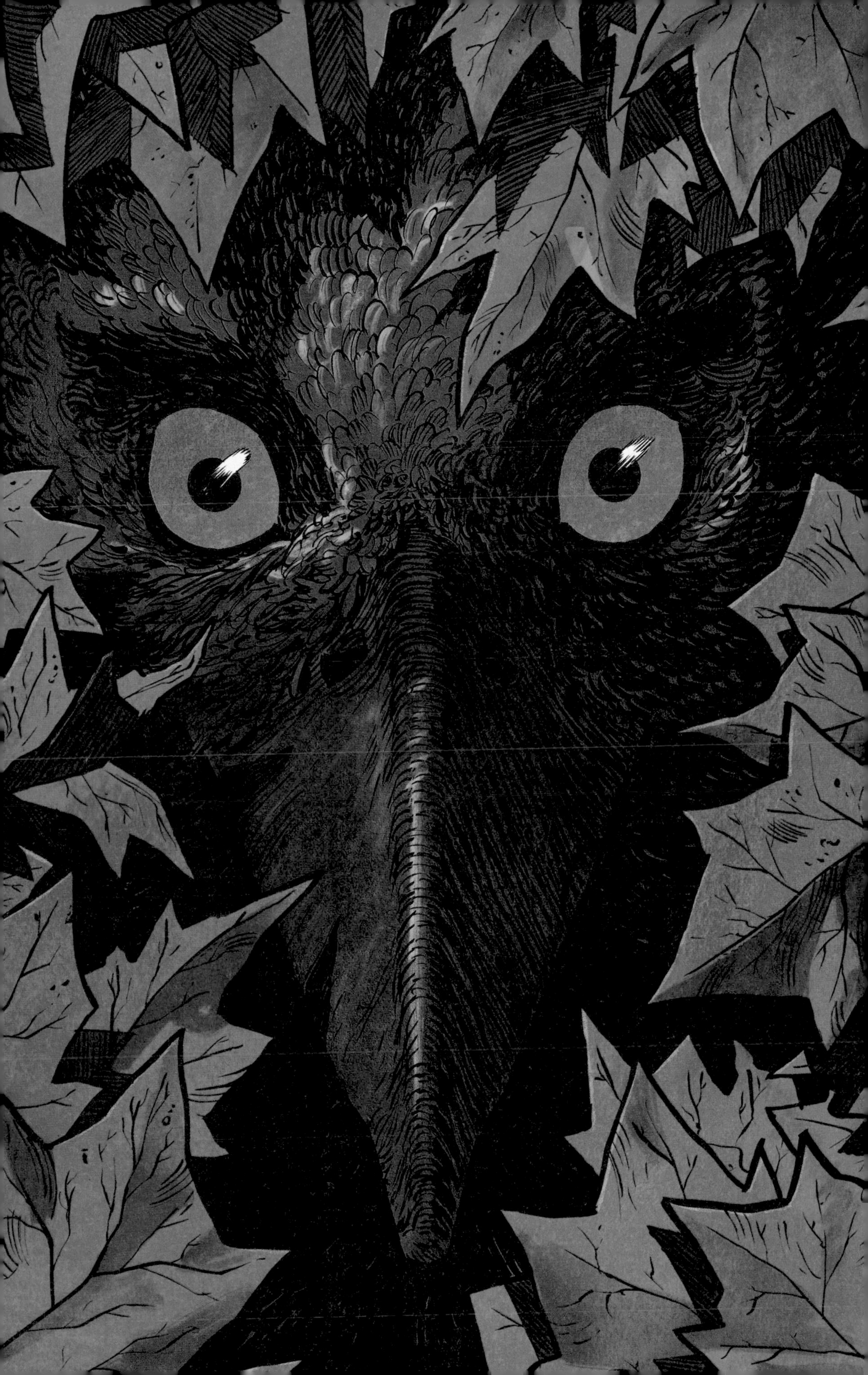

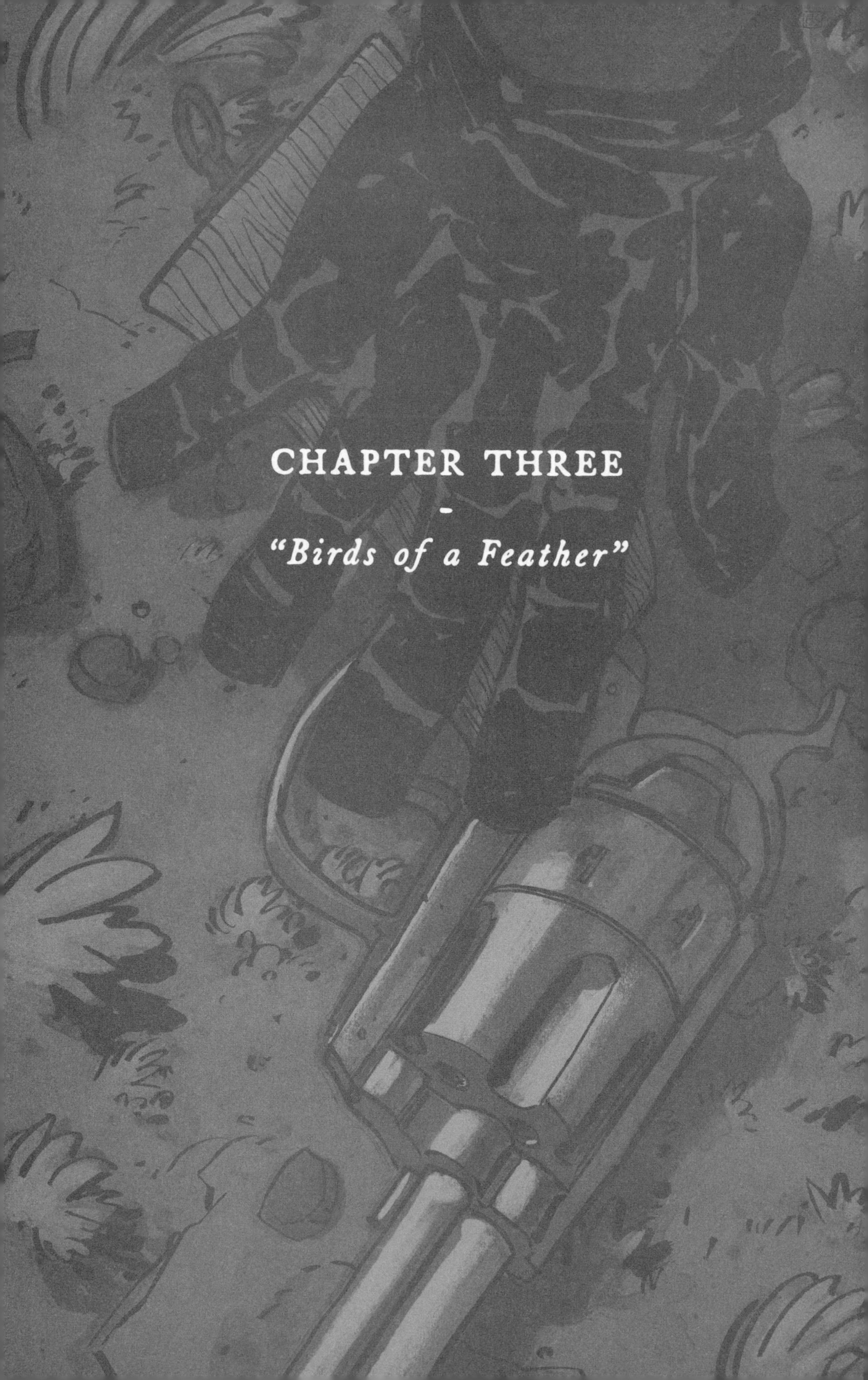

CHAPTER THREE

-

"Birds of a Feather"

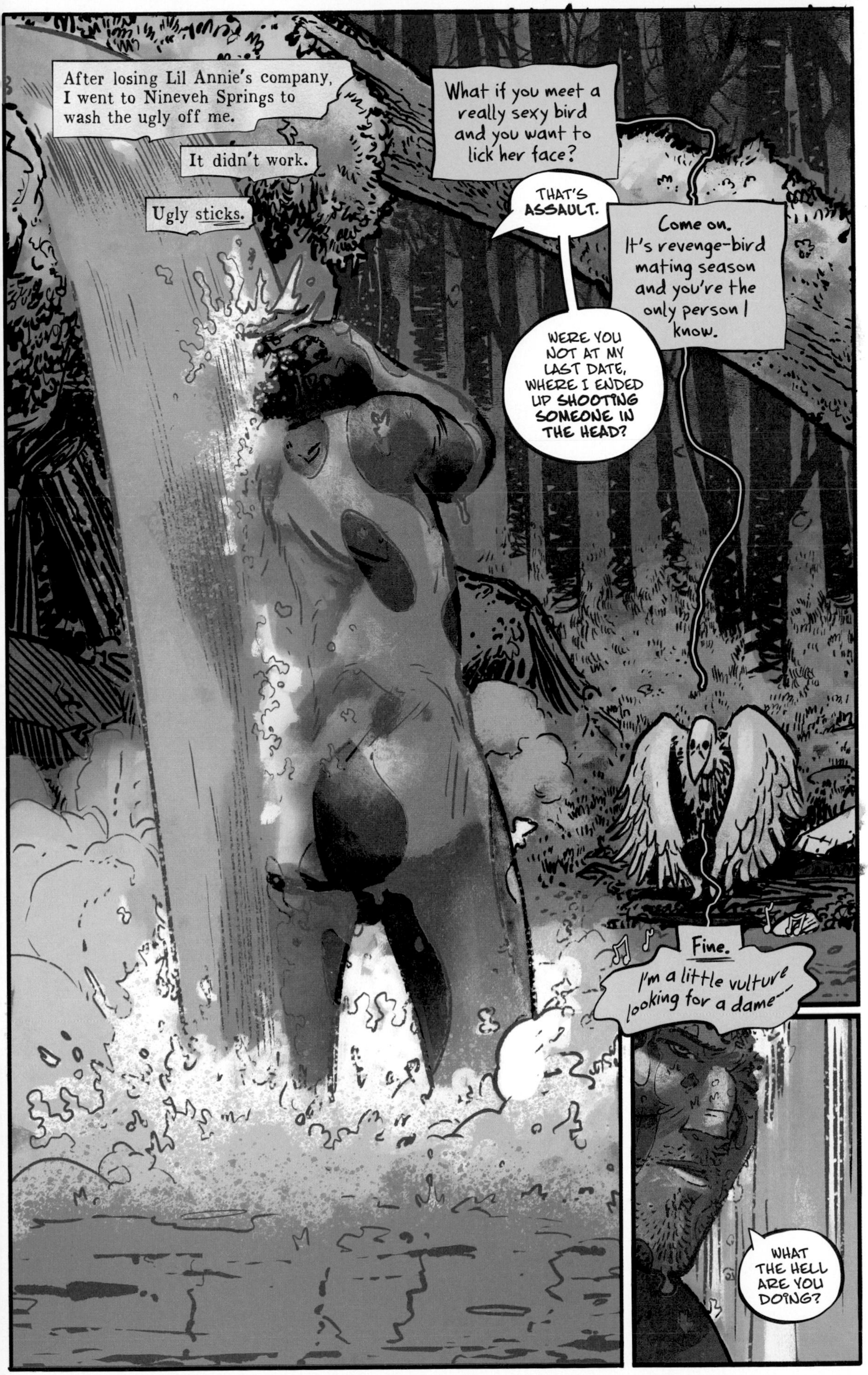
After losing Lil Annie's company, I went to Nineveh Springs to wash the ugly off me.
It didn't work.
Ugly sticks.
What if you meet a really sexy bird and you want to lick her face?
THAT'S ASSAULT.
Come on. It's revenge-bird mating season and you're the only person I know.
WERE YOU NOT AT MY LAST DATE, WHERE I ENDED UP SHOOTING SOMEONE IN THE HEAD?
Fine.
I'm a little vulture looking for a dame—
WHAT THE HELL ARE YOU DOING?

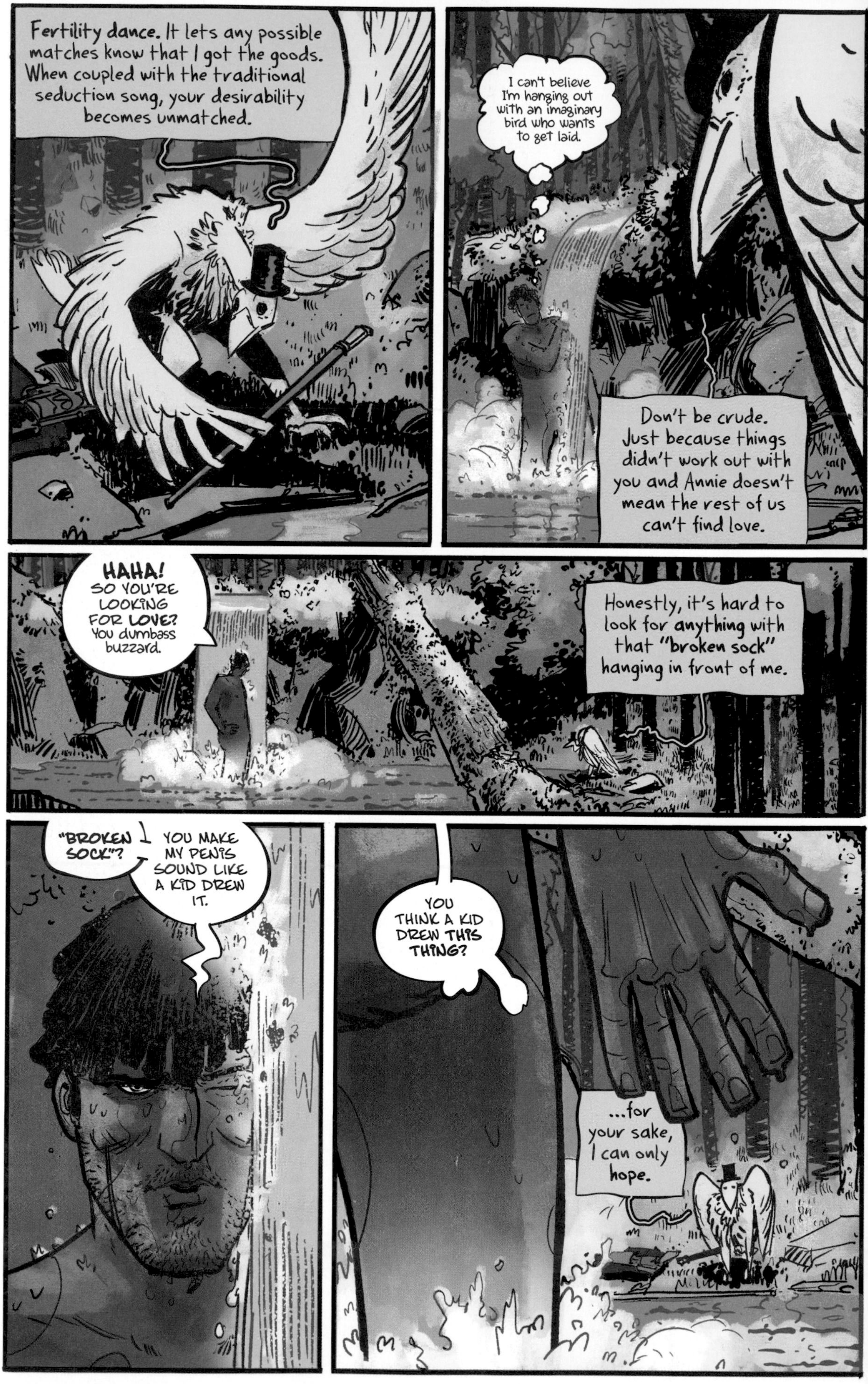

Fertility dance. It lets any possible matches know that I got the goods. When coupled with the traditional seduction song, your desirability becomes unmatched.
I can't believe I'm hanging out with an imaginary bird who wants to get laid.
Don't be crude. Just because things didn't work out with you and Annie doesn't mean the rest of us can't find love.
HAHA! SO YOU'RE LOOKING FOR LOVE? You dumbass buzzard.
Honestly, it's hard to look for anything with that "broken sock" hanging in front of me.
"BROKEN SOCK"?
YOU MAKE MY PENIS SOUND LIKE A KID DREW IT.
YOU THINK A KID DREW THIS THING?
...for your sake, I can only hope.

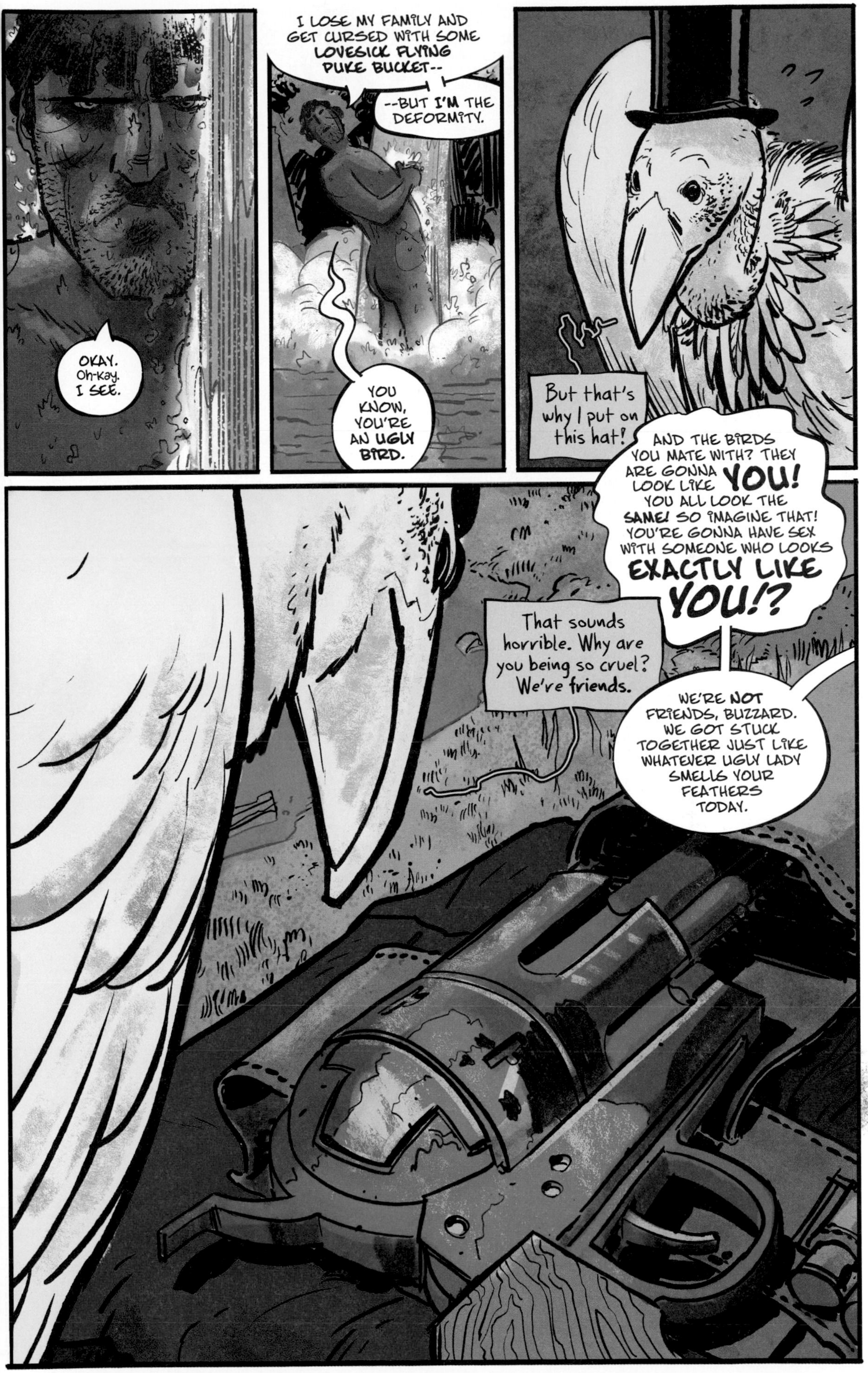
OKAY. Oh-kay. I SEE.
I LOSE MY FAMILY AND GET CURSED WITH SOME LOVESICK FLYING PUKE BUCKET--
--BUT I'M THE DEFORMITY.
YOU KNOW, YOU'RE AN UGLY BIRD.
But that's why I put on this hat!
AND THE BIRDS YOU MATE WITH? THEY ARE GONNA LOOK LIKE YOU! YOU ALL LOOK THE SAME! SO IMAGINE THAT! YOU'RE GONNA HAVE SEX WITH SOMEONE WHO LOOKS EXACTLY LIKE YOU!?
That sounds horrible. Why are you being so cruel? We're friends.
WE'RE NOT FRIENDS, BUZZARD. WE GOT STUCK TOGETHER JUST LIKE WHATEVER UGLY LADY SMELLS YOUR FEATHERS TODAY.

YOU REMIND ME OF DOROTHEA AND WHAT I HAVEN'T DONE YET.

HAD A BEAUTIFUL WIFE AND NOW CURSED WITH A DANCING MAGGOT EATER--

WAIT!

DO VULTURES MATE FOR LIFE?!

Yes. We have morals. Unlike you flesh bags.

You offend us greatly.

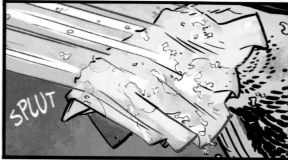

SPLUT

SO, IF YOU MATE, YOU GOTTA GO **LIVE** WITH YOUR VULTURE WIFE? YOU GOTTA LEAVE **ME** ALONE.

In theory. Her parents would have to agree to it. I ask her dad and then bring her mom a fresh carcass.

That's the process.

WELL, COME ON, THEN...

...LET'S GET YOU HITCHED.

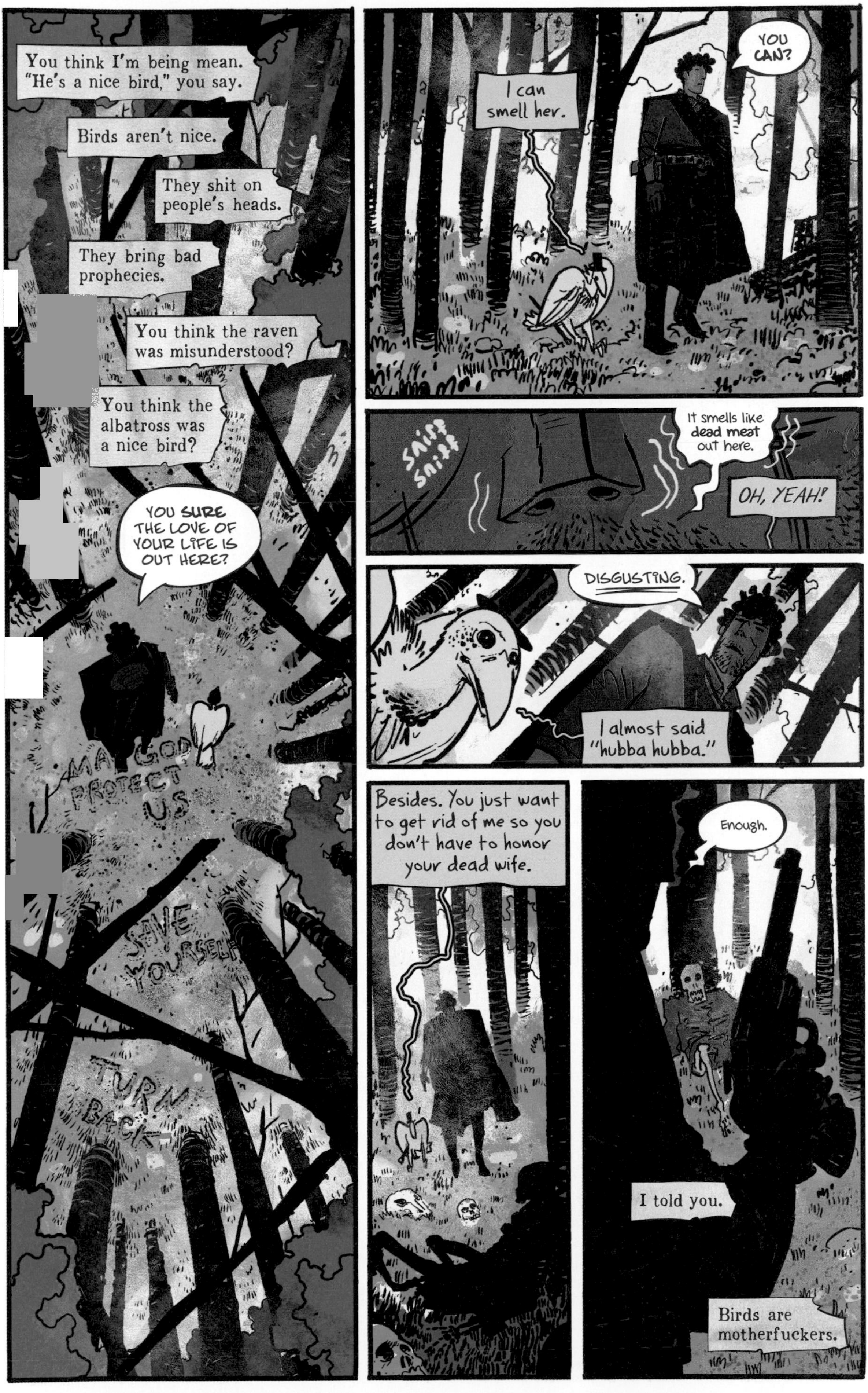

You think I'm being mean. "He's a nice bird," you say.
Birds aren't nice.
They shit on people's heads.
They bring bad prophecies.
You think the raven was misunderstood?
You think the albatross was a nice bird?
YOU **SURE** THE LOVE OF YOUR LIFE IS OUT HERE?
MA GOD PROTECT US
SAVE YOURSELF
TURN BACK
I can smell her.
YOU CAN?
SNIFF SNIFF
It smells like **dead meat** out here.
OH, YEAH!
DISGUSTING.
I almost said "hubba hubba."
Besides. You just want to get rid of me so you don't have to honor your dead wife.
Enough.
I told you.
Birds are motherfuckers.

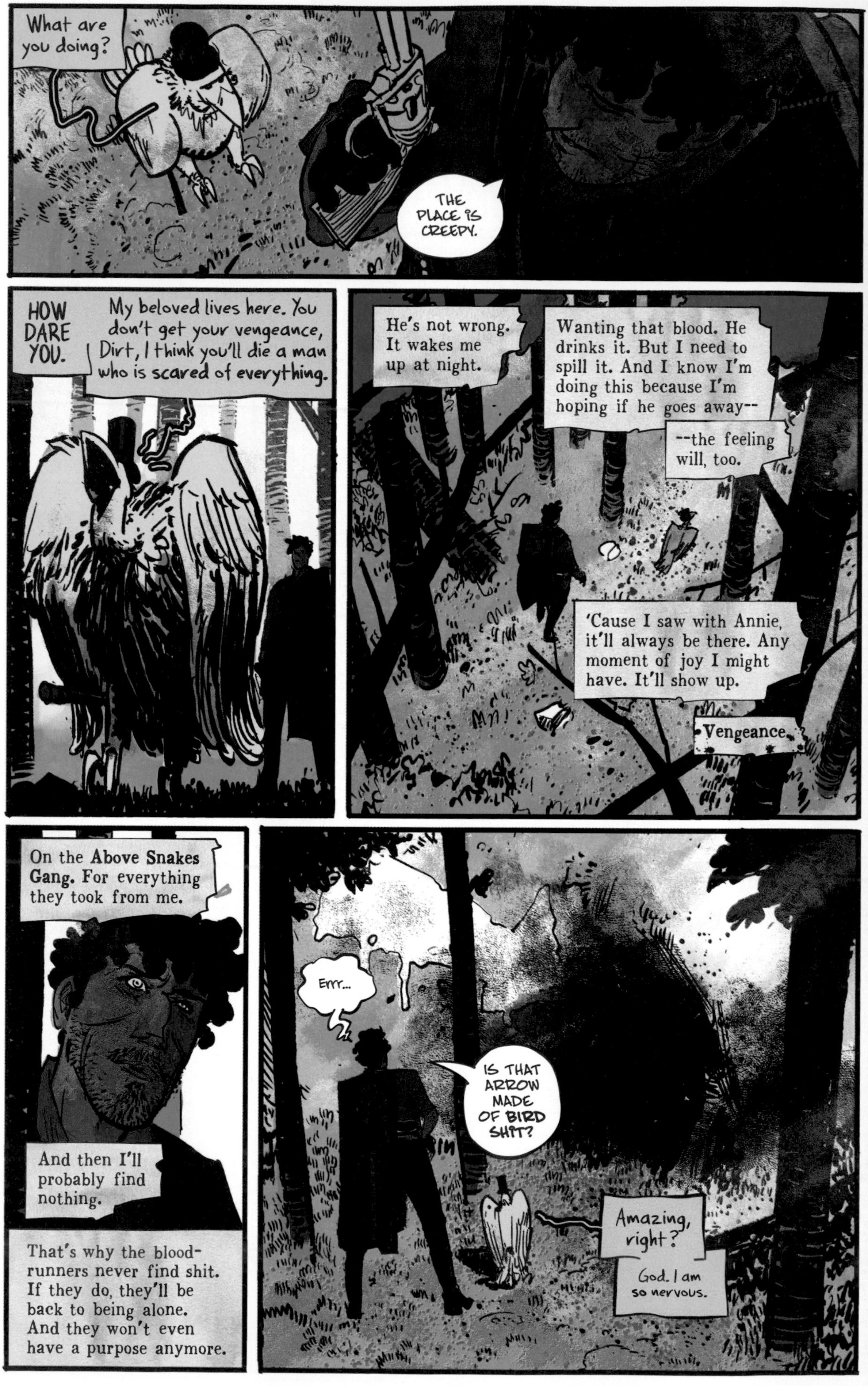
What are you doing?
THE PLACE IS CREEPY.
HOW DARE YOU.
My beloved lives here. You don't get your vengeance, Dirt, I think you'll die a man who is scared of everything.
He's not wrong. It wakes me up at night.
Wanting that blood. He drinks it. But I need to spill it. And I know I'm doing this because I'm hoping if he goes away--
--the feeling will, too.
'Cause I saw with Annie, it'll always be there. Any moment of joy I might have. It'll show up.
Vengeance.
On the Above Snakes Gang. For everything they took from me.
And then I'll probably find nothing.
That's why the blood-runners never find shit. If they do, they'll be back to being alone. And they won't even have a purpose anymore.
Errr...
IS THAT ARROW MADE OF BIRD SHIT?
Amazing, right?
God. I am so nervous.

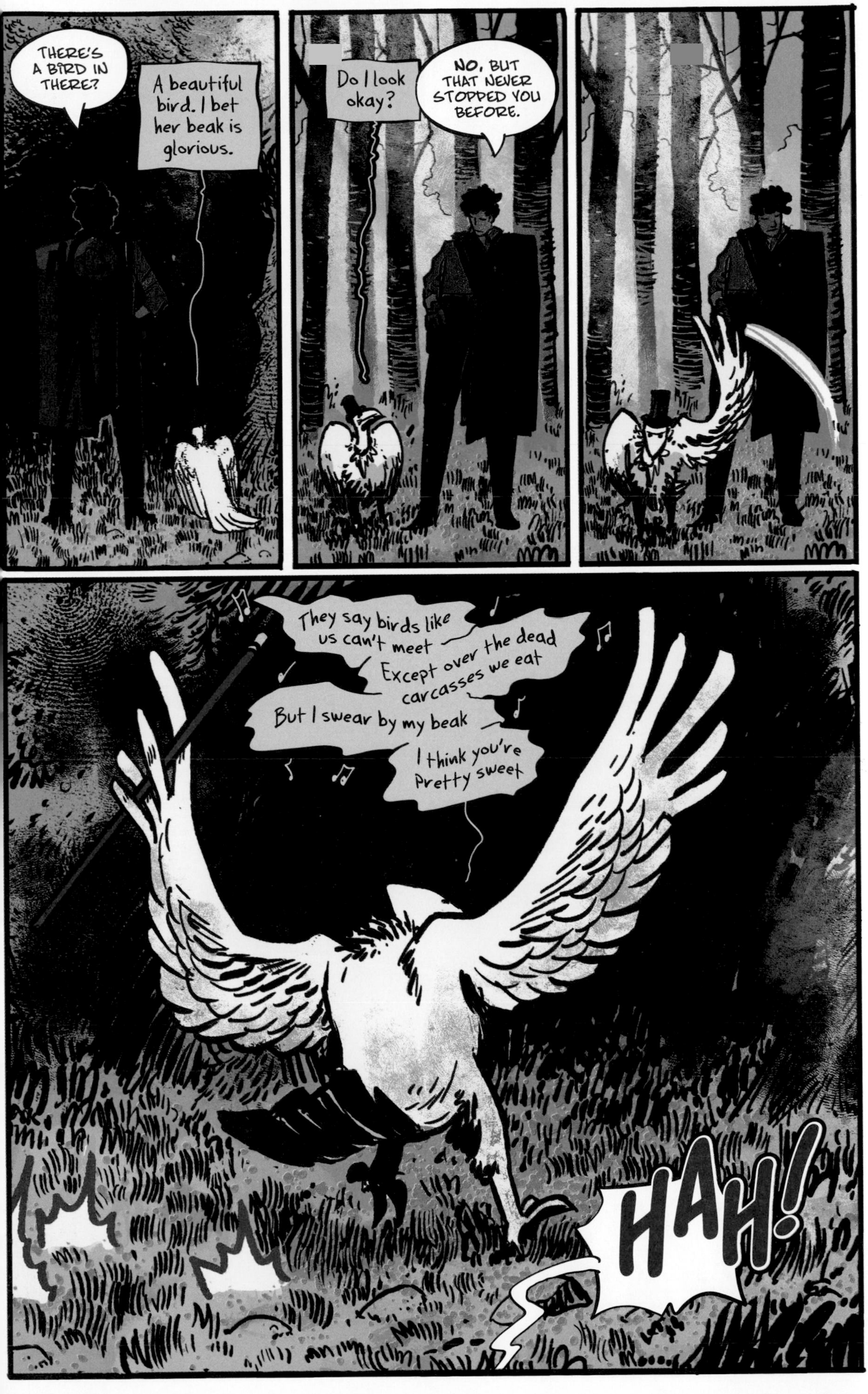
THERE'S A BIRD IN THERE?
A beautiful bird. I bet her beak is glorious.
Do I look okay?
NO, BUT THAT NEVER STOPPED YOU BEFORE.
They say birds like us can't meet
Except over the dead carcasses we eat
But I swear by my beak
I think you're pretty sweet
HAH!

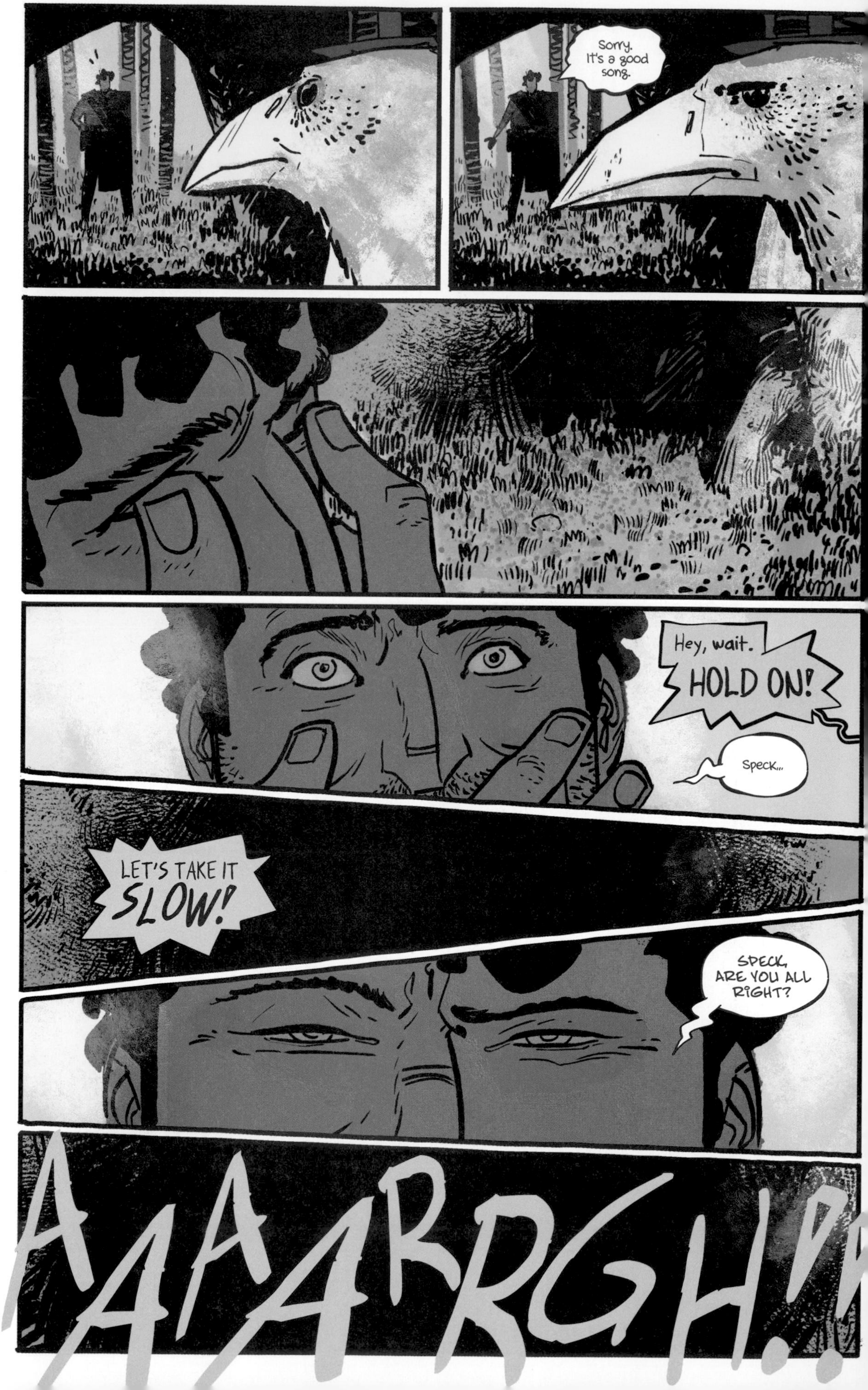
Sorry. It's a good song.
Hey, wait. HOLD ON!
Speck...
LET'S TAKE IT SLOW!
SPECK, ARE YOU ALL RIGHT?
AAARRGH!!

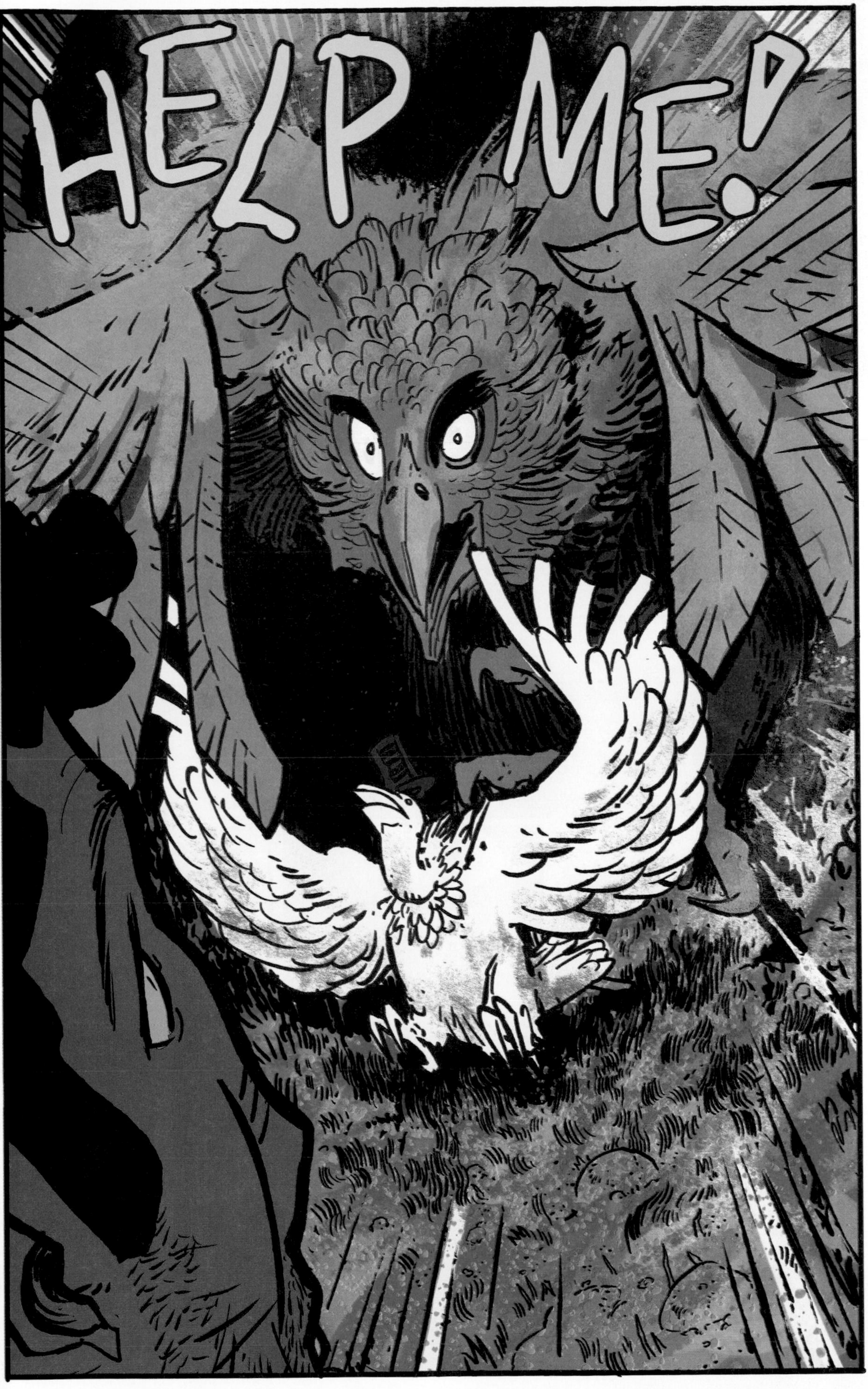
HELP ME!

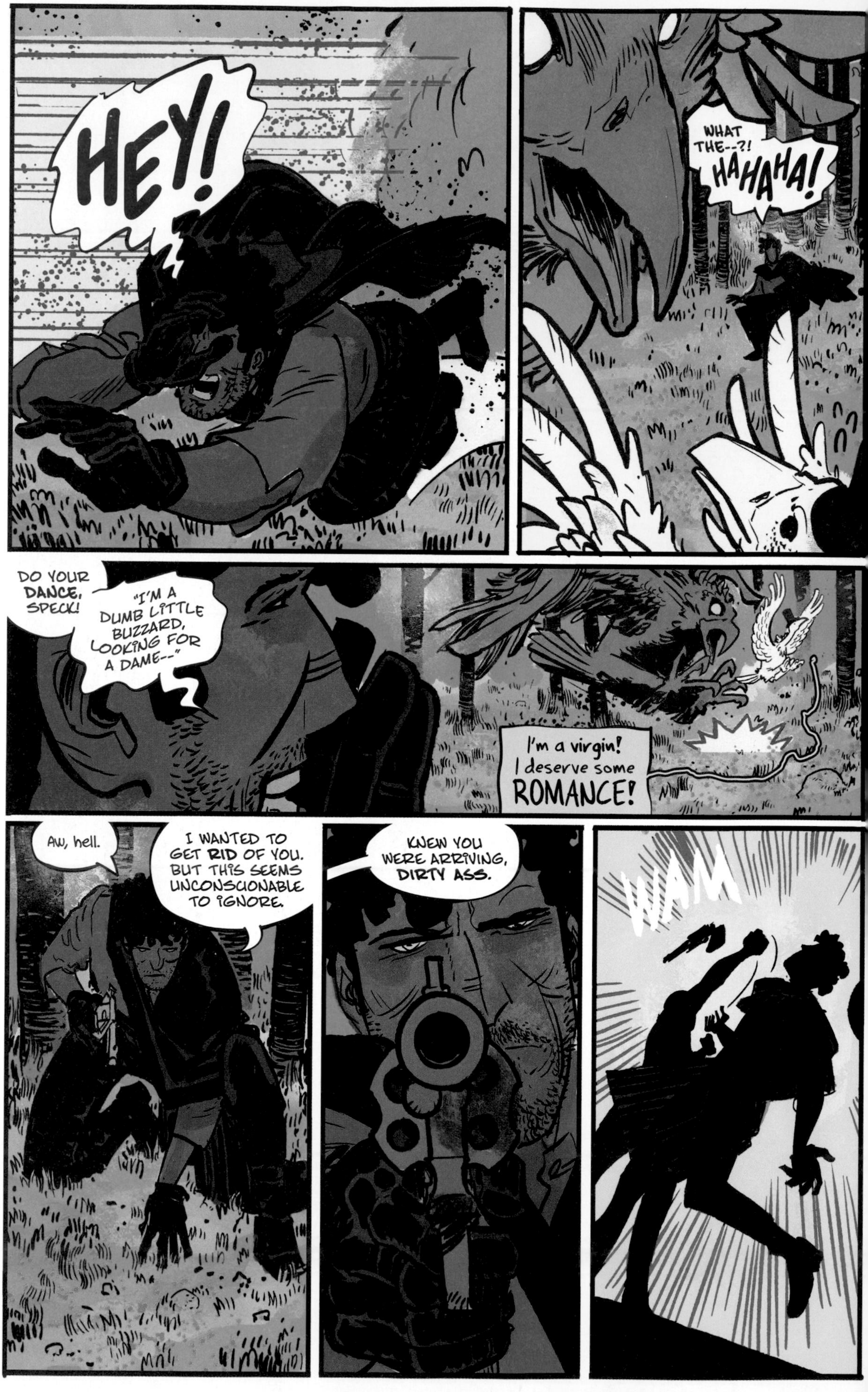
HEY!
WHAT THE--?!
HAHAHA!
DO YOUR DANCE, SPECK!
"I'M A DUMB LITTLE BUZZARD, LOOKING FOR A DAME--"
I'm a virgin! I deserve some ROMANCE!
Aw, hell.
I WANTED TO GET RID OF YOU. BUT THIS SEEMS UNCONSCIONABLE TO IGNORE.
KNEW YOU WERE ARRIVING, DIRTY ASS.
WAM

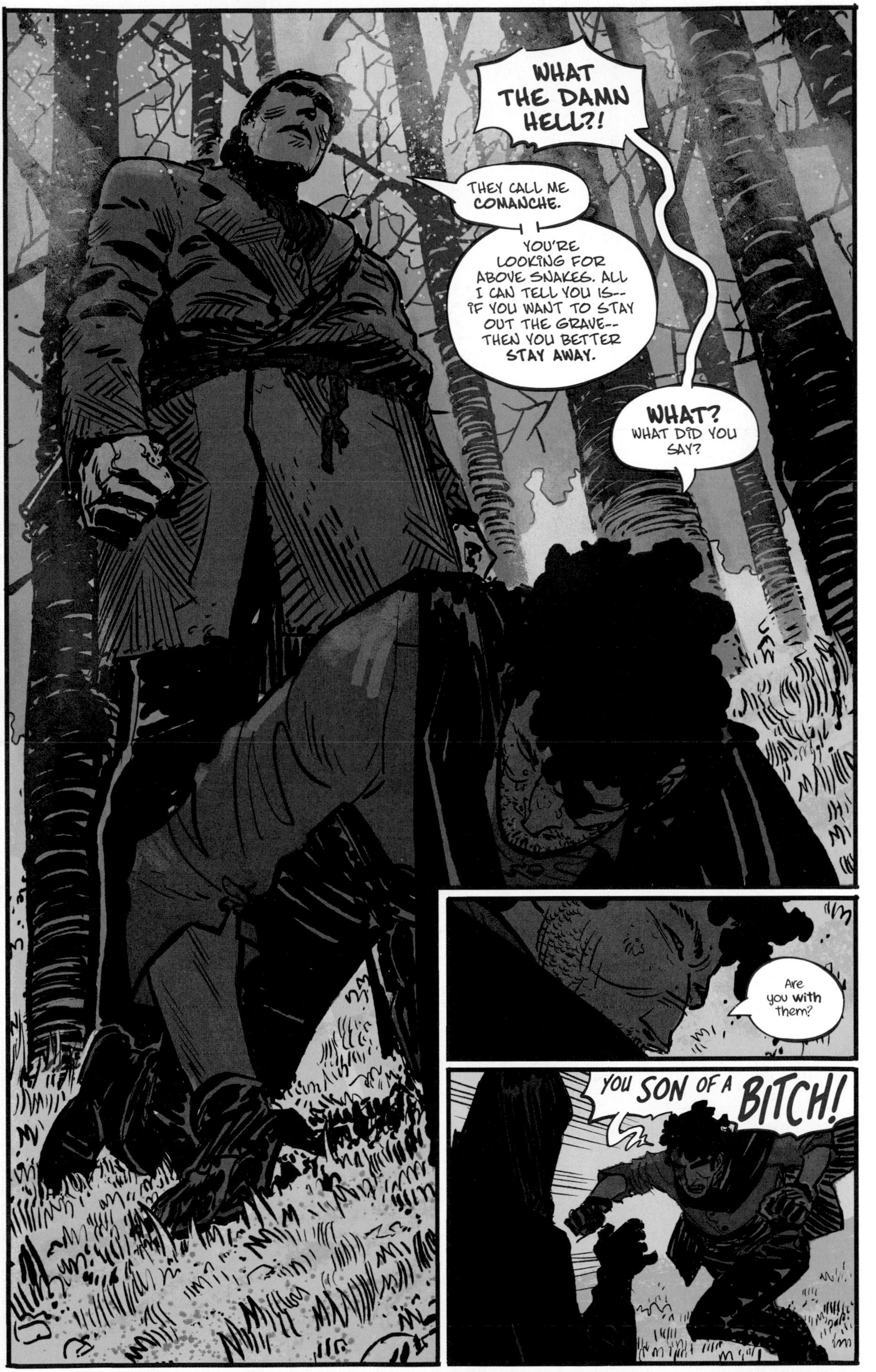
WHAT THE DAMN HELL?!
THEY CALL ME COMANCHE.
YOU'RE LOOKING FOR ABOVE SNAKES. ALL I CAN TELL YOU IS-- IF YOU WANT TO STAY OUT THE GRAVE-- THEN YOU BETTER STAY AWAY.
WHAT? WHAT DID YOU SAY?
Are you with them?
YOU SON OF A BITCH!

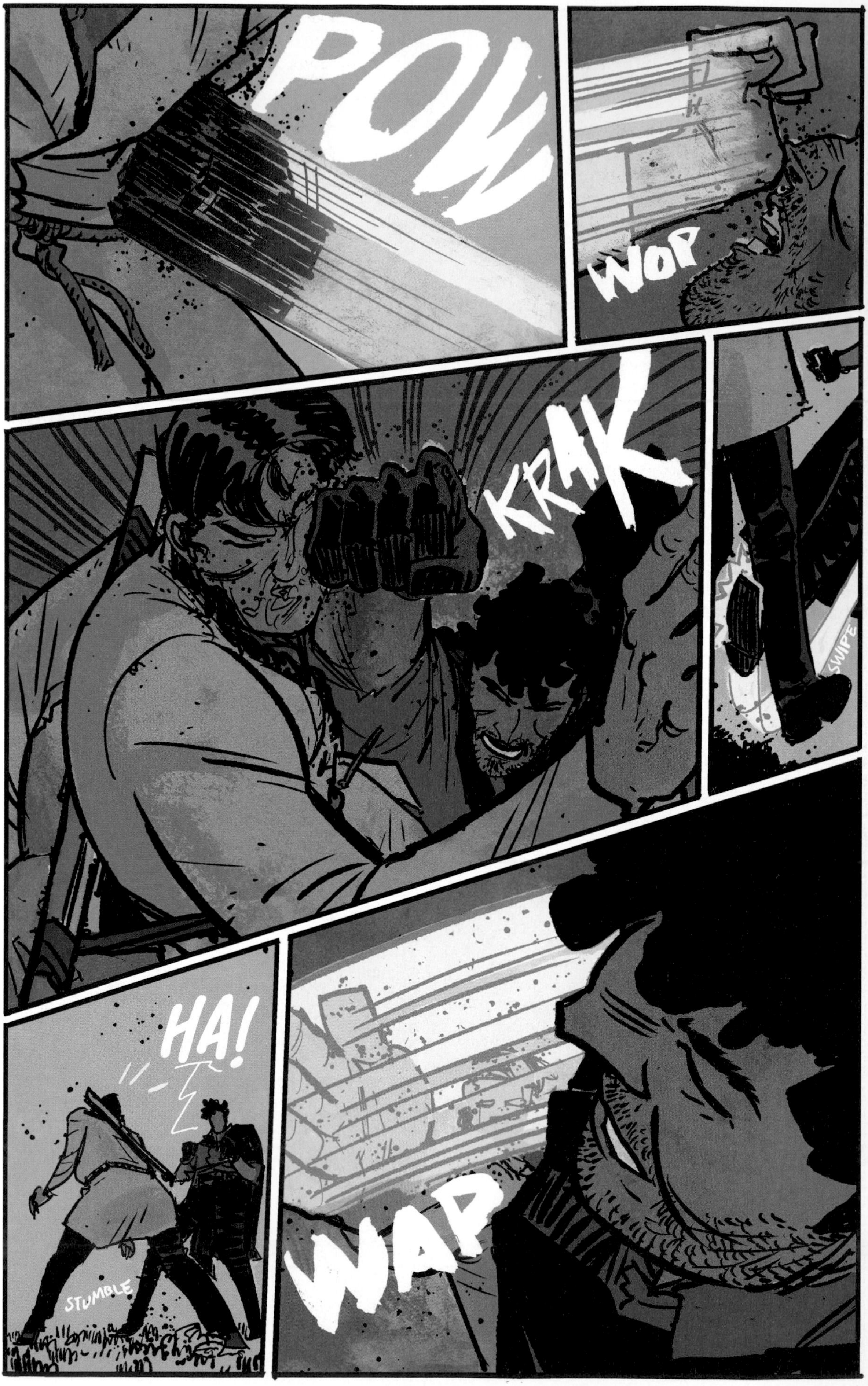
POW
WOP
KRAK
SWIPE
HA!
STUMBLE
WAP

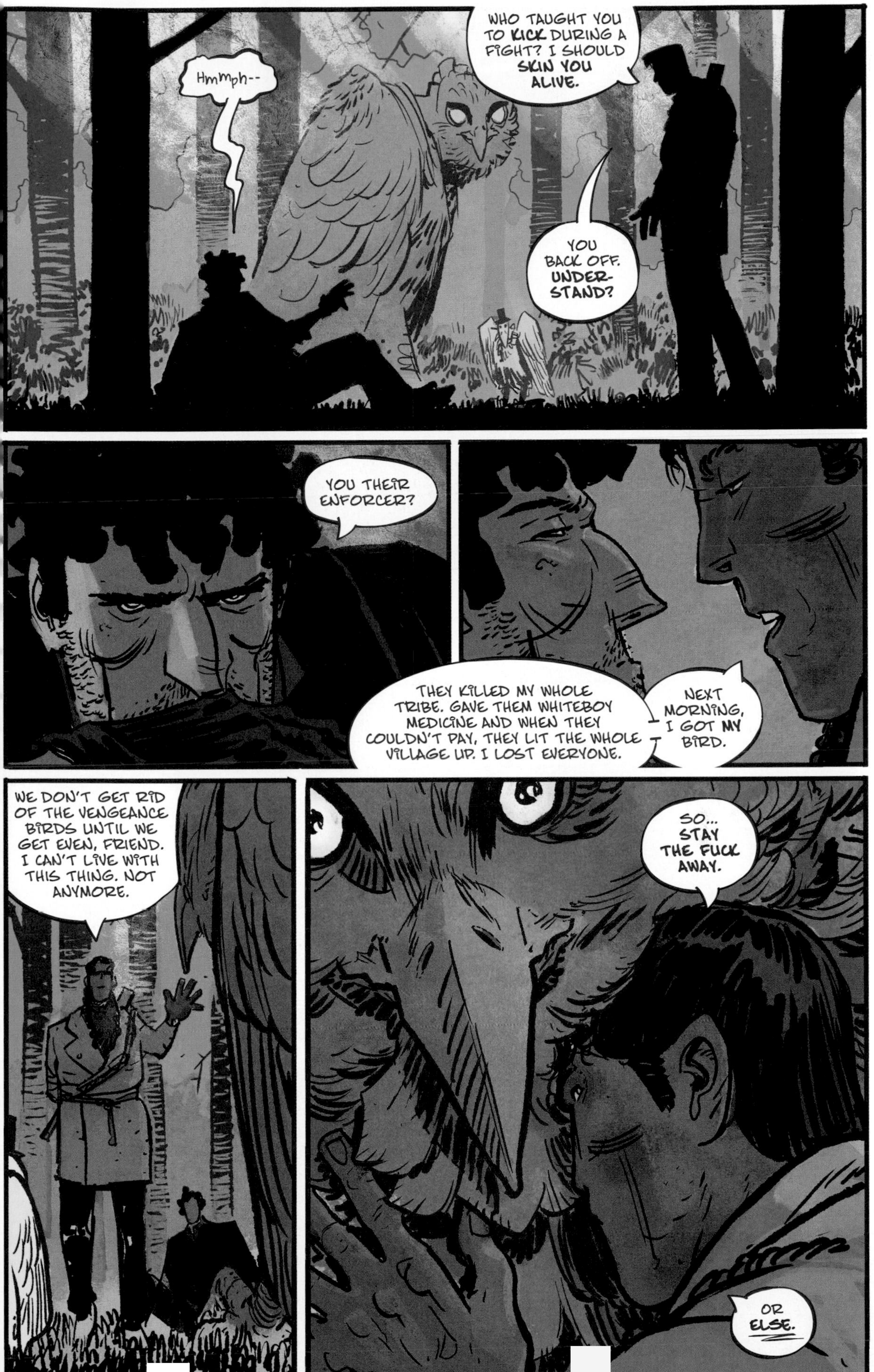
Hmmph--
WHO TAUGHT YOU TO KICK DURING A FIGHT? I SHOULD SKIN YOU ALIVE.
YOU BACK OFF. UNDER-STAND?
YOU THEIR ENFORCER?
THEY KILLED MY WHOLE TRIBE. GAVE THEM WHITEBOY MEDICINE AND WHEN THEY COULDN'T PAY, THEY LIT THE WHOLE VILLAGE UP. I LOST EVERYONE.
NEXT MORNING, I GOT MY BIRD.
WE DON'T GET RID OF THE VENGEANCE BIRDS UNTIL WE GET EVEN, FRIEND. I CAN'T LIVE WITH THIS THING. NOT ANYMORE.
SO... STAY THE FUCK AWAY.
OR ELSE.

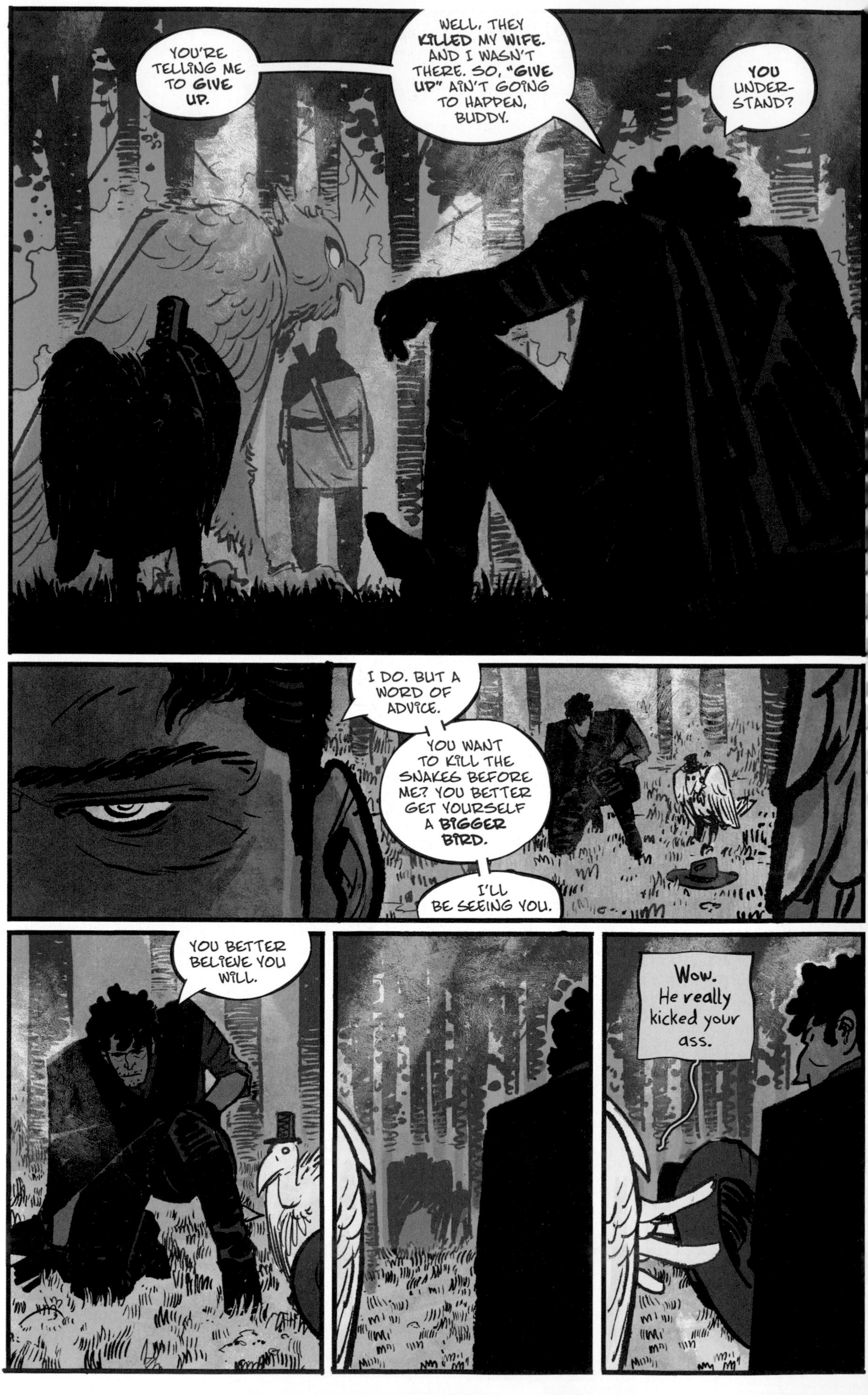
YOU'RE TELLING ME TO GIVE UP.
WELL, THEY KILLED MY WIFE. AND I WASN'T THERE. SO, "GIVE UP" AIN'T GOING TO HAPPEN, BUDDY.
YOU UNDER-STAND?
I DO. BUT A WORD OF ADVICE.
YOU WANT TO KILL THE SNAKES BEFORE ME? YOU BETTER GET YOURSELF A BIGGER BIRD.
I'LL BE SEEING YOU.
YOU BETTER BELIEVE YOU WILL.
Wow. He really kicked your ass.

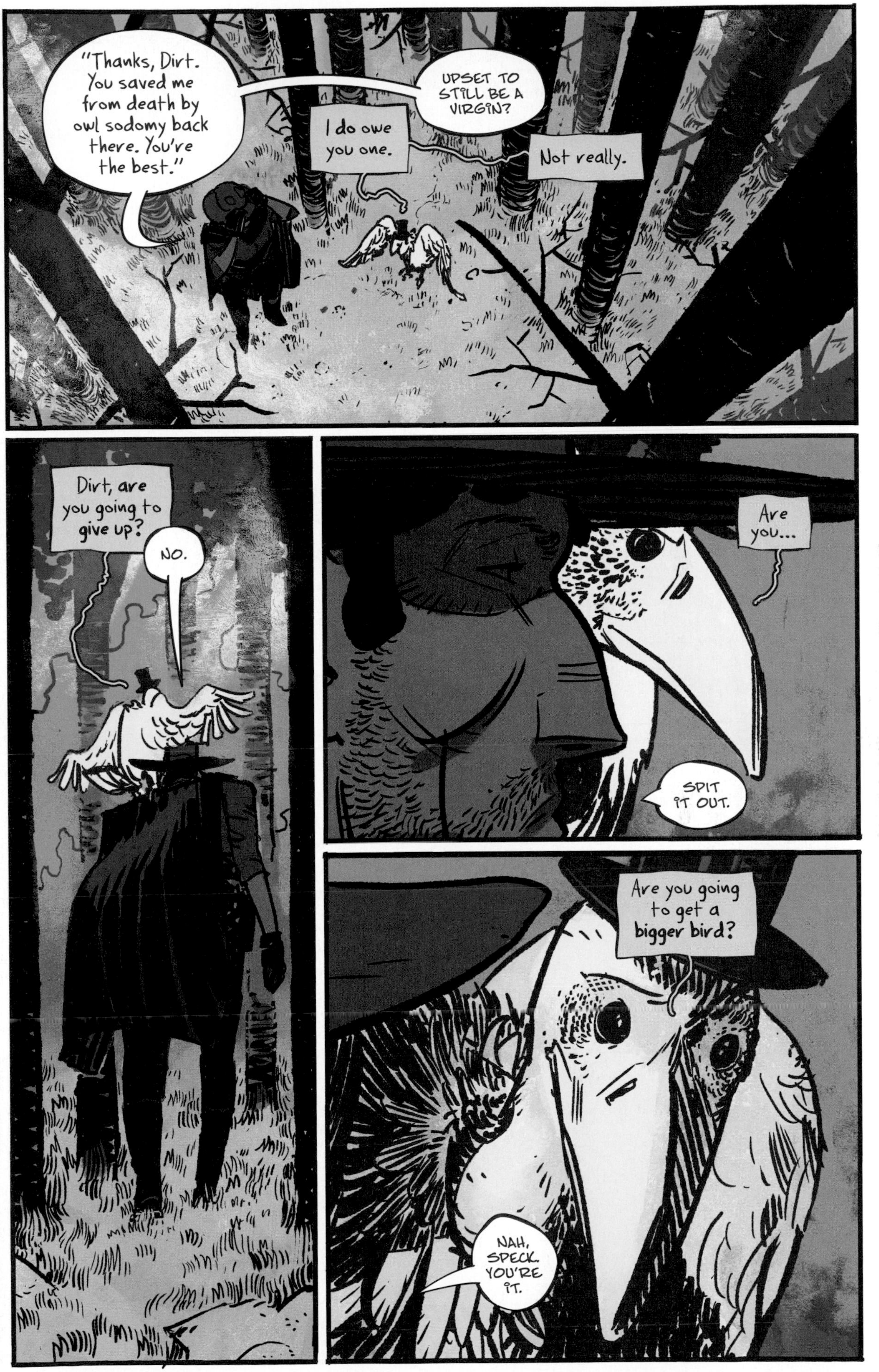
"Thanks, Dirt. You saved me from death by owl sodomy back there. You're the best."
UPSET TO STILL BE A VIRGIN?
I do owe you one.
Not really.
Dirt, are you going to give up?
NO.
Are you...
SPIT IT OUT.
Are you going to get a bigger bird?
NAH, SPECK. YOU'RE IT.

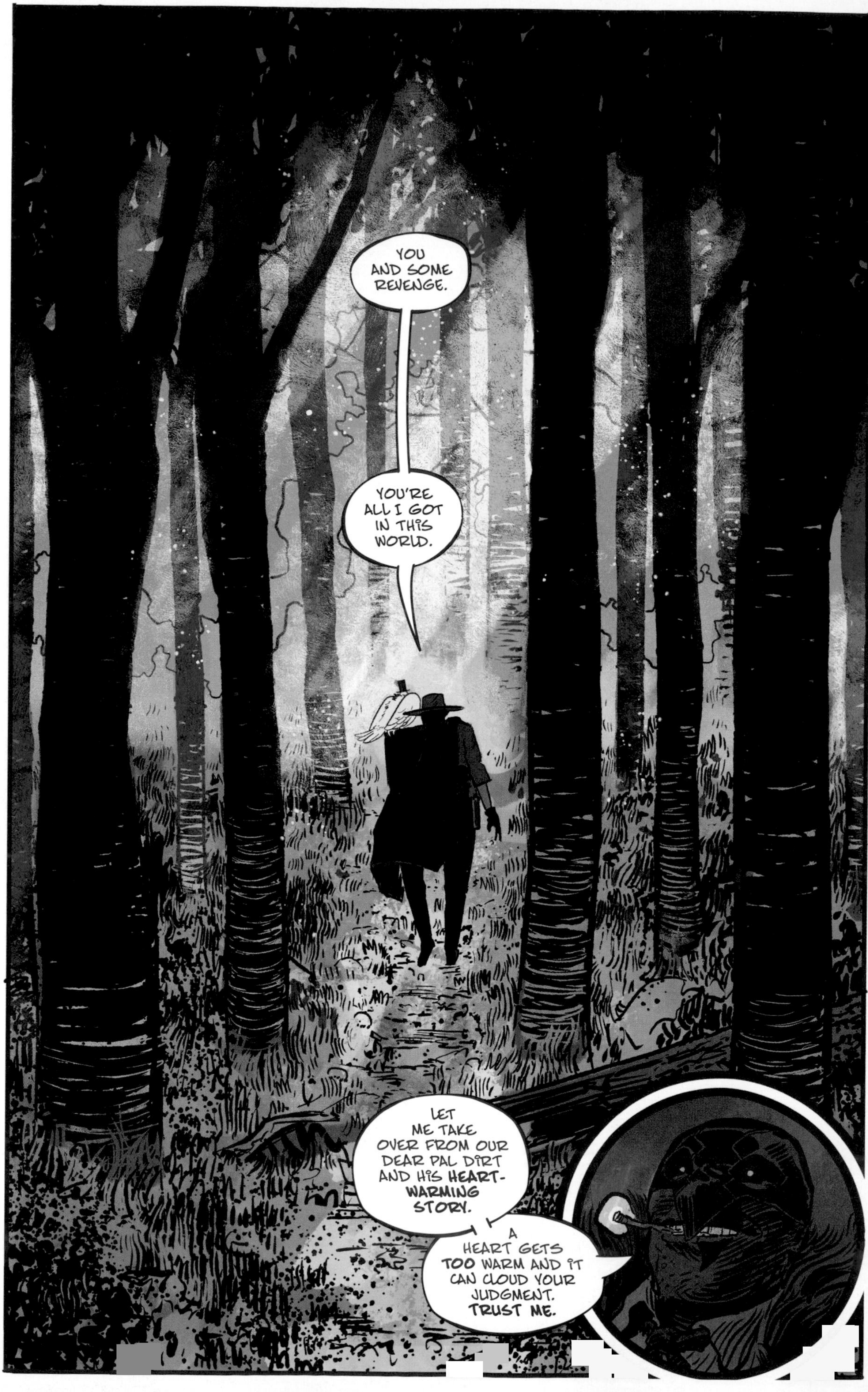
YOU AND SOME REVENGE.
YOU'RE ALL I GOT IN THIS WORLD.
LET ME TAKE OVER FROM OUR DEAR PAL DIRT AND HIS HEART-WARMING STORY.
A HEART GETS TOO WARM AND IT CAN CLOUD YOUR JUDGMENT. TRUST ME.

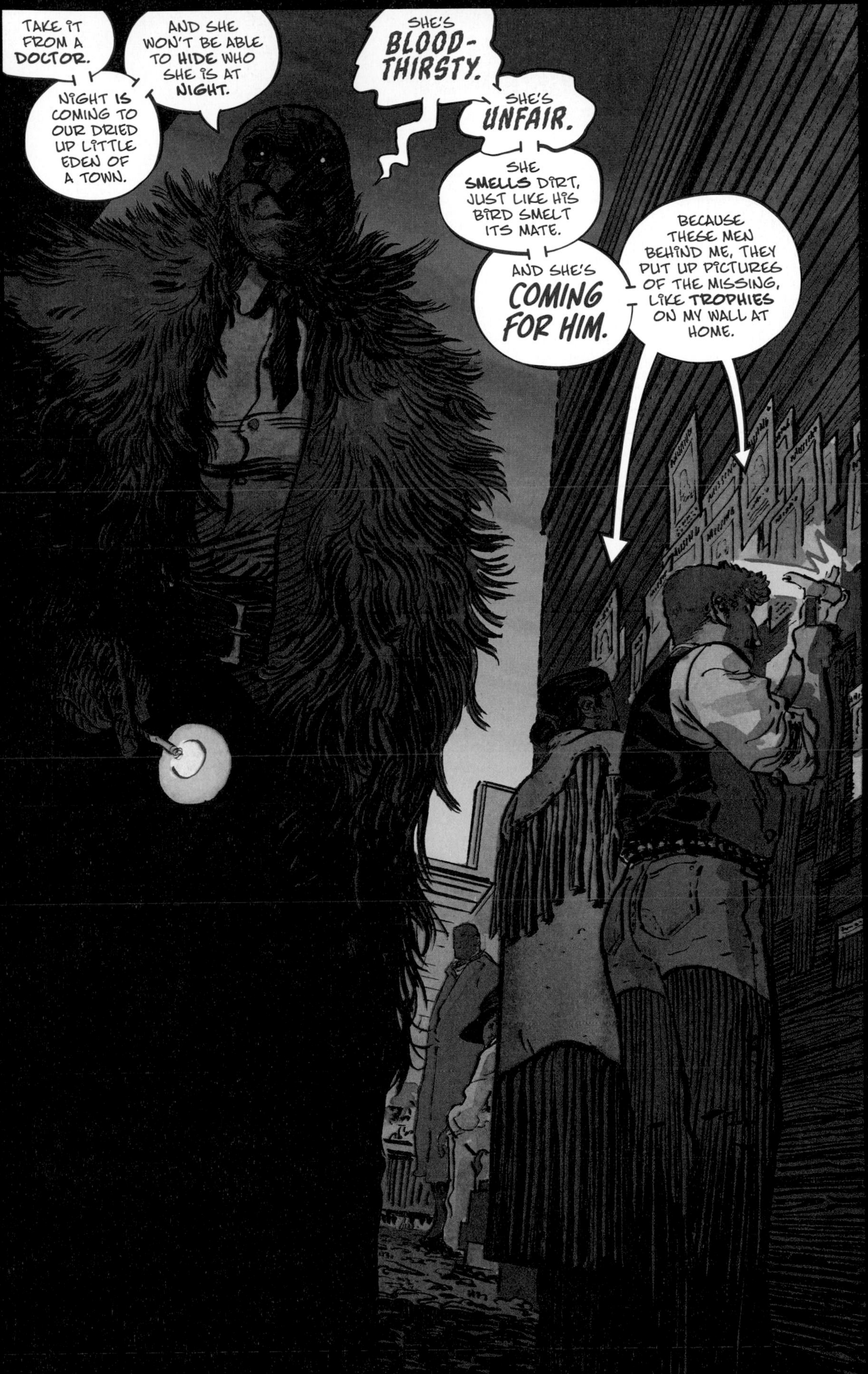
TAKE IT FROM A DOCTOR.
NIGHT IS COMING TO OUR DRIED UP LITTLE EDEN OF A TOWN.
AND SHE WON'T BE ABLE TO HIDE WHO SHE IS AT NIGHT.
SHE'S BLOOD-THIRSTY.
SHE'S UNFAIR.
SHE SMELLS DIRT, JUST LIKE HIS BIRD SMELT ITS MATE.
AND SHE'S COMING FOR HIM.
BECAUSE THESE MEN BEHIND ME, THEY PUT UP PICTURES OF THE MISSING, LIKE TROPHIES ON MY WALL AT HOME.

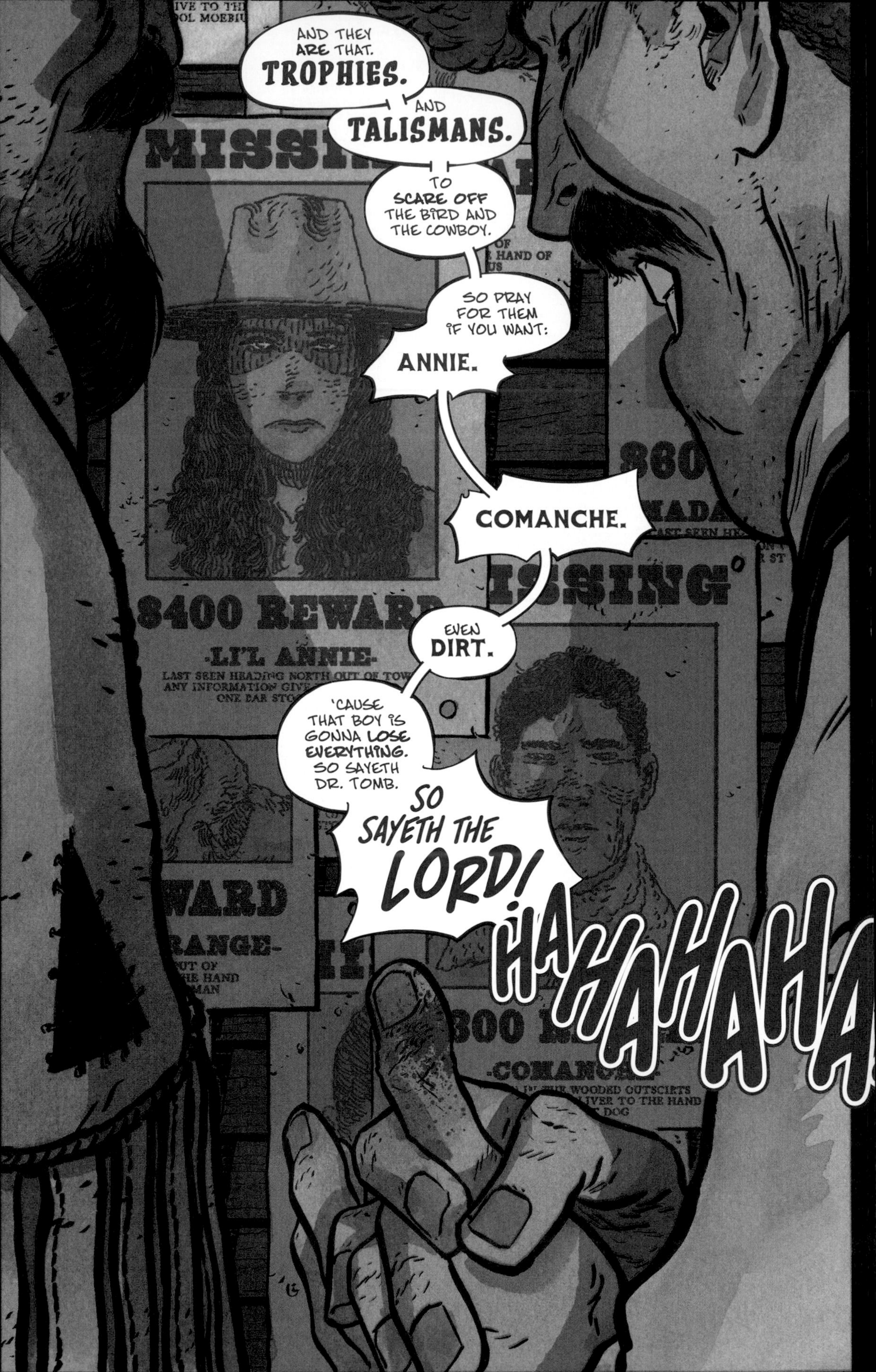
AND THEY ARE THAT. TROPHIES.
AND TALISMANS.
TO SCARE OFF THE BIRD AND THE COWBOY.
SO PRAY FOR THEM IF YOU WANT:
ANNIE.
COMANCHE.
EVEN DIRT.
'CAUSE THAT BOY IS GONNA LOSE EVERYTHING. SO SAYETH DR. TOMB.
SO SAYETH THE LORD!
HAHAHAHAHA
$400 REWARD
-LI'L ANNIE-

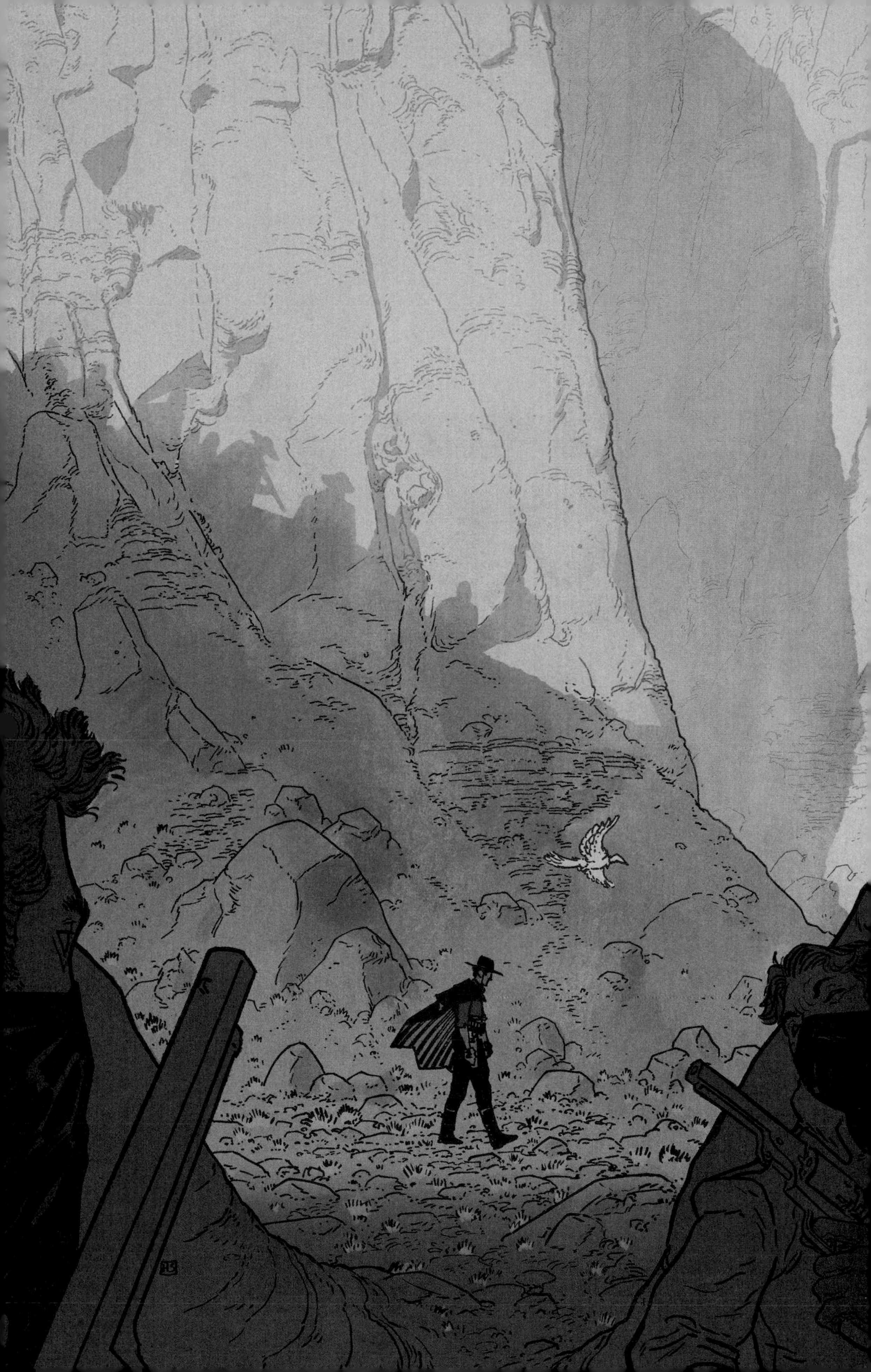

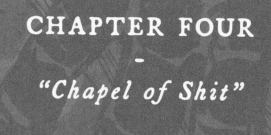

CHAPTER FOUR
-
"Chapel of Shit"

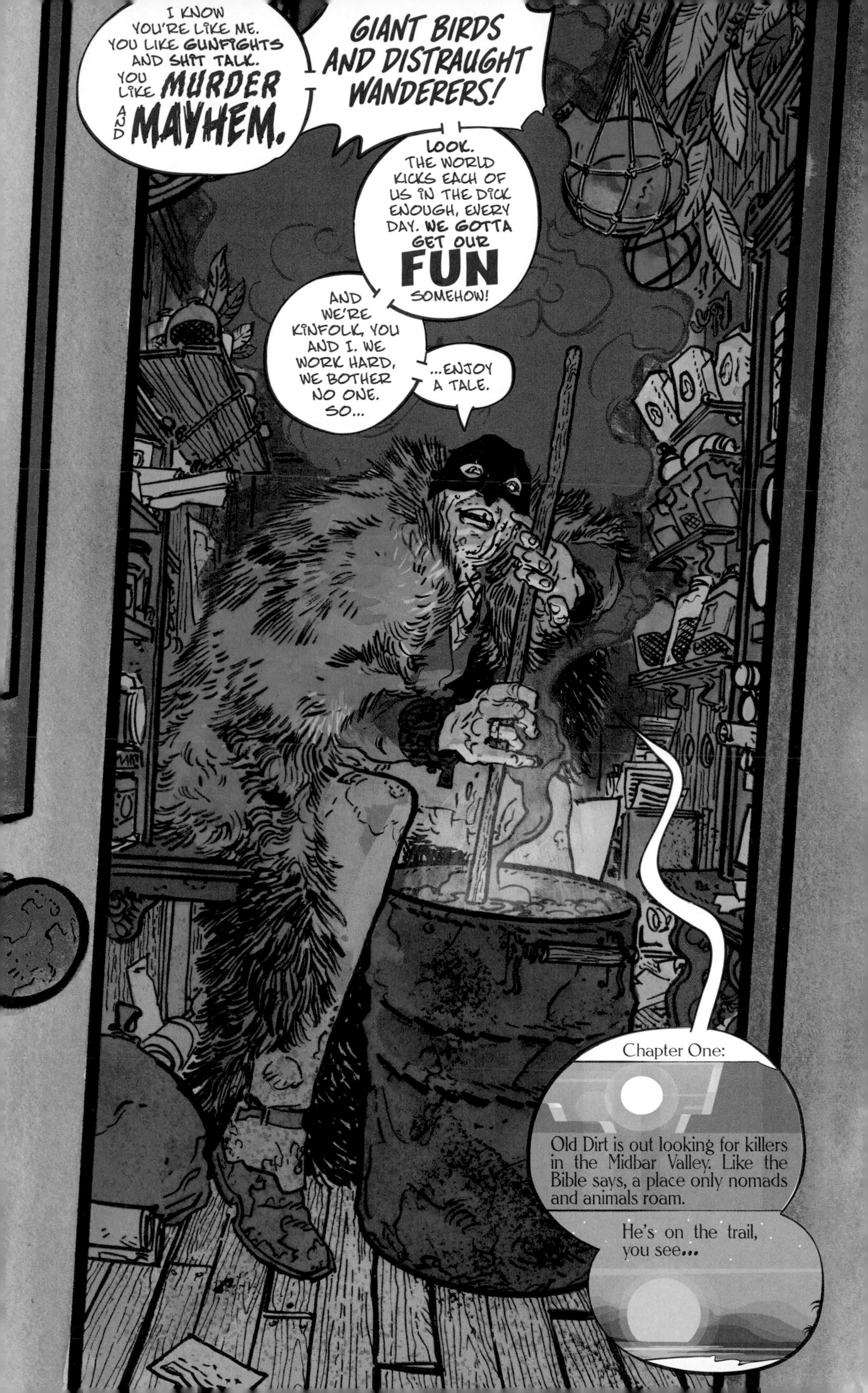
I KNOW YOU'RE LIKE ME. YOU LIKE GUNFIGHTS AND SHIT TALK. YOU LIKE MURDER AND MAYHEM.
GIANT BIRDS AND DISTRAUGHT WANDERERS!
LOOK. THE WORLD KICKS EACH OF US IN THE DICK ENOUGH, EVERY DAY. WE GOTTA GET OUR FUN SOMEHOW!
AND WE'RE KINFOLK, YOU AND I. WE WORK HARD, WE BOTHER NO ONE. SO...
...ENJOY A TALE.
Chapter One:
Old Dirt is out looking for killers in the Midbar Valley. Like the Bible says, a place only nomads and animals roam.
He's on the trail, you see...

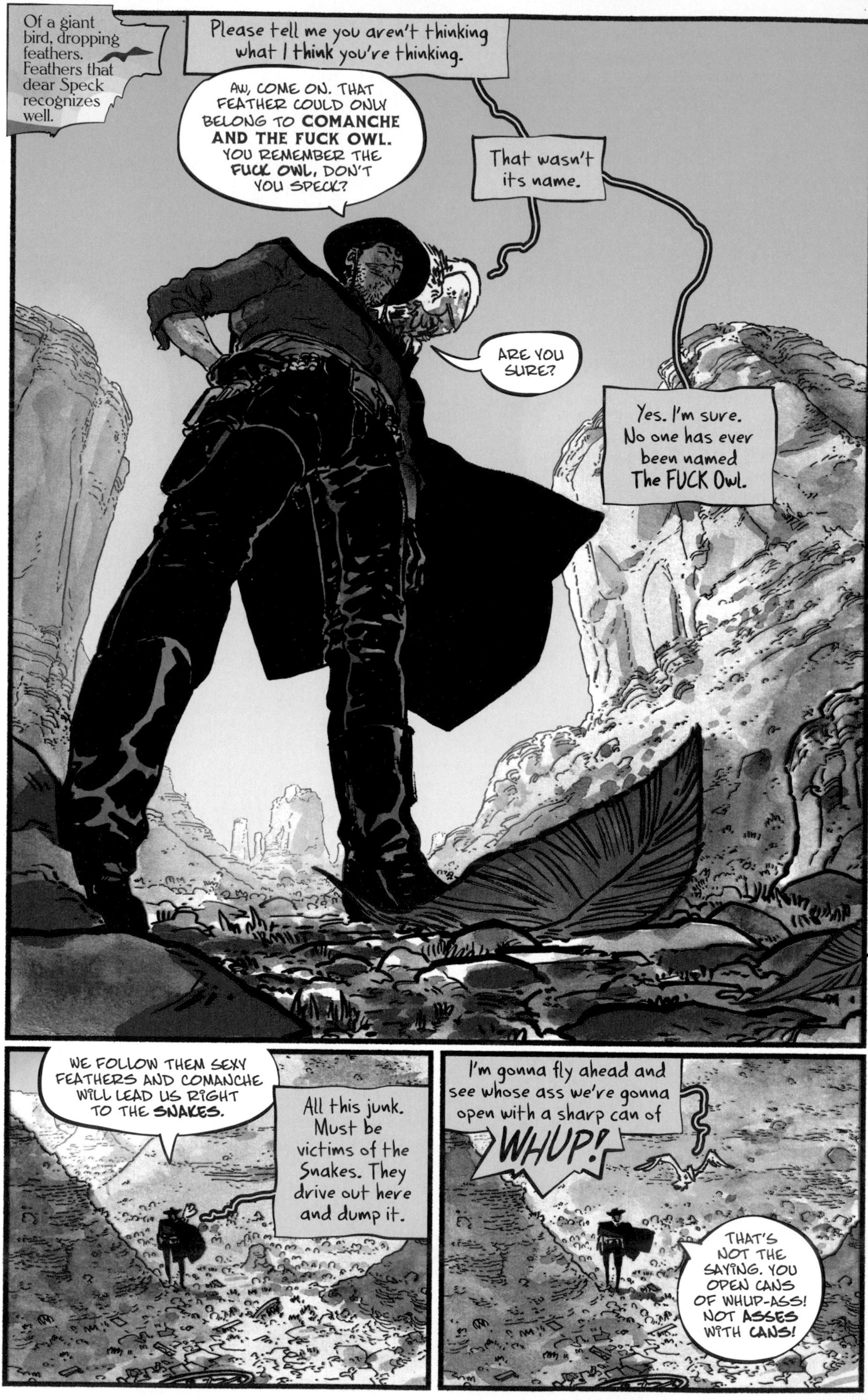
Of a giant bird, dropping feathers. Feathers that dear Speck recognizes well.
Please tell me you aren't thinking what I think you're thinking.
AW, COME ON. THAT FEATHER COULD ONLY BELONG TO **COMANCHE AND THE FUCK OWL.** YOU REMEMBER THE **FUCK OWL**, DON'T YOU SPECK?
That wasn't its name.
ARE YOU SURE?
Yes. I'm sure. No one has ever been named The FUCK Owl.
WE FOLLOW THEM SEXY FEATHERS AND COMANCHE WILL LEAD US RIGHT TO THE **SNAKES.**
All this junk. Must be victims of the Snakes. They drive out here and dump it.
I'm gonna fly ahead and see whose ass we're gonna open with a sharp can of
WHUP!
THAT'S NOT THE SAYING. YOU OPEN CANS OF WHUP-ASS! NOT **ASSES** WITH **CANS!**

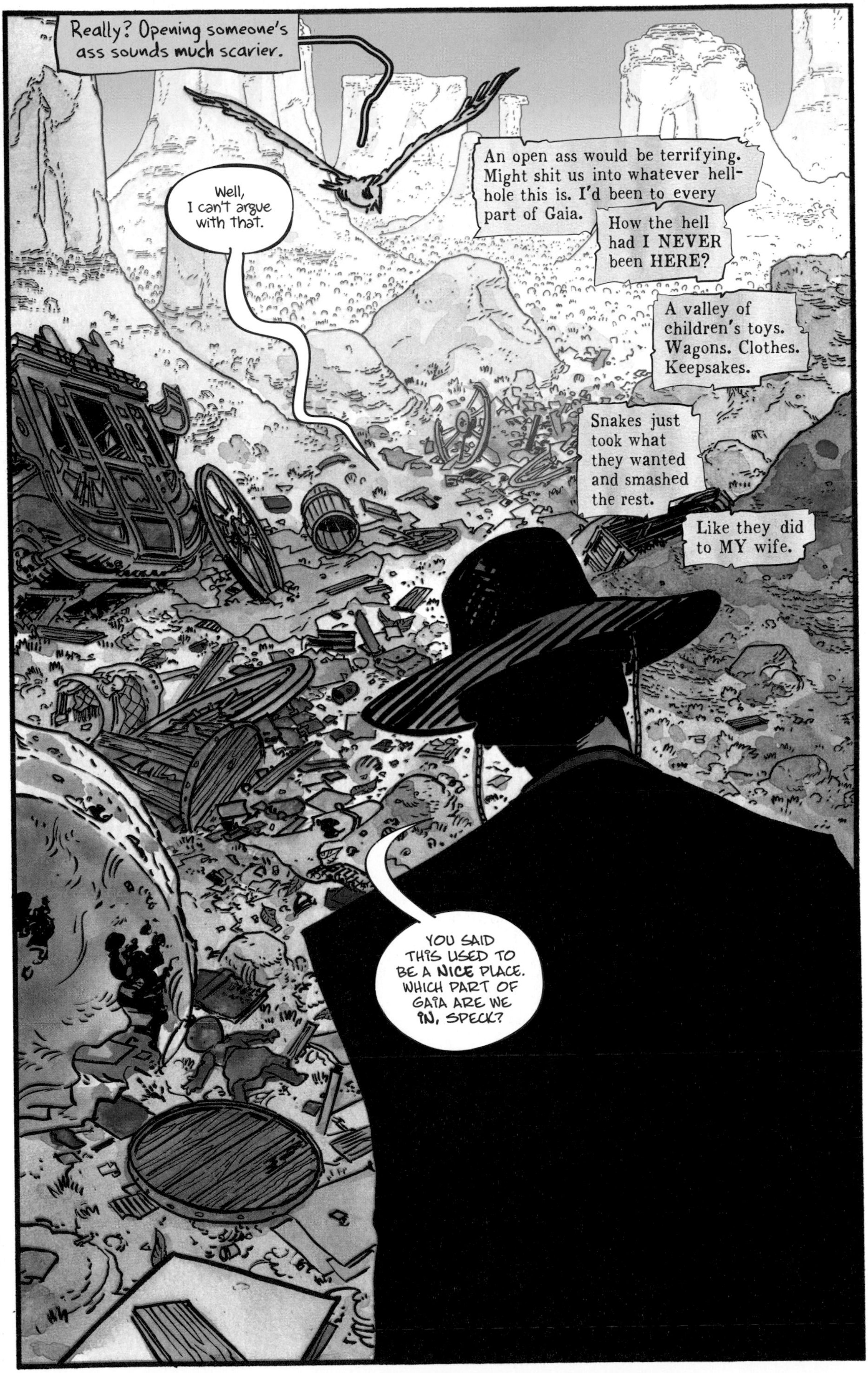
Really? Opening someone's ass sounds much scarier.
Well, I can't argue with that.
An open ass would be terrifying. Might shit us into whatever hell-hole this is. I'd been to every part of Gaia.
How the hell had I NEVER been HERE?
A valley of children's toys. Wagons. Clothes. Keepsakes.
Snakes just took what they wanted and smashed the rest.
Like they did to MY wife.
YOU SAID THIS USED TO BE A NICE PLACE. WHICH PART OF GAIA ARE WE IN, SPECK?

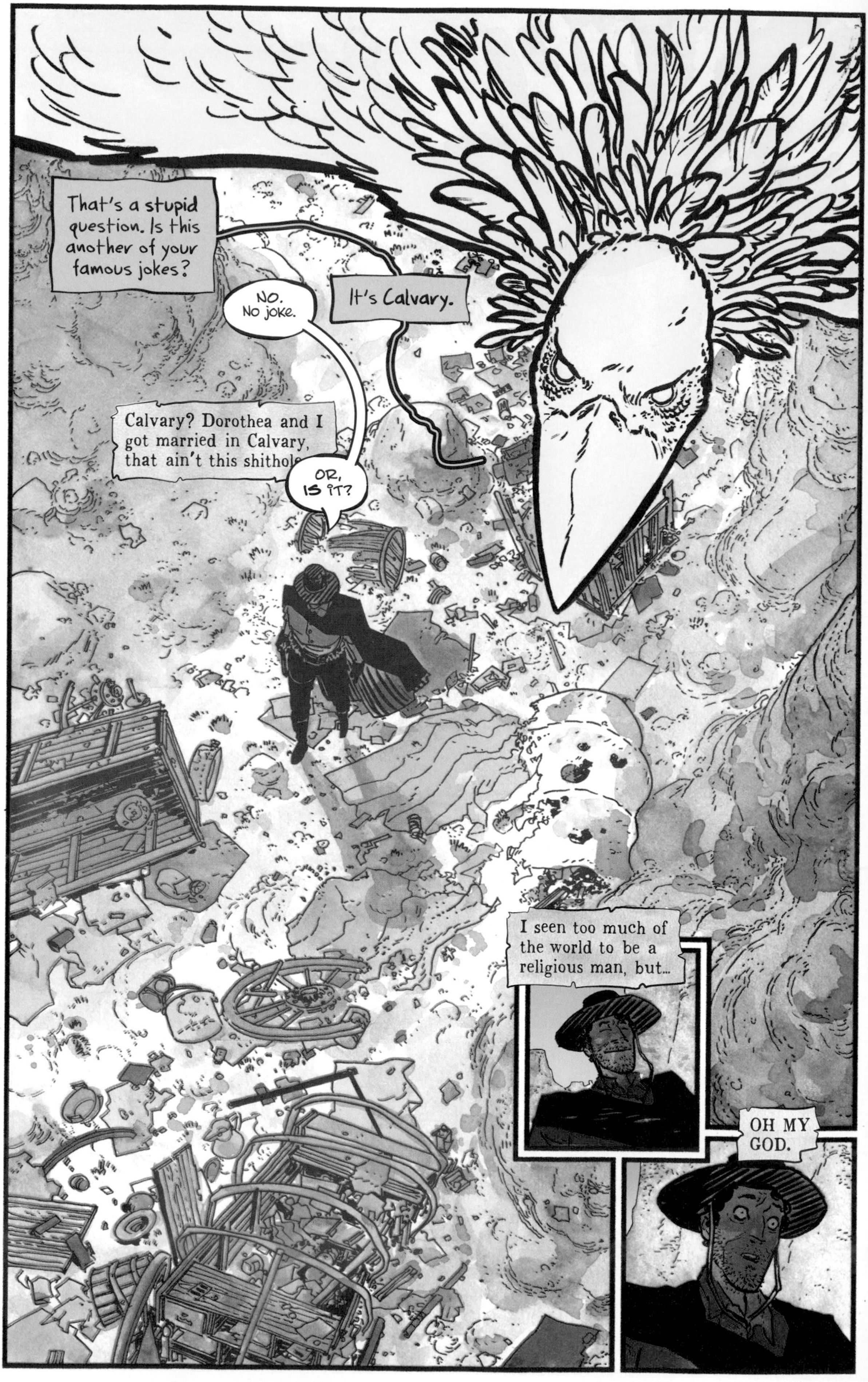
That's a stupid question. Is this another of your famous jokes?
It's Calvary.
NO. No joke.
Calvary? Dorothea and I got married in Calvary, that ain't this shithole.
OR, IS IT?
I seen too much of the world to be a religious man, but...
OH MY GOD.

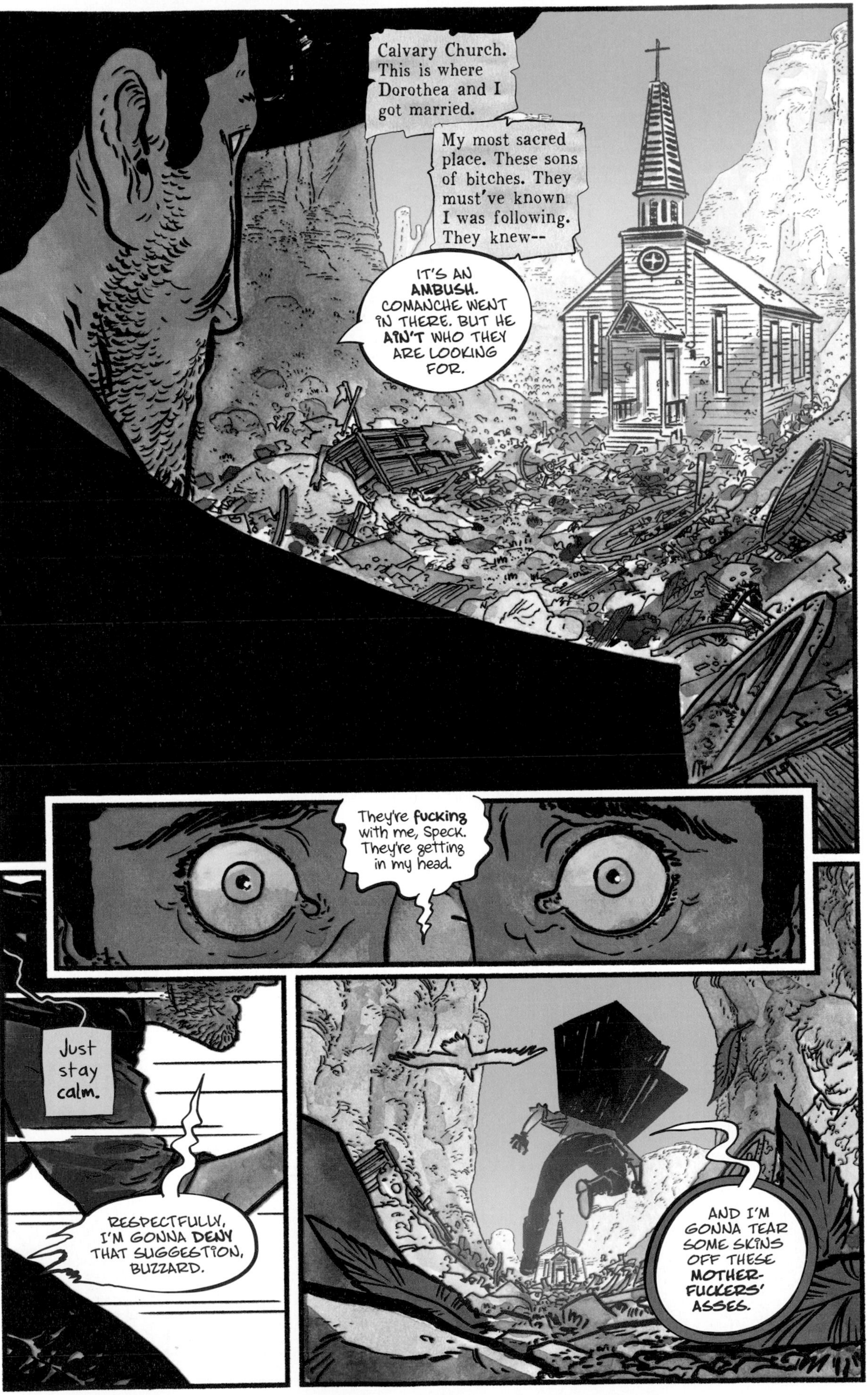
Calvary Church. This is where Dorothea and I got married.
My most sacred place. These sons of bitches. They must've known I was following. They knew--
IT'S AN AMBUSH. COMANCHE WENT IN THERE. BUT HE AIN'T WHO THEY ARE LOOKING FOR.
They're fucking with me, Speck. They're getting in my head.
Just stay calm.
RESPECTFULLY, I'M GONNA DENY THAT SUGGESTION, BUZZARD.
AND I'M GONNA TEAR SOME SKINS OFF THESE MOTHER-FUCKERS' ASSES.

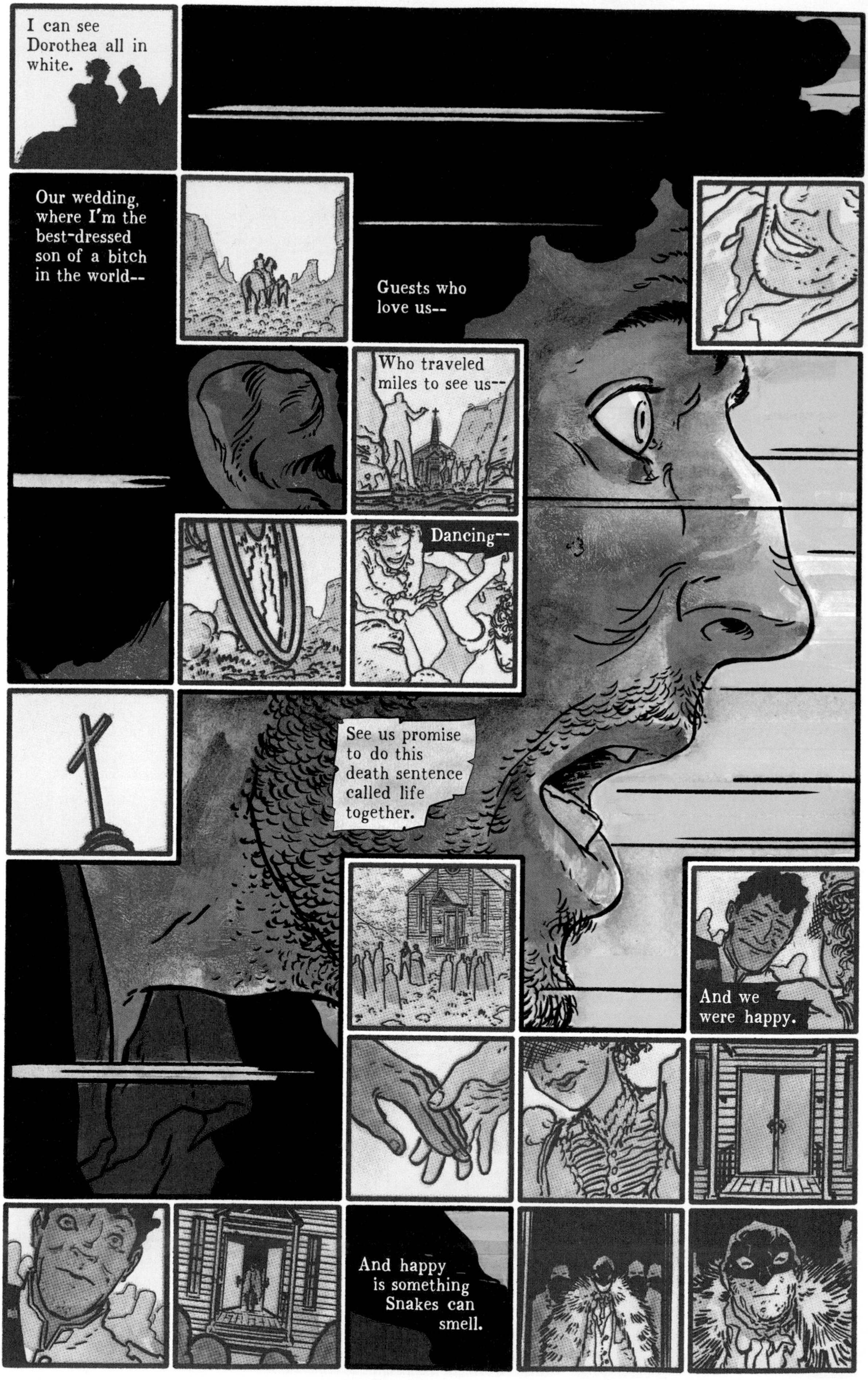

I can see Dorothea all in white.
Our wedding, where I'm the best-dressed son of a bitch in the world--
Guests who love us--
Who traveled miles to see us--
Dancing--
See us promise to do this death sentence called life together.
And we were happy.
And happy is something Snakes can smell.

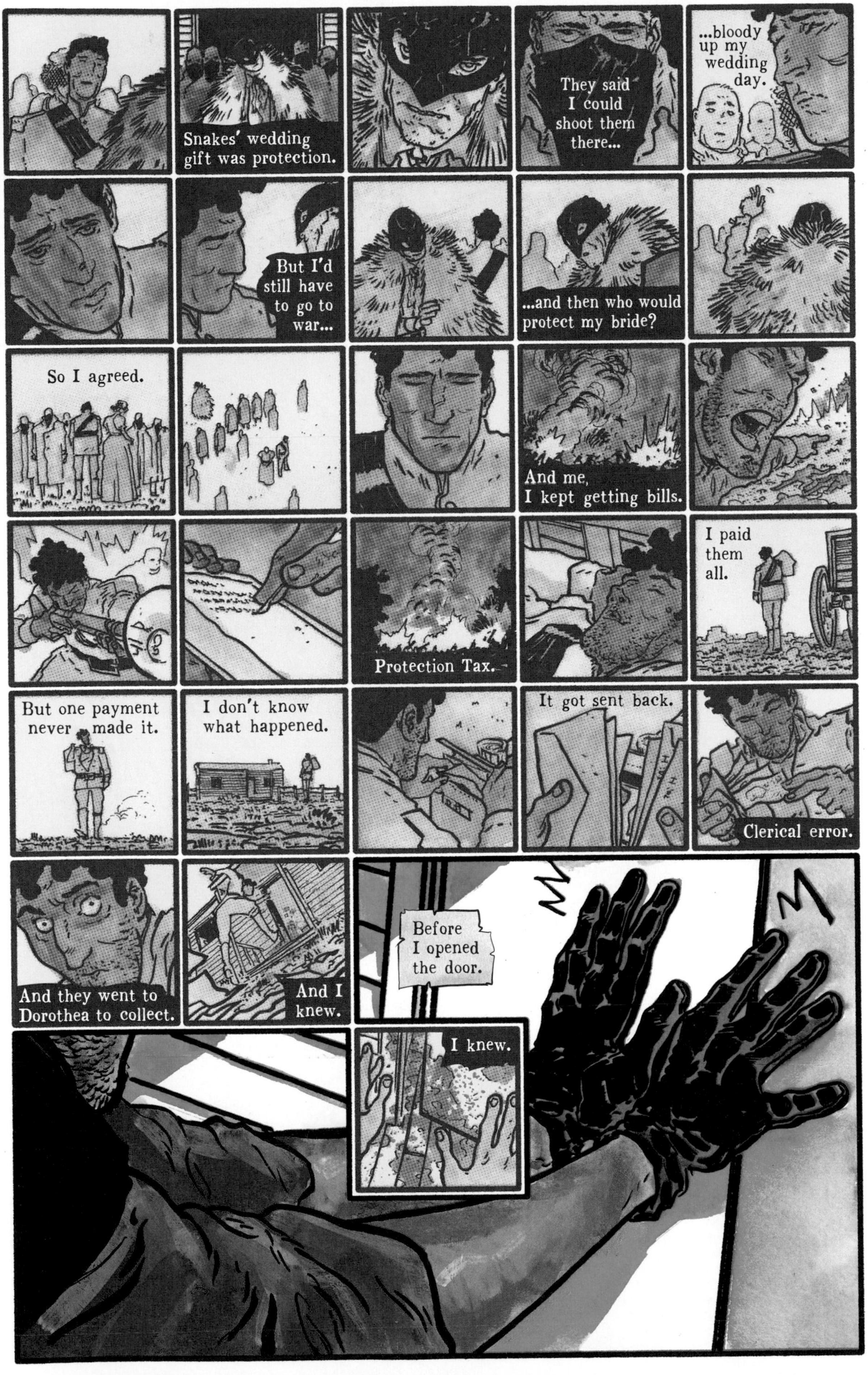
Snakes' wedding gift was protection.
They said I could shoot them there...
...bloody up my wedding day.
But I'd still have to go to war...
...and then who would protect my bride?
So I agreed.
And me, I kept getting bills.
Protection Tax.
I paid them all.
But one payment never made it.
I don't know what happened.
It got sent back.
Clerical error.
And they went to Dorothea to collect.
And I knew.
Before I opened the door.
I knew.

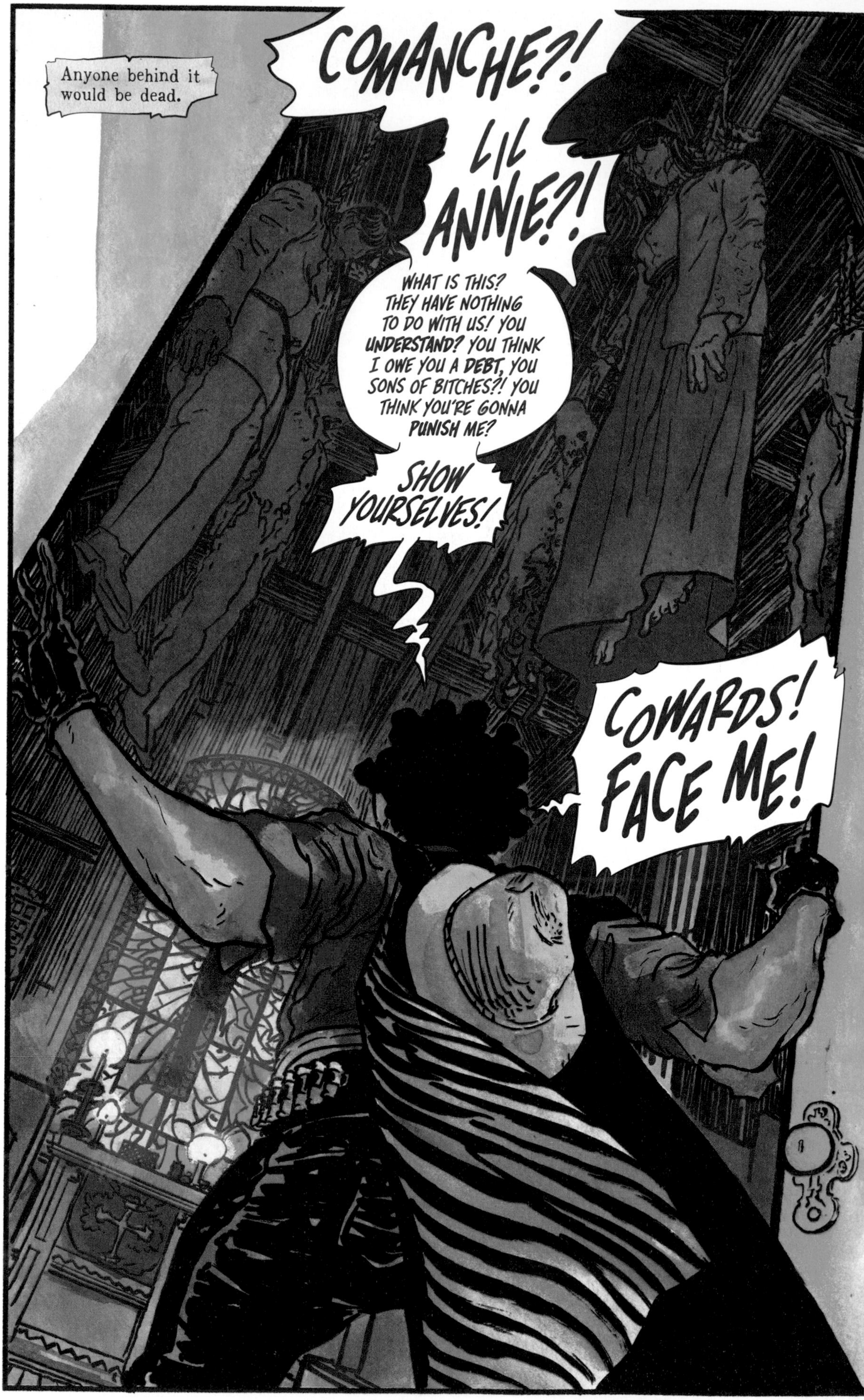
Anyone behind it would be dead.
COMANCHE?!
LIL ANNIE?!
WHAT IS THIS? THEY HAVE NOTHING TO DO WITH US! YOU UNDERSTAND? YOU THINK I OWE YOU A DEBT, YOU SONS OF BITCHES?! YOU THINK YOU'RE GONNA PUNISH ME?
SHOW YOURSELVES!
COWARDS! FACE ME!

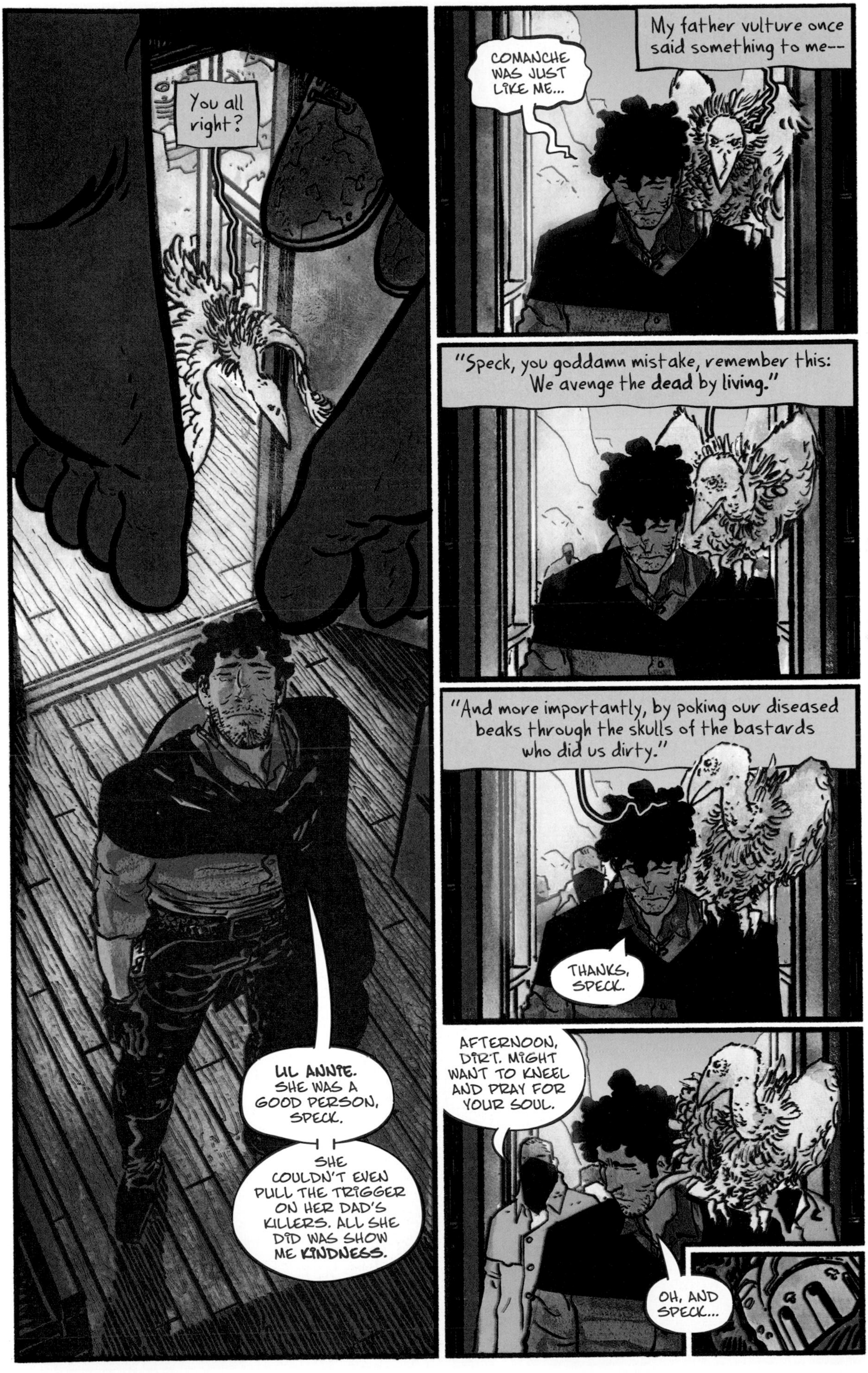
You all right?
LIL ANNIE. SHE WAS A GOOD PERSON, SPECK.
SHE COULDN'T EVEN PULL THE TRIGGER ON HER DAD'S KILLERS. ALL SHE DID WAS SHOW ME KINDNESS.
My father vulture once said something to me--
COMANCHE WAS JUST LIKE ME...
"Speck, you goddamn mistake, remember this: We avenge the dead by living."
"And more importantly, by poking our diseased beaks through the skulls of the bastards who did us dirty."
THANKS, SPECK.
AFTERNOON, DIRT. MIGHT WANT TO KNEEL AND PRAY FOR YOUR SOUL.
OH, AND SPECK...

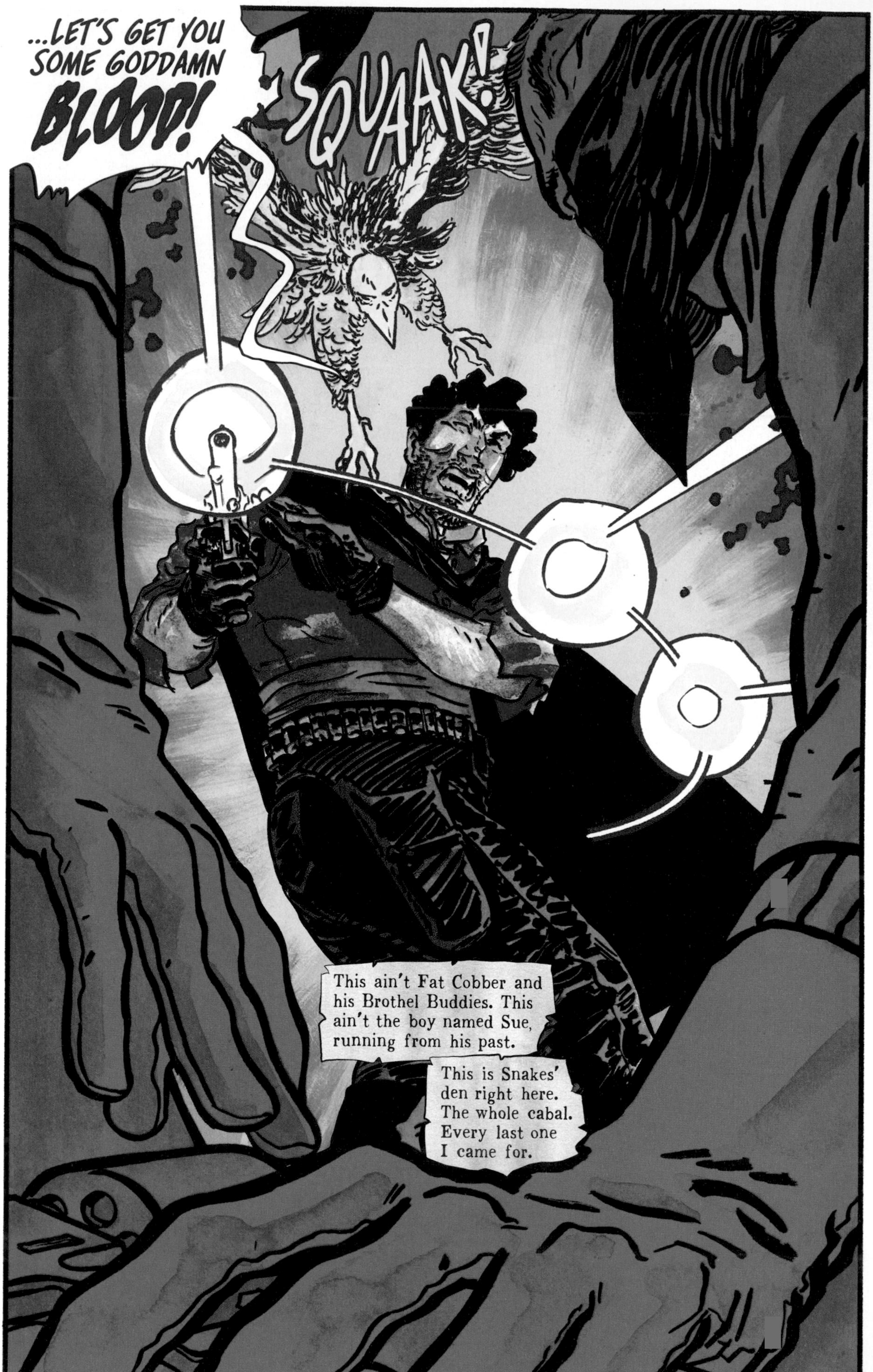
...LET'S GET YOU SOME GODDAMN BLOOD!
SQUAAK!
This ain't Fat Cobber and his Brothel Buddies. This ain't the boy named Sue, running from his past.
This is Snakes' den right here. The whole cabal. Every last one I came for.

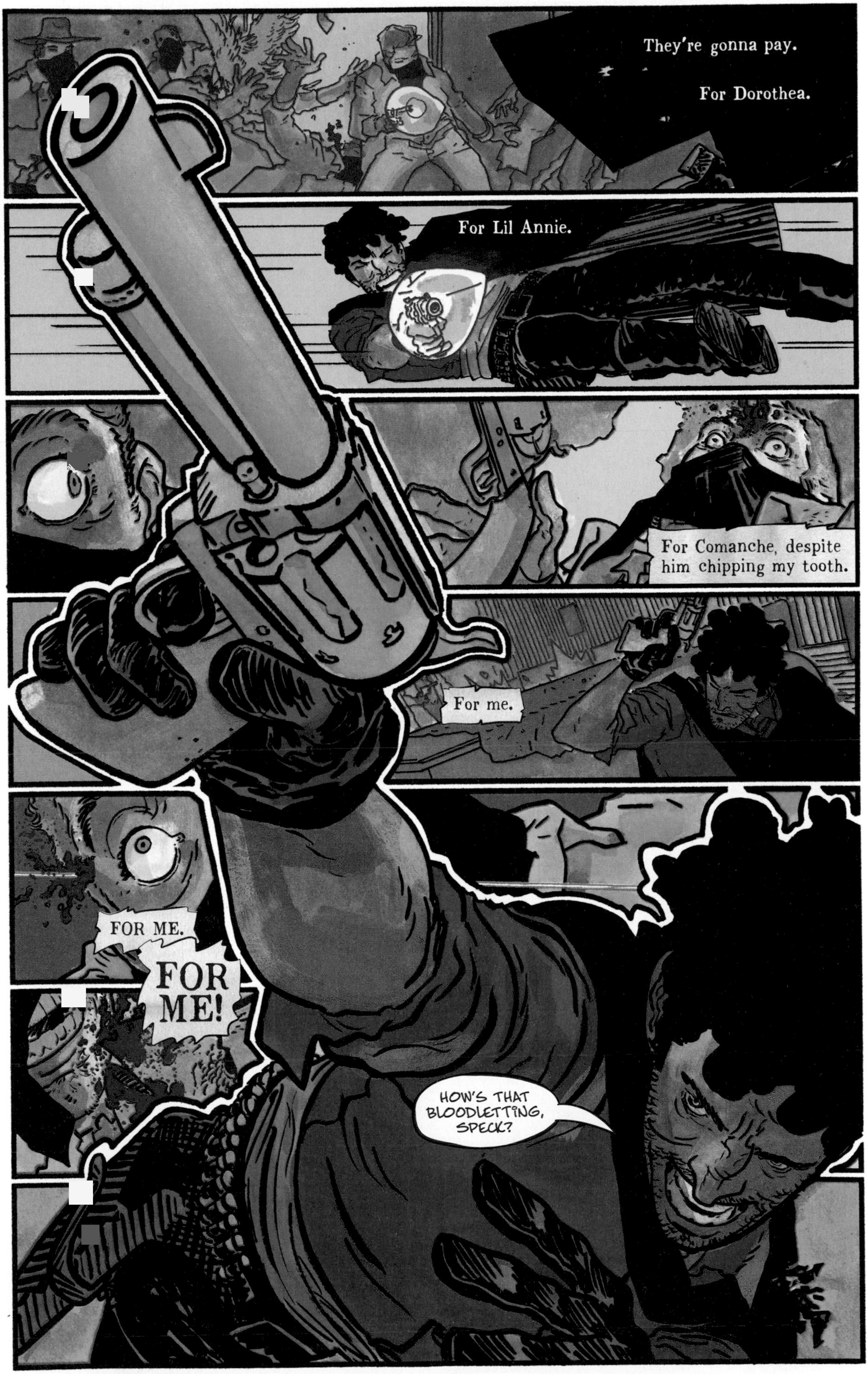

They're gonna pay.
For Dorothea.
For Lil Annie.
For Comanche, despite him chipping my tooth.
For me.
FOR ME.
FOR ME!
HOW'S THAT BLOODLETTING, SPECK?

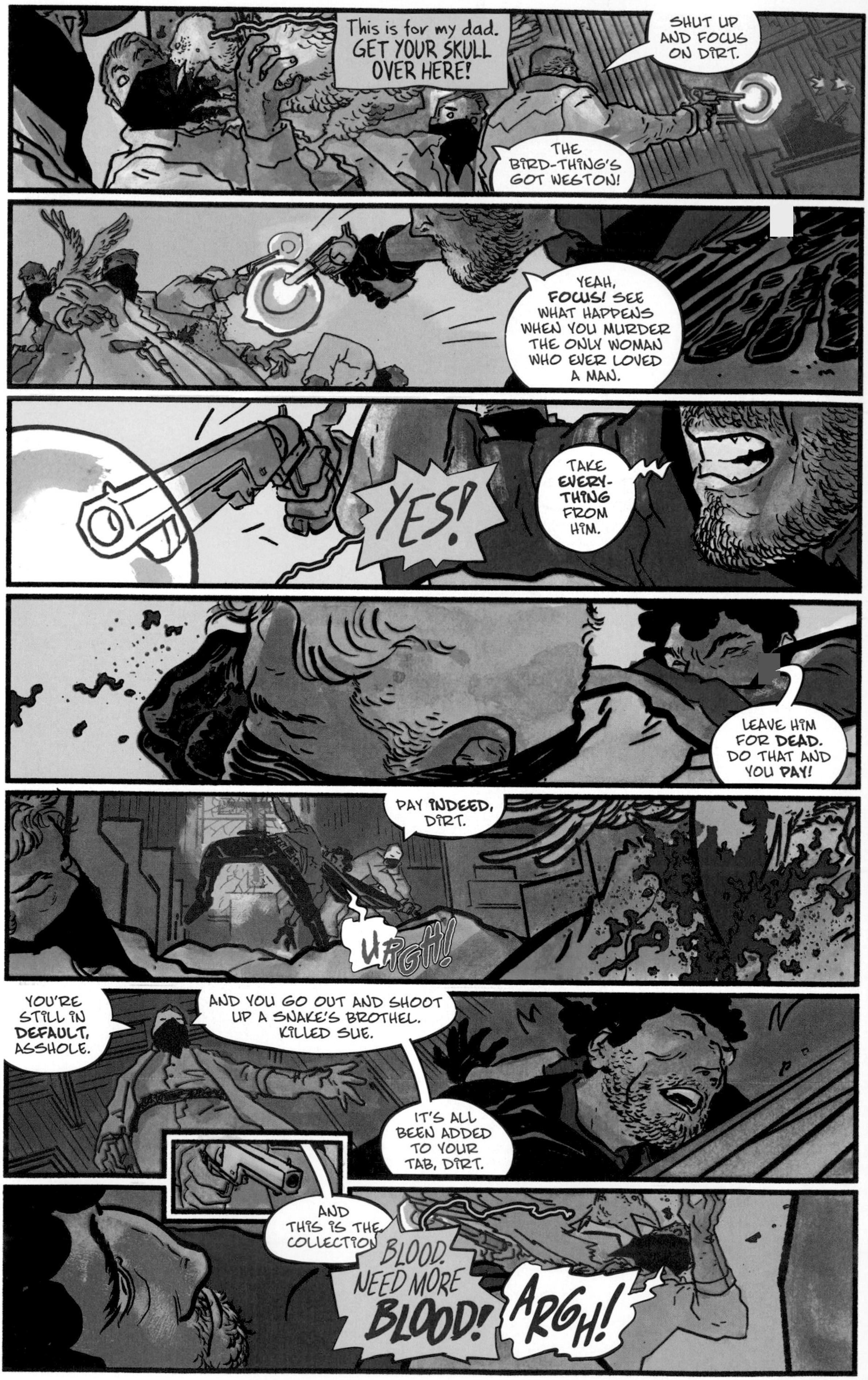
This is for my dad. GET YOUR SKULL OVER HERE!
SHUT UP AND FOCUS ON DIRT.
THE BIRD-THING'S GOT WESTON!
YEAH, FOCUS! SEE WHAT HAPPENS WHEN YOU MURDER THE ONLY WOMAN WHO EVER LOVED A MAN.
YES!
TAKE EVERY-THING FROM HIM.
LEAVE HIM FOR DEAD. DO THAT AND YOU PAY!
PAY INDEED, DIRT.
URGH!
YOU'RE STILL IN DEFAULT, ASSHOLE.
AND YOU GO OUT AND SHOOT UP A SNAKE'S BROTHEL. KILLED SUE.
IT'S ALL BEEN ADDED TO YOUR TAB, DIRT.
AND THIS IS THE COLLECTION
BLOOD. NEED MORE BLOOD!
ARGH!

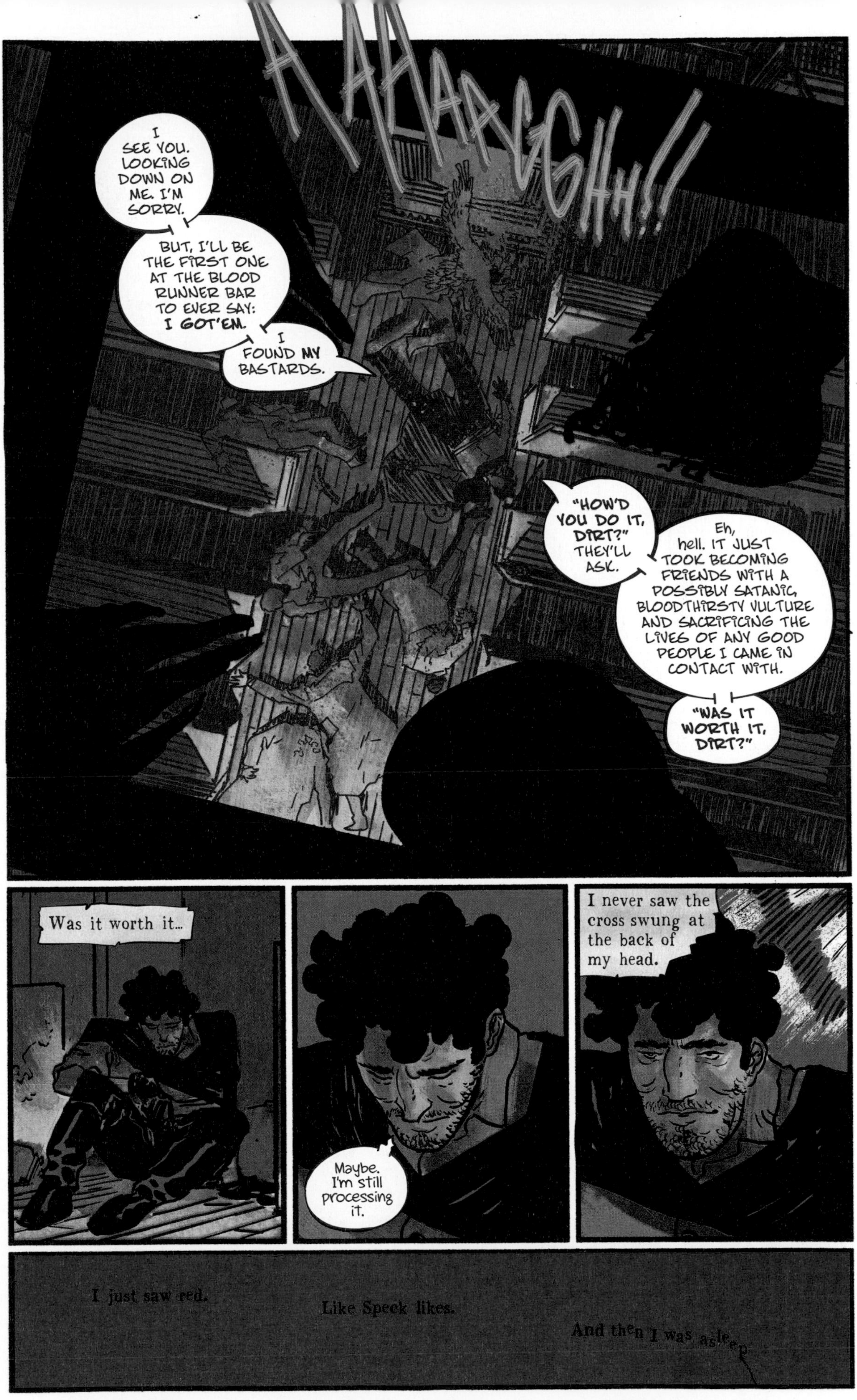
AAAAAGHH!!
I SEE YOU. LOOKING DOWN ON ME. I'M SORRY.
BUT, I'LL BE THE FIRST ONE AT THE BLOOD RUNNER BAR TO EVER SAY: I GOT'EM.
I FOUND MY BASTARDS.
"HOW'D YOU DO IT, DIRT?" THEY'LL ASK.
Eh, hell. IT JUST TOOK BECOMING FRIENDS WITH A POSSIBLY SATANIC, BLOODTHIRSTY VULTURE AND SACRIFICING THE LIVES OF ANY GOOD PEOPLE I CAME IN CONTACT WITH.
"WAS IT WORTH IT, DIRT?"
Was it worth it...
Maybe. I'm still processing it.
I never saw the cross swung at the back of my head.
I just saw red.
Like Speck likes.
And then I was asleep

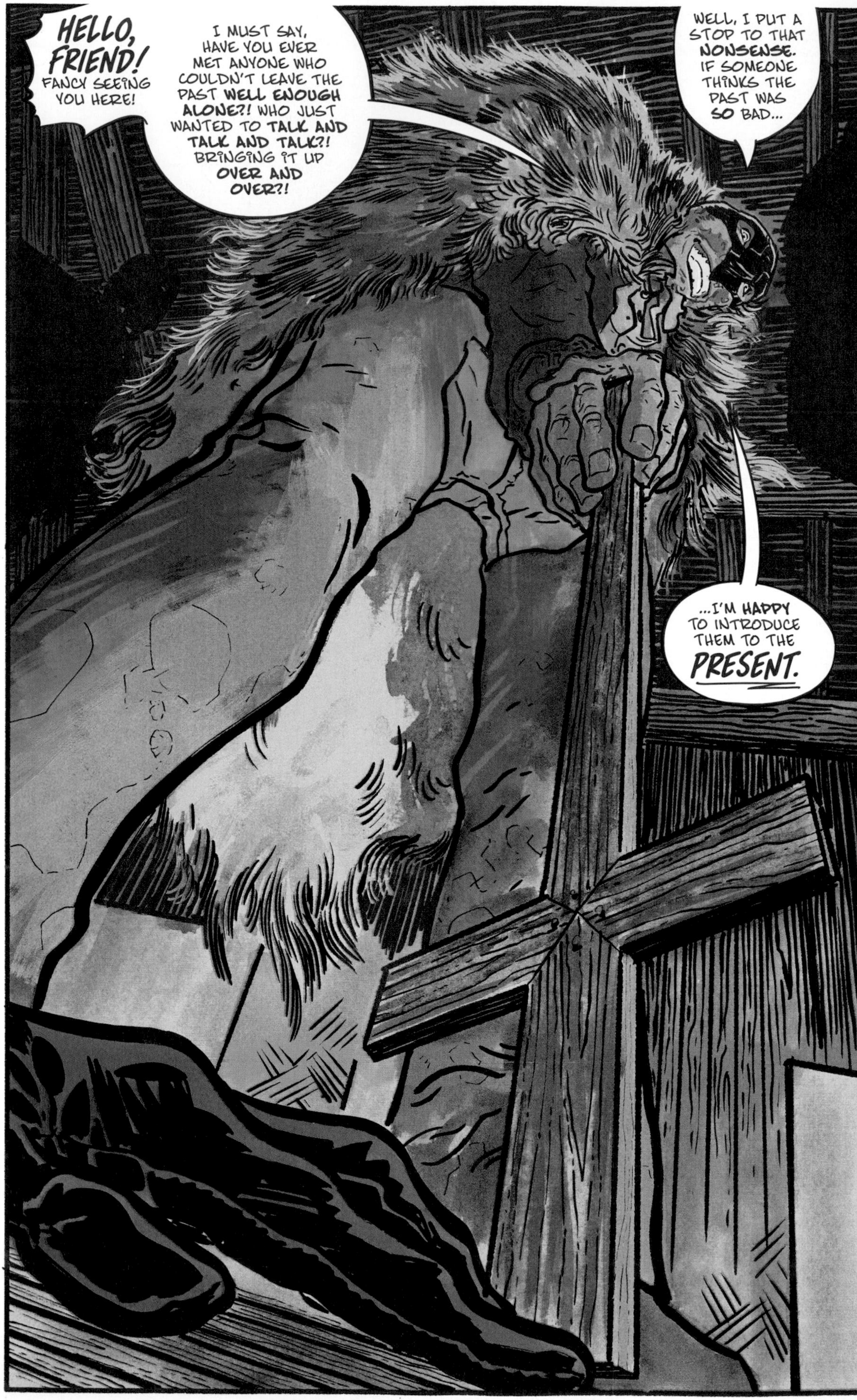
HELLO, FRIEND! FANCY SEEING YOU HERE!
I MUST SAY, HAVE YOU EVER MET ANYONE WHO COULDN'T LEAVE THE PAST WELL ENOUGH ALONE?! WHO JUST WANTED TO TALK AND TALK AND TALK?! BRINGING IT UP OVER AND OVER?!
WELL, I PUT A STOP TO THAT NONSENSE. IF SOMEONE THINKS THE PAST WAS SO BAD...
...I'M HAPPY TO INTRODUCE THEM TO THE PRESENT.

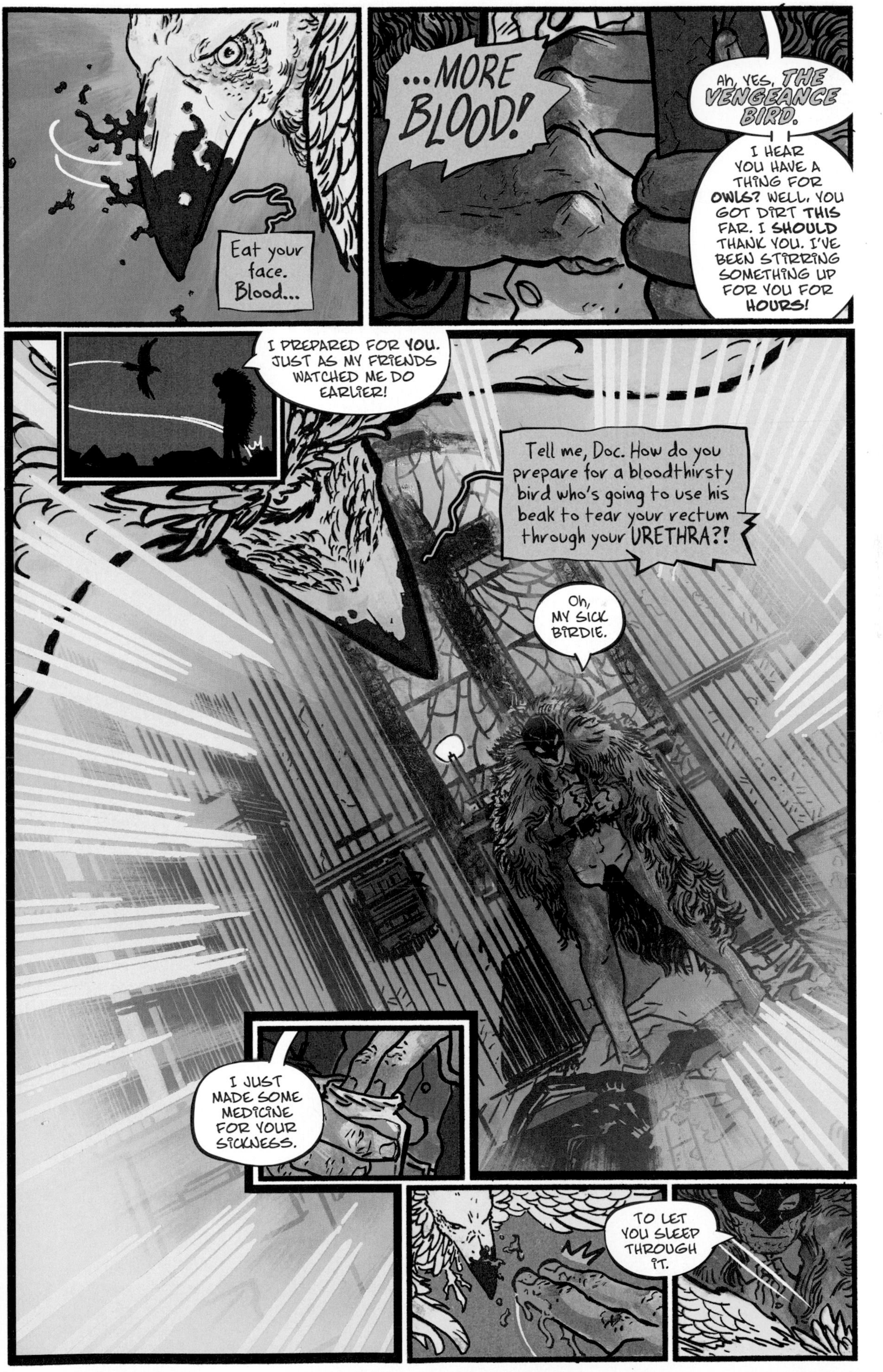
Eat your face. Blood...
...MORE BLOOD!
Ah, yes, THE VENGEANCE BIRD.
I HEAR YOU HAVE A THING FOR OWLS? WELL, YOU GOT DIRT THIS FAR. I SHOULD THANK YOU. I'VE BEEN STIRRING SOMETHING UP FOR YOU FOR HOURS!
I PREPARED FOR YOU. JUST AS MY FRIENDS WATCHED ME DO EARLIER!
Tell me, Doc. How do you prepare for a bloodthirsty bird who's going to use his beak to tear your rectum through your URETHRA?!
Oh, MY SICK BIRDIE.
I JUST MADE SOME MEDICINE FOR YOUR SICKNESS.
TO LET YOU SLEEP THROUGH IT.

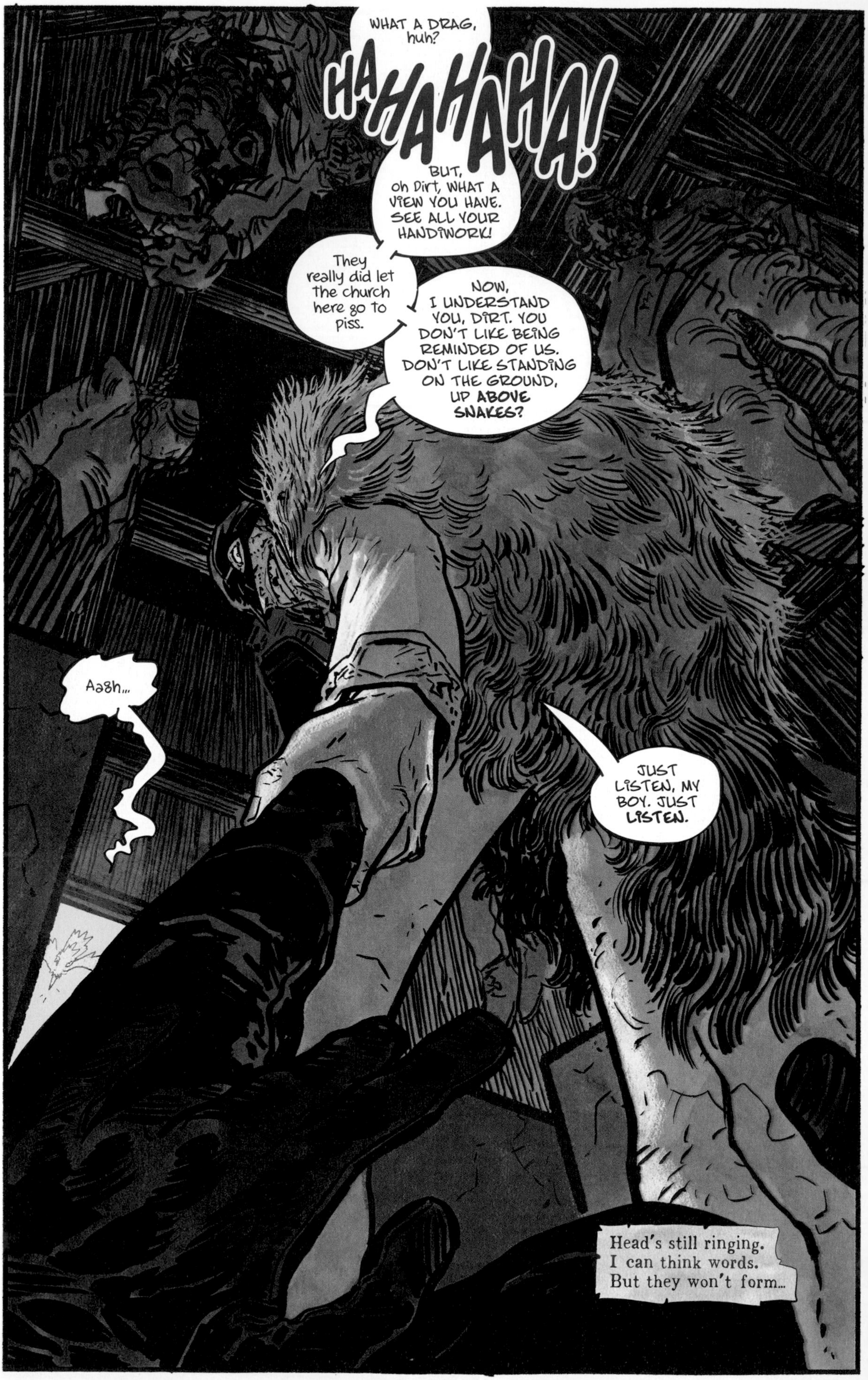
WHAT A DRAG, huh?
HAHAHAHAHA!
BUT, oh Dirt, WHAT A VIEW YOU HAVE. SEE ALL YOUR HANDIWORK!
They really did let the church here go to piss.
NOW, I UNDERSTAND YOU, DIRT. YOU DON'T LIKE BEING REMINDED OF US. DON'T LIKE STANDING ON THE GROUND, UP ABOVE SNAKES?
Aagh...
JUST LISTEN, MY BOY. JUST LISTEN.
Head's still ringing. I can think words. But they won't form...

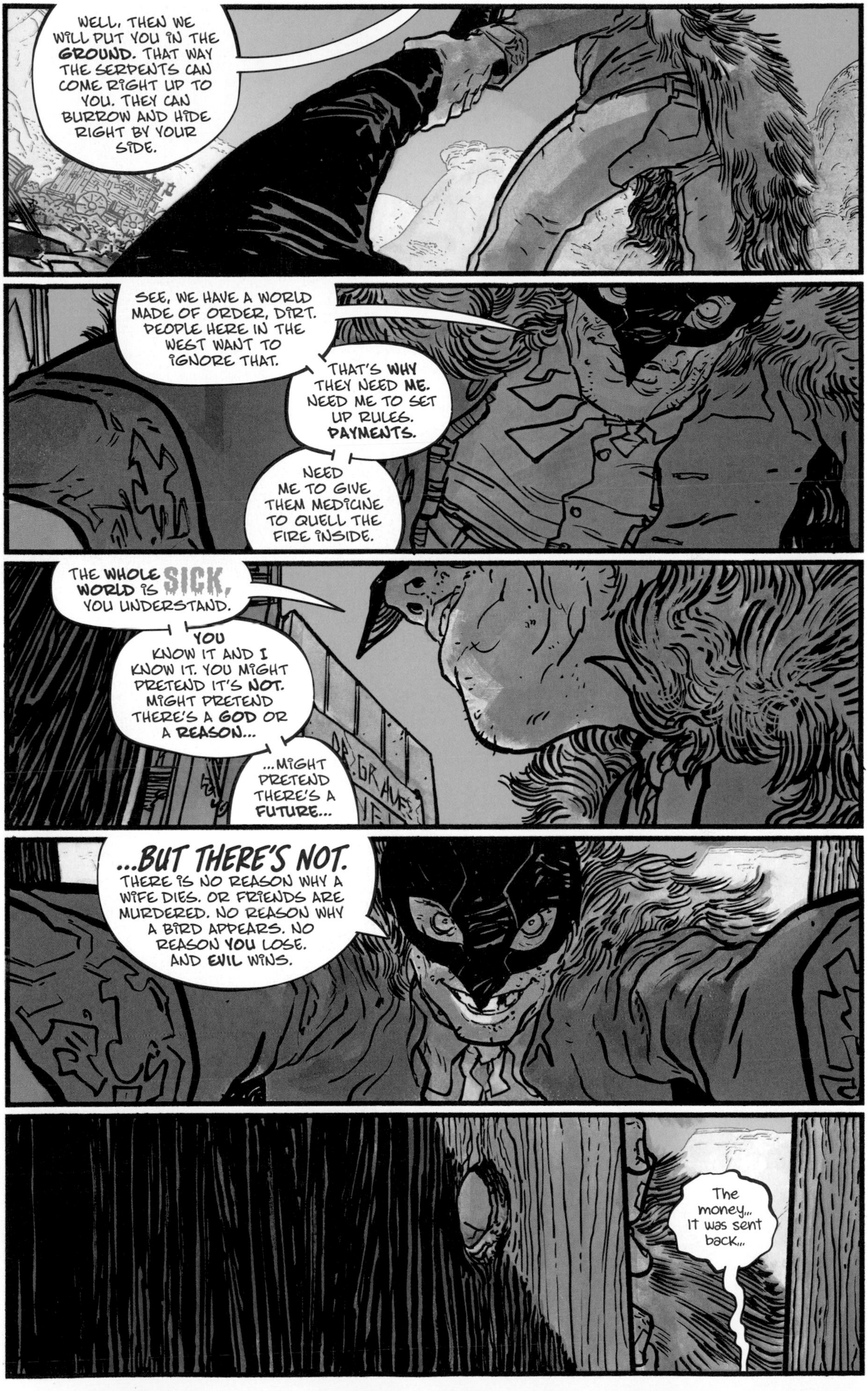
WELL, THEN WE WILL PUT YOU IN THE GROUND. THAT WAY THE SERPENTS CAN COME RIGHT UP TO YOU. THEY CAN BURROW AND HIDE RIGHT BY YOUR SIDE.
SEE, WE HAVE A WORLD MADE OF ORDER, DIRT. PEOPLE HERE IN THE WEST WANT TO IGNORE THAT.
THAT'S WHY THEY NEED ME. NEED ME TO SET UP RULES. PAYMENTS.
NEED ME TO GIVE THEM MEDICINE TO QUELL THE FIRE INSIDE.
THE WHOLE WORLD IS SICK, YOU UNDERSTAND.
YOU KNOW IT AND I KNOW IT. YOU MIGHT PRETEND IT'S NOT. MIGHT PRETEND THERE'S A GOD OR A REASON...
...MIGHT PRETEND THERE'S A FUTURE...
...BUT THERE'S NOT.
THERE IS NO REASON WHY A WIFE DIES. OR FRIENDS ARE MURDERED. NO REASON WHY A BIRD APPEARS. NO REASON YOU LOSE. AND EVIL WINS.
The money... It was sent back...

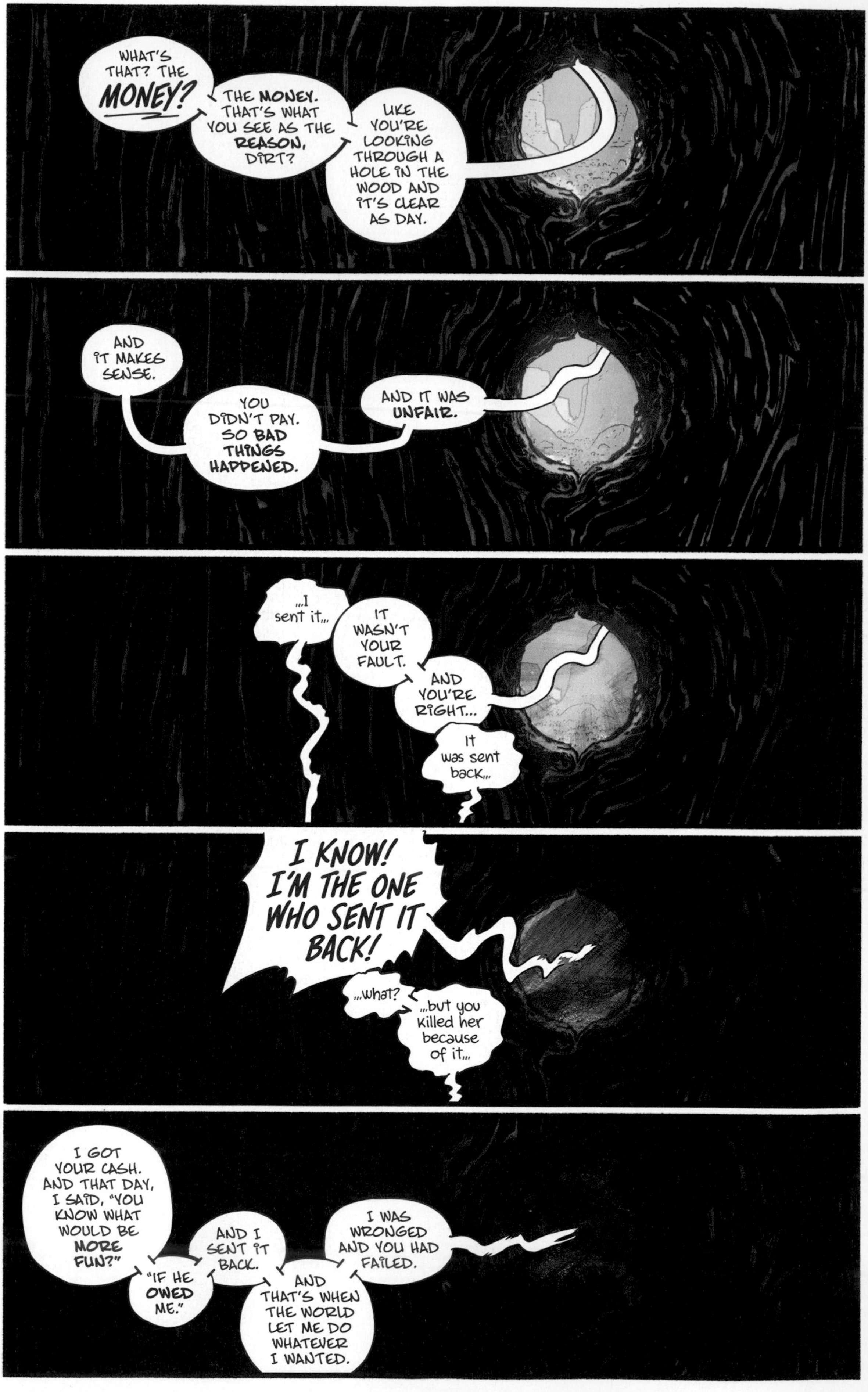

WHAT'S THAT? THE MONEY?
THE MONEY. THAT'S WHAT YOU SEE AS THE REASON, DIRT?
LIKE YOU'RE LOOKING THROUGH A HOLE IN THE WOOD AND IT'S CLEAR AS DAY.
AND IT MAKES SENSE.
YOU DIDN'T PAY. SO BAD THINGS HAPPENED.
AND IT WAS UNFAIR.
...I sent it...
IT WASN'T YOUR FAULT.
AND YOU'RE RIGHT...
It was sent back...
I KNOW! I'M THE ONE WHO SENT IT BACK!
...what?
...but you killed her because of it...
I GOT YOUR CASH. AND THAT DAY, I SAID, "YOU KNOW WHAT WOULD BE MORE FUN?"
"IF HE OWED ME."
AND I SENT IT BACK.
AND THAT'S WHEN THE WORLD LET ME DO WHATEVER I WANTED.
I WAS WRONGED AND YOU HAD FAILED.

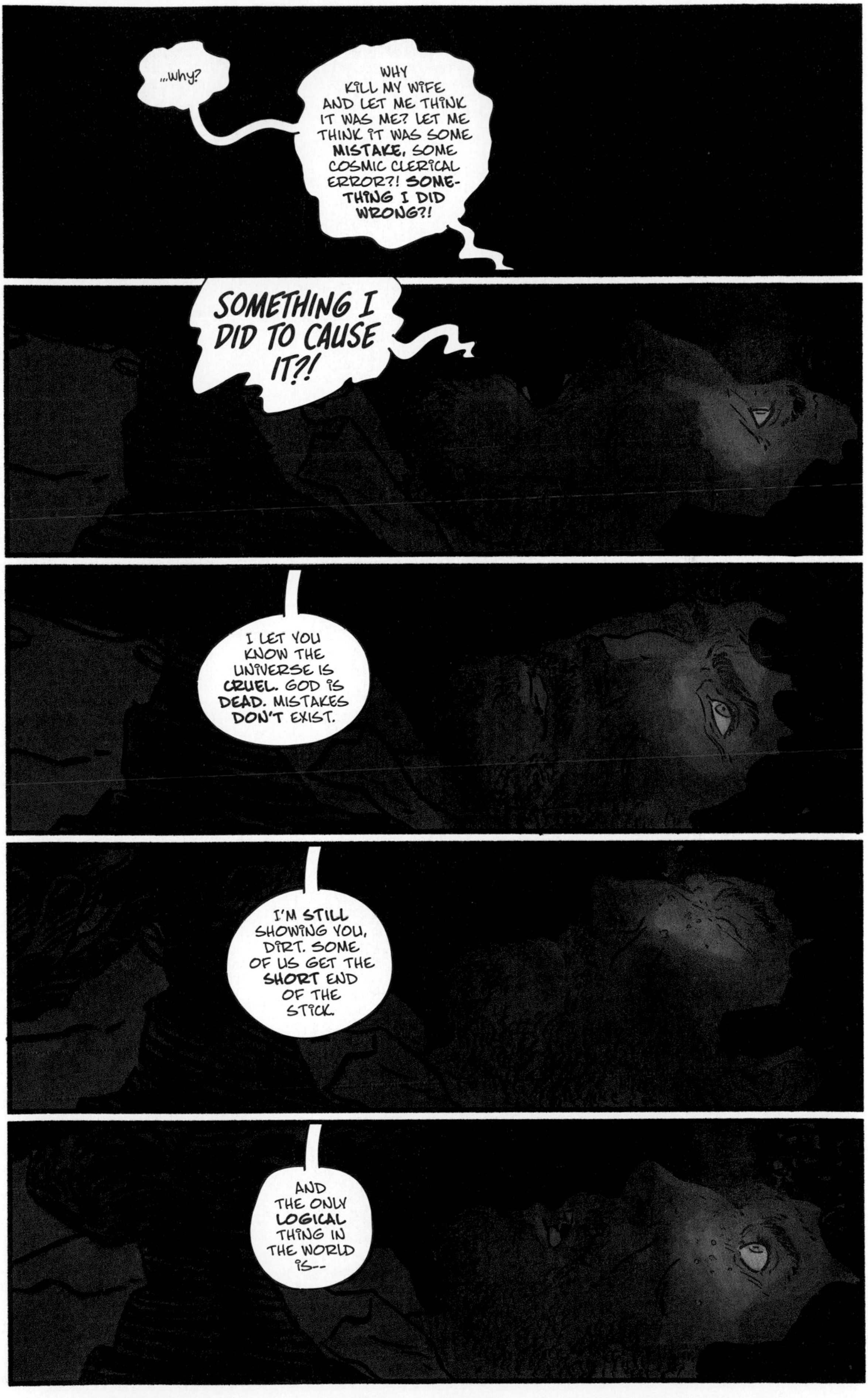
...why?
WHY KILL MY WIFE AND LET ME THINK IT WAS ME? LET ME THINK IT WAS SOME MISTAKE, SOME COSMIC CLERICAL ERROR?! SOMETHING I DID WRONG?!
SOMETHING I DID TO CAUSE IT?!
I LET YOU KNOW THE UNIVERSE IS CRUEL. GOD IS DEAD. MISTAKES DON'T EXIST.
I'M STILL SHOWING YOU, DIRT. SOME OF US GET THE SHORT END OF THE STICK.
AND THE ONLY LOGICAL THING IN THE WORLD IS--

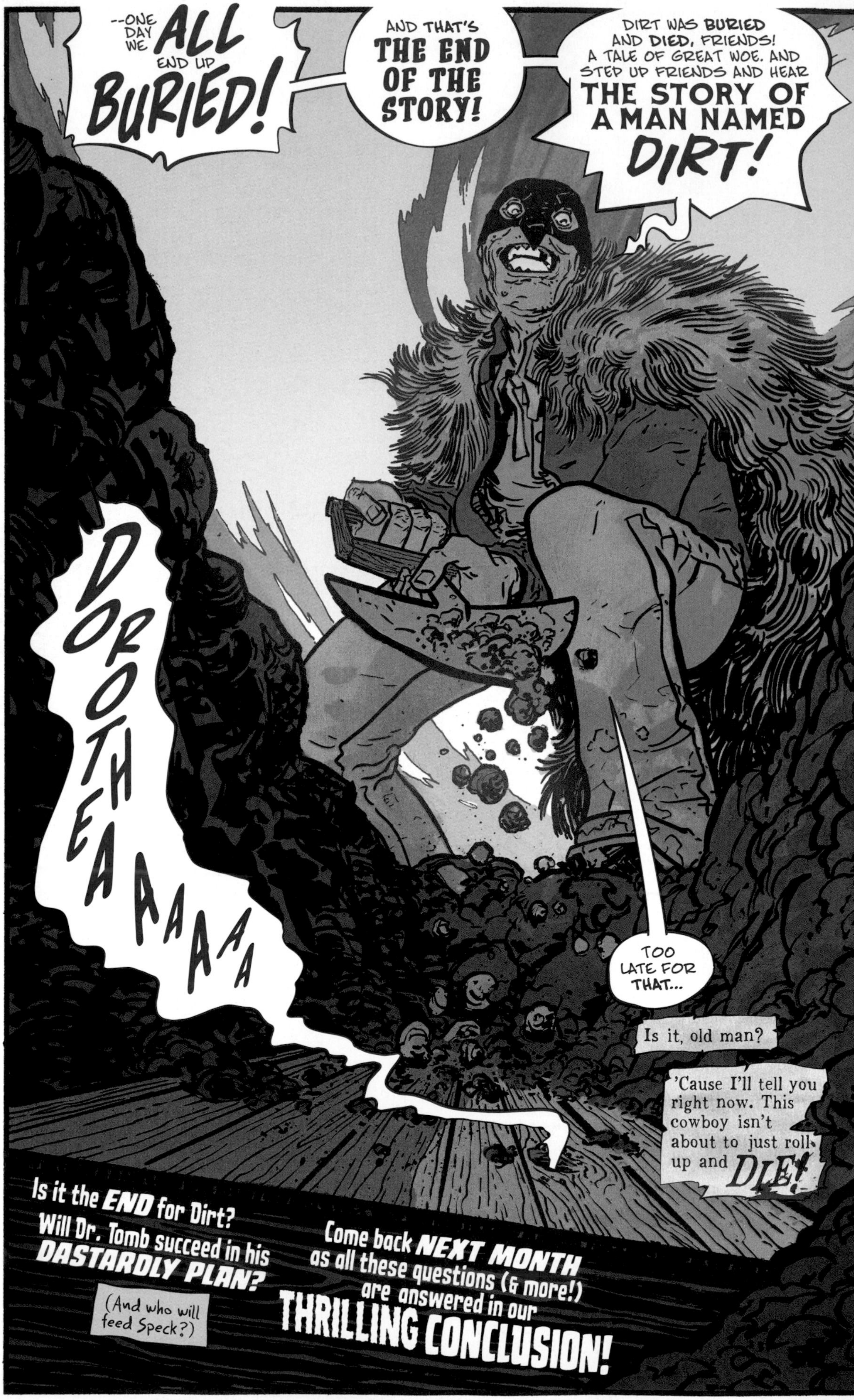
--ONE DAY WE ALL END UP BURIED!
AND THAT'S THE END OF THE STORY!
DIRT WAS BURIED AND DIED, FRIENDS! A TALE OF GREAT WOE. AND STEP UP FRIENDS AND HEAR THE STORY OF A MAN NAMED DIRT!
DOROTHEAAAAAA
TOO LATE FOR THAT...
Is it, old man?
'Cause I'll tell you right now. This cowboy isn't about to just roll up and DIE!
Is it the END for Dirt?
Will Dr. Tomb succeed in his DASTARDLY PLAN?
(And who will feed Speck?)
Come back NEXT MONTH as all these questions (& more!) are answered in our THRILLING CONCLUSION!

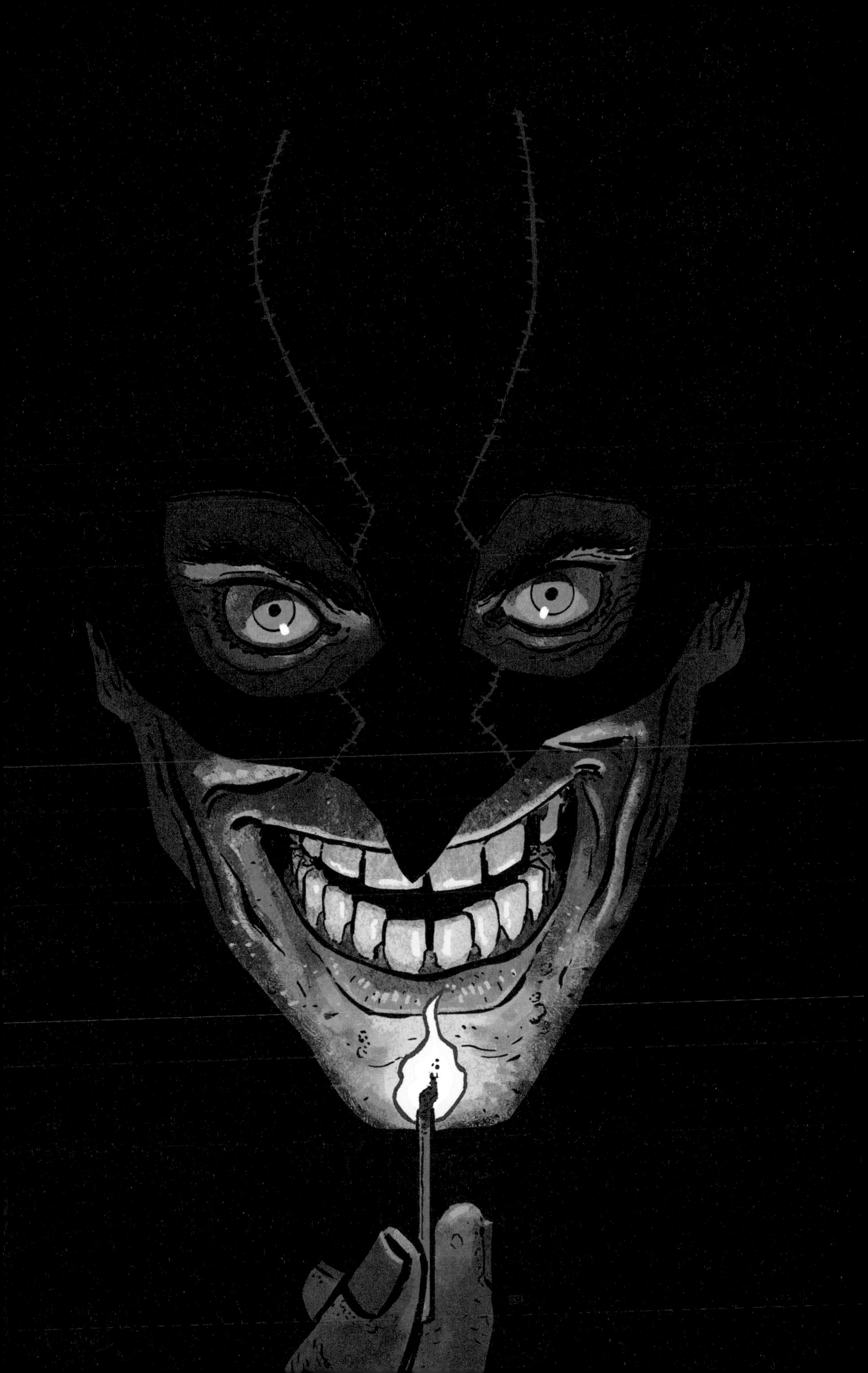

CHAPTER FIVE

-

“Dirty Hands”

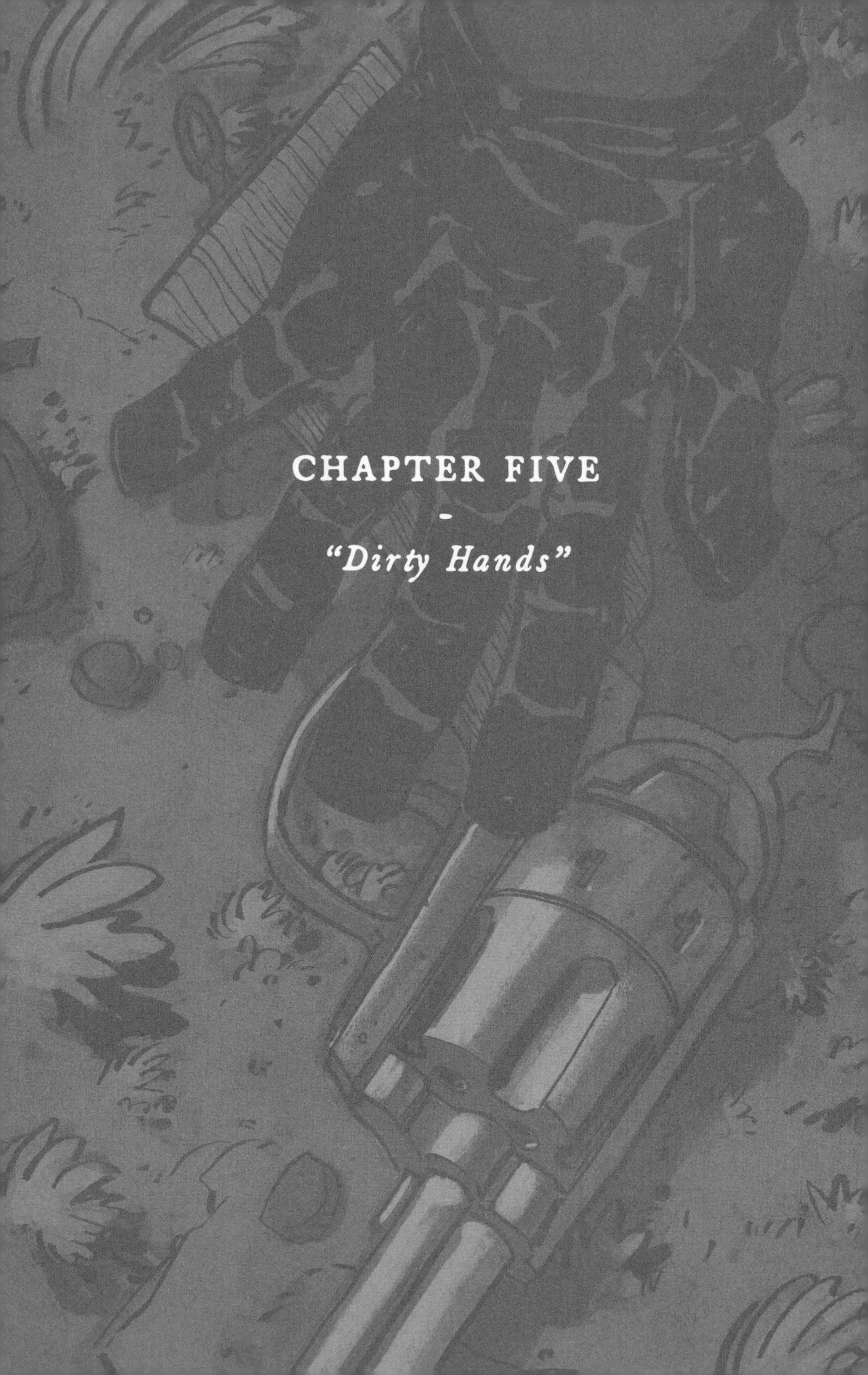

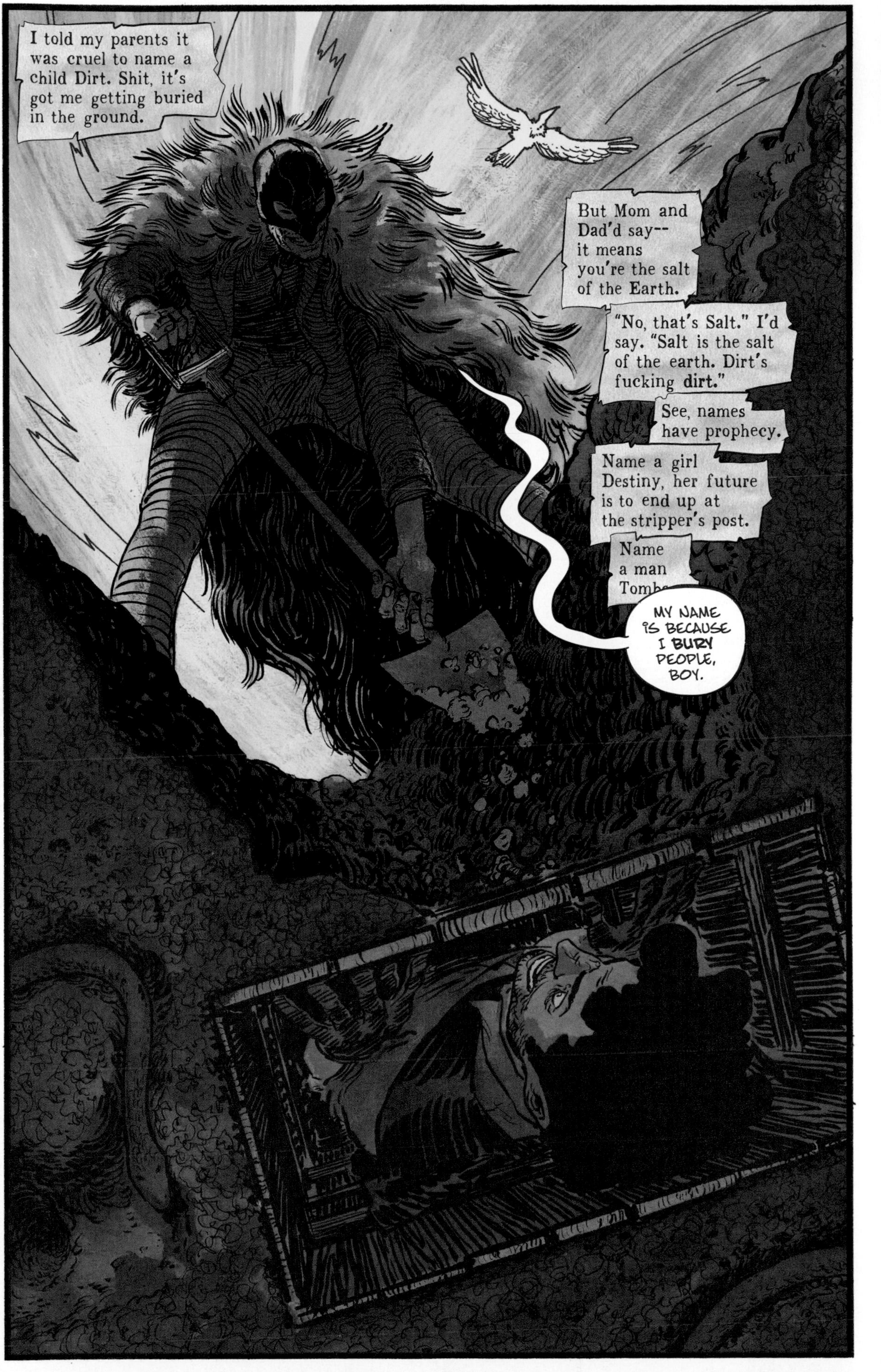
I told my parents it was cruel to name a child Dirt. Shit, it's got me getting buried in the ground.
But Mom and Dad'd say-- it means you're the salt of the Earth.
"No, that's Salt." I'd say. "Salt is the salt of the earth. Dirt's fucking dirt."
See, names have prophecy.
Name a girl Destiny, her future is to end up at the stripper's post.
Name a man
MY NAME IS BECAUSE I BURY PEOPLE, BOY.

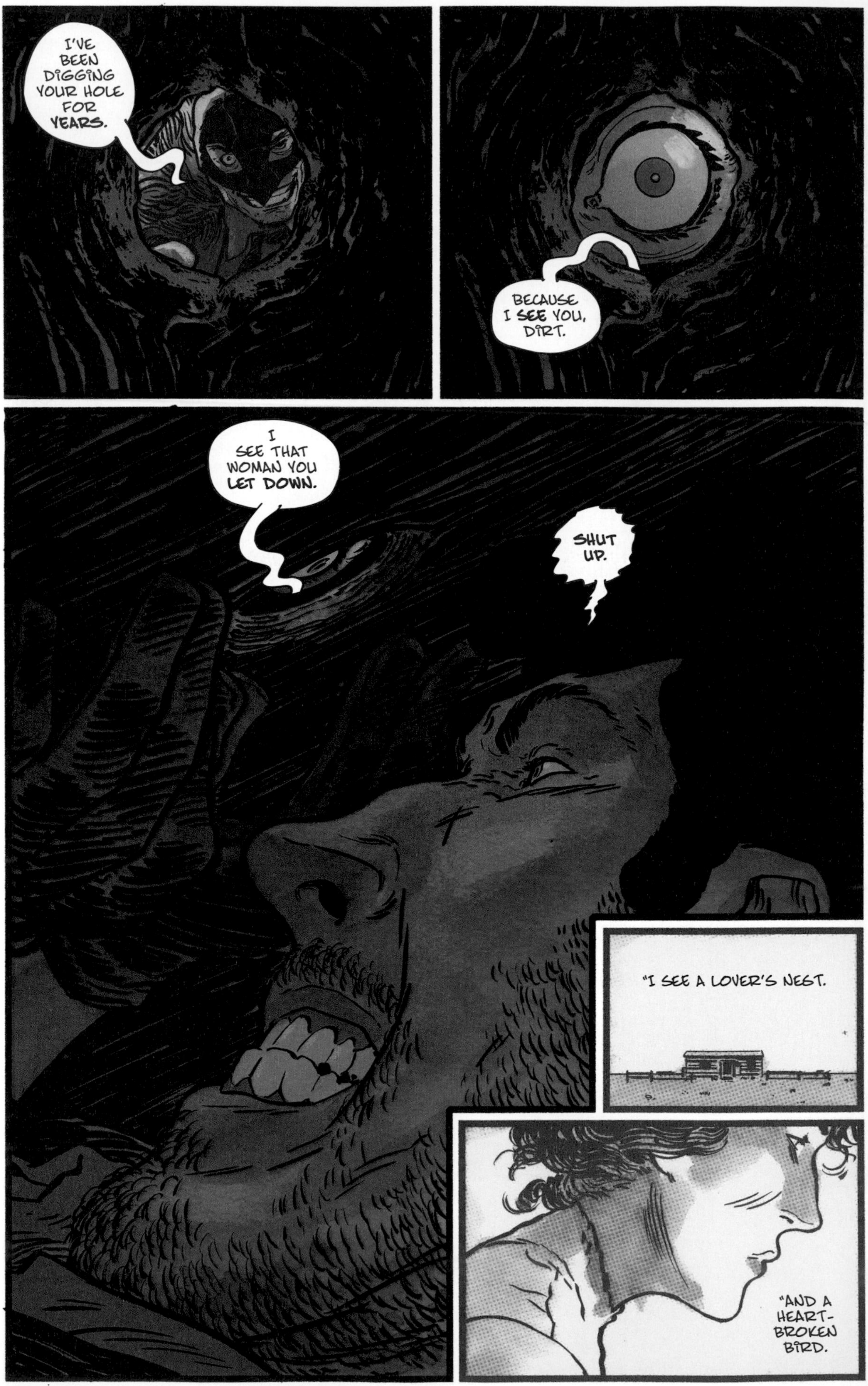
I'VE BEEN DIGGING YOUR HOLE FOR YEARS.
BECAUSE I SEE YOU, DIRT.
I SEE THAT WOMAN YOU LET DOWN.
SHUT UP.
"I SEE A LOVER'S NEST.
"AND A HEART-BROKEN BIRD.

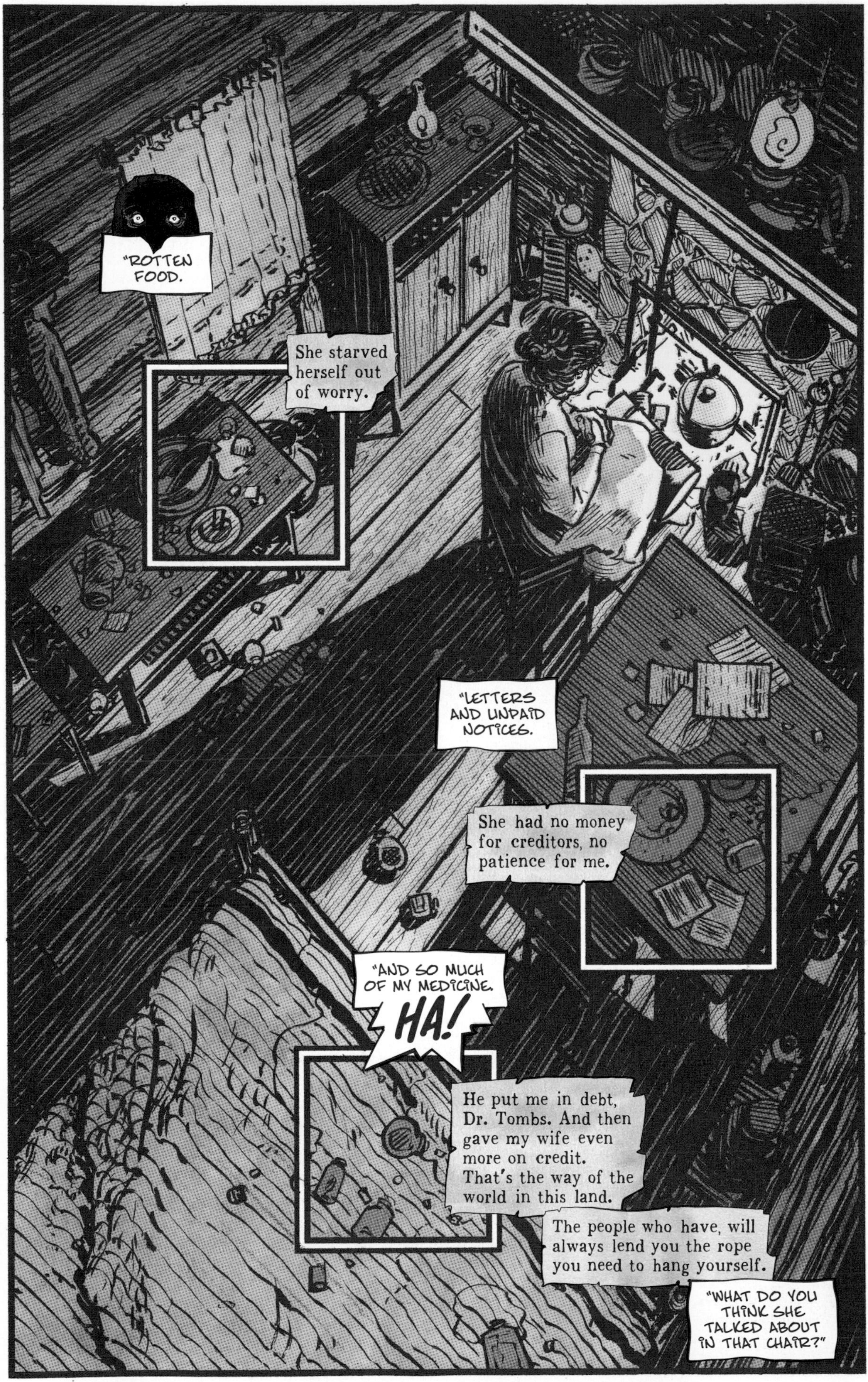
"ROTTEN FOOD.
She starved herself out of worry.
"LETTERS AND UNPAID NOTICES.
She had no money for creditors, no patience for me.
"AND SO MUCH OF MY MEDICINE.
HA!
He put me in debt, Dr. Tombs. And then gave my wife even more on credit. That's the way of the world in this land.
The people who have, will always lend you the rope you need to hang yourself.
"WHAT DO YOU THINK SHE TALKED ABOUT IN THAT CHAIR?"

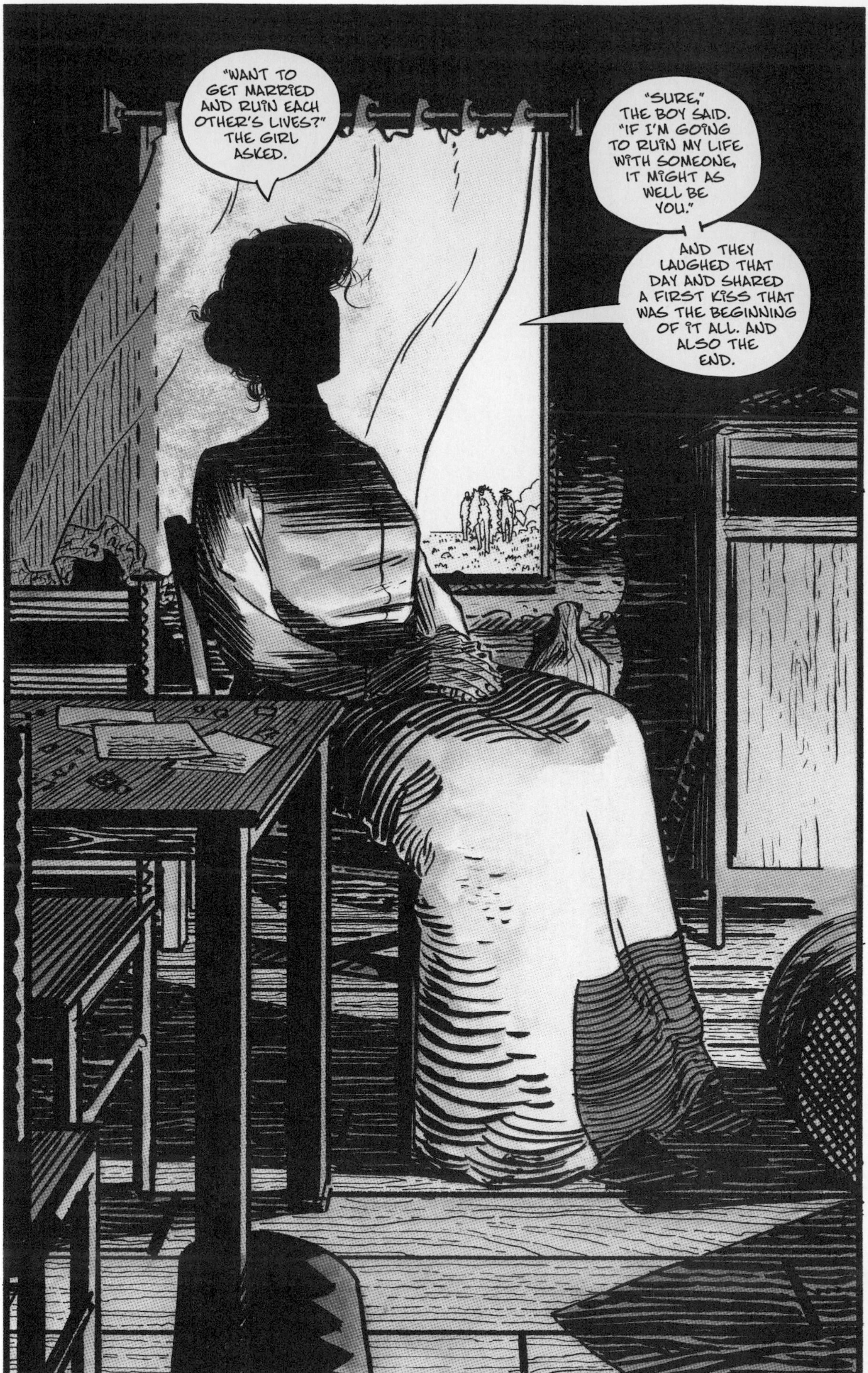
"WANT TO GET MARRIED AND RUIN EACH OTHER'S LIVES?" THE GIRL ASKED.
"SURE," THE BOY SAID. "IF I'M GOING TO RUIN MY LIFE WITH SOMEONE, IT MIGHT AS WELL BE YOU."
AND THEY LAUGHED THAT DAY AND SHARED A FIRST KISS THAT WAS THE BEGINNING OF IT ALL. AND ALSO THE END.

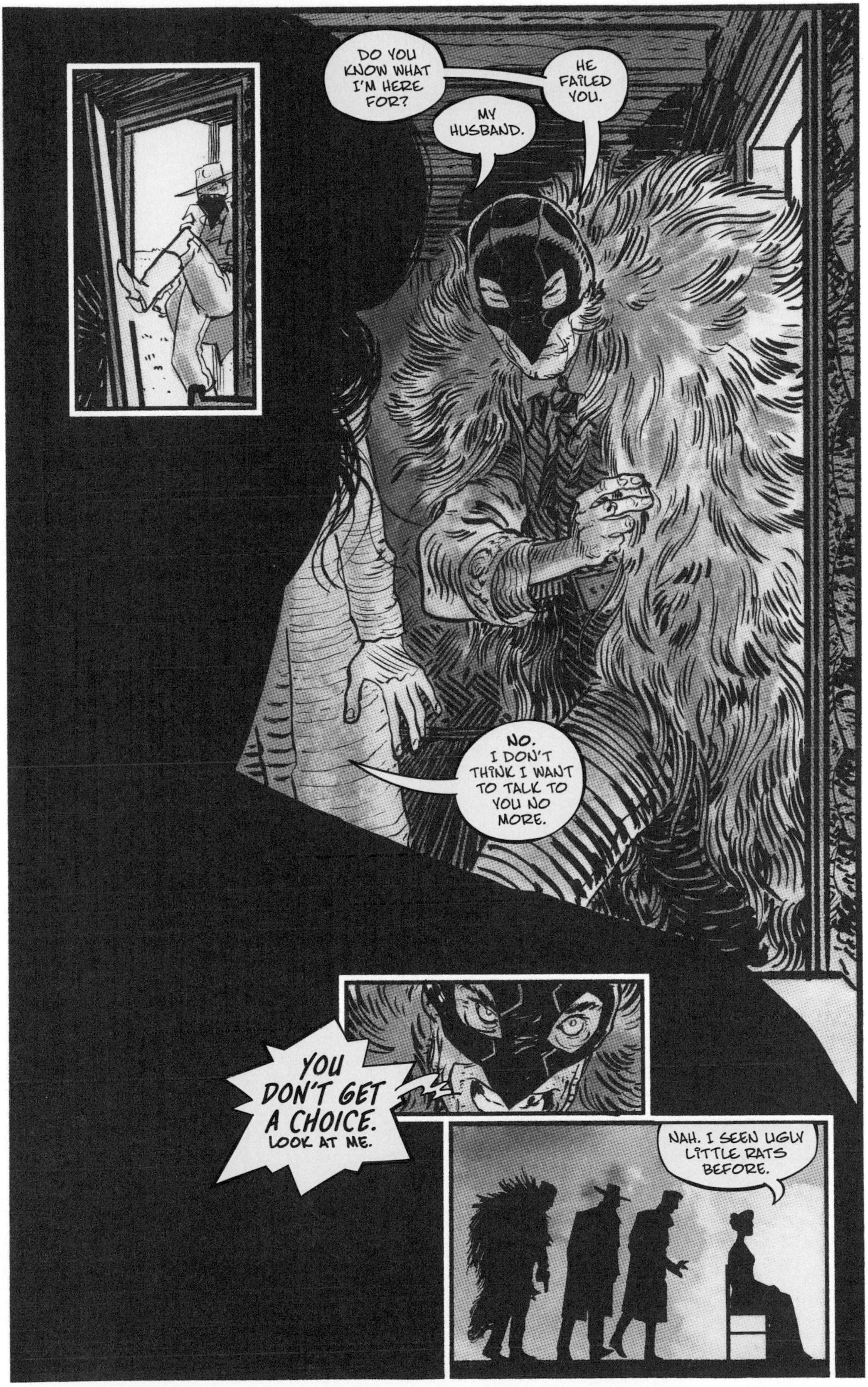
DO YOU KNOW WHAT I'M HERE FOR?
MY HUSBAND.
HE FAILED YOU.
NO. I DON'T THINK I WANT TO TALK TO YOU NO MORE.
YOU DON'T GET A CHOICE. LOOK AT ME.
NAH. I SEEN UGLY LITTLE RATS BEFORE.

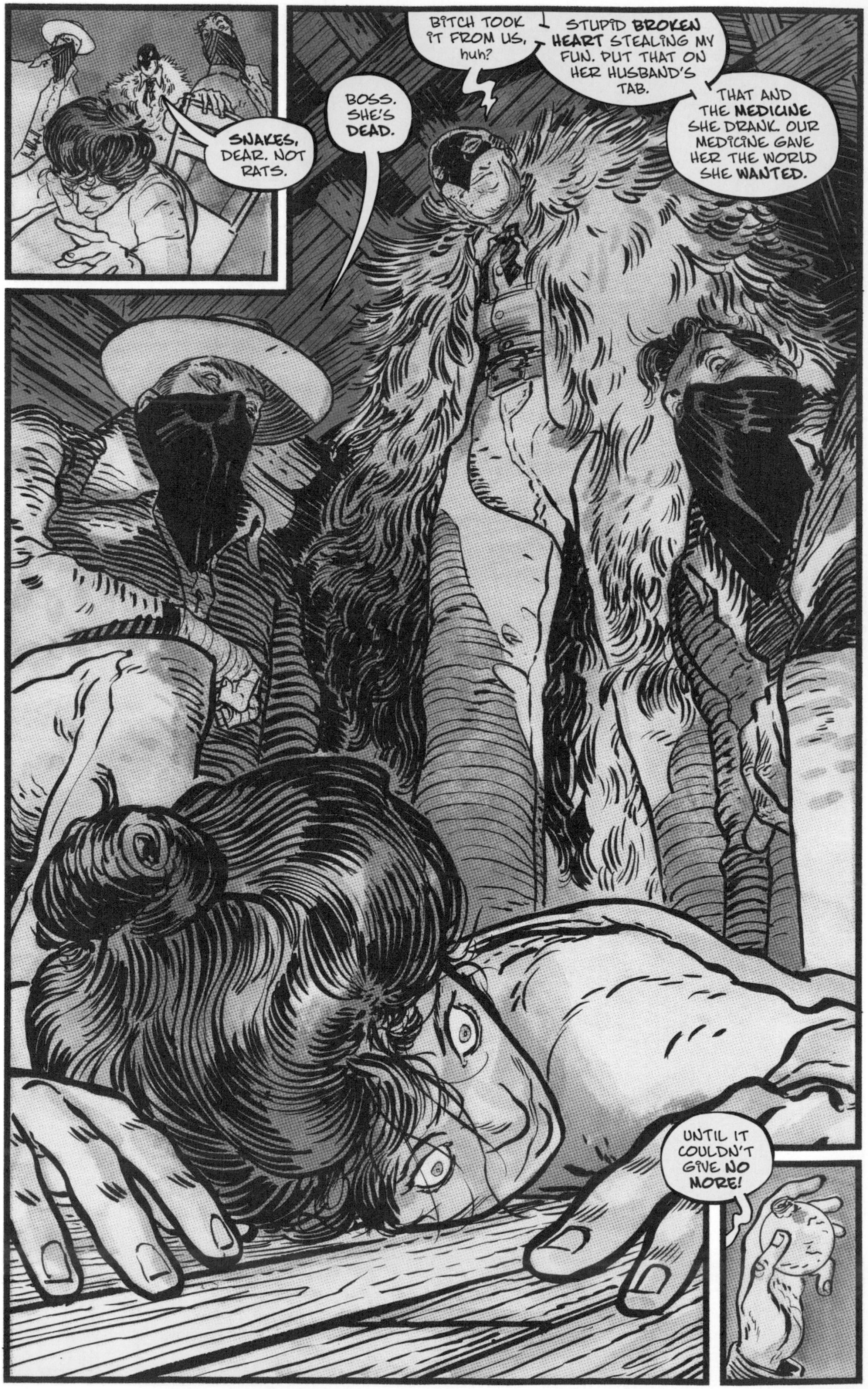
SNAKES, DEAR. NOT RATS.
BOSS. SHE'S DEAD.
BITCH TOOK IT FROM US, huh?
STUPID BROKEN HEART STEALING MY FUN. PUT THAT ON HER HUSBAND'S TAB.
THAT AND THE MEDICINE SHE DRANK. OUR MEDICINE GAVE HER THE WORLD SHE WANTED.
UNTIL IT COULDN'T GIVE NO MORE!

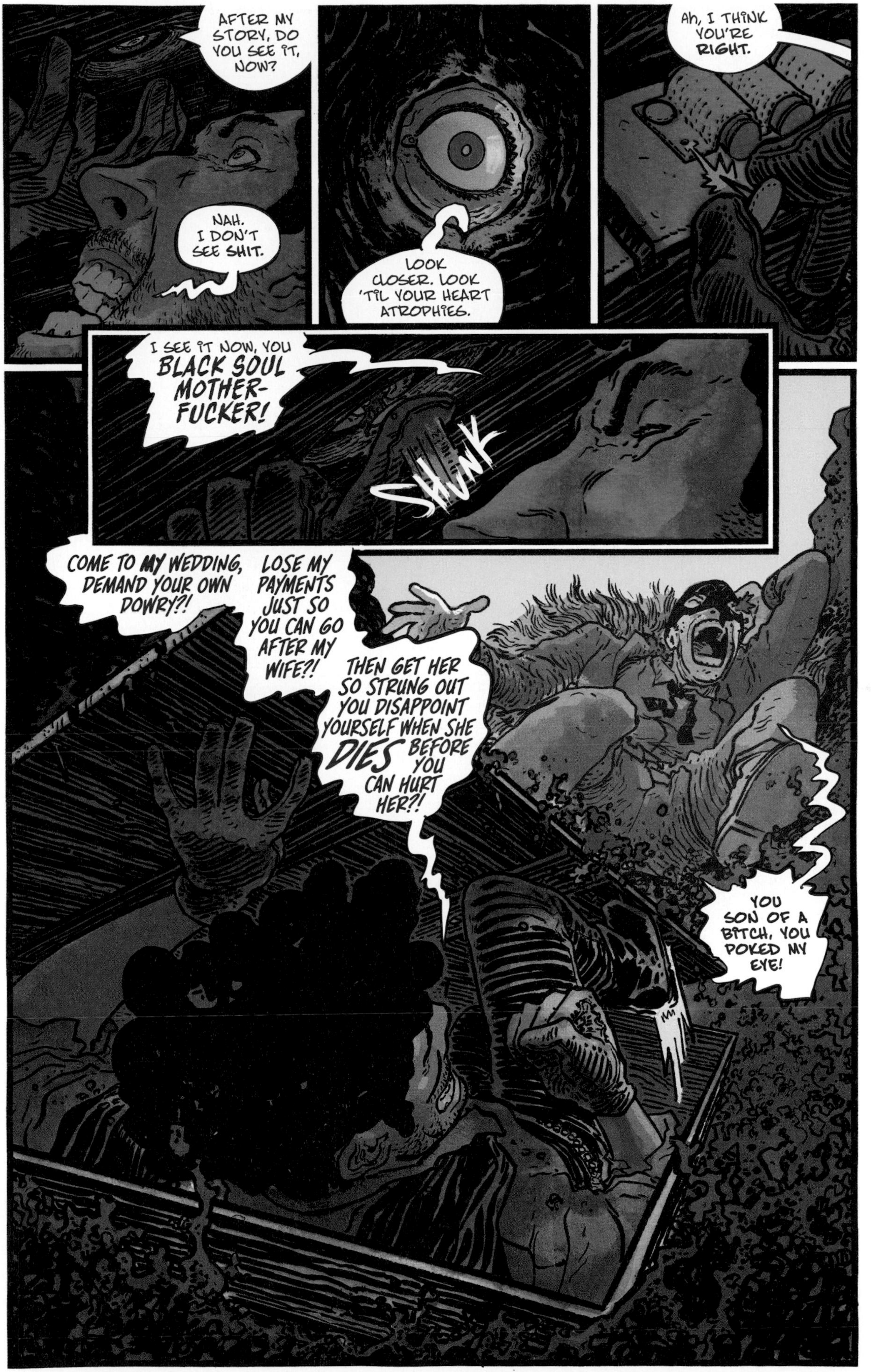
AFTER MY STORY, DO YOU SEE IT, NOW?
NAH. I DON'T SEE SHIT.
LOOK CLOSER. LOOK 'TIL YOUR HEART ATROPHIES.
Ah, I THINK YOU'RE RIGHT.
I SEE IT NOW, YOU BLACK SOUL MOTHER-FUCKER!
SHUNK
COME TO MY WEDDING, DEMAND YOUR OWN DOWRY?!
LOSE MY PAYMENTS JUST SO YOU CAN GO AFTER MY WIFE?!
THEN GET HER SO STRUNG OUT YOU DISAPPOINT YOURSELF WHEN SHE DIES BEFORE YOU CAN HURT HER?!
YOU SON OF A BITCH, YOU POKED MY EYE!

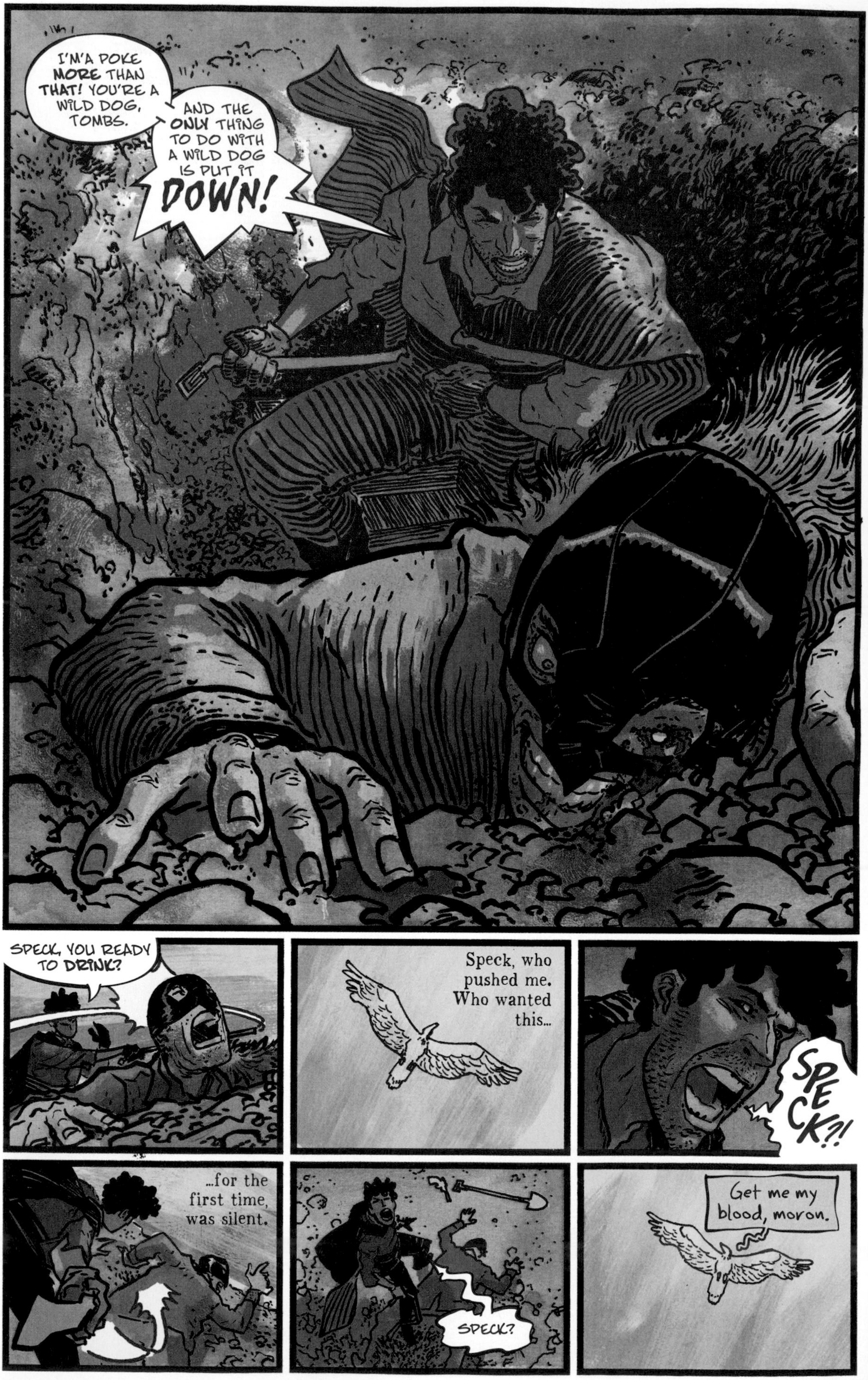

I'M'A POKE MORE THAN THAT! YOU'RE A WILD DOG, TOMBS.
AND THE ONLY THING TO DO WITH A WILD DOG IS PUT IT DOWN!
SPECK, YOU READY TO DRINK?
Speck, who pushed me. Who wanted this...
SPECK?!
...for the first time, was silent.
SPECK?
Get me my blood, moron.

STUPID BIRD, ALWAYS TALKING SHIT--

SMAK

YOU **SICK** BASTARD. PUT YOU IN THE GROUND WITH YOUR **WIFE** AND HER **MELTED BRAIN.**

YOU'RE WHAT'S WRONG IN THIS WORLD. NO RESPONSIBILITY.

ABANDON YOUR WOMAN!

CONJURE THIS **DEMONIC BIRD** AND BLAME **ME!** YOU'RE THE PROBLEM!

HELP!

You know these stories.

You know I waited too long for this.

Remember those impotent-ass Blood Runners?

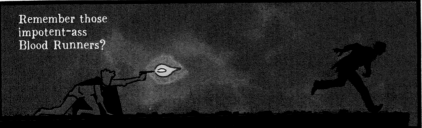

Yeah. I ain't them.

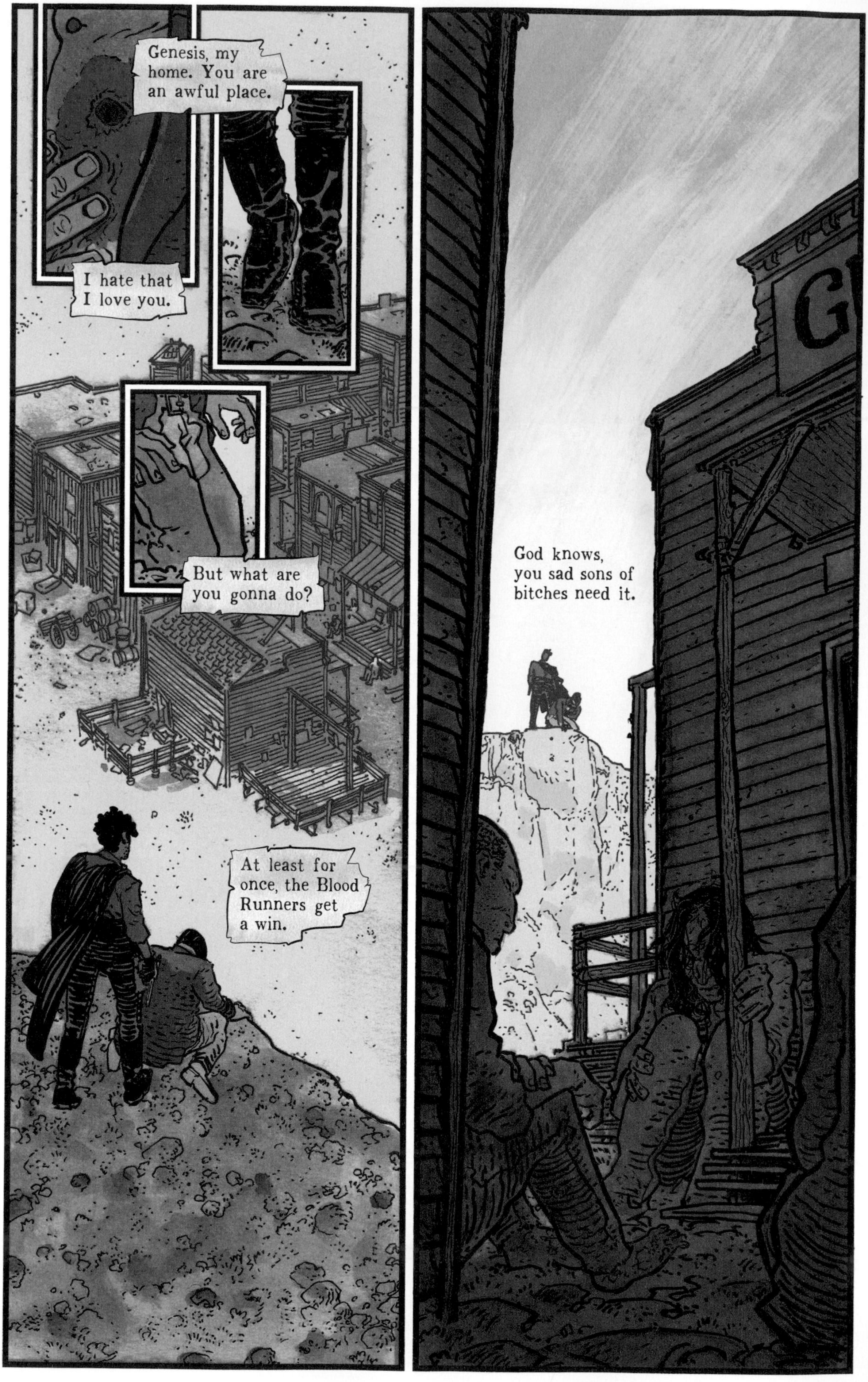
Genesis, my home. You are an awful place.
I hate that I love you.
But what are you gonna do?
At least for once, the Blood Runners get a win.
God knows, you sad sons of bitches need it.
GE

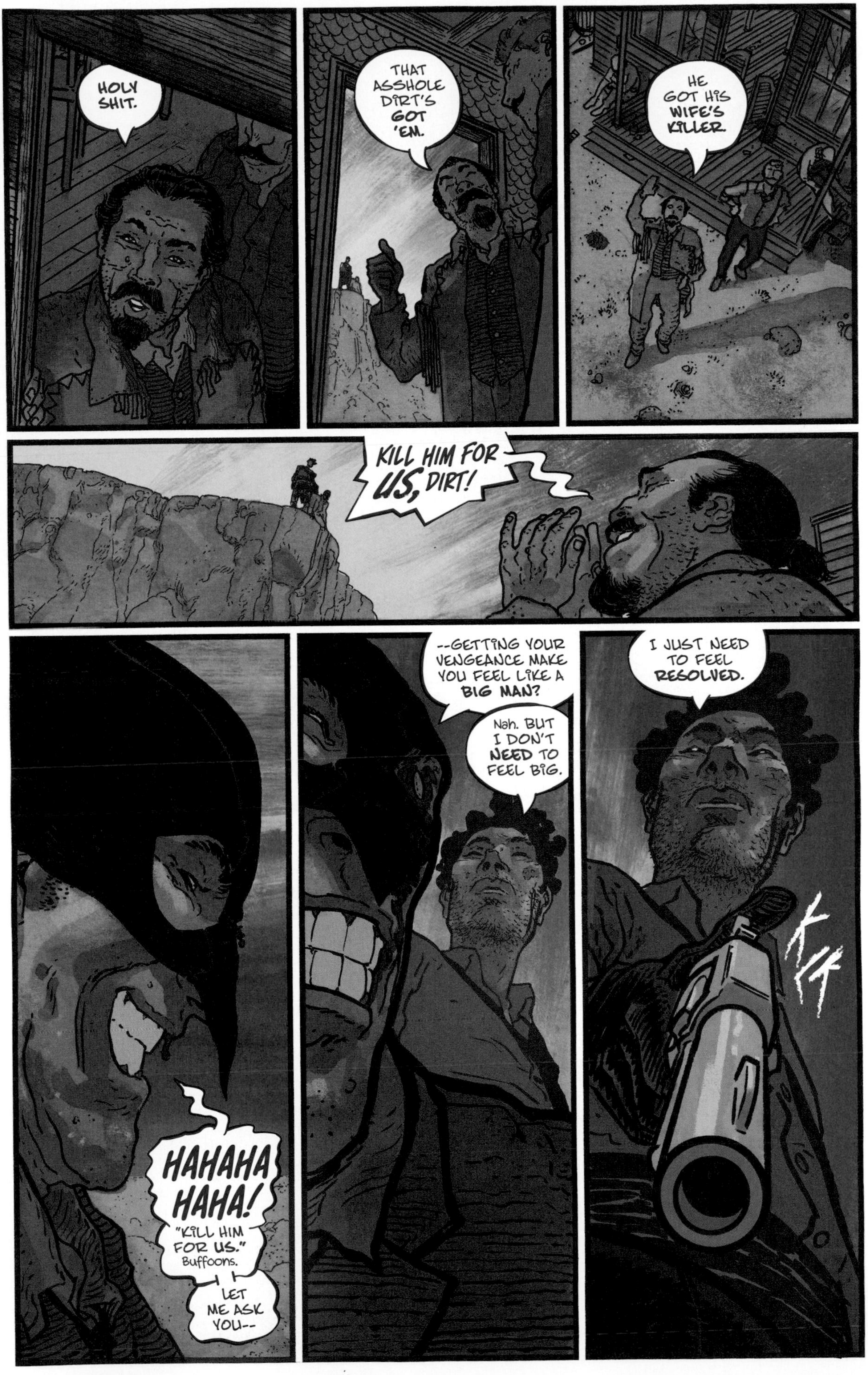

HOLY SHIT.
THAT ASSHOLE DIRT'S GOT 'EM.
HE GOT HIS WIFE'S KILLER.
KILL HIM FOR US, DIRT!
HAHAHA HAHA!
"KILL HIM FOR US." Buffoons.
LET ME ASK YOU--
--GETTING YOUR VENGEANCE MAKE YOU FEEL LIKE A BIG MAN?
Nah. BUT I DON'T NEED TO FEEL BIG.
I JUST NEED TO FEEL RESOLVED.
K-K

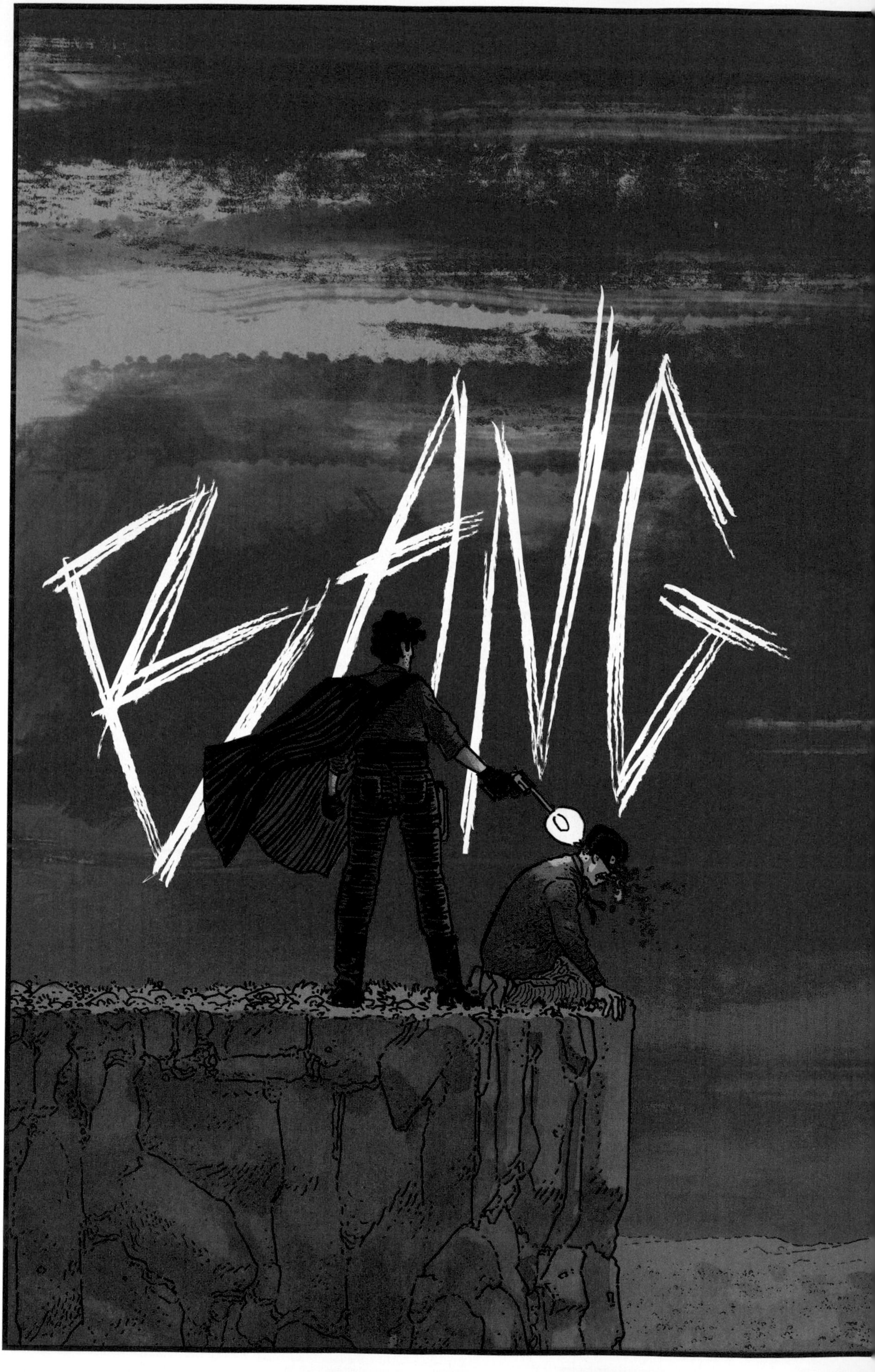
BLANG

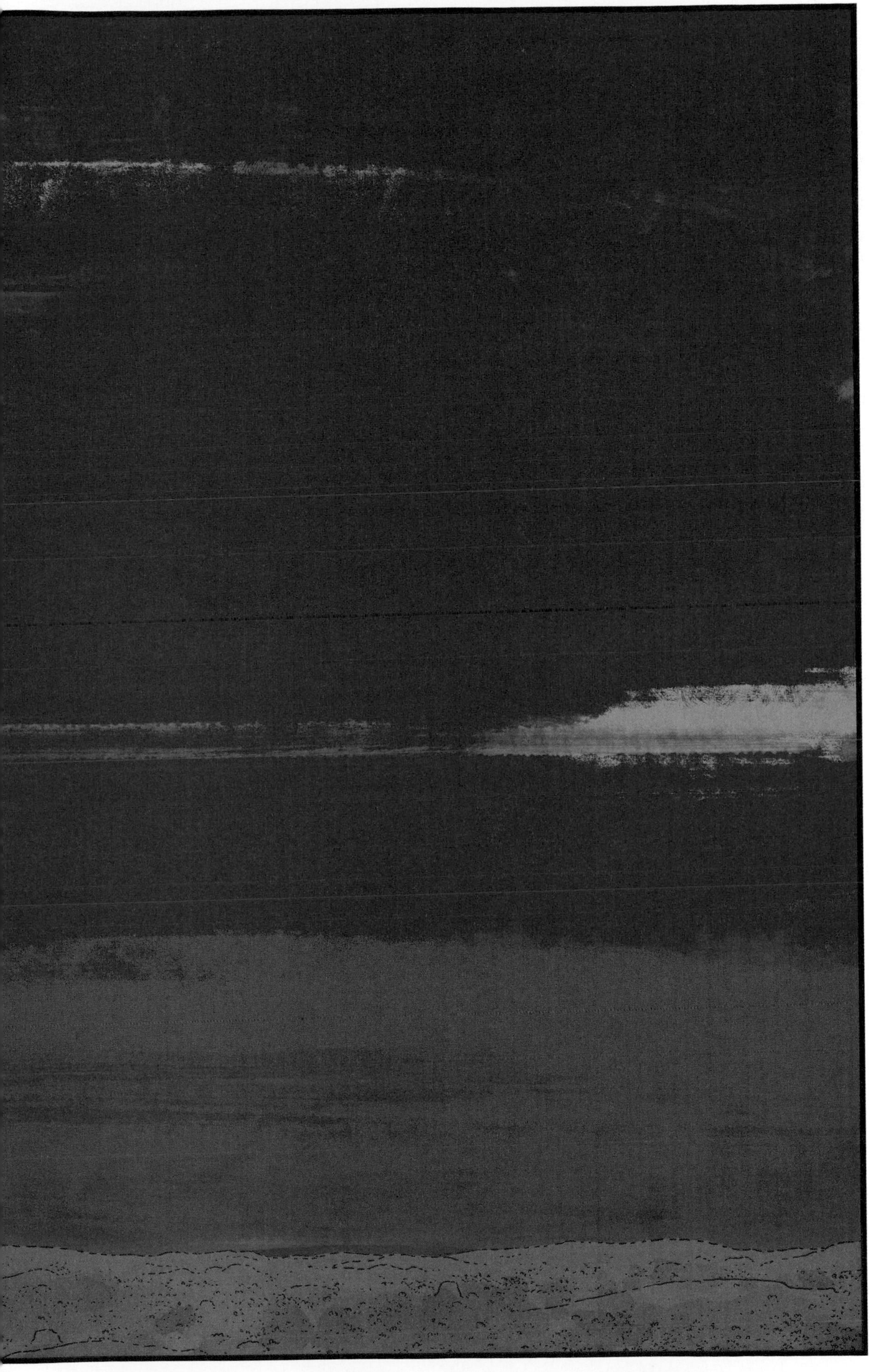

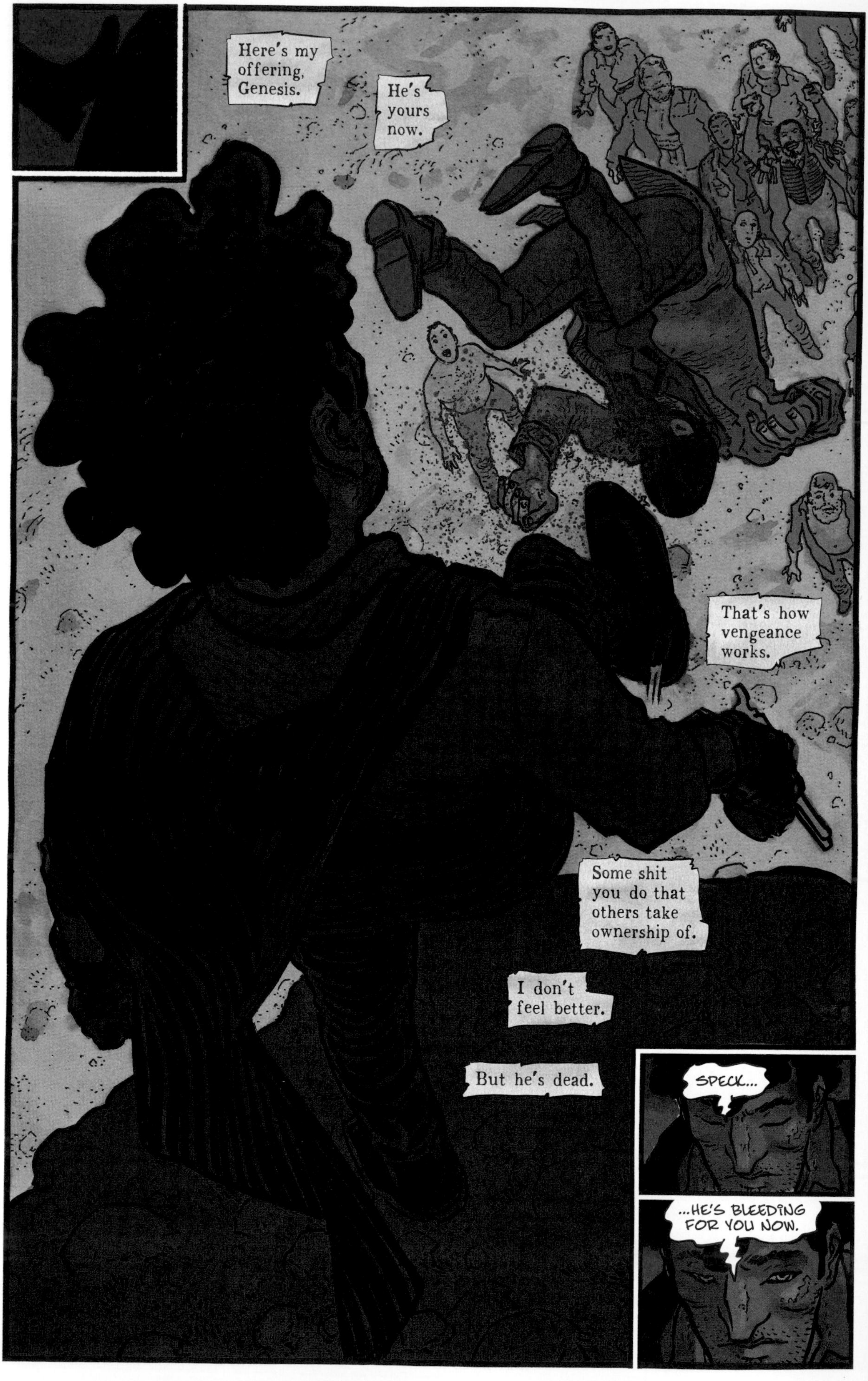
Here's my offering, Genesis.
He's yours now.
That's how vengeance works.
Some shit you do that others take ownership of.
I don't feel better.
But he's dead.
SPECK...
...HE'S BLEEDING FOR YOU NOW.

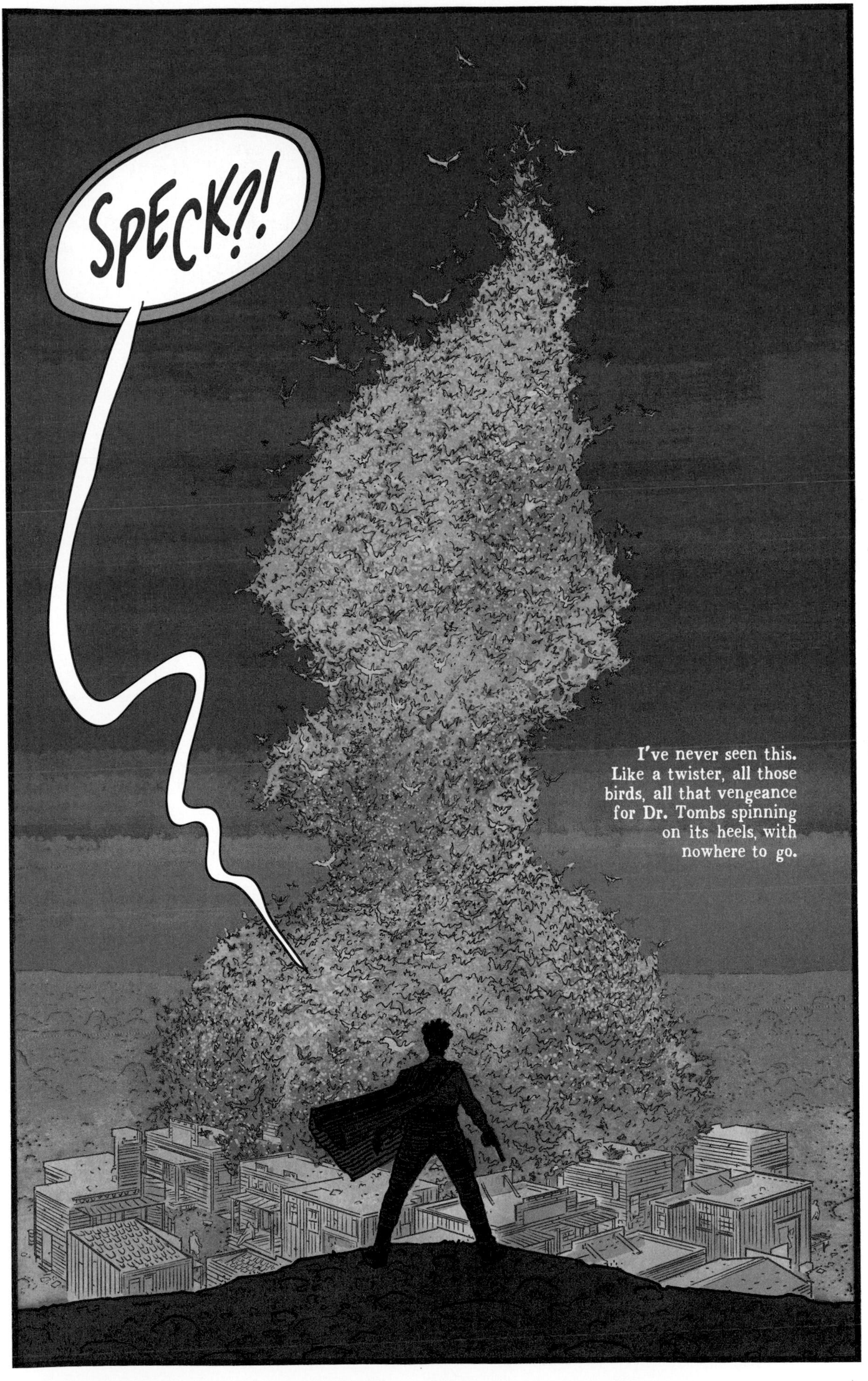
SPECK?!
I've never seen this. Like a twister, all those birds, all that vengeance for Dr. Tombs spinning on its heels, with nowhere to go.

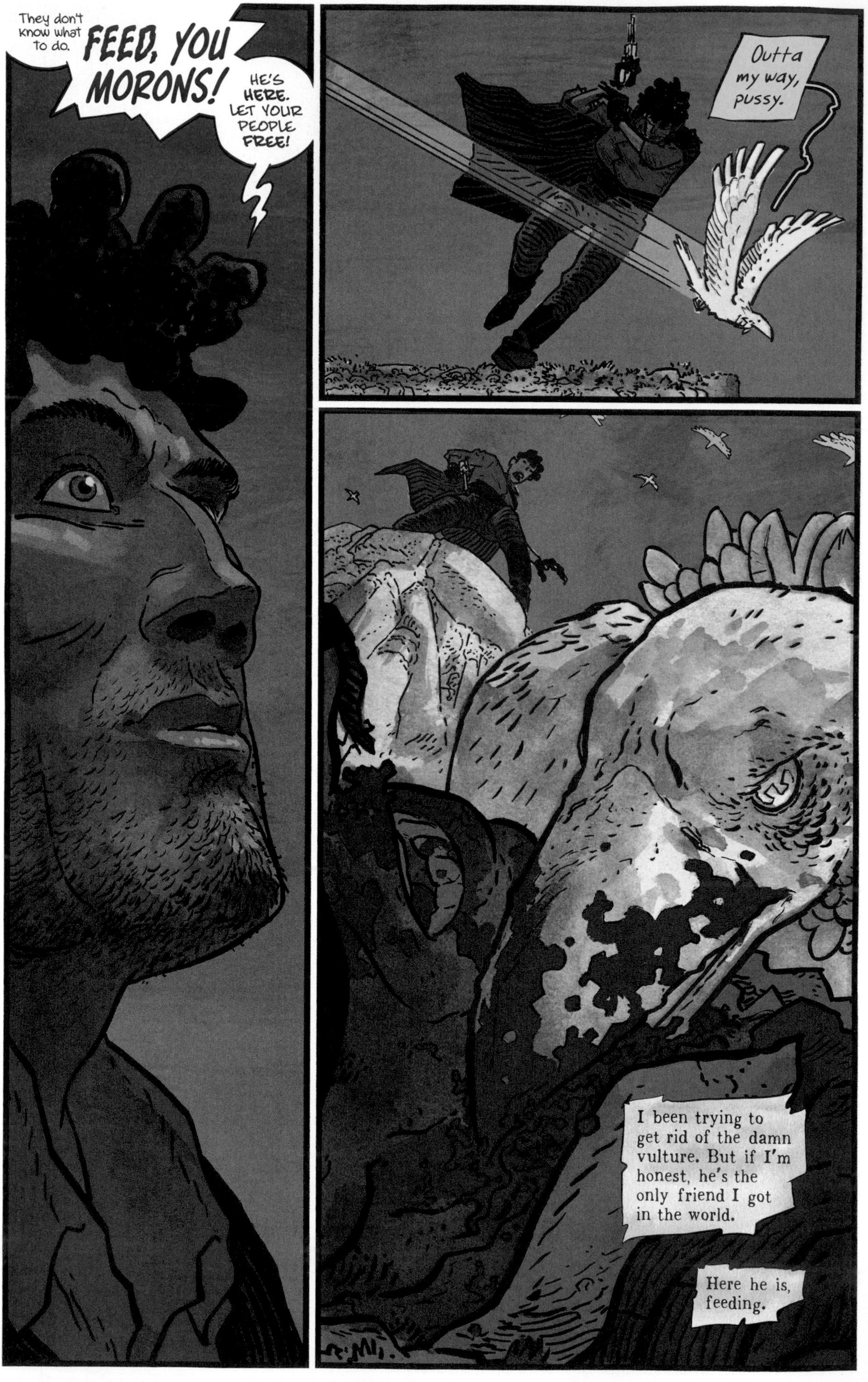

They don't know what to do.
FEED, YOU MORONS!
HE'S HERE. LET YOUR PEOPLE FREE!
Outta my way, pussy.
I been trying to get rid of the damn vulture. But if I'm honest, he's the only friend I got in the world.
Here he is, feeding.

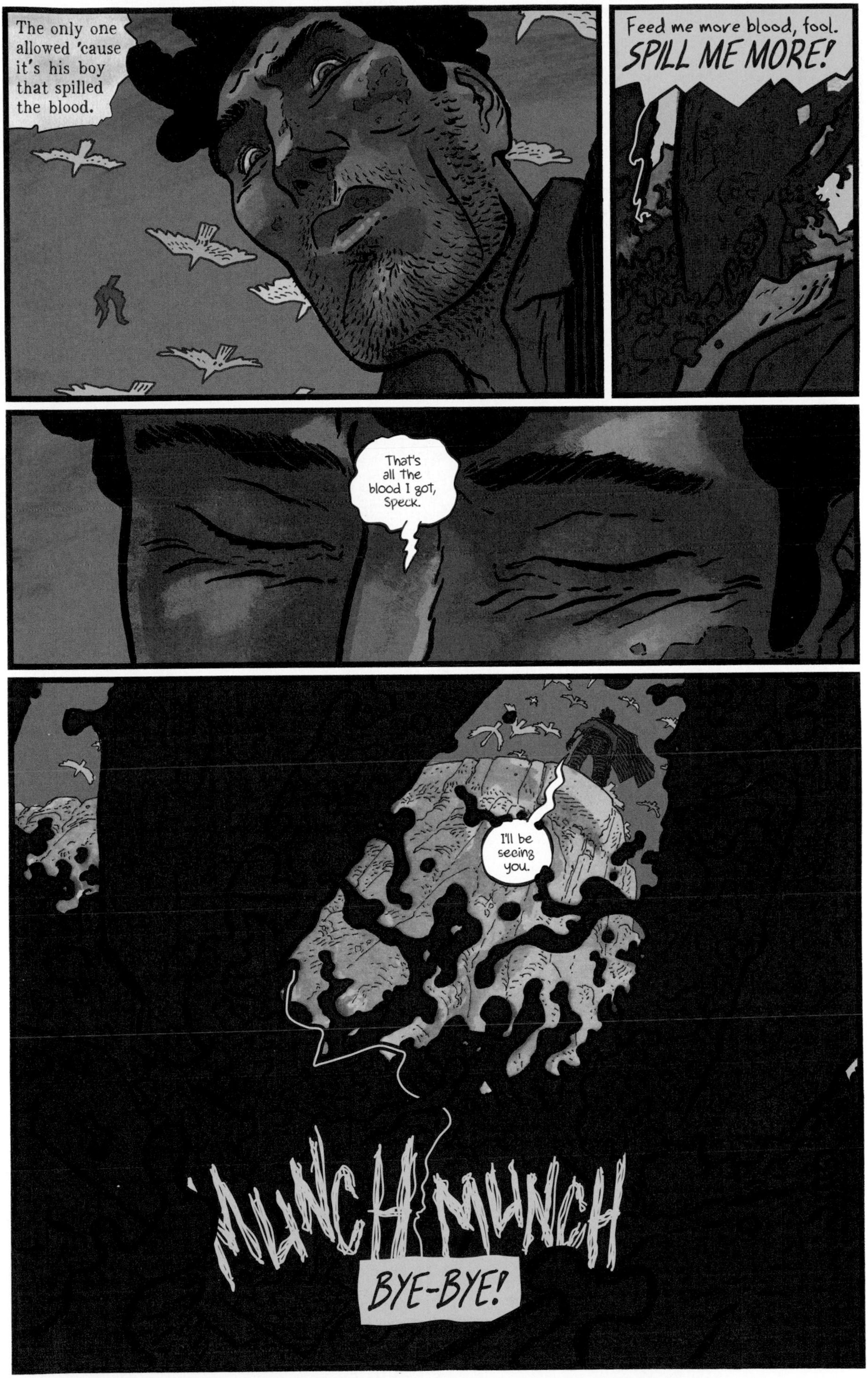

The only one allowed 'cause it's his boy that spilled the blood.
Feed me more blood, fool.
SPILL ME MORE!
That's all the blood I got, Speck.
I'll be seeing you.
MUNCH MUNCH
BYE-BYE!

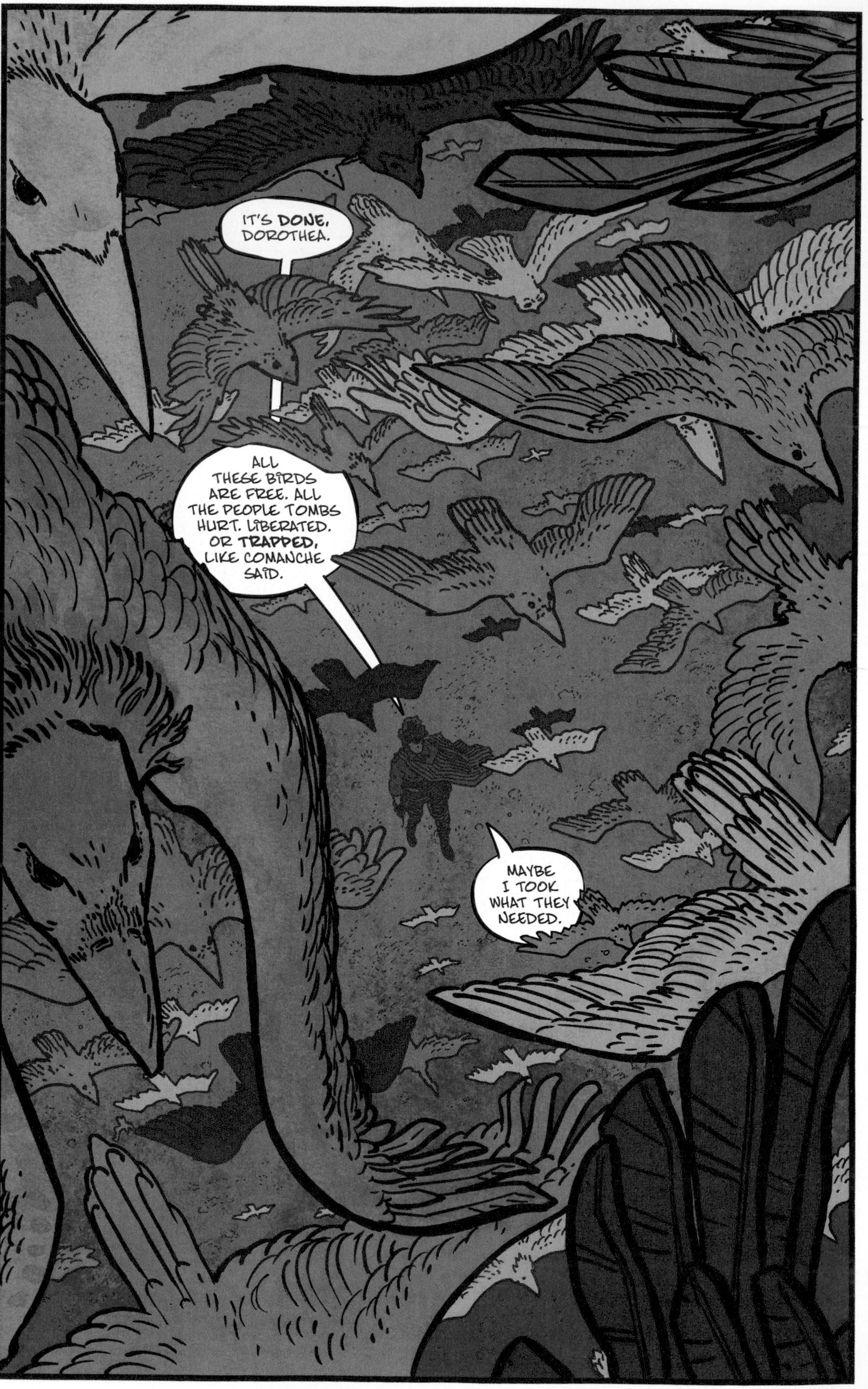
IT'S DONE, DOROTHEA.
ALL THESE BIRDS ARE FREE. ALL THE PEOPLE TOMBS HURT. LIBERATED. OR TRAPPED, LIKE COMANCHE SAID.
MAYBE I TOOK WHAT THEY NEEDED.

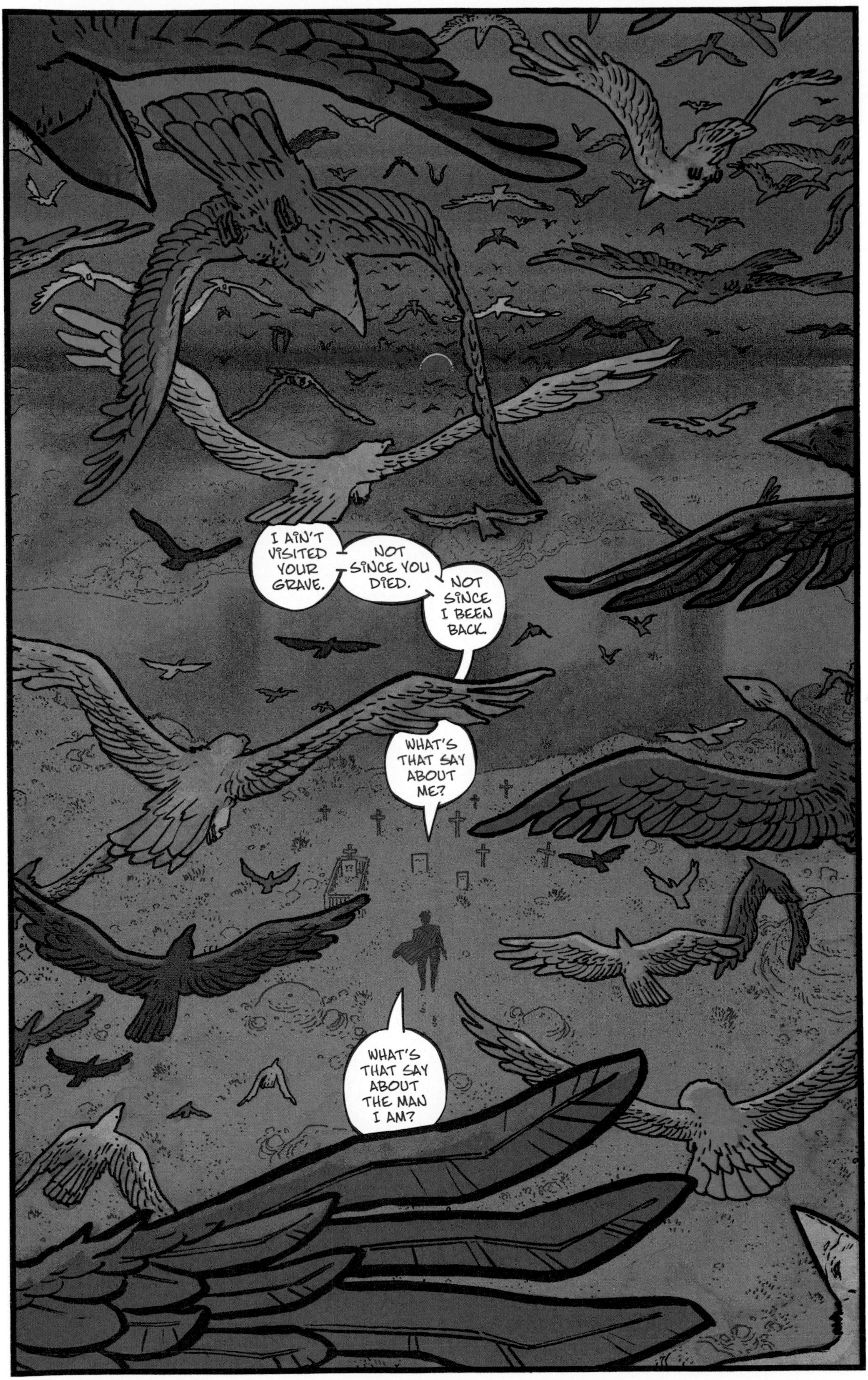
I AIN'T VISITED YOUR GRAVE.
NOT SINCE YOU DIED.
NOT SINCE I BEEN BACK.
WHAT'S THAT SAY ABOUT ME?
WHAT'S THAT SAY ABOUT THE MAN I AM?

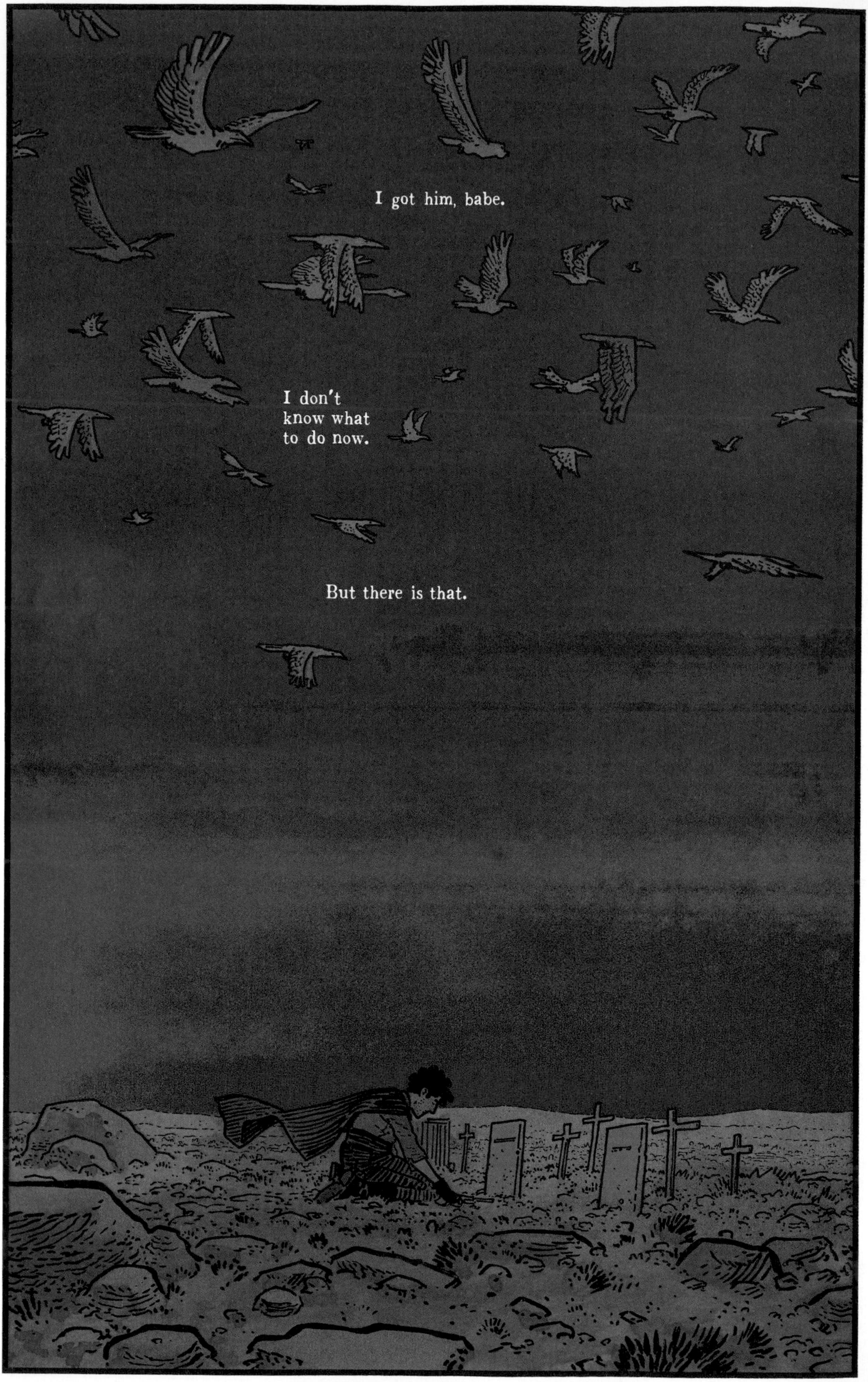
I got him, babe.
I don't know what to do now.
But there is that.

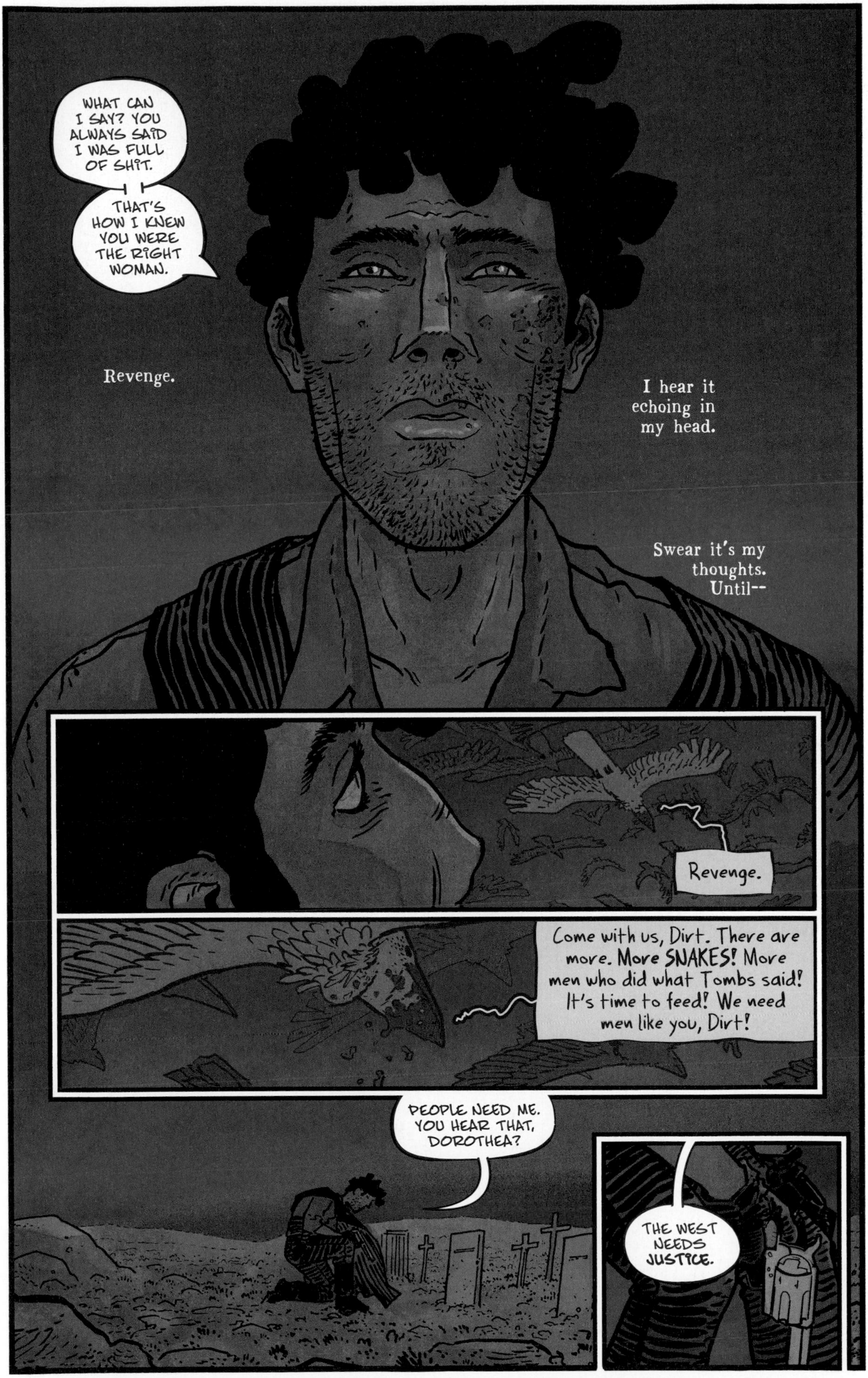
WHAT CAN I SAY? YOU ALWAYS SAID I WAS FULL OF SHIT.
THAT'S HOW I KNEW YOU WERE THE RIGHT WOMAN.
Revenge.
I hear it echoing in my head.
Swear it's my thoughts. Until--
Revenge.
Come with us, Dirt. There are more. More SNAKES! More men who did what Tombs said! It's time to feed! We need men like you, Dirt!
PEOPLE NEED ME. YOU HEAR THAT, DOROTHEA?
THE WEST NEEDS JUSTICE.

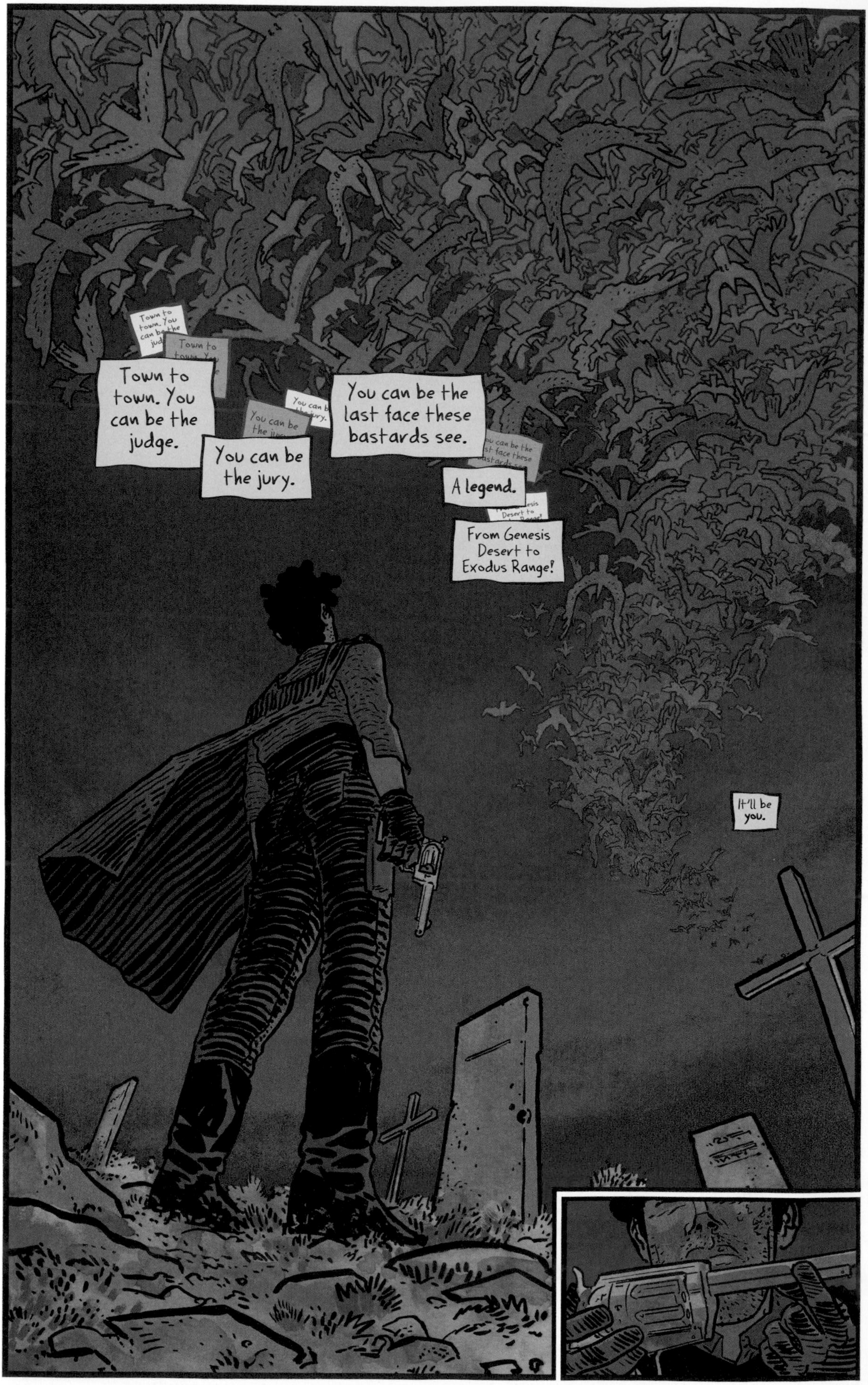
Town to town. You can be the judge.
You can be the jury.
You can be the last face these bastards see.
A legend.
From Genesis Desert to Exodus Range!
It'll be you.

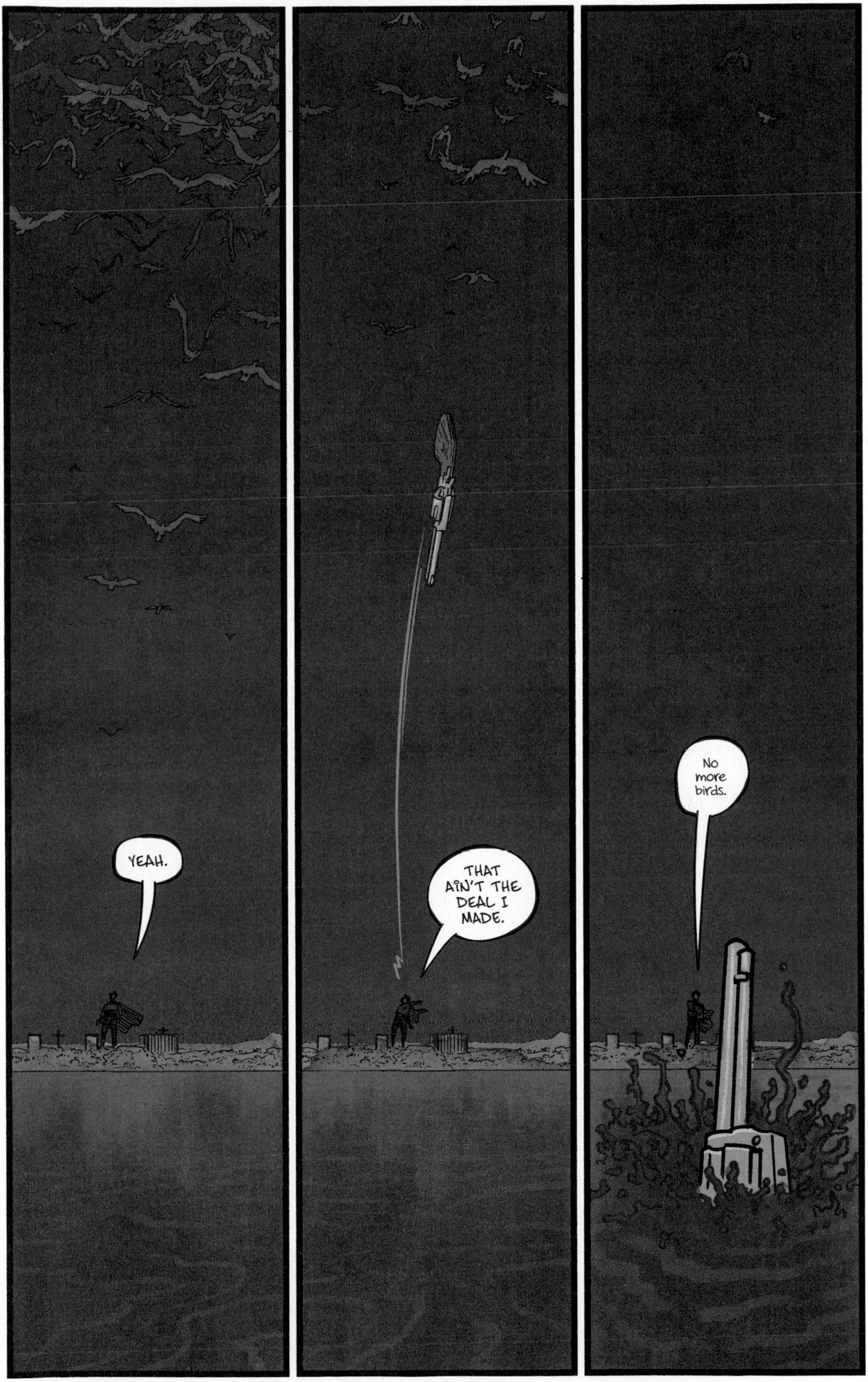
YEAH.
THAT AIN'T THE DEAL I MADE.
No more birds.

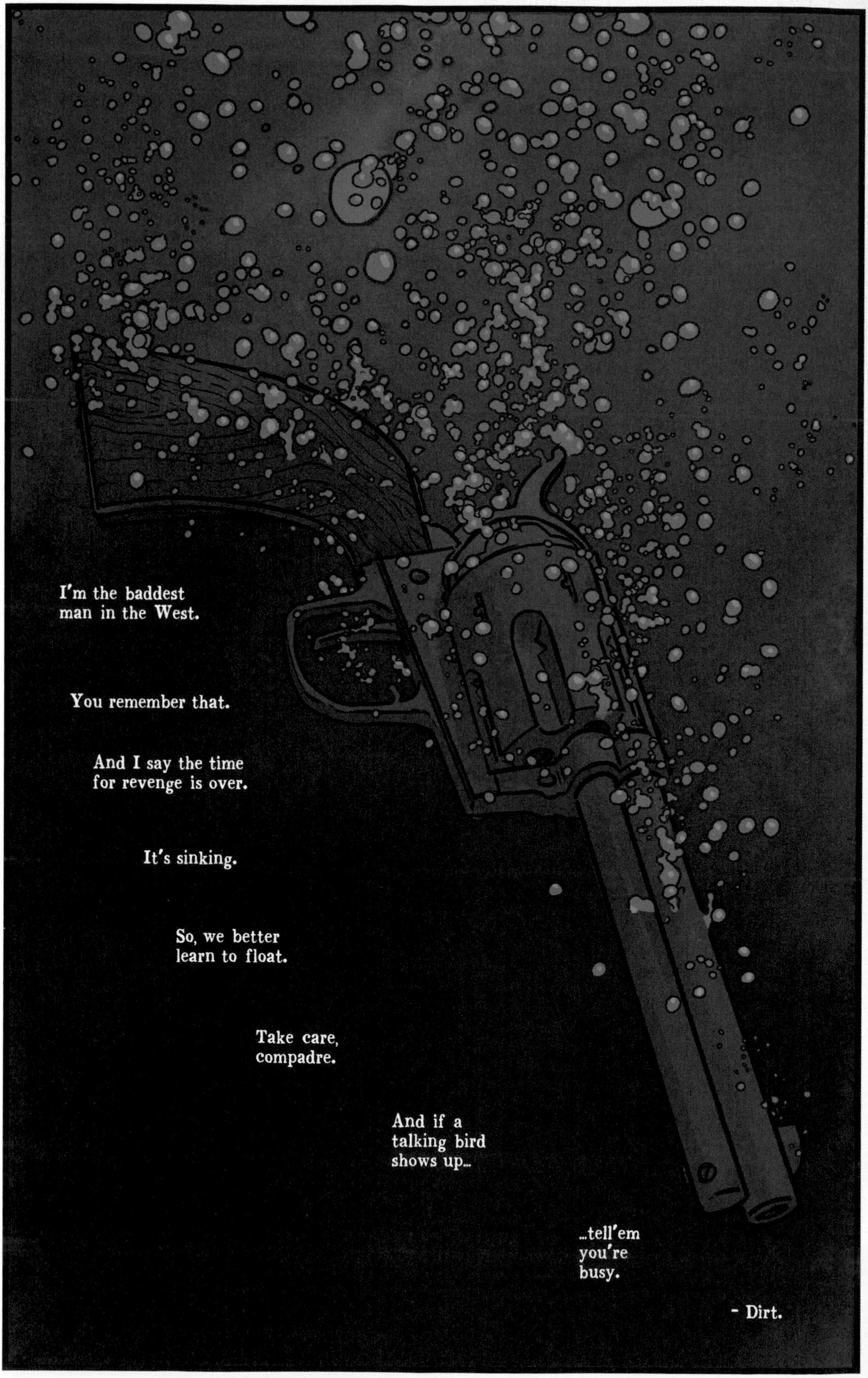
I'm the baddest man in the West.
You remember that.
And I say the time for revenge is over.
It's sinking.
So, we better learn to float.
Take care, compadre.
And if a talking bird shows up...
...tell'em you're busy.
- Dirt.

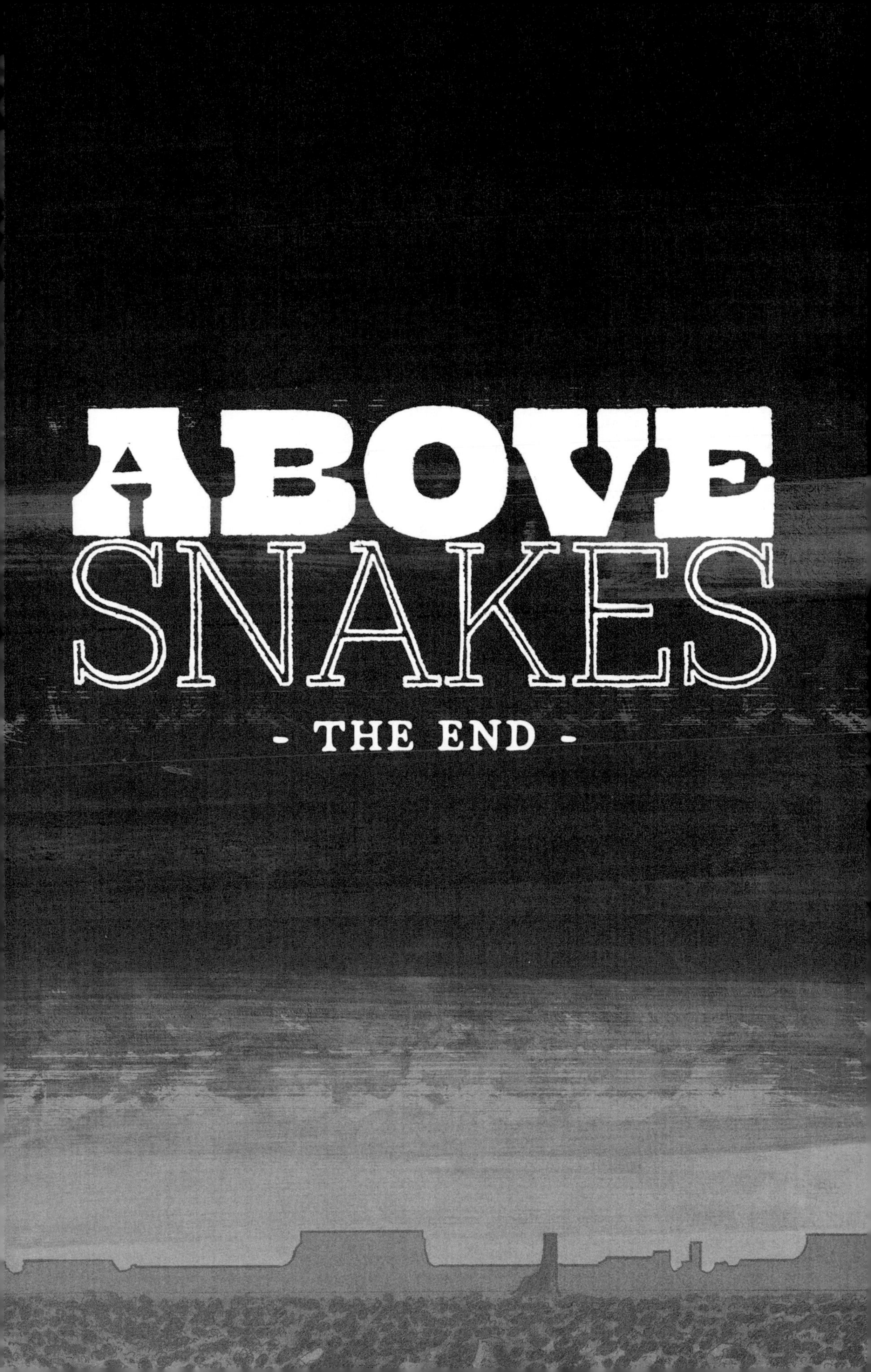
ABOVE
SNAKES
- THE END -

DIRT: And so partner, we come to the end of the road.

Now me, Dirt, I don't know when I'm gonna see you again. So, I'm gonna say some things cowboy to cowboy.

Be honest.

Don't worry about your mistakes, and don't respect people who try to define you by them.

Define yourself.

Make decisions. You won't regret moving. But you might regret standing still.

Get yourself a bird or a dog.

Sing a goddamn cowboy song.

I gotta remember to do these things, too.

It's been a real pleasure, telling this story to you. But now, I'm getting sappy, so I think I should tell a ball joke or insult Speck.

Emotions are hard for cowboys. Read more comics. Speck you got anything?

SPECK: Kill your enemies.

Eat their faces-

Forgive no one!

DIRT: Speck!!! Goddammit. Every time I let you talk, you start talking about faces and eating and murder. Say something nice!

SPECK: Hug your mom.

DIRT: There you go.

SPECK: Unless she did you wrong. Then dig a hole behind your house-

DIRT: GODDAMMIT, SPECK. We're saying good bye!!!!!

SPECK: Okay. Jeez. Good bye.

DIRT: Thanks, Cowboys. I'll see ya when we ride again.

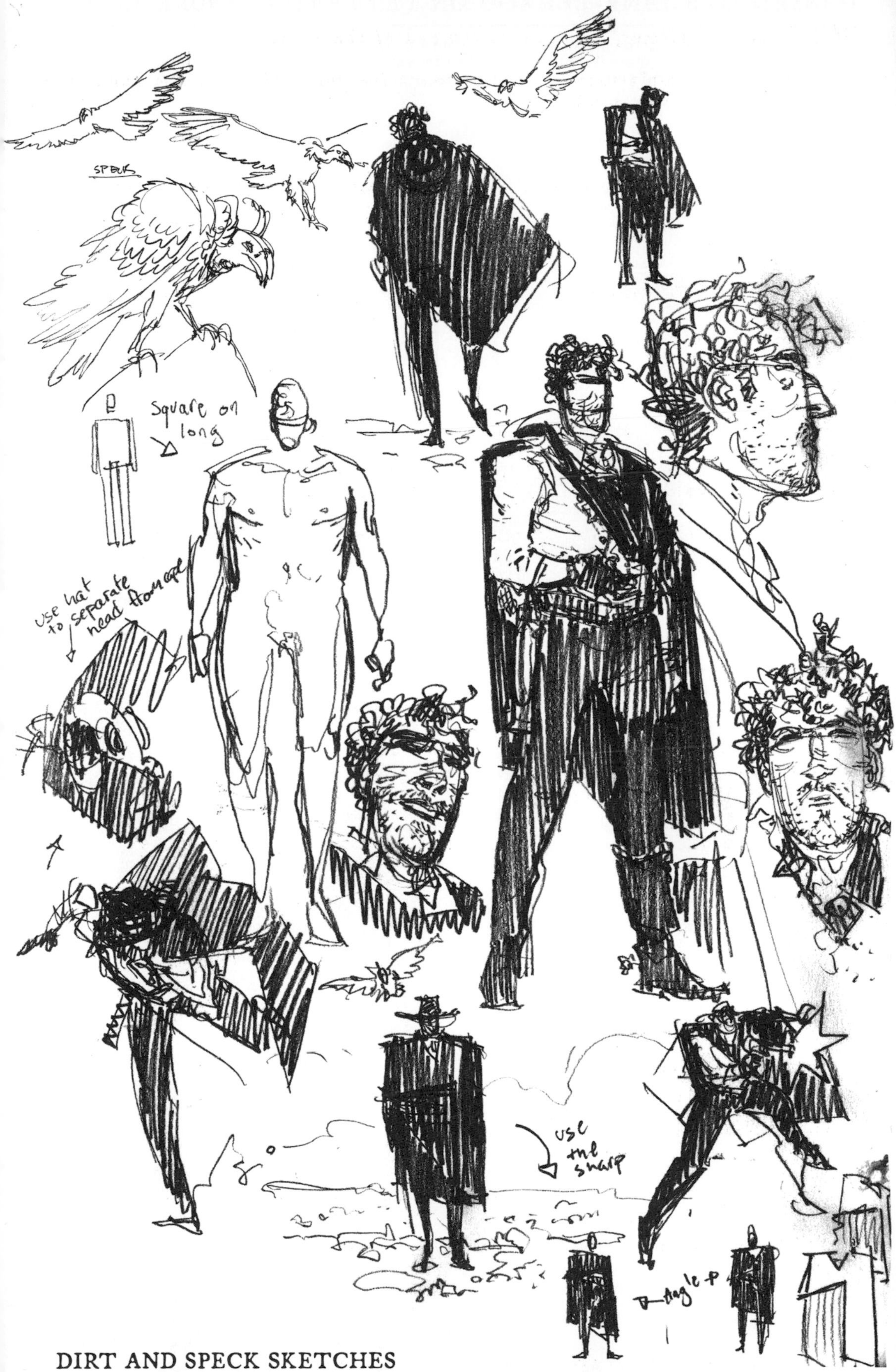
SPECK
Square on long
use hat to separate head from cape
use the sharp
Angle

DIRT AND SPECK SKETCHES

HASSAN OTSMANE-ELHAOU ON LETTERING *ABOVE SNAKES*

The first stage of lettering for me is always figuring out what the style is going to be. This is going to have a huge impact *(obviously I'd say that)* on the way the reader will engage with the book. Not just in getting the lettering to feel 'at one' with the art, but the tone of it can be changed dramatically with different lettering.

1

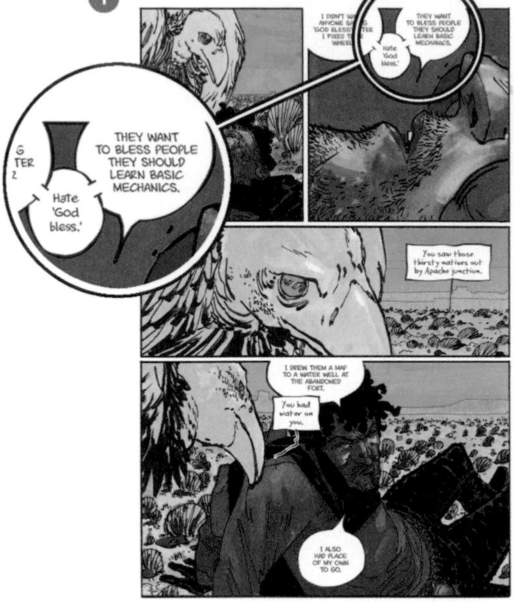

THEY WANT TO BLESS PEOPLE THEY SHOULD LEARN BASIC MECHANICS.
Hate 'God bless.'
You saw those thirsty natives out by Apache junction.
I DREW THEM A MAP TO A WATER WELL AT THE ABANDONED FORT.
You had water on you.
I ALSO HAD PLACE OF MY OWN TO GO.

2

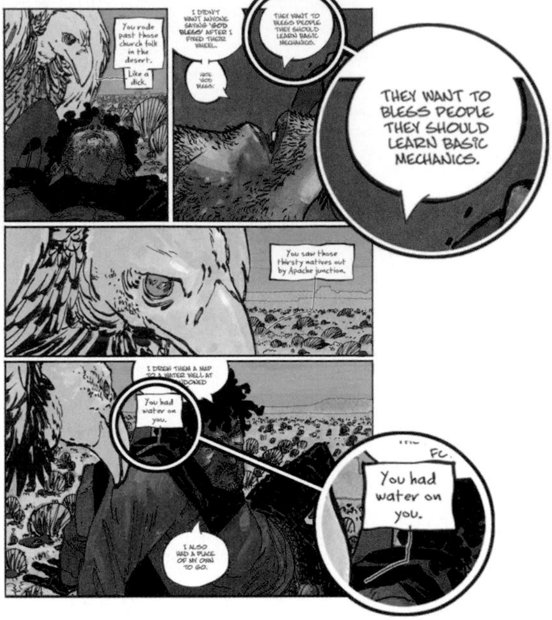

You rode past those church folk in the desert.
Like a dick.
I DIDN'T WANT ANYONE SAYING 'GOD BLESS' AFTER I FIXED THEIR WHEEL.
THEY WANT TO BLESS PEOPLE THEY SHOULD LEARN BASIC MECHANICS.
You saw those thirsty natives out by Apache junction.
You had water on you.
I ALSO HAD A PLACE OF MY OWN TO GO.

I'd previously lettered ***Chicken Devil***, which Hayden was the artist on, and we had a very distinct style for that book. So I knew that Hayden would want something sort of idiosyncratic, unique and dynamic to the book. The first styles [IMAGES **1**, **2**] had that same idea in the voice of Speck, the line tails. But because it felt like (to me) Hayden was channelling some inner-Moebius on Blueberry, I wanted to keep Dirt with these bigger, rounded, more airy balloons with regular tails. It also helped to make that distinction between the 'reality' of Dirt and the vengeance-bird of Speck.

3

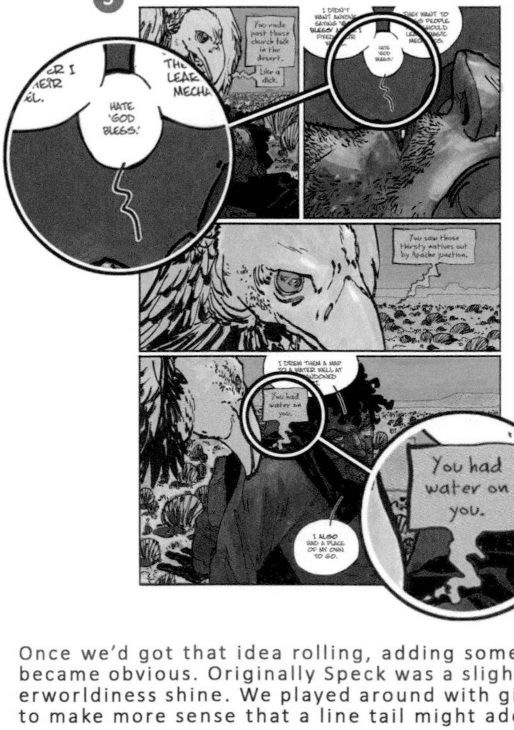

You rode past those church folk in the desert.
Like a dick.
HATE 'GOD BLESS.'
You saw those thirsty natives out by Apache junction.
You had water on you.
I ALSO HAD A PLACE OF MY OWN TO GO.

4

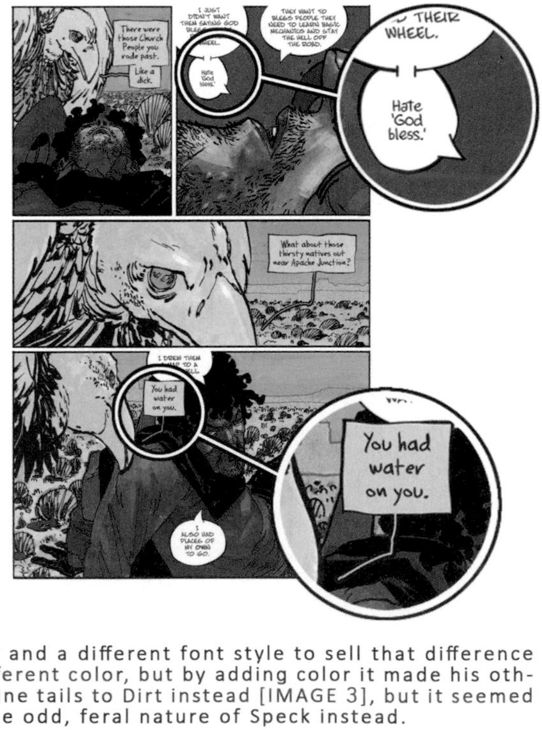

There were those Church People you rode past.
Like a dick.
THEY WANT TO BLESS PEOPLE THEY NEED TO LEARN BASIC MECHANICS AND STAY THE HELL OFF THE ROAD.
THEIR WHEEL.
Hate 'God bless.'
What about those thirsty natives out near Apache Junction?
You had water on you.
I ALSO HAD PLACES OF MY OWN TO GO.

Once we'd got that idea rolling, adding some color and a different font style to sell that difference became obvious. Originally Speck was a slightly different color, but by adding color it made his otherworldiness shine. We played around with giving line tails to Dirt instead [IMAGE 3], but it seemed to make more sense that a line tail might add to the odd, feral nature of Speck instead.

And that's how the lettering of ***Above Snakes*** came to life!

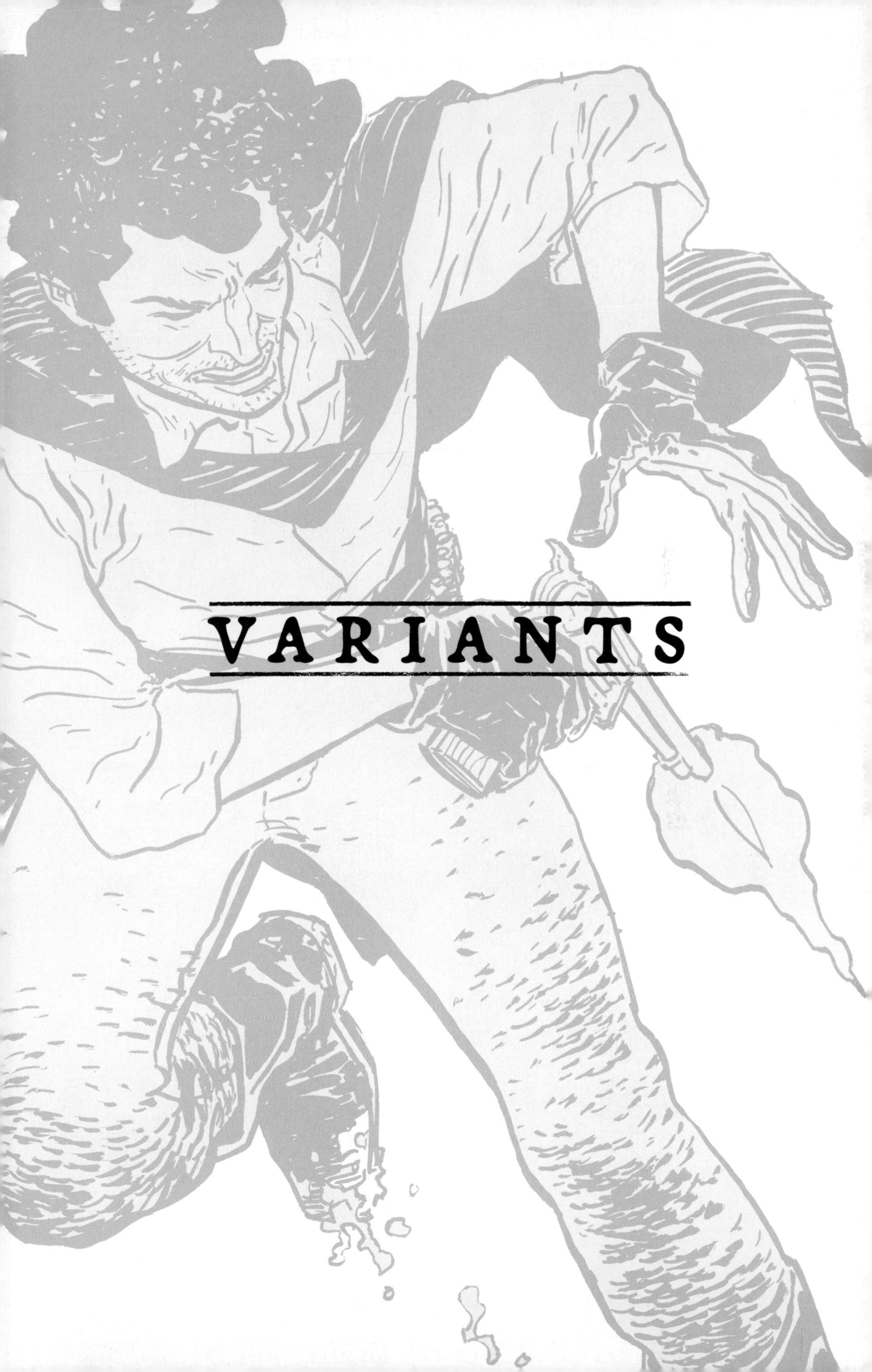

VARIANTS

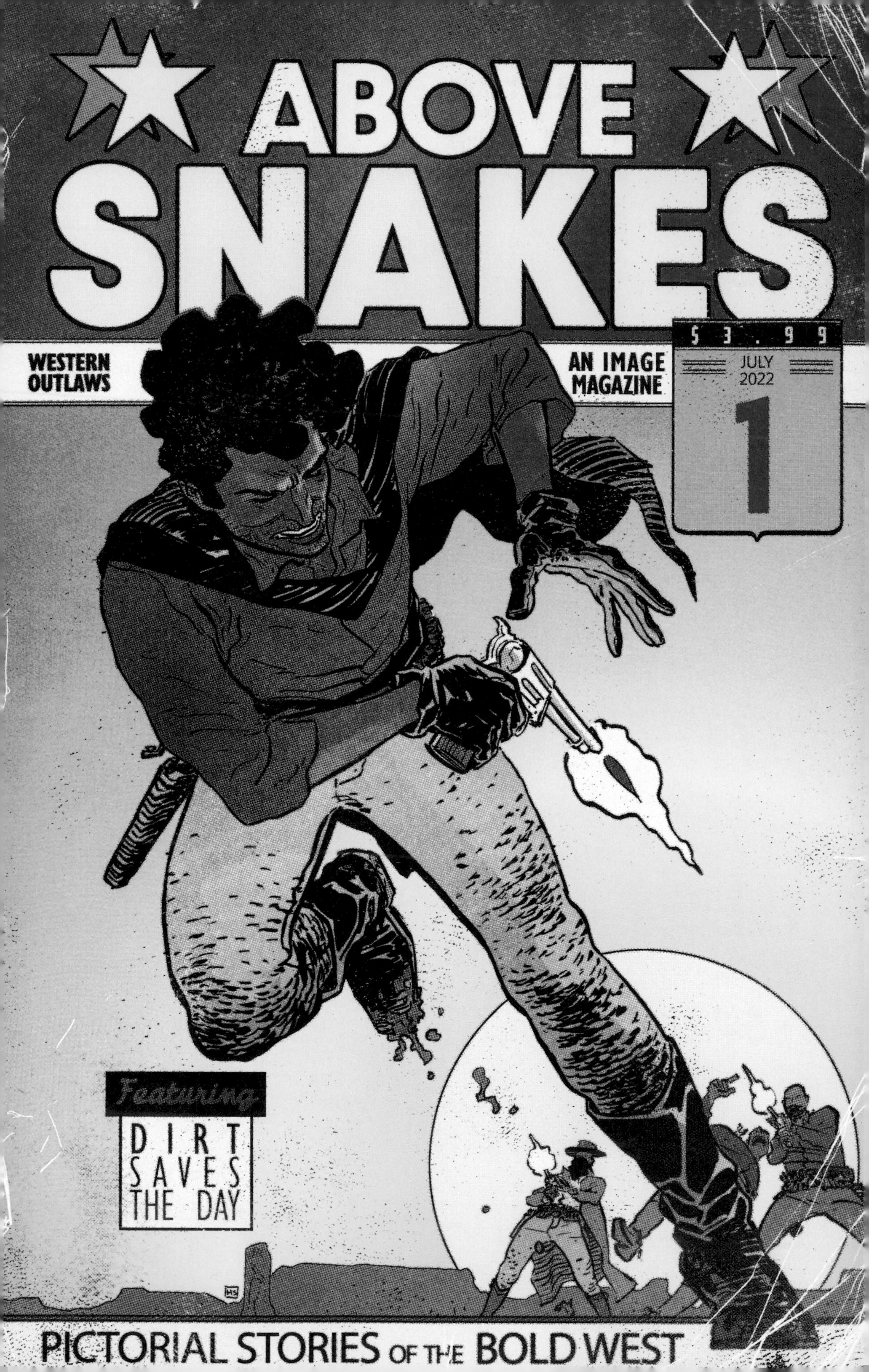
ABOVE SNAKES
WESTERN OUTLAWS
AN IMAGE MAGAZINE
$3.99
JULY 2022
1
Featuring
DIRT SAVES THE DAY
PICTORIAL STORIES OF THE BOLD WEST

SEAN LEWIS HAYDEN SHERMAN

ABOVE SNAKES

HASSAN OTSMANE-ELHAOU

No. 3

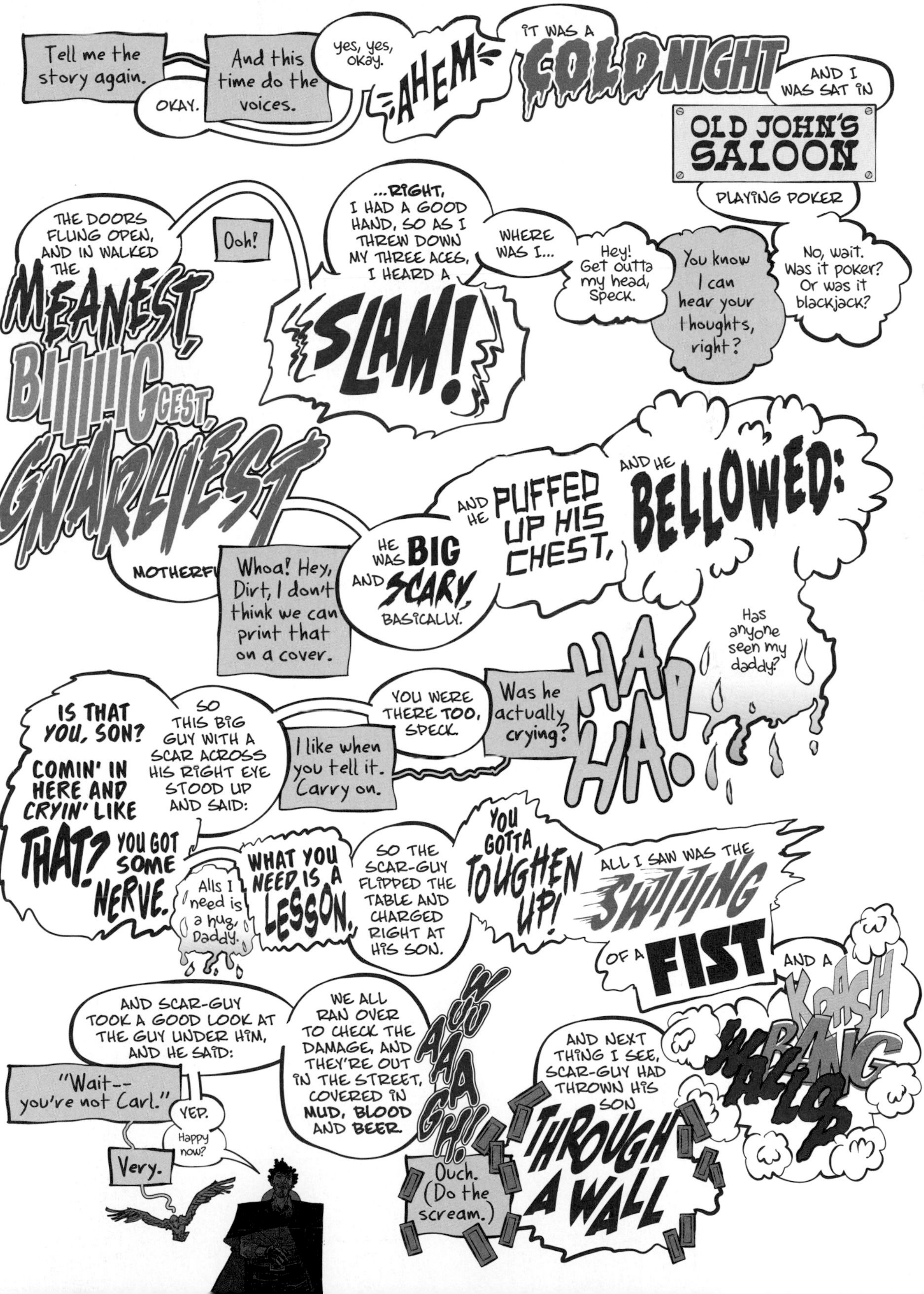

Tell me the story again.
OKAY.
And this time do the voices.
yes, yes, okay.
AHEM
IT WAS A COLD NIGHT
AND I WAS SAT IN
OLD JOHN'S SALOON
PLAYING POKER
No, wait. Was it poker? Or was it blackjack?
You know I can hear your thoughts, right?
Hey! Get outta my head, Speck.
WHERE WAS I...
...RIGHT, I HAD A GOOD HAND, SO AS I THREW DOWN MY THREE ACES, I HEARD A
SLAM!
THE DOORS FLUNG OPEN, AND IN WALKED THE
Ooh!
MEANEST, BIIIIIGGEST, GNARLIEST
MOTHERF
Whoa! Hey, Dirt, I don't think we can print that on a cover.
HE WAS BIG AND SCARY, BASICALLY.
AND HE PUFFED UP HIS CHEST,
AND HE BELLOWED:
Has anyone seen my daddy?
HA HA!
Was he actually crying?
YOU WERE THERE TOO, SPECK.
I like when you tell it. Carry on.
SO THIS BIG GUY WITH A SCAR ACROSS HIS RIGHT EYE STOOD UP AND SAID:
IS THAT YOU, SON? COMIN' IN HERE AND CRYIN' LIKE THAT? YOU GOT SOME NERVE.
Alls I need is a hug, Daddy.
WHAT YOU NEED IS A LESSON.
SO THE SCAR-GUY FLIPPED THE TABLE AND CHARGED RIGHT AT HIS SON.
YOU GOTTA TOUGHEN UP!
ALL I SAW WAS THE SWIIIING OF A FIST
AND A KRASH WHAM BANG
AND NEXT THING I SEE, SCAR-GUY HAD THROWN HIS SON THROUGH A WALL
WUUUAAAGH!!
Ouch. (Do the scream.)
WE ALL RAN OVER TO CHECK THE DAMAGE, AND THEY'RE OUT IN THE STREET, COVERED IN MUD, BLOOD AND BEER.
AND SCAR-GUY TOOK A GOOD LOOK AT THE GUY UNDER HIM, AND HE SAID:
"Wait-- you're not Carl."
YEP.
Happy now?
Very.

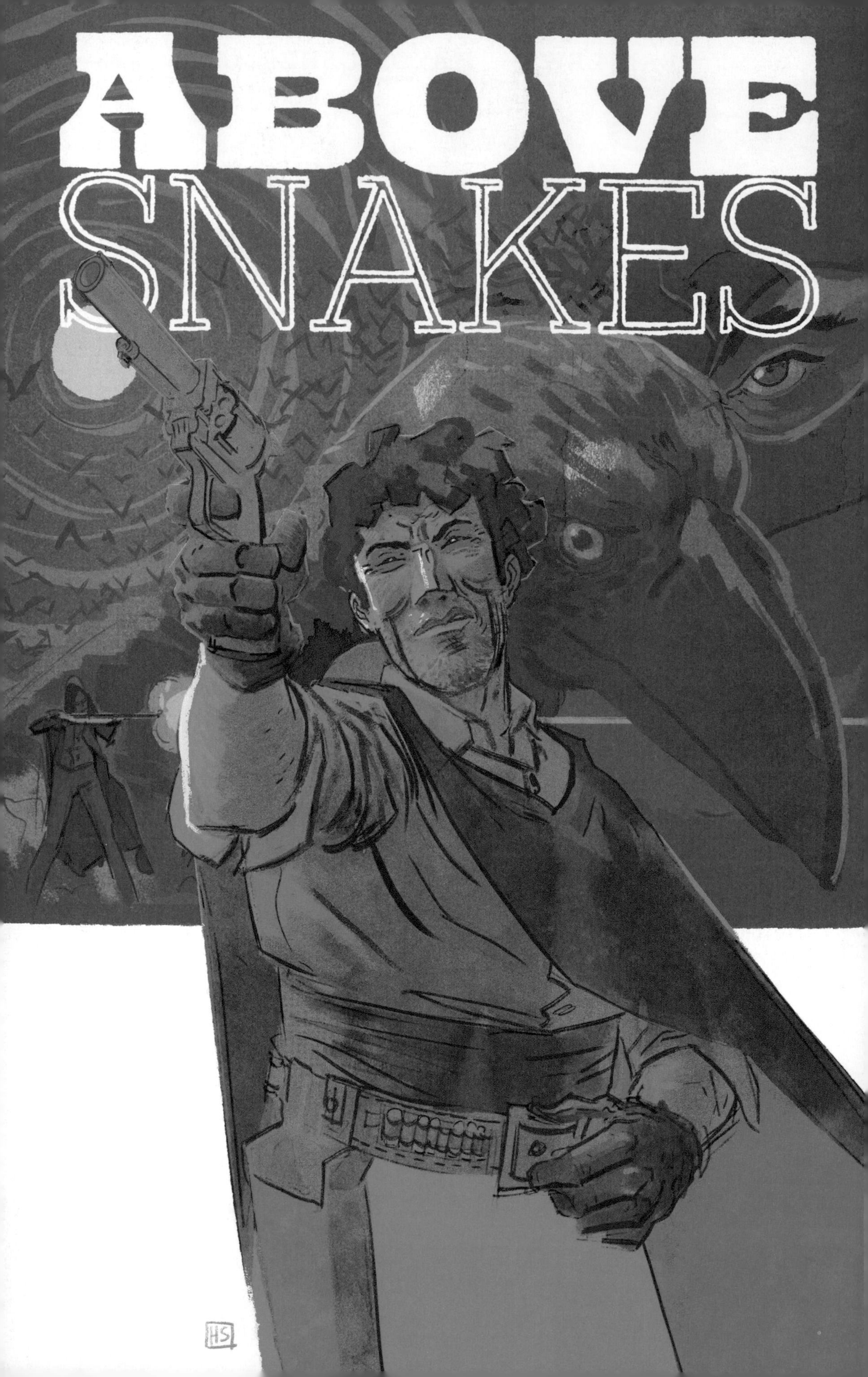
ABOVE
SNAKES
HS